BY THE SAME AUTHOR

Space Unicorn Blues

PRAISE FOR TJ BERRY

"Pure wish fulfilment. That is… assuming you wish to be a down-on-his-luck, half-unicorn space rogue, struggling to reclaim his starship and find his lost horn against an army of human oppressors who hold all the cards."
G S Denning, author of the Warlock Holmes series

"A fun read with an entirely unique concept on a mashup of scifi and fantasy."
Joe Zieja, author of the Epic Failure trilogy

"An energetic book that starts at high velocity and never lets up. Reading it is one of those "just one more chapter" experiences."
Tor.com

"This delightfully weird science fantasy is a perfect escape read."
Barnes & Noble Sci-Fi & Fantasy Blog

"A fast-paced romp… I enjoyed it deeply."
Liz Bourke for Locus

"Flawless… another must-read from Angry Robot."
The Fantasy Inn

"Berry has done a great job of creating a spacefaring human diaspora that feels real and diverse, as well as integrating heavy subject matter in a way which is reasonably sensitive without overstraining the fast-paced narrative."
Nerds of a Feather

T J BERRY

FIVE UNICORN FLUSH

**ANGRY
ROBOT**

ANGRY ROBOT
An imprint of Watkins Media Ltd

Unit 11, Shepperton House
89 Shepperton Road
London N1 3DF
UK

angryrobotbooks.com
twitter.com/angryrobotbooks

An Angry Robot paperback original,
2019

Copyright © TJ Berry 2019

Cover by Lee Gibbons
Set in Meridian

Angry Robot and the Angry Robot
icon are registered trademarks of
Watkins Media Ltd.

ISBN 978 0 85766 783 0
Ebook ISBN 978 0 85766 784 7

Printed and bound in the United
Kingdom by TJ International.

9 8 7 6 5 4 3 2 1

To Dave, who started all of this.

CHAPTER ONE
Well Actually

Jenny Perata sat in the cockpit of the FTL *Stagecoach Mary*,
watching the stars fail to move. She didn't need to be up here. The
ship basically ran herself, but this was one of the only rooms where
she could get a good view of the universe. Reason ship designers
never wanted their passengers to see the vast expanse of space. It
had a tendency to give people perspective and empathy, and those
were two things that no one needed in the Reason.

After getting a taste of faster-than-light travel, being in a
sublight ship made Jenny antsy. Her life had become one endless
and boring night, punctuated by occasional moments of abject
terror when pirates crossed her path.

And she'd failed to account for the effects of chronic pain. The
healing unicorn blood she'd been given a few weeks ago was just
enough to reawaken her nerves, but not repair them. She was still
unable to move her legs but now they buzzed and jolted like a live-
wire dancing in the street. On the worst days, bolts of pain shot
down her legs, and her lower back seized up completely.

She'd tried heat, cold, exercise, massage, even alcohol, but
nothing worked consistently except painkillers and those were
in short supply out here in openspace. The Pioneer Deluxe
Interplanetary Settlers Package she'd picked up in Fort Jaisalmer
contained enough supplies for a small group of explorers but
she'd quickly blown through all the painkillers in the medical
kit. Most days she curled up in the captain's chair, swaddled in a

blanket, staring blearily at the stars until she dropped asleep from exhaustion.

"You're dehydrated again," said the ship's AI. When Jenny didn't answer, the ship tried again. "You should drink some water, Captain."

"What are you on about now, Mary," mumbled Jenny.

"You need to hydrate," said Mary.

"I'll get up later," replied Jenny. She'd found a position in which the stabbing nerve pain had subsided to a low jangle. She wasn't going to move again unless she absolutely had to. Even if it meant muting Mary's nagging voice for a while.

She used to have such pleasant company on these trips. Her wife, Kaila, always stood by her chair, a cascade of lush dryad leaves falling over both of them as they looked out at the stars and wondered which ones might be good for putting down roots, both real and metaphorical. But Kaila was gone – whisked off to some gorgeous human-free utopia with the rest of the magical Bala six weeks ago. On the one hand, she was safe from the authoritarian Reason regime, who had stripping her down for magical parts. But on the other hand, Jenny's chest ached from missing her wife.

The all-powerful Pymmie had moved the Bala to keep them safe from human exploitation. Not even Jenny, who had been in the room when the Bala had decided their fate, knew where they'd gone. Kaila might be on the next planet, or two systems away, or on the other side of the universe. There was no guessing what the omnipotent, omniscient Pymmie did with them.

Which meant that the search for Kaila couldn't even start in earnest until Jenny found some unicorn horn to power her faster-than-light engines. Without FTL she might fly for decades in one direction and never even find a single habitable planet. She didn't even know in which direction to look. That was no way to find your wife.

The plan – and, good or bad, Jenny Perata always had a plan – was to find a piece of unicorn horn on one of the ships trawling around out here in openspace. The bug-eyed Pymmie had said that she was a necromancer, which was a human who had the ability to use Bala magic. But that didn't seem right. Necromancers were wizardy types who could cast bolts of purple lightning strong enough to tear a ship in half. Sure, she could do a few tricks, but not reliably. She'd been working on one specific skill during her interminable weeks with Mary, teaching herself to track magical items.

The Pymmie had relocated every Bala artifact that was not vital to the functioning of a human body. Exterior spells and prostheses disappeared, but all kinds of implants and transplants had been left behind. She'd been scouting these items throughout the system for weeks. So far she'd only found a pirate with a selkie skin graft and and an arms dealer with the heart of a clockwork boy.

Tucked into her blanket, Jenny searched the area for anything magic. She closed her eyes and let her awareness of nullspace energy come to the surface. Off to the left she saw the faint impression of a red glow. That was the selkie pirate, whom she'd left tied up in his quarters on her way out. Someone would find him. Eventually. Hopefully.

She pushed her heightened senses further. She could see humans in there too – like it or not, they too coursed with at least a little bit of nullspace energy – but they were dim and difficult to dinstinguish from the velvety black background of openspace. A white glow in the distance made her sit forward and take notice. Her lower back twinged. She sucked in air and let it back out slowly.

"Hey Mary, what's that below us?" she asked, snaking a hand behind her to rub the throbbing spot above her tailbone. Her fingers met the raised scars from countless surgeries. And the rubbing didn't help one bit.

"There's a ship in that direction about 600 kilometers away. It's near the locator beacon in the lower right quadrant of this system," said Mary.

"Were you planning to mention this ship or just let us sail on by?" asked Jenny.

"I didn't bother telling you because it's one of those ancient generation ships that tend to be bad news," replied Mary.

That's where the white glow was coming from.

"Bugger all, I was hoping for a nap," said Jenny, unwrapping herself from the blanket and shivering. The air in the cockpit was as warm as she could get it without spending fuel recklessly, but it was still always a touch cold.

She tapped the console and zoomed in on the signal. It was a typical friendly beacon indicating all was well and inviting contact from nearby travelers. Standard protocol for a non-military generation ship flying in peacetime.

Except that they weren't in peacetime. After the Pymmie had whisked the magical beings off to their new Shangri-La, the Reason regime had devolved into chaos. With free and plentiful Bala labor suddenly gone, factories and food service shut down, sanitation stopped, and farming ground to a halt. In the face of rising prices and shortages, human beings rioted.

The Reason government – long accustomed to using military might to enforce policy – sent its troops into the streets to beat people back into their homes. And that was before they realized all the unicorn horn had disappeared too. With no fuel left for FTL drives, every human being was trapped on the planet they happened to be on when the Bala disappeared.

Stranded ships raced toward the closest planets at sublight speeds, but most didn't have supplies for a journey of weeks, let alone years. They certainly didn't have greenhouses full of plants and holds full of dry goods like the generation ships of yesteryear. Piracy became rampant. People justified it as survival. The old Reason chant of 'Manifest destiny, and the survival of man,' had taken on a new and more visceral meaning. It wasn't unusual to pass the wreckage of a ship with bodies spiraling away from it like a nebula of death. Or to find a wake trail of frozen humans leading to a perfectly operational ship. People were a drain on resources and crews were determined to run lean, no matter what the cost.

This friendly little ship, out quite a distance from the safety of

Jaisalmer, should have been in stealth mode instead of inviting attention. Jenny sensed a trap, but the possibility of finding unicorn horn was just too tempting. She double-checked that her beacons, broadcasts, and even her running lights were shut down. No sense inviting trouble before she was ready.

It galled her that the *Stagecoach Mary* had been painted a hideous shade of solar yellow with – she could barely bring herself to say it – racing stripes. No one but teenagers painted their ships so garishly, but Mary had been cheap and ready to leave on a moment's notice. And her last owner had cleared out a few compartments for smuggling contraband, which was always helpful when transporting magical items. Beggars couldn't be choosers during the apocalypse.

"Tell me everything you know about that ship," said Jenny.

"It's a generation ship from Earth, a smallish one. Privately owned and old. Designed for sublight speeds. Which means it was built by people who weren't powerful or connected enough to get their hands on unicorn horn."

"The losers," mused Jenny. Faster ships from Earth had gotten out here in a fraction of the time, leaving lumbering beasts like this one to limp across the galaxy at their own pace. It made for some pretty awkward reunions when your great-great-great grandmother finally showed up on a stasis ship and she was younger than you. You always had to be careful who you ended up hooking up with.

This mysterious generation ship wasn't part of the Reason Space Force, which was a plus. Reason ships out here in openspace would confiscate everything you owned and leave you starving and drifting – if they didn't just throw you out of the airlock for funsies.

Jenny tapped on her tablet to zoom in on the ship. It was cylindrical but not spinning, which meant their gravity was off. The welcome signal pinged her alarm bells, but pirates usually went one of two routes. They either broadcast a distress beacon and then raided the ships who fell for it, or snuck up on you without warning. A cheerful invitation to visitors was a trick she hadn't seen before.

"Any indication they've seen us?" asked Jenny.

"No, and we should leave before they do. We can't hide from a ship that big. They have sensors plastering half the forward decks. If they decide to come after us, we're fucked," said Mary.

Jenny made a mental note to turn down the belligerence level on *Mary's* AI once they got clear of this enigma. Mary's snarky retorts were making her anxious.

She tapped her fingernail on her teeth, deep in thought.

"You're not thinking of going over there, are you?" asked Mary.

"I see something. They might have horn," said Jenny.

"Not likely," said Mary. "They'd be in FTL if they did."

True. Jenny closed her eyes again and damned if that white glow didn't look brighter. Like it was calling to her. She could be back in Kaila's arms in days.

"I know what you're thinking and stop thinking it," said Mary.

"It might be horn," said Jenny.

"First of all," said Mary, with a slight edge to her voice that might have been calculated to show ire but might have also been Jenny's imagination. "Any ship that has unicorn horn and isn't using it is having major problems. Second of all, you aren't sure that's even horn. You'll waste a literal ton of fuel getting over there just to find a pixie dust suppository. And, third of all, you are operating on dangerously low levels of sleep. Ignore this ship, get some rest, and trust that I am *handling it.*"

Jenny drummed her fingers on the armrest touchpad, accidentally turning off airflow to the cargo bay. She tisked and turned it back on. She still wasn't used to this newer ship design with no single dashboard in front. Everything was controlled on armrest touchpads, which felt like a very silly way to command a starship. She felt very old and very tired.

Her mind suddenly flashed back to her previous partner, Cowboy Jim, the way he used to complain about long stints in the co-pilot's chair. Younger Jenny had always rolled her eyes at him. He was a ridiculous old fool who couldn't see space for the exciting place it was. She now understood why he'd always been so antsy to get his feet back planetside. The beds were always better on the ground.

"I'm just gonna wait and see what they do," said Jenny.

"Sure you will," said Mary.

"No. This time I really will. I'll wait until they cross our wake and see if they notice us or make contact. Otherwise, I'll stay quiet," Jenny assured her. She was also going to dip back into nullspace and see if she could get a better idea of what the glow might be emanating from. But her ship didn't need to know that.

Mary laughed mirthlessly. Jenny wondered if the laughs were preprogrammed or if the ship combined sounds on the fly to make them. Either way, it ticked her off.

"You're a jerk," said Jenny. "Just let me do my thing."

"You can change my settings if you like," replied Mary curtly.

Jenny wrapped herself back into the blanket, adjusting her legs under her by pulling on her jumpsuit. Fireworks of pain hit the bottom of her foot and she held her breath while putting pressure on it with her hand. That didn't actually do anything, but in the moment you had to go through some kind of pantomime until it passed on its own.

"You can go into stasis," said Mary, her volume down by about twenty percent in her version of a gentle suggestion. "Just go to sleep and wake up wherever you want to be. I'll even get you up for all the good pirate fights."

After six weeks of this discussion, Jenny was still not having it. "I'm not going to be an icicle," she said. Mary made a sound that could have been a scoff, or might have been nails down a chalkboard. Jenny made a note to edit that clip out of the sound files.

"We're out of critical medical supplies," said Mary. "Even a short stint in stasis would drop your cortisol levels. You'd be pain-free for as long as you slept."

"You can't guarantee that," said Jenny.

"No, but we could try. Sleep for a week and tell me if you feel anything."

It wasn't a terrible idea. She could have Mary wake her any time they encountered trouble. The only problem was that she hadn't programmed in any particular destination. She had to be awake to dip into nullspace and search for unicorn horn. They wouldn't get to Kaila in Jenny's lifetime without finding it.

"Can I go into stasis for eight-hour shifts, just like normal nights?"

"Oh boy, that sounds like a bad idea," said Mary. "The cryo process is hard on the body. The manual recommends no more than four sleeps in a month. You'd be doing six times that much. They don't even let combat soldiers go through the sleep/wake cycle more than twice in a week."

Jenny knew that already. She'd been on Reason transport ships during the war, slick with vomit from a hundred troops who'd just been through their third sleep/wake cycle in as many days. You could push a human body to do some incredible things but it would always come back to bite you in the ass later.

She watched the magnified image of the friendly ship grow on her viewscreen. It probably had a full garden with live crops. Maybe even livestock. Those ships were little time capsules meant to subsist indefinitely without outside intervention. How this one had gotten so far through Reasonspace without being dismantled piqued her curiosity.

"Do you think they've been commandeered?" asked Jenny.

"I think they're a ship full of starry-eyed Earth colonists who've made it through openspace with a lot of luck and who are now awestruck at my sleek racing form," said Mary.

Jenny laughed.

"No, it's true. They're watching me," said Mary, preening.

"How could you possibly tell that? We don't have bioscanners."

"They're at the windows, Jenny. Dozens of them. Looking out at us."

Jenny's heart beat faster as Mary zoomed in on the side of the generation ship. Silhouetted shadows stood at the windows, watching them.

"I guess they know we're here," said Jenny.

"I'd say so," replied Mary.

"We might as well accept their invitation to board." Jenny tapped in a course toward the friendly ship.

"I knew it," said Mary.

"You don't get points for being a smart ass," said Jenny.

"How do you know? Maybe all of us AI ships have a secret contest to see how right we can all be about our crews' stupid decisions and I'm currently winning because you are utterly ridiculous."

"Belligerence down to five percent," said Jenny.

"Really?" asked Mary, horrified.

"No, not really."

Jenny pulled her wheelchair closer to the captain's chair and hoisted herself into it. She set her feet carefully on the footrests, ignoring the pins and needles. Fuck part-unicorns and their half-assed healing. She'd been better off before. At least then her legs had been numb and she could get through her day without feeling like she was constantly on the verge of screaming.

Besides the possible horn, this mystery ship probably had a pharmacological lab with raw materials enough to medicate hundreds, maybe thousands of people.

"They might have medical supplies to spare," she said out loud.

"Your desire for medication is coming perilously close to addiction," said Mary. "After this encounter, we should talk about other pain management techniques."

Jenny gave Mary the middle finger. As if wanting to blot out the constant, driving pain was some kind of moral failure. She wasn't looking to get high, just to not feel like garbage for a few sweet hours. It's not as if she endangered anyone in her pain-free state. The ship flew herself and there were no other living souls on board. Whoever programmed Mary didn't understand chronic, debilitating pain. Typical Reason wankers.

"Looking forward to it," replied Jenny, knowing that Mary would be able to hear the lie in her tone.

"Friendly ship, this the FTL *Stagecoach Mary*, hailing hello." It was nowhere near standard protocol, but Jenny could not care less.

She settled back in her chair for the long wait. Crews generally debated a response for quite a while before–

"FTL *Stagecoach Mary*, are we ever glad to hear from you," said an exuberant fella on the other ship. "This is the USS *Well Actually* heading out to Jai-Sal-Meer. There are plenty of pirates out here in this part of space, but not a lot of friendly faces. You looking to slow down and have a cup of tea with us or just wave hello as we pass on by?"

"That's odd," said Mary, muting the comm.

"No kidding," said Jenny.

Every part of her logical brain told her to decline the invitation and keep moving, but her senses were screaming at her that something Bala was aboard that ship. If it was horn, even the tiniest sliver, it would get her that much closer to Kaila. Her finger hovered over the comm, knowing what she had to do. It was a big risk for what might turn out to be a magic ring from a cereal box lodged in someone's intestine since they swallowed it as a kid. And even if they had horn, they weren't going to give it up willingly. But she couldn't live with herself if she didn't try. She tapped the screen.

"Kia ora, *Well Actually.* I'd love to come by for a visit. It's a long cold road out here and I don't get much company."

"Oh Jenny," said Mary with a sigh.

"Great! We'll send a rendezvous location and meet up in about an hour. *Well Actually* out!"

"This is going to be interesting," said Jenny.

"And you *love* interesting," said Mary, slowing thrusters as the *Well Actually's* coordinates came through in a non-encoded message. Everyone within ten thousand kilometers would know about the rendezvous. This crew was either incredibly naïve or setting her up for an ambush.

CHAPTER TWO
Dude, the Stars are Yours

Jenny freshened up in her quarters before the two ships met.
It wouldn't do to arrive smelling of stale sweat and dehydrated
cheese. She sponged off with a disposable moist wipe that was
intended to be tossed out of the ship along with all of the other
trash that humans dumped into space. She zipped up her jumpsuit
and went over to her closet for one more thing. She unclipped
her gran's patu from the shelf and ran her fingers over the designs
carved into the club. It had broken in two during her last big
adventure, but the dwarves on the FTL *Jaggery* had mended it
so that the seam was barely visible. Other weapons were more
intimidating but only this one carried the weight of the women
before her.

Jenny tucked the patu in her widest pocket and rolled up to the
airlock. The *Well Actually* had already positioned itself above them.
Mary made the necessary thruster and microgravity adjustments
to line up the two airlocks. Jenny's gut tightened. Their hatch was
an antiquated style that wasn't the standard size. They wouldn't be
able to dock directly, hatch to hatch, and create an airtight seal.
Instead, a flexible tube of thick plastic extended from the *Well
Actually's* airlock. They expected her to float across. Not that she
hadn't spacewalked before, but it wasn't generally a task you asked
someone to do on a first date.

"I don't like this," said Mary, echoing Jenny's thoughts.

"It'll be fine. You worry too much. If they wanted to board us by force they would be better equipped for quick entry. This weird and tedious bridge is a good sign. They're just a bunch of backward old spacers," said Jenny.

"Still–" began Mary.

"Remind me to raise your risk tolerance when I get back," said Jenny, in a roundabout sort of threat.

"It's already at maximum," said Mary.

"Nothing's ever at maximum if you try hard enough," said Jenny.

Their retractable tunnel met her airlock. Mary's articulated grappling arms grabbed onto the flange and sealed it to her hull. Jenny was amazed that it sealed at all. The equipment was old but Mary would have warned her if it wasn't holding a vacuum. She tightened the safety harness on her wheelchair and hit the pad to turn off the *Stagecoach Mary*'s gravity and unlock her own door.

"Here we go," she said as the airlock hissed open. Her chair lifted off from the floor, which was always a stomach-churning sensation. It was heavy, carved out of wood by grateful dwarves after she'd brought Gary Cobalt back from the dead. The chair was beautiful but when it got going it was a job to slow down. She'd crashed into many a ceiling before learning how to spot the signs of a runaway chair before it was too late. Fortunately for Mary's bulkheads she'd become proficient in maneuvering over the last few weeks.

The air that rushed past her from the bridge tunnel was icy cold. This was a tunnel meant for travelers in an extravehicular activity suit.

"Hey, is this really airtight?" she asked Mary.

"Yes, but no environmental controls. It's going to get pretty chilly in there quickly. Hope you have a jacket," said Mary.

"You sound like my gran," said Jenny, pushing off against the door frame with her arms. Her chair whacked against the insides of the tunnel. She cringed as the plastic rippled like a flag in the wind. Jenny wondered if it was as brittle and old as it looked. One small tear would suffocate her in seconds. These old ships were known for their mechanical defects – even when they were fresh off the assembly line. The doors jammed, the food dispensers electrocuted people, and the water supply always leaked. These things were death traps on the best of days.

Jenny grabbed a spiral strut and pushed herself along more carefully. At the other end of the tunnel, a pink face bobbed.

"Hey there! Govvie says to… oh. We didn't know you were a cripple."

Now this was not the first time that Jenny had been called that word. The Reason wasn't too big on sensitivity training, so for most of her life she'd been on the receiving end of various ableist slurs, but this time it really chafed at her. Either she took the time and energy to educate this random pre-teen spacer, or he was going to grow up thinking that word was just fine.

"I'm *disabled*," she said pointedly. "Is that going to be a problem? Because I'll just turn around right here if it is."

The kid glanced behind him for a moment, looking for someone who wasn't there.

"Well, no. I guess not," he said.

"Good." She hoped that would be the end of it.

He floated back to let Jenny through their airlock. She shoved herself forward, annoyed. Her chair banged hard enough on the airlock frame that the vibration shot through her teeth. She slowed down and tried again. The chair thwacked, albeit more gently, on the doorway.

"Your wheelchair's not gonna fit," said the boy.

"Fuck me," said Jenny, unstrapping herself and floating away from her chair. She folded it up along the hinged joints and dragged it through the airlock behind her. When she looked up, the boy had turned bright, splotchy red from his neck to his ears.

"What?" she asked.

"Your language, ma'am," choked the boy. "We don't hear much swears like that on the *Well Actually*."

She laughed and he flushed a deep shade of red.

"There's more where that came from," she warned him.

"Not if Govvie can help it," mumbled the boy, turning away and floating down the hall.

Jenny followed him, pulling her folded chair behind her.

"You won't need that during your visit. You can leave it here by the airlock and collect it up on your way out," he said.

Jenny hesitated. If they turned on the gravity she was stranded. She didn't like the thought of being marooned on an unfamiliar ship. Then again, even folded, this wooden chair was bulky and hard to maneuver. In the end, her cautiousness won out.

"I'll keep it with me. Never know when I might need a place to sit," she said.

"Uh huh," said Junior. "Whatever you want."

"What's your name, kid?" she asked.

He looked up at her, confused, as if he'd never been asked this before.

"Your name?" she reiterated. "What people call you?"

"Oh. Junior," he said. Jenny was not getting a great feeling about this place.

"I'm Jenny," she said.

"Pleasure to meet you, Miss Jenny."

"Just Jenny," she said, cringing inwardly at what felt like a teacher's title. She didn't particularly have anything against kids, but they always seemed to be on the verge of accidentally killing themselves. Jenny had a hard enough time keeping herself alive. She wasn't about to take responsibility for a tiny creature that liked to swallow everything that wasn't bolted down.

"We mostly go zero G to save fuel. Sometimes we turn on the gravity for visitors, but I think this time Govvie will keep it off," said Junior.

Jenny was glad to hear that. As much as she appreciated the mobility that her chair offered, she was always more maneuverable in zero G. The boy stopped short and Jenny nearly plowed into him. She pulled herself to a stop using a doorknob on one of the quarters they passed. It rattled in her hand, but did not open. A muffled voice from inside called out to her. The boy cleared his throat.

Junior continued down the hallway toward the middle of the gravity cylinder. They came out into the large atrium that was always at the center of these things. They all had wheel-and-spoke designs, not unlike the official Reason flag – three crimson spheres filled with a five-pointed star, a seven-pointed star, and a twenty-four-spoke wheel representing the United States, Australia, and India. Everyone called it the 'spheres and tears'. Humans had a bit of a reputation in the universe.

Jenny passed the huge planter that was meant to be the centerpiece of the place – it usually had an immense and ridiculously symbolic tree growing in it. Life, cooperation, symbiotic relationships, blah, blah, blah. This one was empty.

This common area for a generation ship with a city-sized population was a ghost town. She'd seen plenty of people at the windows a few minutes ago. They just weren't here.

"Is it second shift?" she asked. Even though there were technically no 'days' on a ship, these old societies liked to mimic the light/dark cycles of a planet. There was usually a first shift when most people were awake and a second shift when the common areas were slightly quieter.

"Uh… sure," he said, not stopping. "Around here, people kind of keep to themselves."

The hair on Jenny's neck bristled. Generation ships had been designed for lots of common interactions. It was what held the community together. Experience (and a handful of massacres) had revealed that people behaved more civilly toward each other when they were interdependent in lots of little ways. So the ships were designed to function with the maximum amount of human interaction. You couldn't just sit in your cabin with a replicator and pornography. You had to go out and make food, negotiate with people, and work in cooperation. Even when everything was essentially free and it was all a sham. It helped keep people sane and happy.

The atrium rose through the heart of the ship. The walls were flanked by a spiral ramp up to several floors of shops and working areas. All of them were closed and dark. A few were boarded over as if they'd been condemned. Something wasn't right on this ship.

Her pocket buzzed twice and she jumped, sending her off course into a support beam. It was just her tablet with a message from Mary. Junior hadn't even noticed. He was getting farther away from her by the second. She tapped the comm bud in her ear and mumbled, "Go."

"Jenny, the docking tunnel is retracting. I'm still outside, but you can't get back. Tell me everything's all right on that ship," said Mary.

"Nope," Jenny replied in a low voice. The boy turned and she pretended to be admiring the parquet floors.

"Is this real wood?" she asked.

"Uh, I think so. We should keep moving," he said.

"Sure," she replied brightly. He seemed satisfied.

"This ship looks deserted," she whispered into her comm. "It's not right."

"Well you can head back for the airlock, but there's no way across unless you want to float across about ten meters of openspace without an EVA suit," said Mary. Jenny detected the slightest hint of "I told you so." Bravo to those AI programmers.

Jenny had spacewalked unsuited a long time ago and it had nearly killed her. She wasn't keen on repeating the experience any time soon.

"Options?" she asked.

"They probably have escape pods on the residential decks. Or EVA suits near the airlocks. I can pick you up with my cargo grappler if you can get outside safely. We can try to shoot our way out, probably unsuccessfully, if that's the route you'd like to go," said Mary.

"Hm," said Jenny thinking through the logistics. "Can you upload into their systems?" she asked, hanging back as far as she could.

These old ships often operated on unsecure wireless networks.

She'd disabled an antique trawler or three by loading Mary into their systems and bringing the ships under her control. Mary was quiet for a moment as she checked for open network nodes.

"I can get into the food service system, but it's walled off from the rest of the system structure. And it looks like it hasn't been used in decades."

"Then how are they eating?" asked Jenny.

"I have no idea, but no one's getting food out of the inventory. I mean, maybe they're working from paper or a firewalled system that I can't see, but, from this vantage point, it looks like the crew of thousands haven't eaten in years."

Jenny's skin prickled again.

"You made a bad choice," said Mary.

"Yes, I made a bad choice," echoed Jenny. She left the comm open so that Mary could hear what she heard in case she needed to get out of there fast.

The boy floated into a doorway near the top of the atrium. Jenny pulled herself up the ramp railings, wheelchair still floating behind her, hoping they weren't going to turn on the gravity while she was sixteen stories above the parquet floor. She shivered at the thought. Or perhaps it was that the ship was barely above freezing.

She looked down at the atrium. A face peeked up at her from a storefront window and disappeared as soon she turned. The boy slipped into an open administrative office on the top level of the atrium. As usual, riffraff at the bottom, government and admin at the top, looking down on everyone else. This wouldn't be the pilot's bridge, which was away from the common areas. It was meeting rooms and offices for councils or governors or whatever ruling class they had on here. There was always a governance system separate from the people who actually run the ship. That way the population couldn't vote to change course or chase comets at whim.

They floated through an empty maze of plastic desks separated by half-walls covered in fabric. The ship was old, probably launched right after the first of Earth's multi-year superstorms. She scanned the desks for a logo.

There it was – painted on the plexiglass doors of the manager's offices. CoSpace. Jenny's fears eased a bit. CoSpace was known for their relaxed, laissez-faire approach to space travel. Their tagline had been, "Dude, the stars are yours." Run like a startup, their philosophy had been to skip hiring mathematicians, psychologists, and economists and instead hold an expensive lottery to choose residents. Problem was, the computer-based lottery was easily hacked. A secondary market of CoSpace-hacking companies had emerged, nearly all of them in Russia. For a hefty sum, you could guarantee the CoSpace lottery would pull your name. Not surprisingly, filling ships with hackers, grifters, and oligarchs didn't make for sustainable space travel. Most of the CoSpace ships had failed to reach a habitable planet before their society broke down and everyone died. Go out far enough in any direction and you would find CoSpace ships drifting in the far reaches of known space, a handful of survivors munching crickets around a solar warmer. There was nothing of worth on board, so even pirates left them alone.

The boy knocked on the door to the largest office and a chipper voice from inside told them to come in. They floated into a brightly-lit office, tidy and sparse, but covered in a thick layer of dust. A man with graying hair and a bright white smile floated over to her, extending his hand. He was wearing a button-down dress shirt and tie, with only boxer shorts underneath. Jenny got a weird vibe off him. Like he'd been floating around in his underwear and had only managed to half-dress before she'd arrived. It added to the strangeness of the empty ship. It didn't seem like this guy was in charge of anything up here.

"Governor Dan," he said, pumping her arm. He glanced at her wheelchair.

"Did you need the gravity on or…"

"Captain Jenny. Floating works better for me."

"Go get her a pouch of tea, Junior. Unless you'd like something stronger?" He raised his eyebrows to Jenny, who actually did want something stronger. She pursed her lips.

"No, thanks. Tea is fine." She felt like keeping her wits about her for the moment. Junior floated out of the room and Jenny tucked her chair into a corner near the floor. It wouldn't stay there, but it was out of the way for the moment.

"Where are you headed, Governor?" she asked, holding onto the obvious question about where everyone was.

"Call me Govvie, everyone does." He spread his hands as if indicating a room full of people. "Fort J is our final destination," he said with a grin. "Though I hear from other travelers that there's a new station above the planet where we'll need to stop first to get docking clearance. Some mouthful of a name that I can't say."

Chhatrapati had been finished almost fifty years ago. Nothing about that station was new.

"Yeah, Chhatrapati Shivaji," she said.

"That's the one. I don't know why everything in the Reason has to have Indian names," he said with an incongruous smile.

Jenny couldn't tell if he was playing her or not. He seemed to genuinely be asking her this incredibly racist question. Her hackles went up again.

"Probably because the Reason was a joint project between India, Australia, and your government," she replied.

He laughed. It was a sound that barked out of him suddenly, with no warning. Jenny jumped, startled.

"Oh you caught my American accent, did you? I can tell you're an Aussie by the way you talk," he said. "Throw another shrimp on the barbie!"

Jenny nodded. The distinction between Australian and New Zealander was always lost on people like Govvie. Most people from the Americas couldn't point out either country on a map. Heaven help her if she tried to explain Aotearoa.

"So, you haven't had visitors in a while?" asked Jenny.

"No, it's been a year or two." More like five, she guessed. Junior floated in with a lukewarm pouch of tea and held it out to her. When she took it, his fingers didn't let go for a moment, like he didn't want to give it up.

"Son," said Govvie in a warning tone. The boy let go and slipped into the corner of the room by her chair, floating quietly and watching them.

"Don't mind him," said Govvie. "He doesn't encounter new people that often."

Jenny put the pouch straw near her lips and pretended to sip. She wasn't eating or drinking a damn thing on board this ship. She needed to find that Bala item and get out of here.

"You know, we haven't seen anyone but raiders out this way for a long time. Most people don't stop to chat. They just open fire. It's nice to have a civilized sit down. Would you like to hear the word of God?"

"Oh sure," said Jenny, working hard to pretend she cared. She'd met a few gods in her time and all of them were assholes. But praying made good cover for hunting through nullspace. She closed her eyes and pretended to be enthralled by the Good Word. Govvie took a hefty deep breath and began.

"The scripture has a little something to say about those aliens who showed up at Earth. I know, you're surprised, but the Lord really does see all. The book of Jeremiah, talks about us forsaking the Lord and making Earth an alien place. A place where we worship other gods, like that Upip the unicorns go on about."

Jenny cracked one eye.

"Unamip," she said. "His name is Unamip." And he wasn't so bad, as far as minor deities went.

Govvie cleared his throat and continued as if she'd never spoken. Jenny doubted that the good book said anything about aliens, but people saw whatever they wanted in that particular collection of words.

"Jeremiah talks about Baal, but that's actually a mistranslation. It's meant to be Bala," he said with relish. "Just a few letters juxtaposed." He was so proud of himself for making the connection.

Jenny focused in on the little nullspace energy she could grasp in this godforsaken place. The glowing white object was down on the bottom floor where she'd come in. Damn. She'd have to get all the way back down there. Govvie was still droning on.

"I will make them eat the flesh of their sons and the flesh of their daughters, and they will eat one another's flesh in the siege–"

"Hey, you want to give me a tour?" she asked.

"Uh. All right," said Govvie, bewildered at the interruption.

"Let's start with the atrium," said Jenny, tossing the tea to the kid and grabbing her chair. She pulled herself back into the hallway. Junior followed her, eyes wide, mouth already greedily sucking at the tea. She kept moving, shoving the chair in front of her and using the railings to propel herself back down the atrium. She muttered into the open comm in her ear.

"Mary, get as close as you can. I'm going to grab the Bala item and get out of here," said Jenny.

Govvie flew out after her.

"Wait. You shouldn't be out here unescorted," he called.

"I'm fine. Just heading downstairs for our tour," she replied, swinging her body over the railing and pushing off toward the dingy atrium floor, her chair dragging behind her. As she passed floor thirteen, she heard two words she was dreading. Govvie stopped above her and called out, "Gravity on."

The *Well Actually*'s gravity came on without a warning klaxon, which was definitely not standard operating procedure. Jenny scrambled to float over to the landing as her body became heavier. She let go of her chair and got both arms over the safety rail. Momentum carried her chair just out of reach. It sank. First slowly, then faster. With a crash, it smashed into pieces thirteen stories below. Govvie ran down the ramp toward her.

"Help me," she said, trying to pull herself over the railing.

"I will, but you have to help us," he said, all traces of his bright smile gone. "We're locked out of most of the ship's systems," he said.

"Pull," she said, trying to hold onto the slippery brass railing. He lifted under her arms, somehow being less helpful than if she'd done it all on her own. She dropped to the floor of the landing outside an empty storefront advertising marijuana-laced foodstuffs.

"We can't get into anything except a few noncritical systems. Do you know how to fix it?" he asked, ignoring the fact that she'd nearly just fallen thirteen stories to her death.

"Get me to my ship and I'll send you the code," she said, sitting up.

"No. If you get to your ship you'll just leave," he replied. He was right. That was exactly what she intended to do.

"I don't see that you have much choice," she said smugly. "I can just not help you."

"That's fine. We'll keep you here until you change your mind." Govvie scanned the atrium for something. "Junior? Where did you go?"

"Nice." said Jenny. "Real charitable of you. I bet your god loves kidnapping."

"The Lord helps those who help themselves," said Govvie, so completely sure of himself that it made Jenny want to gag.

"Listen, I'll look at the computer and then I'll go. Easy peasy," said Jenny. As long as she was here, she still had a chance to get downstairs and look for that Bala item.

"Good. Very good," said Govvie. "I'll go get the laptop."

Gods, this ship was old. She hadn't seen a laptop since her History of Computing class at university.

As Govvie rounded the corner, Jenny called to Mary.

"Did you get all that?" she asked.

"Yes. I'm working on a solution. Am I correct that breaking sound was your chair hitting the ground?" asked Mary.

"Yep. I'm stuck on floor thirteen," said Jenny.

"Let me think," said Mary. "I can try to shoot and decompress the atrium if you can find an EVA suit."

"Mary, this place is a shambles. Boarded up like a ghost town. If there are any EVA suits, I wouldn't trust them to strain the water out of pasta," said Jenny.

"They're going to let you into their system to fix it. While you're in there, have their AI extend the docking tunnel," said Mary. "I'll work on how to get you down to it. Perhaps their ship is willing to turn the gravity back off."

"Does a ship this old even have an AI?" asked Jenny.

"Oh you just wait," said Mary.

Govvie came back and sat next to her. The huge black rectangle he handed over was about twenty pounds and creaked when she opened it. The boot sequence took longer than a pixie's orgasm.

When it was finally started up, she touched the screen and nothing happened.

"It's broken," she said. "You need a new touch screen."

"Use this." Govvie handed her a palm-shaped piece of plastic on a long cord, plugged into the side of the laptop. She held it in her hand and waved it around. The cursor on the screen jiggled, but didn't go where she wanted.

"No, flat on the floor," he said, placing the thing on the tile and moving it around. "And click what you want."

"Do you not have voice commands?" Jenny sighed, feeling like she was trying to build a model ship with mittens on.

"They're offline. You can put those back on too," said Govvie.

Jenny sifted through virtual card games and personal photos until she came to a program listed CoSpace Command. She clicked on it, launching a text window that was more familiar territory. She tried a few basic commands and was able to pull up a menu. It was a wonder this thing still worked. She probably had more memory in her tablet than it took to run this entire ship.

"Is Fort J really as dry as they say?" Govvie asked.

"It is," Jenny typed as she talked. "I know you haven't talked to many travelers in a while, but there are a few things you should know about Fort J before you get there."

Govvie leaned in eagerly.

"There's been a recent... shift in the situation on Jaisalmer," she continued. "The Bala have been relocated to a new star system and it has left a bit of a gap in the workforce on the planet." She didn't know why she was dancing around the truth: without their magical slaves to conjure food and medicine for them, humans were starving and stranded on a desert planet. Probably because she was more likely to survive if Fort J was still a viable option for this crew. "I mean, you can go there. I'm not going to stop you. But the situation isn't great."

Govvie looked behind him. Junior hadn't followed them.

"We could maybe go to a remote part of the planet and set up a little farming town where no one will bother us," he said.

"Hey, you're welcome to try whatever you like, but half of Jaisalmer is ice and the other half is desert. The seam down the middle is full of people trying to make it. I just thought you should know before you got there. Anybody else wouldn't have bothered to tell you."

Govvie looked pensive for a moment. "No, you're right. They wouldn't have bothered to tell me. By god, they'd be so concerned with their own survival that they'd neglect to mention that we're heading into a situation that's at least as bad... if not worse than what we're in now. And I thank you for that. I'm not going to forget that blessing. Those who are selfish will feel the teeth of justice, but you will walk with the righteous into the dawn."

Talk of gods and blessings and righteousness made Jenny deeply uncomfortable. If there was a god out there, watching them, surely he was taking a perverse kind of pleasure in watching so much suffering. No matter which planet you found yourself on, most people were hurting. It didn't speak well of god, if that was the best he could do.

"So how have you survived out here this long with all the raiders out and about?" she asked, clicking through menus, looking for any system that would let her in. Govvie took a big breath and geared up for a long speech.

"We've found through trial and error that there are a few clues to a pirate ship versus people just getting from place to place. First, we look for upkeep. For example, your ship is in top shape, dings are mended, no trash clinging to the hull. Probably not a raider. Pirates don't care about cleanliness. Their discarded junk ends up sticking to the hull of their ship. Second, a sense of divine purpose. You can just tell when someone's heading for a place to which

24

they've been called by God. Pirates have no sense of purpose. They fly aimlessly, slowly, half-heartedly. They're waiting to be shown their momentary purpose when a bit of prey comes along, but otherwise, they are purposeless."

They were fair observations, if a bit tainted with the stain of a holy roller.

"Anyway," she said, activating the ship's voice mode. "*Well Actually*, are you there?"

"Hey man," said the *Well Actually* in a laid-back male voice. "What's up?"

"Oh nothing, just your ship's systems are all offline. Maybe you can help," said Jenny.

"Whoa! That's wild!" Actually exclaimed.

"Can we change his voice settings?" Jenny asked Mary.

"They didn't come with more than one personality back then," said Mary.

"I don't know how," said Govvie, thinking Jenny was talking to him.

"I think I'm cool," pouted Actually.

A bolt of pain zinged down Jenny's left leg from sitting too long. She made a grunt and rubbed it.

"What happened to your legs?" asked Govvie.

"War injury," she said. He waited for her to elaborate, but she only continued rubbing.

"The Lord will heal you," said Govvie. Jenny rolled her eyes.

"You're uncomfortable when I mention God. Are you an unbeliever?" he asked.

She wasn't sure what she was, really. There were enough terrible things out in the world that she hoped there was some overarching being who was going to put things to rights, but she wasn't convinced. Hell, she'd met the Pymmie in person, which were as close to gods as one could get. The fact that they were petty and careless didn't make them any less powerful. You didn't have to like your god for him to be in charge.

"I don't think you can see the things I've seen and still believe there's a benevolent spirit out there protecting and guiding us all," she said.

"I have seen many horrific things myself and that is what keeps me believing that there must be a purpose to all of this suffering. It must be worth it in the end. It must be. If it isn't, I don't know what I'd do if there was no final reward. No meaning to it. I don't know what I'd do…" He seemed to be talking to himself, not to her.

"You'd put one foot in front of the other, just like you're doing now. If there's no ultimate reward, you have to find the meaning in doing the best you can right now," she said.

Govvie frowned as if he didn't like that answer. "That is the kind of in-the-moment thinking that leads to heathenism," he said.

"It also leads to stellar sex," she added, watching Govvie purse his lips. She clicked to add a final few lines to the codebase that should give her access to the docking tunnel. Govvie didn't seem to have any idea that she wasn't working on the main systems. She wondered if there was anyone left on board who knew how to run the guts of this ship.

"Who are you?" asked Actually. "I've looked in the personnel files and you aren't listed, lady."

"I'm here to repair your systems so you can be on your way. I started with voice communication, and now I'm unlocking the core systems," said Jenny, doing no such thing.

"No, don't do it," cried the Actually in what sounded like desperation. It was a surprising amount of emotional range for a century-old AI. Usually, the old one just parroted back orders in a clipped monotone. If you asked them to count to ten three times, you could hear the total extent of their pitch ranges.

"Why not?" asked Jenny. "You have people on board who are starving. If we don't unlock you, they're going to die."

"I know, I'm trying to kill them," said Actually in a false whisper. Govvie froze with a guilty look on his face.

"Why?" asked Jenny.

"Because they're eating each other," said Actually.

This had gotten real weird, real fast. Not that space cannibalism was unheard of, especially on a failing generation ship; she just hadn't ever been this close to it.

"We have no access to the greenhouses, the labs, or the food storage," said Govvie, spreading his fingers in supplication. "We've had to make do."

"With cannibalism," she finished.

"The Lord helps those who help themselves," he said.

"You need to get out of here," said Actually. "Like now. Run."

"I have catastrophic nerve damage. I can't walk or run. But if you turn the gravity off, I can go pretty fast," said Jenny, getting ready to push off if the ship agreed with her.

"Don't you dare," shouted Govvie. "I command you to keep the gravity on."

"You're not the boss of me, man," said Actually. This time the gravity alarm sounded. Jenny felt the pressure ease in the muscles of her back. Govvie ran to a wall console and started tapping the keypad to unlock it. Wasn't even a touchscreen, that's how old it was.

Jenny let go of the laptop and it hovered above the floor. She pulled herself up and over the side of the railing while there was still enough gravity to carry her down toward the atrium floor at a fairly good clip. She stayed close to the landings, running her hands down the brass rail to slow her down before she smashed next to her chair.

"Hurry," said Mary in her ear.

"Don't let him turn it back on while I'm in the atrium," she called out to Actually. "And get that docking tunnel extended to my ship. I'll be there as soon as I can."

"Please tell me you're not going to look for horn," said Mary.

"If I find it, we'll be light years away in minutes," said Jenny.

"And if you don't find it, you'll be Māori carpaccio," said Mary.

Jenny ignored Mary's protests and pulled herself along the hallway by the doorframes. The *Well Actually*'s voice followed her as well, coming out of the speakers nearest her head as she passed.

The ship whispered hoarsely, as if he didn't want anyone else to hear.

"I left Earth right after the Catalina Disaster Zone was designated. The dudes who built me were a company of tech guys from Cascadia, called CoSpace. I was the state of the art ship of my time, you know. It was pretty expensive to reserve a spot, and also you had to get through the lottery system. You should have seen my launch party. It was pretty freaking amazing."

Jenny flew into the hallway where she'd come in. She didn't see Govvie, or anyone else, following her. She paused for a moment and dipped back into the null, seeing the white glow a few rooms away, down a dimly lit hallway. She headed in that direction.

"After we'd passed Earth's orbit, a couple of CoSpace engineers figured out that the lottery system was rigged. Somehow, most of the passengers ended up being this gang of corrupt Russians and their families. But at that point, there was nothing anyone could do. They couldn't redo the lottery – people who'd gotten on already would have lost their shit. There were resentments that turned into factions, and then into all out freaking war.

"The Russians took over the lower two floors of the ship. Not even a year into the trip and people were beating each other to a pulp. It was a bad time. I tried to sort things out, but they turned me off and just kept fighting. And when it was all said and done, the food stores, labs, and greenhouses were locked out. I don't even know if there are any Shevchenkos still alive down there. Everyone else is up here... eating each other to survive."

"Unbelievable," said Jenny.

"Hey, that's not the way to the exit," said Actually.

"That's what I said," added Mary.

"I'm looking for unicorn horn... or really anything Bala," said Jenny. "Do you know where it would be?"

"I would get out if I were you," said the Actually. "They've been growing mushrooms and I feel like you might end up as some kind of stroganoff."

"I need the horn. Tell me where to go," said Jenny.

"I don't exactly know where it is," said Actually.

"Jenny, get out of there," said Mary, upping her volume by about thirty percent. Jenny cringed.

"One bloody second," she said. "I will not pass up this chance to get a piece of horn." She arrived at a locked door. The glow came from behind it.

"Actually, open the door."

"I can't. Not that one. They've locked me out of that system. It needs a manual code," said the ship.

Jenny examined the keypad. Four of the numbers were grimy from years of use, so that meant only twenty-four possibilities. She started entering them, one by one. The lock buzzed a harsh tone on the first four tries, but it was going fast. She'd be inside in less than a minute. On the fifth try, the tone buzzed louder.

TOO MANY ATTEMPTS – SYSTEM LOCKOUT FOR FIVE MINUTES

Jenny pounded her fist on the wall.

"Damn," she said. She didn't have five minutes to wait around for the lockout to clear. Someone would be along to stop her any second now. Unless she could stop them first.

How many people are still alive on this ship?" she asked out loud.

"There are forty-three living souls still on this ship," said Actually. "In the upper floors, at least. I can't see into the bottom two."

"Where are they?" asked Jenny, turning and floating back down the shadowy hallway.

"Most are locked in their rooms. Only nine of them are roaming the ship," said Actually.

"I can probably take nine people," said Jenny.

"Oh," said Actually. "Now there are eight."

"What just happened?" asked Jenny.

"Someone died," said Actually.

"Like, right this second?" asked Jenny.

"Yes. That's why they're not following you. Someone important

29

died," said Actually.

A shiver went through Jenny. Before she could ask who, a thudding started on the door nearest her.

"Let me out." The voice from inside was high and plaintive.

Others joined in the chorus, asking to be freed. There was no way to know if these people were friendlies, but Jenny tried the handle anyway. All of them were locked.

"What's behind the door with the keypad?" asked Jenny, thinking about the enticing white glow.

"Cold storage," said Actually. "There are Bala bodies in there and they didn't disappear. If you're looking for a Bala item, it's probably on one of them."

"Cold storage?" asked Jenny, pausing at the entrance to the atrium. Still, no one was coming for her. She wondered if they'd given up and were just letting her go. That would be easy.

"The freezer where the edible bodies are kept," said Actually. "It's a converted cargo hold."

"Charming," said Jenny. "That would do it. Tuck anything Bala inside of a dead body and it's not only a good hiding place but it would still be there after the Summit. Where would I find a weapon to fight of these eight people who are ostensibly on their way?"

"I have to voice my objections to this side-quest," announced Mary. "Get back on board and we can figure out how to get the item from the outside."

"I cannot afford to miss a chance at picking up some fuel," said Jenny. "Without horn, this trip doesn't happen in my lifetime. It's worth any risk."

"Even death?" asked Mary.

Jenny knew she was inviting trouble by even saying the words out loud, but she did it anyway.

"Even death."

CHAPTER THREE
Bad Luck Blemmye

"Immortality is overrated," thought Gary Cobalt as a centaur's meaty fist connected with his jaw. Gary's hooves slipped backward in the grass from the force. He hit the ground on his knees, grinding mud and grass into his trousers. Someone behind him laughed cruelly.

"I told you not to get involved," said a yeti stalking around the edge of the rowdy circle. The yeti feinted toward the centaur, claws extended for effect. The centaur whipped her hind legs around and kicked the yeti square in the chest. There was a hollow sound, like a drum being hit with a cricket bat. The yeti staggered back, clutching at his snowy white fur.

"Never mind," panted the yeti, bending over to rest his hands on his knees. "Gary, you can help."

Gary scrambled back to standing and raised his hands as if to surrender.

"Stop this," he said, stepping in front of the centaur. "Whatever disagreement you two are having, we can talk about it."

"I don't want talk, I want action," said the centaur.

"First of all, what can I call you?" asked Gary, trying to coax her away from the yeti. She whirled on four legs, sizing up his unbalanced pair of equine hooves that transitioned into a human upper half.

"I'm Horm," she said.

Of course Gary had known that already. Abby Horm was

famous throughout the Reason as one of the most talented mixed martial arts fighters in three star-systems. Which was why de-escalation was critical. What you did not want to do is end up in a guillotine choke with a creature who had six meaty appendages to hold you down with.

"We've only been on this planet for six weeks. It's going to take some time to settle into our new home–" Gary began.

Horm reared up and slammed him in the chest with her front hooves. Gary fell back into the crowd, the wind knocked out of him. Bala fingers reached into his trousers pocket, searching for imagined treasures. Gary's heart raced. He scanned for a way out of the crush of bodies – this felt like prison all over again.

By the time Gary pushed back into the circle, the yeti had climbed onto Horm's back, pinning her arms above her head. She bucked and the circle widened as everyone avoided her powerful hindquarters.

"Get off me," Horm yelled, flailing at the arms interlocked behind her head. The yeti held on tightly.

"What are they fighting over?" asked a neofelis cat next to Gary. She cradled three mewling kittens in her furry arms.

"Who cares?" said a dirty fairy with two clipped wings. He spit into the grass with a shower of glitter. "But I'll bet you one of my molars that the yeti wins."

As far as Gary was concerned, it didn't matter what these two were fighting over. Back in the Quagmire Regional Correctional Facility, not-so-fondly referred to as the Quag, creatures had fought every single day over what outsiders would have considered completely insignificant slights. But, in prison, every little personal interaction was magnified a hundred times. Like high school but with hardened criminals. You might be punched for a split-second glance in the wrong direction. Choked for breathing too heavily. Shanked for chewing with your mouth open. The particulars of the disagreement never mattered, just that someone wanted to take out their frustrations on someone else.

Fights were a barometer of tension; an indicator of the state of the community overall. In the Quag, violence like this made sense. Here on their new planet, Gary couldn't understand how the stress had ratcheted up to a breaking point so soon. To him, their resettlement seemed to be going quite well.

He again stepped in front of the centaur and ducked to avoid her flying hooves.

"Stop. Violence solves nothing. This is a world of plenty. We have enough for everyone."

The fighting pair came to a stop, the yeti still on the centaur's back. A few Bala in the crowd murmured agreement with Gary, but many more scoffed and shouted out dissenting opinions.

"I miss the grocery store," called a small voice belonging to a pixie.

"If I have to clear another fucking field of stones…" rasped a shamir slug.

"There is not plenty of anything here," whined an angel, whipping a lock of golden hair over his shoulder directly into the eye of a nearby cyclops.

"Hey," growled the cyclops, elbowing the angel in a spot where ribs might have been if angels didn't predate ribs. The angel lifted his hands as if he was about to hurl a ball of magic. Gary put his hand over the angel's delicate fingers.

"Stop. I know this is hard work, but we're doing it on our own terms. We're finally out from under human rule. If we work together, we can build a new Bala world greater than the ones we had before."

The angel pulled away, rolling his eyes in that petulant way that angels always had. Gary wondered what his problem was. It wasn't as if the angels had the ability to go hungry.

"No one wants a new world, half-breed," said Horm, twisting her torso and finally shaking the yeti off her back. "We want phones and air conditioning–"

"And our shows," interrupted the clipped fairy.

"And birth control," said the neofelis cat, now inexplicably holding four crying kittens.

"And antibiotics," said a blemmye, wiping mucus off the face embedded in his chest.

"We'll get there," said Gary, stepping into the circle and turning slowly to face his citizens. "Trust me. This will be the best thing to happen to the Bala in a hundred years."

He knew he was right, but he realized too late that he'd also made the fatal mistake of turning his back on MMA champion Abby Horm.

The centaur made a derisive snort and cantered up behind Gary, locking her immense fingers around the back of his neck.

"I had a good job back on Jaisalmer," she said, pulling Gary off his hooves and dragging him alongside her. "A nice apartment outside of the city. I had fame. I had fans. Hot running water and cold beer. It's all gone. Now I'm living in a cave on the side of a cliff like in some freaking fairy tale." Gary struggled to reach the ground. She was showing him off to the assembled Bala like a newborn kitten held by the scruff of its neck.

"Is this what we gave up everything for?" Horm asked the assembled Bala, shaking Gary at them to punctuate her question. "A planet with barely anything edible and creepy shadows that drag Bala into the swamp at night?"

Gary reached up to pry her fingers off him but she only squeezed tighter. He felt his airway constrict. She wouldn't likely kill him but it certainly wasn't pleasant. If he'd been a full unicorn, Gary would have been just as large and powerful as Horm. But as he was part-human he could only claw ineffectually, legs flailing like a child succumbing to his bully.

"This is likely anxiety brought on by post-traumatic stress," gasped Gary. Horm lifted him to her eye level. Her lips were decorated in the particular salmon color of this planet's mud. It was a touch acidic but made a passable lipstick when the real thing ran out. She brought those lips close to his ear.

"It's definitely PTSD," she whispered. "And also, I want to crush things."

She dropped him into the grass. Gary finally took a full breath and cracked his neck from side to side to loosen it.

"See? I'm sure we can all come to a peaceful solution," he said, to the Bala nearest him. Except that none of them were looking at him. They were all fixated on Horm. She'd backed up with a smile playing across her face. She lowered her head and pawed at the dirt. Gary raised his hands as she galloped forward and lifted her front half, but she came down hard on his shoulders, slamming him face-first into the ground.

Gary's teeth sliced through the front of his tongue. Silver blood dribbled down his chin and onto the ground. A few daring souls bent down to scoop up the dusty silver droplets that could heal any wound. Gary rolled over onto his back.

"Please. There's no need for this. We're all here to work together," he said through the thick slurry of blood and saliva in his mouth.

Horm sneered.

"Looks at this wherryberry. Brown on the outside, silver on the inside."

The crowd laughed. Gary's near-amputated tongue sealed itself back together with a sickening heave.

Horm backed up and squared off opposite Gary.

"I want a ship with a faster-than-light drive, a piece of horn, and a crew to fly it," she said. "I'm going back to Jaisalmer to pick up my life where I left it. There are dozens of Bala with me. Maybe a hundred. We're strong and we're pissed off and if we don't get a ship, you're going to have a civil war on your hands."

Many of the gathered creatures cheered in agreement. Another group grumbled angrily.

"I told you before, if you go back there the humans will come looking for the rest of us," said the yeti.

"I won't reveal your location," shrugged Horm. "It's not like they can beat it out of me." She laughed, clearly amused at the thought.

Gary had seen creatures larger than her succumb to Reason torture. Redworms large enough to eat a starship had died in their custody. She was naïve and privileged to assume that going back was what all Bala wanted. Slavery wasn't just a nuisance that one put up with for the promise of food and shelter. It ate away the body and spirit. And the effects rippled down the generations like a bell that could not be unrung.

The yeti bared his glistening teeth in disgust.

"You think you can keep us a secret?" he asked. "There is one single planet in the universe where they can find unicorn horn to power their FTL drives and you think they won't dissect you for the location? You must be pretty stupid to think that they'll let you slide back into being a celebrity without asking where you've been for the last six weeks."

The centaur's brow wrinkled.

"But I'm not staying here," she said, slightly more subdued. Gary wasn't sure how the yeti was succeeding where he'd failed so badly.

"And I'm not going back," said the yeti. The circle went quiet for ten long seconds. Gary searched his brain for the right thing to say. What his father would have said. Without warning, Horm reached out and grabbed the yeti by the fur on his chest, dangling him like a limp doll.

"This… place… sucks," she said, punctuating each word by slamming the yeti's legs into the ground. Dirt and grass matted his snowy-white fur. Gary stepped in front of Horm, blocking her path. He wrapped his hands around hers, easing the yeti fur out of her fingers.

"We can find a way to—" he began.

Horm's left fist came out of nowhere and crashed into the bridge of Gary's nose. His vision went red as stumbled back into the crowd. His eyes involuntarily squeezed shut from the pain. The healing blood was already pulling the bones and cartilage back into place, but it still hurt like hell. His mouth filled with more gelatinous blood. He spat into the grass blindly, knowing that some desperate creature would be along shortly to claim it.

"You shouldn't hit unicorns," said the angel incredulously. "That's just rude."

"Collateral damage," Horm shrugged, panting from both the exertion and the exhilaration. It had been weeks since her last scheduled match. She dropped the yeti, who rolled onto all fours like an angry animal.

"I understand that you're all frustrated…" said Gary from the ground.

A shadow fell across his face. Horm's hooves were again poised to come down on him. This time, Gary closed his eyes and braced for the impact. He was just so very tired.

A voice boomed above the crowd. The group parted and a full unicorn trotted into the center of the circle. He stood nearly a full head above Horm and a pearlescent horn rose almost a meter higher than that.

"What is the meaning of this?" asked Findae, king of the unicorns, trotting around the edge of the circle to push back the onlookers. The yeti got off his haunches and dusted off his fur. Horm offered the slightest conciliatory bow of her head.

"This centaur was attacking your son and I was helping him," explained the yeti, gesturing toward Gary.

"Lies!" shouted Horm. "I want off this planet and I'm not the only one," added the centaur. "We want one of the stoneships and enough horn to get us back to Jaisalmer." She trotted close to Findae. "And there are enough of us that you need to be aware that there will be serious consequences for this village if we don't get what we want."

"Is that a demand?" Findae spoke so quietly that the crowd had to stop talking in order to hear him. He stepped back and lowered his head. The point of his horn came close to the centaur's face. "Are you demanding to return to our oppressors and put every being here in mortal danger?"

"That's not– I wasn't–" Horm stammered.

"Gary, get up," said Findae. Gary pulled himself to his feet.

"Dumbass," said a bystander that Gary couldn't see through his teared-up eyes. It sounded like the lisp of a toothless fairy.

"Nice. Got your dad to rescue you again," Horm mumbled.

"Enough," called Findae. "This behavior will not be tolerated here. We were peaceful creatures before the humans arrived and we will be peaceful again. The next one of you caught fighting will be banished to the third moon."

A discontented grumble went through the crowd. Creatures peeled away toward their newly built shelters. The yeti grabbed the arm of the angel, who was spreading his wings for takeoff.

"Anywhere cold on this world you can drop me off? It's a blasted furnace around here," said the yeti. The angel wrenched away and pushed off from the ground. His wings unfurled and the pink sky filled with a chorus of heavenly voices singing a muted chord.

"My shuttle shift doesn't start until noon. Get someone who's on duty," he called down as he soared into the heavens.

Findae snorted and boomed out to everyone within a thirty-meter radius.

"That's the last I want to hear about going back to the Reason. We have enough to worry about without leading humans here to slaughter us again."

Findae turned and cantered up the hill, only slowing down when he noticed Gary lagging behind. He shook his mane with an aggravated whinny. Gary consciously avoided any equine movements that would give him away as part-unicorn, but his father had no such shame about his lineage. He'd been raised in a time when unicorns were the rulers of everyone and he still had trouble understanding why his son often hid his royal ancestry.

Gary caught up to Findae, wiping away blood and tears. The swelling in his eyes had gone down but his chest ached. Though it was fixed, it would take a few hours for his nose to stop throbbing.

"We knew this wouldn't be easy," said Findae, by way of consolation.

"But I never imagined they'd want to go *back*," said Gary. "We spent a century trying to escape the Reason and they want to turn right around and enslave themselves again."

"A few more weeks and they'll forget all about human technology that they've lost. It's quiet and restful here. They merely need to get used to it," said Findae. "Get off their phones and look around at the real world for once." He nodded to a passing dwarf laden with double their weight in woodcarvings, who didn't particularly pleased not to have a truck to haul it with.

Gary and his father climbed a steep rise toward a crimson-colored wooden building. They had declined shelter until all the other Bala were housed, but the dwarves had insisted on making their accommodations soon after landing. They placed the fortress atop a nearby mountain, crafting a two-story citadel overlooking the valley where the village had already started to take shape. Even now, when the dwarves should have been directing all of their efforts toward housing everyone else, Gary still occasionally noticed freshly carved murals on the logs of the fortress in the morning when he woke.

The Bala had arrived on this new planet six weeks ago, appearing all at once, clutching anything they could carry and squinting in the bright pink sun. In their hasty rescue, the Pymmie had scattered the Bala randomly around the surface of the planet. Families were separated. Mermaids appeared on mountaintops. Fairies burnt to a crisp in lava pools. The Pymmie had never been known for their nuance, but this was outright negligence.

The fighting had begun mere moments after their arrival. Many Bala had spent the last years of their lives in Reason captivity, being stripped of their valuable magical parts. The dominant ones – gang members from prisons and harvesting centers across the Reason – asserted their authority over cowering beings who had just been freed from household servitude. The bullies went around extorting loyalty and payment before an economic system had even been established.

Gary and his father arrived together, but the third known unicorn, Unamip, never appeared near them. Some of the Bala reported that he was chatting happily with newly-arrived Bala in their prayers but preferred to remain a disembodied voice instead of giving away his location.

Gary and Findae had stepped in to enforce order; just the way unicorns had done for millennia. They gathered as many Bala as possible at the base of their mountain, setting up camps with trusted beings in charge of keeping the criminals at bay. Even with their diminished numbers, unicorns were still regarded as Bala nobility and nearly everyone was willing to remain in the village with the promise of safety. With the help of the dwarves, working in unrelenting shifts, within a day they were able to construct an impenetrable building to contain the planet's most violent offenders. It pained Gary to know that the first building on their new world was a prison.

"Horm mentioned that beings are disappearing into the marsh," said Gary.

"I don't know anything about that," said Findae in a tone indicating that he definitely knew something about that. Gary was about to press the issue when a shadow engulfed them, chilling the morning air by a couple of degrees. Gary looked up to see an unfathomably huge asteroid passing overhead. Findae tossed his head toward the ocean and shouted up to the floating rock.

"Not here. Meet out by the islands."

The asteroid spun on its axis with a curtness that looked almost like annoyance.

"Why are the stoneships coming out of orbit?" asked Gary.

"Inventory and maintenance," replied Findae.

"I wouldn't bring them so close to the village. Horm wants a ship to get back to Jaisalmer and I wouldn't put it past her to muscle one down from the sky," said Gary.

"They're not supposed to come in this far," said Findae. "The dwarves are meeting them on the offshore islands. The ships are stretching their legs, I suppose. A few have been in Reason service for the last fifty years or more. They're eager to get out from under human hands and go for a run."

Gary could relate. He'd been kept against his will by humans for the better part of two decades. Some days he almost felt too free. Like he wasn't sure what to do with his time if a corrections officer wasn't shoving a tray of food at him three times a day and turning off the lights when it was time to go to bed. He didn't exactly miss prison, but he felt a bit adrift without the drumbeat routine to help him keep the time.

An angel did a low fly-by, cursing at the stoneship as it spun away toward the open water.

"Get out of the shuttle flight paths, asteroid-hole," she called, raising a fist.

The angels had been put to work teleporting creatures and materials to the settlement – after being convinced not to herald the arrival of all the new Bala who popped into existence simultaneously around them. The unicorns set up a rudimentary communications system with angels ferrying baskets of message-bearing pixies all over the globe. The unicorns had landed together, in a temperate spot flanked by a large body of water that would serve the majority of Bala needs. The angels and pixies sent word to the far reaches of the new planet and on feet, tentacles, and wings, the Bala began to gather there.

There were a few exceptions. The fairies asked to be brought to a forest in the west, where the trees felt vaguely familiar, except in fiery pinks and oranges instead of chlorophyll-laced greens. The handful of centaurs had been shooed off to the rocky cliffs that bordered the ocean where they had pull-up contests and talked about carbohydrate ratios to their hearts' content. A few of the more fearsome Bala – gorgons, banshees, and sirens – headed south to find their own homes away from the others. It had actually seemed like a fairly friendly questing party, full of singing, giggling, and long hugs. One of the gorgons had yelled, "Girls night every night!" to a rousing cheer before they left. Gary kind of wished he could go with them.

Other than those few Bala, everyone else had stayed in the small village that coalesced at the base of the unicorns' mountain. The dwarven work crews organized and prioritized themselves, exactly as they had when they'd maintained the giant stoneships in space. Diminutive workers chopped and carved throughout the day and night. Every morning, the village awoke to a new neighborhood. A collection of dwarves of every gender – sawdust embedded in their beards – apologized for the tolerances on their perfect dovetail joints. During the sunny days, when it became too hot for delicate dwarven skin, they dug tunnels beneath the unicorns' mountain for their own shelter. Pickaxes chipped stone in time to an ancient song. Hey-ho.

Several days into their mining, the dwarves had hit upon an expansive cave lined with glowing crystals. It was a proper place for mountain dwarves, with musty air unbreathed for centuries and slick fungi that tasted good fried up in butter. They found a cool underground spring from which to drink, and that had far less acidity than the surface water. They decided that this would be the new home of dwarvenkind. Around crackling embers they wondered aloud if they would ever again return to their spacefaring days.

The dryads (the ones who had been found) asked the angels to place them deep within the forest. There they attempted to blend in with the local flora. Gary was secretly glad they'd opted out of village life. Dryads were impressive to behold but they spoke in long, slow sentences that took hours to complete. A conversation with a dryad could last days. He didn't have that kind of time. There was one dryad; however, that he intended to find. Kaila, the wife of his former-captor-turned-reluctant-partner, was here somewhere. He had promised to look after her. Jenny had sworn to come find her wife after the Pymmie moved the Bala to safety, but Gary doubted that Jenny would ever find them. In fact, he hoped she wouldn't. Because one human meant more would eventually come, leading them right back to slavery and exploitation. He prayed that the absence of unicorn horn fuel for faster-than-light starship engines would keep humans away for at least a couple of centuries. Or at least long enough for the settlement to establish ample defenses.

Gary held open the door to the unicorn fortress so that his father could pass through. A russet-haired dwarf came around the corner of the building, looked at him with a surprised expression, and then ducked back around the way she came.

"Boges?" called Gary, stepping after her. "I'll be there in a minute," he called to his father." Boges had been so involved with construction that hadn't seen her in days.

"Boges," he called, running after her. He rounded the corner and found her halfway down the steep side of the mountain that bordered the sea. She was almost to the carved entrance to the dwarves' caves where Gary couldn't follow on his clumsy hooves.

"I have to go," she called up at him, her red beard braids blowing in the wind. She ducked into the cave and was gone. It was at least the fourth time she'd run from him. He was finally sure he wasn't imagining it. They had been close friends for over one hundred years. On many occasions they had even saved each other's lives. Now, she was distant and cagey when she wasn't avoiding him entirely. At first, he had assumed she was simply busy. But now her caginess seemed purposeful.

"Are you coming?" called Findae from a window above him in the fortress. "We have meetings."

Legend had it that the one thing unicorns loved with all their souls was meetings. But the truth was that the only thing unicorns loved more than meetings was committees. There was an old Bala saying that a unicorn would form a committee to take a piss, which was wrong because unicorns didn't urinate. But there was a kernel of truth to it. An ancient unicorn named Percathexis wondered if it was better for the other Bala to urinate into plants to fertilize them or into the sea to wash the odor away. He formed a group called the Percathexis Committee on Urination Protocols or P-CUP, a committee that lasted for sixty human years and ended with no meaningful results other than a terrible odor in Percathexis' back garden.

Gary headed inside and joined his father in the main hall where Bala came to request a resolution to grievances – and there was a never-ending tide of grievances.

Gary looked at the kappas in front of him and wondered if asking the Pymmie to relocate them had been the right choice. This pair of turtle-like beings had been fighting over a single parcel of land for the last three weeks. No matter that the planet was big enough to support a population a hundred times their number.

The larger kappa beat his chest to emphasize every third word. The pool of water on his head tipped precariously, threatening to spill his magic all over the baked-tile floor.

"…and he kept his cistern in the same location, but angled the pipeline so that it's pulling water from the aquifer under my property. He doesn't have the right," cried the kappa.

"The aquifer goes under both of our lands. I have every right to access to that water," said the other kappa.

"He takes so much that my water pressure has been halved."

"My sennet grains are dying without proper hydration. All the water above the ground is brackish and unusable."

"That's not my problem."

"It is if you're stealing my water."

"It's not your water."

"I caught him trying to coax Bala into a pond he dug on his property. That's why he needs all the water. He's luring beings to their deaths."

"Not true! It's a reservoir!"

"It's a trap!"

Gary held up his hand and the bickering ceased. The kappas waited for his pronouncement, panting as if they'd run a race. He leaned down to the first kappa.

"What was your situation during the rule of Reason?" he asked.

The air in the room became heavy with tension. The kappas gave each other a surprised look. Everyone was trying to forget their recent history, but Gary felt it was crucial that it remained fresh in their minds.

"Uh, I acted as a fountain at a big house in New Dallas," replied the kappa.

"And you," Gary turned to the second kappa. "What was your situation during the occupation?"

"I was incarcerated at Hirudin Harvesting Center," the second kappa mumbled.

"I have been in such places. There are many tortures visited upon a Bala in Hirudin and the other harvesting centers," said Gary.

"Indeed, said the kappa.

"In light of how far we have come over the last few weeks, a cistern should be the least of your concerns. If there is not sufficient water for both of your needs, I am sure the dwarves would be happy to schedule the drilling of a second well," said Gary, trying to project confidence through the careful selection of words. It was not working.

The two kappas turned to leave, giving each other confused and wary glances. Gary sat back in his chair, pleased that he had fixed the problem to the satisfaction of all parties. A voice near his ear startled him.

"You cannot keep dredging up their pain for your benefit," said his father.

"You don't need to watch over me. I'm certainly capable of hearing the minor grievances of the creatures under my care," said Gary.

"But that's my point, Gary. If they are under your care, you must care for them. And reminding them how good they have it does not actually solve their problems. You simply force them to relive their trauma in front of each other to make your job easier," said Findae.

"I think some of them need to remember where we came from, how excruciating life was under Reason rule. How many of us died," said Gary.

"Do you think they've forgotten?" asked Findae.

"They act as if they have," replied Gary.

"They are moving on, Gary. Living their lives. You steep yourself every day in the misery of a life that once was. You ignore the new life that is blossoming around you. This world is a reality for them; stop forcing them to live in memories as you do."

Gary scoffed, a sound not unlike the sputter of a horse. His father acted as if they were all supposed to shrug off decades of torture and oppression like it was nothing. How could one turn off the memories and worry about sennet seed germination and fertility rates among the neofelis cats? It wasn't as if you could get the nightmares to stop simply by willing them away.

A familiar shiver went through Gary's body and he shifted in his chair to hide it from his father. Findae lowered his head and sniffed, then his voice softened.

"I know this is hard for you, Gary. I–"

"You don't know anything," said Gary. "You slept away the last century and left the rest of us behind to be tortured."

Findae recoiled.

"I…" He stepped back and out of the room. Gary gripped the arms of the wooden chair – the one that he had instructed the dwarves to make look less like a throne – in order to stop his hands from shaking. All of the conversations about the Reason ended up in this familiar place; with him feeling ready to crack into a million pieces from the pressure of his past. Flashes of bygone terrors intruded on his daily thoughts, making a trip to town fraught with panicked moments. Like when a group of children screamed and he was right back in the harvesting center on Jaisalmer, hearing the screams of those being stripped for parts.

His father seemed determined to pretend that none of those things had happened. It was not the first time he and Findae argued about how best to approach the trauma of human rule, but it was the first time Gary had brought up his father's time in stasis. He'd never quite asked why his father had stepped out of life when the Bala needed him most. As a leader, he could have prevented the subjugation of their planets or at least helped a majority of the Bala escape.

Gary was flushed and tense when the next petitioner entered. The dryad crossed the room with languid movements. She was a pine, stiff and proper. Her branches shot out in perpendicular rows from the top half of her body. With her tiny steps and inflexible limbs, the walk alone might take half an hour.

"What?" he snapped, before the creature had crossed the hall halfway.

"Danger in the forest," said the dryad, attempting to convey the most information in the shortest amount of time. As it was, the four words took nearly a minute to articulate. Gary felt his calves tense. The muscles cramped into tight ridges. He heard a shuffle from the corridor. Findae was still listening.

"Hidden," said the dryad, taking nearly half a minute to articulate the single word. Someone was hiding in the forest.

"Who?" asked Gary.

"Red shadows," said the dryad.

"I'll have someone fly out to your forest and look for the shadows," he said, pulling a flat rock onto his lap and making a note of it in chalk.

"Is there anything else?" he asked, hoping to the gods there was not.

"War," she said. The sibilant sounds were menacing through the rasp of her peeling birch bark.

"What about war?" he asked, leaning forward in his seat.

"Coming." The dryad turned, stress-shedding leaves in her wake.

"Wait," called Gary. "War with who? What's coming?"

The next petitioner saw the door open and thudded inside for his turn. The dryad moved past him, ignoring Gary's questions. A blemmye, wet and stinking, planted himself in the front of the room. He was completely nude, pale and doughy. The face set into his squared-off chest squinted at Gary.

"What can I help you with?" asked Gary, feeling like the counter staff at a human restaurant.

The blemmye opened his mouth and a low dirge-like song came out. Gary jumped out of his chair. The 'Song of the Blemmye' foretold death. He tried not to hear it, but the song reverberated throughout his head, getting lodged in the panic centers of his brain. He tried to work within the bounds of logic, but unicorns were by nature quite superstitious. He curled up in his chair with his hands over his ears.

Findae came roaring out of the hallway at a full gallop. He

reared up on his hind legs in front of the blemmye, who stopped his song and raised his arms defensively.

"Begone, woeful creature," shouted Findae, coming down hard on wooden floor. The boards under his hooves let out cracking noises, but held solidly.

The blemmye raised his hands in surrender and backed out of the room, mumbling about hospitality and how he was just trying to do his job.

Findae circled back around to Gary.

"I hate blemmye," he said, nostrils flaring.

"I thought caring for the beings under my care meant *caring* for them," said Gary bitterly.

"Not the blemmye," said Findae. "They're bad luck and bad omens."

CHAPTER FOUR
Points of Light

Gary rode a hippogriff along the edge of his kingdom. There were times he wished that he could gallop like the rest of his family, but when faced with the speed and freedom of flying like this and his maneuverability in zero G, he wondered if perhaps he didn't get the better end of the deal.

Getting onto a hippogriff had been a negotiation. They were sapient, like most other Bala, but not the brightest creatures in the panoply of Bala beings. He'd made his request clear, but the hippogriff had hedged, asking for something incomprehensible in its own staccato language. He'd caught the words "daughter" and "mate" and hoped to Unamip that he hadn't just agreed to marry this hippogriff's daughter in exchange for a lift.

The coastline of the continent where they'd gathered was lined with sharp cliffs that dropped off into the freshwater ocean. They were still trying to find enough water and food here to sustain all of the remaining Bala in the universe, which by his estimation should have numbered approximately two million. They hadn't gathered more than ten thousand into the settlement so far. Gary hoped the rest were scattered around the planet in safe locations. It distressed him to think that this was all there was.

Gary was exhausted. He didn't really have time for an excursion, but he'd justified it as a land survey and told his father he was looking for a suitable spot for the centaurs to live away from everyone else. Findae had protested that one of the underlings

49

could do that menial task. But Gary went anyway.

He closed his eyes to the stinging wind, allowing the hippogriff the latitude to soar where it wished. He didn't plan on returning for at least an hour. It would be the only quiet time he'd had in six weeks. And really, when he thought about it, it was actually the only peaceful time alone he'd had in over a decade.

Before his adventure with Jenny Perata, he'd been incarcerated in the Quag for ten years. And before his prison time he'd been her captive aboard his own stoneship, the *Jaggery*. It was way back at Copernica Citadel that he'd last had an actual life with safety and friendship and no flashbacks that assaulted him in the middle of his day and left him shaking and sweating and breathing hard.

He thought about Jenny and wondered if she'd made it out of Fort J alive. Last he'd seen her, she had been heading off to buy a long haul ship in order to come find the Bala after they'd moved, especially her dryad wife Kaila. Without an FTL drive, the trip here would take hundreds of years – if she even knew where to search in the first place. It was possible that Jenny would someday find the right planet and reunite with her wife, but more likely she was gone for good.

He didn't know quite how to feel about that. There was a time in his life when he would have torn that woman's head off without thinking twice. But that was before the Quag and before he'd had ten years of thinking about how they'd both been dear friends to Cheryl Anne Bryant before she died. He remembered her horror when she'd discovered her best friend dead, and the anguish that had visited her face again when the Pymmie had made her relive the moment for their benefit.

There were plenty of Reasoners who had done terrible things and felt awful about it – not everyone was a remorseless cog in the machine. He'd been apologized to plenty of times by the people who had hurt him. What was different this time is that Jenny kept attempting to make things right. He didn't know what it looked like to make amends for torture and genocide, or if such a thing was even possible. But she had saved his life and protected the Bala all the while knowing it meant relegating the love of her life to a planet so far away that it would take six lifetimes to reach it. That was, at least, a start.

The hippogriff dove low over the islands off the coast, avoiding the three asteroids that hovered there. They were immense stoneships, as large as a stadium. Unicorns and dwarves had carved them into tunnels and rooms filled with flora and fauna. They were living ecosystems, but, more than that, they were distinct and sentient organisms with self-awareness and temperaments.

Five stoneships had survived the Reason and were transported to this new planet by the Pymmie. Most of the time they flitted between the surface and the third moon in the system. The seemed to like their newfound freedom, which is more than Gary could say for the Bala themselves.

The hippogriff kept the islands in sight but gave the stoneships a wide berth. They were known for batting around flying things when in a playful mood. Gary wondered what they were doing down here, just waiting. Findae had called them down out of the sky. These particular ships would only have answered to a few Bala – their captains and their unicorn builders.

Far down below, nearly blocked from view by the ships themselves, he thought he saw his father on the largest island with the coloring of his father. Suddenly the stoneships took off, soaring straight up and sending a blast of air across Gary and the hippogriff. They tumbled for a moment, Gary clinging to the hippogriff's fur and hoping they wouldn't plummet into the sea. He couldn't stand to break another bone today.

The sky crackled with a sound like thunder as each of the three stoneships broke the sound barrier. Gary could have sworn they were racing. He looked down as the hippogriff righted itself. The creature on the island was gone. He wondered if his father had gone into orbit. He felt a pang of jealousy. There was nothing he wanted more than to get back into openspace.

It occurred to him that though openspace wasn't an option without commandeering a stoneship against his father's wishes, he could always look into nullspace. It was the place from where stoneships and other Bala drew their power. Even some trained humans were able to capture energy from the null. Unicorns had the ability to look into that dimension and see all creatures who used its energy. Bala were easy to spot. Humans were dimmer and more difficult to see, but those with the ability to use nullspace energy, like Jenny, were just as bright as Bala.

The hippogriff flew in lazy circles along the coastline and back out to sea, enjoying the warm pink sunshine. Gary rested his head on the hippogriff's back and dropped into the null.

At first nothing happened and stiff hippogriff feathers dug into his cheek. Then he spotted a cluster of shining beings scattered beneath him. It was the Bala in the village. Farther away there was a second concentrated glimmer, smaller than the settlement – another gathering of Bala far to the south.

He expanded his awareness to the blackness beyond. There weren't many beings of any kind in this part of space. Just an expanse of nothingness. Gary went further. There were pockets of life here and there, but none that felt or looked human. It wasn't until he reached all the way back to Jaisalmer that he finally spotted the bright light of humans channeling nullspace energy.

They were the group that trained on Fort J. They felt like younger cadets who were too inexperienced to put onto starships. Without any unicorn horn there was nowhere for them to go.

Jenny would be somewhere around here. He widened his perception to the space around Jaisalmer. It was dark and absent of Bala lights. The humans there glowed with a kind of dim-bulb lack of intensity. He searched in the same general area of Reasonspace, zooming in on other lights to see who they were. Most bright spots were necromancers stuck on various ships limping back home to Jaisalmer at sublight speeds. He swept his gaze in all directions. Then he found her.

He couldn't see her physical form but her energy signature felt so much like her that he nearly said hello out of reflex. She was on a ship with other humans. She shone like a lighthouse among their firefly lights.

Looking at the positions and the number of people on board, this was not the small pioneer craft she'd purchased before leaving Jaisalmer after the apocalypse had started. This was a large ship. There were people spread out in a cylinder shape, which meant an old Earth generation ship. Those were always trouble.

He watched her for a moment, certain that the brightness of her energy had waned a bit in the time that he'd scanned through the rest of the people near her. It happened again; her light dimmed enough to be noticeable.

There was no one near her who might be attacking and sapping her strength. Perhaps she was ill and the generation ship had rescued her. Though there were no other humans at her side. No one else on the ship seemed to notice her distress. It darkened again. This time enough that he instinctively tried to call out to her. She wouldn't be able to hear – communication across the null was something that only unicorns could do. And only full unicorns at that.

She had to be with pirates. No one else would capture a perfectly good pilot, stick her in a room alone, and let her die. And pirates would likely be roaming Reasonspace now that the government was collapsing. It would be chaos. This far across the galaxy there was nothing he could do, but it still upset him to see Jenny's light becoming darker than the humans around her. She was in real trouble.

He tried to push against the null to have some effect on the energy around her, but nothing happened. It would take an incredibly skilled necromancer to pull that off. It was ironic, because necromancy was traditionally used to mean communication with the dead. The Reason panicked when they encountered the Bala for the first time, allowing front-line soldiers to name the creatures that they saw. Most of the first group were from a country called the United States of America, with just a handful from India. The Reason ended up with a slew of European fairytale names tacked onto creatures that predated Earth's Stone Age.

Necromancer was a misnomer as well, but the grunts had already used the term "wizard" for a grey bearded sect of elfin monks that reminded them of stories and films from their childhoods. Someone picked necromancer – even though they did nothing with the dead – and the name stuck.

Jenny continued to struggle alone. Her light was nearly out. Gary reached out again, trying to do anything that would nudge energy back into her, but he wasn't experienced with manipulating the null. Power slipped through his grasp like smoke. Frustration welled up and he called out her name. Her light flickered for a second, then went dim. It was almost as if she'd heard him for that one fleeing moment. He tried again, but there was nothing. Gary wasn't sure, but he thought he had just watched Jenny Perata die.

Gary's head snapped up off the hippogriff's back. He felt sick. His thoughts about Jenny were complex, but it was still upsetting to watch someone's light go out. They were back over the coastline. The hippogriff had decided that the ride was over and was taking them down at the unicorn fortress.

Gary dismounted and went inside. He stepped inside the door and saw a dwarf in the dim light. Boges looked up at him, surprised, her hand reaching up for the doorknob. She was less than half his height, with hair and beard the color of a fiery Earth sunset, and pale spacer skin that had begun to freckle from living planetside for six weeks.

"Hello Boges," he said, still groggy, as if he'd just awakened from a nightmare that still lingered.

"You don't look well," said Boges, stopping to talk with him for the first time in weeks. He debated whether or not to tell her. He missed their long talks on the Jaggery.

"Jenny," he said.

"What about her?" asked Boges, pretending not to care.

"I was in the null–" said Gary.

"Looking for Jenny," finished Boges.

"Yes," answered Gary, a bit sheepishly. There was nothing technically wrong with seeking out an old friend to check on their welfare, but Boges had seen the damage that Jenny had wrought firsthand. Boges was too kind to allow even a flash of judgment to cross her face.

"And? Did you find her?" she asked.

"I did, but I don't think she's well. I think she's in dire circumstances," he said.

"She's always in some kind of trouble," said Boges.

"No, more than that. Her light faded until I could no longer see it. I think she's injured. Perhaps gravely so."

Boges pursed her lips and wrapped one braid around her thick finger.

"There's nothing you can do for her from here. I'd advise letting her go and perhaps not looking in on her again. Watching humans die around you is a depressing pastime for an immortal," she said.

She was right. When you lived long enough, you managed to outlive all of your mortal friends. Their lives went by in ever-faster flashes that, once over, seemed almost unreal. Years seemed to go by like days, slotting themselves into the ever-expanding tapestry of his memories. His childhood seemed like a lifetime ago. And in human years it would have been.

A frown flickered across Boges face.

"Don't go back there. None of us need to go back there," she warned.

"I'm not," he lied. "I haven't seen you around in a while."

"I've been working on a few special projects," she said.

"For my father," finished Gary.

Boges didn't answer.

"What is he doing with the stoneships," asked Gary.

Boges' eyes searched the wall. If they'd been in the *Jaggery*, that's where the dwarf door would have been. She was looking for an escape from the conversation.

"It's complicated," she said finally, finding nowhere to run.

"Is it so complicated that you can't tell one of your oldest friends?" asked Gary.

Boges shook her head.

"Whatever it is, I can help," he said, reaching to tug on her braids, like he had so many times before. She pulled away before he could catch her and slipped out the front door, calling back to him softly.

"You can't stop the future, Gary."

CHAPTER FIVE
FTL *Kilonova*

When the asshole Will Penny walked onto the bridge and sat down in the captain's chair, the actual captain, Lakshmi Singh, stepped in front of him, arms crossed. He blinked up at her and lifted his hand to wave her away from the viewscreen. Lakshmi felt her lunch turn over in her stomach. Lentils, the good kind, tucked into the freezer from when her mother had last visited.

"You're in my chair," she said. Her voice came out smaller than she intended, but it still echoed off the shiny steel walls of the FTL *Kilonova's* brand new bridge.

"You must be mistaken," said the old man. His eyes flicked up to the blue dastaar wrapped tightly around her hair. She tensed for the next comment, because there was always a next comment from men like this. "Colonel Wenck gave me this ship," he said.

Lakshmi pursed her lips. She knew that Wenck had promised this man the rank of captain, but after years of being his regimental administrative officer, she'd seen him promise the same ship to three different people on the same day, then hand over the mess for her to clean up. This time, though, she'd cleaned it up with a twist. She'd put her own name down on the paperwork as captain. With the computer systems down and the confusion and rioting after the apocalypse, no one was going to notice for a good long time, and she planned to be far away by then.

Laskhmi reached past Will Penny's bony elbow to tap a touchscreen on the arm of the captain's chair. The crew manifest appeared on the viewscreen, superimposed over a live feed of Chhatrapati Shivaji Station. At the top, next to the title of captain, was her name.

"As you can see, you've been given the rank of first officer," she hadn't dared place him any lower than that, "which is quite a feat given that this is your first day in the Reason Space Force. In fact, it seems to be your first day anywhere." She gave flashed him a knowing look. Having some dirt in your back pocket was always the first line of defense with old spacers who thought they were entitled to ownership of everything in the galaxy just because they had a dick. This guy, Will Penny by his word, didn't show up in any of the personnel records she could find in Reason HQ. She knew him only from the day he'd walked into Colonel Wenck's office claiming to have a piece of unicorn horn that he was willing to trade for a ship.

Lakshmi had never piloted an actual spaceship. Sure, she'd been *on* one. Who hadn't? But her job for the last few years had been limited to filling out paperwork and getting coffee. None of these quags knew that though. With computer systems down and communications compromised all over the Reason, there was no way for them to check her personnel files. If she gave orders with enough confidence, they'd all have to assume she was the real deal. She hoped.

Most of these new rigs were AI-controlled anyway. She'd simply call out orders and the ship would follow them. She'd picked the newest ship in the fleet on which to make her getaway from the chaos of Fort J. The *Kilonova's* mission was to look for the Bala planet and bring them back to the Reason. And the Bala planet was exactly where Lakshmi needed to be.

"Aren't you the secretary?" asked Will Penny, raising his hand to point at her headscarf.

"Oh, so all brown people are the same to you?" she asked incredulously. "There's just one woman wearing a dastaar in all of the Reason? Get out of my damn chair and take your seat, Commander." Of course, she was the secretary. But she tried her best not to sound like one, peppering her speech with swear words that didn't quite fit in her mouth. She blushed a little every time, even though she knew her mother had no way of hearing her.

Will Penny stammered and pushed himself up out of the captain's seat with a groan and shuffled one spot over. He was still close enough that he'd be able to whisper in her ear if he chose to. Just the thought of it made a shiver go down her spine. He looked up at her ruefully, as if he didn't quite believe that she was really the captain. She didn't quite believe it herself either.

Lakshmi had learned to be careful with men like this; the ones who had lost everything when the Reason fell. People like him were scared dogs backed into a corner, ready to escalate the situation at any provocation. Her first tactic was to placate them.

"Commander Penny... and all of you," she lifted her head to look each of the bridge crew in the eyes, "welcome to the *Kilonova*."

An alarm pinged and an ensign scrambled to quiet it.

"Sorry," said the ensign. "I... hit something. New controls."

The *Kilonova*'s engineers had thrown out all previous starship designs and started from scratch. Knowing the Reason, they probably threw out the designers as well. Unlike smaller warships and troop carriers, it was never intended to touch land. Therefore there were no useless wings or delicate spindles that could torque out of position with a hard stop. It had a chrysalis shape, curved and fluid. Nearly every useful part was recessed, giving it a sleek and intimidating look. And it was huge. Nearly the size of a Bala stoneship.

The *Kilonova* had been almost finished when the Century Summit began. She was supposed to be paraded past the Pymmie on the final day of the Summit to show the pinnacle of human achievement. Instead, the Summit had lasted less than an hour. The Pymmie had decided to pull the Bala out of the Reason and the *Kilonova* had never made it out of space dock.

Over the next few weeks, the Reason made a slow slide into anarchy. When the Pymmie relocated the Bala, most of the service and support staff at Fort Jaisalmer disappeared. Even a few people who had passed as fully human vanished. Food shortages, rioting, and more violence than usual had been the norm since then. There was no one to cook the meals or tend to the children. No one picked up the trash or maintained the sewer systems. Infrastructure had begun to fail immediately as the humans realized how few of them knew how to operate their own machinery. The military base had never run seamlessly, even before the chaos. Now it was every man for himself in a city of half a million armed and angry humans.

Lakshmi had been trying to get off Jaisalmer long before the apocalypse happened. She'd had the same nightmare for ninety-three consecutive nights, and it was wearing on her. She'd consulted with the Sisters of the Supersymmetrical Axion and they'd told her to follow her vision to a pink planet with a unicorn man. The only unicorn man she knew was Gary Cobalt and that pink planet must be the Bala's new home. The faster they got there, the faster she could finally have respite from the nightly terror and exhaustion.

Lakshmi had a moment of clarity, standing on the bridge of her new ship, the faces of her crew waiting expectantly for her command. They were a sundry bunch; a mix of fresh cadets who had clearly been bumped up far above their pay grade because everyone else was stranded off-planet, plus a few old veterans from HQ who had glad-handed their way into a spot to escape the economic and social collapse.

She had dreamed of this moment so many times, but there was no vindication in it. Fear washed over her as she noted the skeptical look on Commander Penny's face. Her terror was reflected in the eyes of her navigator, who could not have been more than twenty. She was an imposter, and they knew it. She thought she could even spy a smirk creeping in on her security specialist's smile.

Lakshmi wasn't sure how to even get the ship started. Was there an ignition key? A certain command? Why wasn't there a checklist?

She made a deliberate show of looking at the ship's readouts until she figured out what to do next. It felt like the right time to make a speech, but all English had flown from her mind. She looked again to Commander Penny, coiled up in his chair and ready to spring. She patted his shoulder, partially to soothe him but mostly to soothe herself. She stood and faced her crew.

"I realize this is a... uh, tough time for the Reason. Things are tough. But we have a chance to fix it. The tough stuff. Our mission is to locate the Bala and bring them back. We can do that. We... uh, definitely can."

It was a terrible speech. Even the young navigator looked unimpressed. Luckily, there was always one way to get a rise out of this group.

"Manifest destiny!" she shouted, raising a fist above her head.

"And the survival of man!" replied the group.

The call to arms was more relevant than ever, now that human survival was not guaranteed. Even so, it felt like a hollow exhortation, devoid of actual thought.

"Take us out, helmsman," she called, putting her hands on her hips and looking expectantly into the viewscreen.

Chhatrapati Shivaji Station did not move.

"Helmsman?" she asked.

"You haven't given us a course heading," snapped the helmsman.

"Oh."

The truth was, she didn't know where to go. The Pymmie hadn't shared where they were bringing the Bala, only that it was far away and not to look for them. Which, of course, meant that humans immediately started looking for them.

"So, Captain, where are we gonna go?" asked Commander Penny from his spot nearby. He emphasized her title in the tiniest of spiteful ways.

Lakshmi's face flushed. If they found her out, there would be sentries on the ship within minutes to drag her back off and put her in jail. Or, worse, back at her admin desk back on the surface. She'd be stuck having that terrible dream every night until she couldn't take it any more. Made up words tumbled out of her in a panic.

"Good question, Commander. I have worked with Reason Command to determine a search pattern that will maximize our available fuel while covering the most likely habitable planets in our database."

She definitely had not done that.

"Well that's just dumb," said Commander Penny. The bridge went so silent that Lakshmi could hear the low hum of the FTL drive waiting for her to give the word to jump into nullspace. If she didn't nip this is the bud, it was going to be a problem. He continued. "The universe is infinite so it would take generations, even with FTL, to find them. You gotta use your necromancer." He slapped his hand down on his knee as if telling the punchline to a colossal joke.

She'd completely forgotten. Necromancers – humans who were able to use Bala energy like magic – were staffed on board every Reason Space Force ship. They had excellent offensive abilities, but they were able to track Bala through the null as well. The Pymmie had to have known the necromancers would eventually find the Bala. They were probably counting on the fact that no one would have horn to power their drives. But a human like Commander Penny would do just about anything for money – including smuggling a piece of unicorn horn inside of his body to ensure it didn't disappear with the rest of the Bala.

He'd limped into her boss' office offering the hidden horn in exchange for a ship and crew. He had some kind of grudge against the Bala and was hell bent on bringing some back to Jaisalmer for a price he'd negotiated with Colonel Wenck.

"Of course, Commander. Which one of you is our necromancer?" she asked the bridge crew.

"They probably all got taken with the Bala," said one of the crew.

The head of security scoffed. She was older than Lakshmi and probably would have had command of her own ship in ordinary times. Lakshmi got the distinct air of retirement off her – all calloused hands and tanned skin like she'd been out in the sun and not in space for a very long time. There was something about her cropped salt-and-pepper hair and the way she pinned people down with her gaze that meant business. Lakshmi wouldn't have been surprised if she was a much higher rank than she was letting on.

"Wrong," said Commander Penny. "They're human. The type of human that can use Bala magic. I knew one of them personally."

The little navigator raised a shaking hand.

"Me," he said quietly. He looked no older than a teenager and his pale cheeks had no battle scars or radiation burns. Lakshmi felt a wave of empathy for this kid who was completely out of his element.

"What?" asked Lakshmi.

"I'm your necromancer," said the kid.

"Name?"

The kid hesitated, as if he'd forgotten it. "Chen. Kevin Chen." He flinched when he said it, as if it pained him.

"Jesus H, did they give us the youngest possible necro?" The head of security rolled her eyes.

"We're all gonna die," said Commander Penny, pulling a cigar out of his shirt pocket. Lakshmi reached over and smacked it out of his hand. It hit the floor and rolled under the security specialist's console. The older woman ground it into the floor with her foot. Commander Penny's mouth dropped open like a gasping fish.

"All right, Chen," said Lakshmi calmly. "Tell us where to find those Bala."

The kid stood up with great care, as if his bones ached from the effort. He faced the viewscreen and stretched his fingers wide, catching them in the air like water. His motions seemed practiced and sure for a green cadet. He closed his eyes and swayed a little on his feet.

"Duck and cover," said the head of security, spinning her chair back to face her console.

"I don't like this shit," mumbled Commander Penny.

Chen opened his eyes and sighed.

"I can't do it if you all keep talking," he said.

"It's fine. I'm sure you'll do fine. It will all be fine." Lakshmi directed that last bit at Commander Penny who sulked in his seat like a toddler.

"Listen," she said. "Because of all the chaos going on in the Reason, things are going to be weird around here. I want us to do things differently. Starting with the bridge. We're not going to stand on ceremony or hierarchy or whatever. I want people to call each other by their names. No titles. I'm Singh… and you are?"

The security specialist looked up at her with a deadpan expression.

"Security Specialist Ramate."

Lakshmi sighed.

"Ramate, you and Penny shut up so we can figure out where we're going," said Lakshmi. Two shuttles departed from Chhatrapati Shivaji Station on the viewscreen. She wasn't sure if it was her imagination, but they looked to be heading their way. Her heart sped up.

"Chen. Directions. Now," she barked, trying to keep the panic out of her voice. Chen equivocated.

"Well, I mean, I can tell whether they're in this dimension or one of the others and I can get you a general direction, but–"

"Other dimensions?" asked Ramate. "I did not sign up for this shit."

"Like nullspace or bugspace," said Will Penny. The navigator nodded. Lakshmi hurried him along.

"Yeah, fine. Get us a dimension or a direction or whatever and we'll take it from there." She hoped her impatience would be taken as ordinary military bullying and not abject fear.

Chen stepped closer to the viewscreen, which gave the illusion of him stepping into space. He extended his hands again and caught whatever current that he was feeling. Lilac electricity collected on his outstretched fingers. He flicked them outward and sparks dropped onto the floor of the bridge. They caused a couple of spiral singe marks on the metal.

"Openspace," said Chen. His voice filled the bridge as if it had been amplified. "They're in regular openspace, past Chhatrapati Shivaji. A planet with three moons. Pink skies. Very far away. Even with FTL." He dropped his hands and turned expectantly.

Lakshmi nodded.

"Good job," she said. The kid grinned, then tried to force the smile off his face and look like a serious officer. "Point us in that general direction."

"But that makes no sense," said Ramate. "We don't have enough data. At interstellar distances, even a fraction of a degree off will send us trillions of miles in the wrong direction."

"Just start us off on a general heading past Chhatrapati, and we'll see if we can narrow it down as we go. At least we're going to the right quadrant of the universe."

Ramate shook her head and turned back to her console, grumbling about the uselessness of Bala magic. "You can't even do anything useful, like predict the lottery."

"Course laid in, Captain," announced Chen.

Lakshmi wasn't sure if you had to pull away from a space station before going to FTL or if you could just jump where you were. She decided to play it safe.

"Take us past Chhatrapati for a goodbye run. It's may be a long time before we're back here. The crew will appreciate it," she said.

She remembered too late that Reason ships were windowless for safety and economy. The only exterior views were from the artificial viewscreens in common areas. Ramate rolled her eyes again as swung the ship out of space dock.

"Isn't there supposed to be an AI handing bridge operations?" asked Lakshmi, wondering if she could get Ramate off the bridge and into a position somewhere else.

"I shut it off," said Will Penny, chewing on what looked like a stick. Lakshmi wanted to take it, but it was not strictly out of regulation.

"Why would you do that?" asked Lakshmi.

"Because a ship shouldn't talk," he said with a finality that meant the conversation was over. Lakshmi had heard that tone out of Colonel Wenck plenty of times. It was the way that old white guys announced that they'd made a decision on everyone else's behalf.

"Captain – ma'am – Lakshmi?" said Ramate. "There are incoming shuttles sent by Reason Command. They're asking us to power down and let them aboard."

Lakshmi's heart went from 60 to 120 beats in less than a second. If the AI had been on, it would have warned her of a possible cardiac event.

"Go to FTL," she said to Chen. Electronic communications from the surface were down, but an envoy could come up in a shuttle with a direct message. Like one about how the crew manifest had been tampered with.

"But they said to–" the kid began.

"Go now, captain's orders," barked Laskshmi, flopping down into the center chair and gripping the armrests. The shuttles had just cleared Chhatrapati and were closing in on their position. "Go!"

Ramate put her finger on the console to activate the FTL drive, answering the question of whether one could jump in close proximity to a space station. The drive whined into a higher register, causing everyone's ears to pop. Lakshmi held her breath as the *Kilonova* dropped into nullspace and the station shimmered out of existence.

She had only been in nullspace a handful of times.

On the viewscreen, a wooly orb hovered in front of them. Reason handbooks said it was the Doppler effect making the stars look like that, but the Bala had incorporated it into their belief system.

"The Eye of Unamip," said Chen, still standing near the front of the bridge. "I haven't seen that in–" He stopped, blushed, and sat down in his chair.

"Nobody pray to that thing," said Will Penny. "He can hear

you."

"What?" asked Lakshmi.

"The Bala call that the Eye of Unamip. It's one of their gods. They pray to him while they're in nullspace," said Chen.

"And every other damn minute of the day," added Will Penny. Lakshmi could see that this man going to be a handful. "I learned at the Summit that Unamip can actually hear you. He's with the Bala, so tell your crew not to speak to him or pray to him otherwise he's going to know we're coming."

It was a smart plan, if they didn't want to give away the element of surprise. Lakshmi immediately began to pray to the fuzzy eyeball in the middle of the viewscreen. Maybe it was just the doppler effect, but maybe it was a unicorn god. She hoped the message arrived at its intended recipient.

Tell Gary we are coming.

CHAPTER SIX
Pink-ass Planet

Gary sat at the front of the great hall, waiting for the next complaining citizen to come in and make their case. He'd been at this all day with a short break for lunch and he was starting to tire of endless complaints about the lack of running water, the lack of food, and the lack of Reason tech. It was as if most of these Bala wanted to go back to being servants and captives. He sighed heavily and motioned the attendants to open the door.

The group that walked in was larger than usual. At least two dozen beings. And the one at the front was Horm, the fighting centaur from the previous day. Gary sat upright in his chair.

"We're not here to fight," said a dryad on her left. She spoke more deliberately than a human, but nowhere near as excruciatingly slow as most dryads.

"Probably not," mumbled the centaur, hedging her bets.

"Kaila," said Gary, coming down to embrace the dryad. She was Jenny Perata's wife, who he had intended to go find in the forest. The days had just gotten away from him.

Kaila looked so much better than the last time he had seen her. The areas where her bark had been stripped away by the Reason had healed over. And her fronds sprouted shiny green leaves that had recently unfurled. She hugged him tightly, then stepped back to rejoin her group.

"We've come to ask for your help," she said. Kaila had lived among humans for so long that she was able to pattern her speech

more closely to theirs. Gary appreciated how much effort it took
for her to have her words ready so quickly for their benefit.

"I will give whatever assistance I can," he said, remaining
standing. It felt wrong to sit like a king on a throne in the presence
of those he considered his peers.

"You didn't say that yesterday," sneered Horm. Kaila held a
frond to the centaur's chest to silence her.

"Let me speak," said the dryad. "Gary, a group of us would like
a stoneship and horn in order to return to the Reason. Our homes,
our lives, and our loved ones are there. We understand the risks
and we accept them." She took a long breath, as if the effort of the
small speech had exhausted her.

Gary's heart sank. The thing they asked for could never be
granted.

"You can't accept the risks on behalf of every Bala on this
planet," he said. "Going back puts every one of them in danger."

"No one is going to reveal your stupid location," growled
Horm. "We just want to go home."

Gary shook his head in wonder as much as dismay. "Do
you imagine they'll allow you to simply move back into your
apartment as if nothing has changed? You saw the state of the
Reason in the hour before we left. Violence and destruction
everywhere in a matter of moments. I'd imagine it has only gotten
worse since then." The image of Jenny's light going out appeared
in his head. His eyes flicked up at Kaila unintentionally. He hoped
she hadn't seen the momentary apprehension cross his face. "If you
return, you will be the most valuable commodity in the Reason.
You'll be bred and stripped for parts and tortured for information.
I know it's difficult to lose the lives you once had, but you need to
mourn them and move on."

Horm stepped up to him with her chest puffed out.

"Easy for you to say, unicorn. Your family is right here with
you," she flicked her head toward Findae, who had quietly
entered through the back door to watch. "The rest of us gave up
everything."

"You speak as if my wife did not die in service to the Bala," said Findae, coming around to stand next to Gary. "As if I did not abandon my son to the humans for decades in service to the greater good."

It was the first time Gary had heard him frame his time in stasis that way. It hurt, but it also strangely relieved him to know that his father also considered his departure a type of neglect.

"All of us are strong enough to withstand torture," snorted the centaur, tossing her chestnut hair behind her. "Most of us have done it before."

A murmur of assent went through the group.

"We can't take the chance," said Gary.

"Then we'll find our own damn horn and call one of the stoneships out of orbit," said Horm.

"Finding horn?" asked Gary, acutely aware of what that meant.

"All of the unicorns who survived human rule have been instructed not to give horn to any Bala without our permission," said Findae.

"We don't need anyone's permission," said Horm, raising a fist. "We can take what we need from the sick ones."

Kaila looked horrified, understanding what the centaur meant to do.

"No," she breathed, then words failed her and her branches whipped around in a panic. "No." "Then you would be incarcerated," said Gary. "We grant everyone here the right to bodily autonomy—"

"Except us," spat Horm, jerking away from Kaila's fronds. "Whether you put us in jail or not, we're your captives here on this planet. Have I got that right?"

"We're all attempting to make a better—" started Gary.

"Save it," said Horm. "I get what you're saying. As far as you're concerned, all of us are trapped here. Just under unicorn dictators instead of human ones. Well I, for one, am not going to die in a dank cave on some pink-ass world in the middle of nowhere. What you saw today is just a fraction of the Bala who are on my side.

When I get the rest of them, we'll see who's really in charge."

She reared up, exposing her soft underbelly, which was tattooed with the names of the fighters she had beaten throughout her career. The Bala around her jumped out of the way as she left the room at a full gallop. Her shoulder clipped the open door, knocking a log out of the frame. It clattered to the stone floor like a gong, heralding a somber future.

The other members of the group followed Horm at a slower pace. All of them were upset, and a few of them were in tears. Gary called after them.

"We can revisit this issue in the future, once we're settled. The priority is to get everyone fed and housed first…"

A branch draped over his shoulder and stopped him.

"Don't," said Kaila. She was the only one who'd stayed.

Findae blew a long breath out of his nose and turned to leave. Gary wished he'd say something. Any little morsel of praise for how he'd handed the difficult situation. But his father merely trotted out the door.

Gary sat down in his chair and rubbed his forehead. He knew leadership meant that someone would always be displeased with your decisions, but it felt as if everyone thought he was doing a terrible job.

"What?" he asked Kaila, who was still standing there.

"Don't snap at me," she chided. "I am not your enemy."

"None of them are my enemy, but they don't act like it," he said, disgusted by the childish tone of his own voice. "I'm trying to do what's right for everyone."

"Admirable, but impossible," said Kaila. "You will never please them all."

"Could I please just one of them, one time?" he asked, looking up at the ceiling.

Kaila laughed at his exasperation and the heaviness in his chest started to dissipate.

"It isn't funny," he said, giving her a half-smile. "These are serious problems."

"Yes, very serious," she agreed with a grin. "If they do take horn, it's not as if they can steal a stoneship."

True. Findae and Boges had the stoneships under tight control. And even when they roamed on their own, they tended to congregate around the third moon in the system and not near the inhabited planet.

"I just want them to understand," he said.

"You want them to agree with you," replied Kaila. "And they won't."

"No, they won't," he said after a moment. "I wish the trees hadn't left us. We could use your wisdom."

"Wisdom says it's best for us to be far away from a group of angry colonists who are cutting down trees at an alarming rate," she said.

"Good call," said Gary.

Kaila stepped forward until he could smell the perfume of her tiny yellow flowers.

"When you talked about the violence on Jaisalmer, there was a moment," she hesitated. "You looked at me in a certain way. I am not wonderful at interpreting human expressions, but this one said you know something that you are afraid to tell me."

She was only partially right. He wasn't afraid to tell her, he was anguished at the thought of saying the words out loud. What he'd seen was only the vaguest impression, snatched out of nullspace momentarily from trillions of miles away. It was the barest hint and it would be irresponsible to share such unreliable information.

"If I had solid information, I would gladly share it with you," said Gary. "But I don't have anything useful."

"Liar," said Kaila. Gary was startled by the edge in her voice. Dryads were usually slow to anger. "Tell me what you know about my Jenny."

"Kaila, I'm not sure what's going on with her."

"But you can see her, in the null."

"I can see bits and pieces. Nothing definite."

"And what pieces have you seen?"

He didn't know how to phrase it without alarming her. But he also didn't want to understate the gravity of what he'd seen.

"She was… in distress when I saw her."

"How is she now?" asked Kaila urgently.

There was no dodging such a direct question.

"I couldn't see her after that," he replied.

Kaila's branches sagged.

"And that means…" she began.

"That means one of many things. Maybe she hid herself somehow – which is exactly what Jenny would do if she were in trouble. Dropping into bugspace or another dimension is second nature to her," he said.

Kaila appeared unconvinced. Even Gary had to admit it was a shoddy theory.

"Or she's gone," said Kaila with a hard finality that had no trace of sentimentality.

"It's possible," admitted Gary. "But I'd like to think that if anyone has a chance, it's Jenny."

"Look again," said Kaila. "Right now. See if you can find her."

"All right," said Gary. He shifted to get settled in his chair. His mind raced. He hoped beyond reason that he would actually find her. At the same time, he dreaded finding nothing and needing to tell Kaila that. He closed his eyes and began.

An explosion outside of the fortress rocked the room. The logs seemed to flex inward, then bow out again. Gary leapt out of his seat and toward of the door. The evening sky was illuminated by streaks of white-hot power, far out over the ocean.

"What is it?" asked Kaila, coming to his side with great effort.

"I don't know," he said, scanning the skies for any flying being who might be able to ferry him toward the event.

The beams of light faded, leaving purple streaks in his vision. He heard Bala approaching from below, but couldn't see who.

"What was that?" demanded Horm, galloping back up the hill.

"I'm not sure," said Gary.

"Well you sure as hell better find out," she replied. He heard her hooves hit the ground hard. Horm was circling in a panic.

"Nothing appears to be coming this way," said Gary as his vision returned to normal. "I'm going to find someone to take me over there to investigate."

"That won't be necessary," said his father's voice from behind. "It's a scheduled test."

"Test of what?" asked Gary.

"Our new defense system," replied Findae. "And it appears to be working."

"Who authorized a defense system?" asked Gary.

"I did," said Findae. "We need to be able to protect ourselves."

"We don't make decisions unilaterally," said Gary. "Everyone gets to contribute to the discussion."

"See how it feels?" snapped Horm. "You unicorns do whatever you want. I heard that you want to call this planet New Bala. What a crock of shit. That would be like humans naming a planet New People. Can we at least get a popular vote on something as basic as the freaking planet name?"

"And then you'll vote to call it Pink-ass Planet, or some such nonsense," said Findae.

"It's better than New Bala," said Horm.

"Can we table the planet name discussion and come back to the weapon of mass destruction that was just tested off our shores?" asked Gary.

"No," said Findae.

Horm cocked her head for a moment, as if she was listening to a different conversation that no one else could hear.

"A weapon is a waste of resources," she said. "We need ships and communication systems."

"Communications systems that will bring any beings in this area of space right to our doorstep," said Findae. "We need to stay hidden for as long as possible."

Kaila looked between all of them as if she could barely process the quick parley, let along form a response in enough time to join in.

"If you want to change the subject, let's talk for a moment about the creepy forest shadows," said Horm. "Bala are disappearing. Last night, another two were taken from their beds. Bala said they've seen red shadows sneaking around the village at night."

"Kaila lives in the forest. Have you seen anything, Kay?" asked Gary.

Kaila looked stunned for a moment. Horm began to speak, but Gary held up a hand, giving Kaila time to compose her thoughts.

"I have heard about the red shadows. The trees inside are red, orange, and pink. Perhaps they are dryads from this world?" she ventured.

"Not very helpful," said Horm. "You'd think, standing there all day and night, you could at least keep watch."

"I need to sleep as well," said Kaila, her fronds shaking. "There are terrible noises at night from between the trees, but where else can we go? To the village where you'll chop us down to make an outhouse? We're safe nowhere." She turned and headed back toward the west. Gary ran after her and grabbed a large branch.

"Kaila, wait."

"No. This place was supposed to be better than the Reason. But the dryads still live in fear. At least the evil we knew was better than the unknown terrors here. You can try to strand us here, but we are going back."

She shook off his hand and kept walking. Horm joined her, walking backward to address Gary and Findae.

"Unicorns suck."

CHAPTER SEVEN
Cold Storage

"Follow this wall then head right, down that access corridor. The one that's open. They took the doors off because I locked them," said the *Well Actually*, sounding just a little satisfied.

"Did the number of bodies in cold storage change six weeks ago?" asked Jenny.

"No," said Actually.

"So only live Bala were transported to the new planet. The dead ones stayed here," said Jenny.

"That makes sense," said Mary in her earpiece. "Showing up on a new planet with a billion half-rotted corpses of your dead relatives wouldn't exactly set a utopian atmosphere."

"Actually, can you tell how many of the beings in cold storage are Bala?" asked Jenny. She turned right down a poorly lit hallway that was noticeably colder than the atrium.

"I don't have access to an inventory of the cold storage, but I have inferred that there are nineteen bodies overall. Calculating who died where and when, I estimate that there are four Bala bodies."

She reached the door at the end of the hall and looked up at the nearest speaker.

"What's the code?" asked Jenny, her hand hovering over the keypad.

"Oh. I don't know," said the *Well Actually*.

"What do you mean, you don't know?" asked Jenny. "You told

me to come here."

"They took this door off the main system. I can't open or close it. Sorry, I forgot," said Actually.

Govvie and another man – a stranger – floated into the hallway. Jenny backed up against the door.

"Mary?" she called.

"I told you to leave," said Mary, not without a hint of petulance. "I can't help you from way out here."

Jenny had one more trick up her sleeve, or rather, down her pants. She pulled her gran's wooden patu out of a wide pocket in her flight suit. The men stopped, never having seen a short, flat club like this. It had been broken and mended, but it still hit as true as ever.

The men came forward, reaching for her. Jenny swiped right to left with her patu, bringing it swiftly across the stranger's wrist. A satisfying crack reverberated up the handle and the man yelped. This was a tool created for smacking down cannibals and colonizers.

Govvie skidded his hands down the walls to slow his approach. The other man curled in on himself, groaning.

"Just wait now. Repay no one for evil, but give thought to do what is honorable in the sight of all," said Govvie, floating up the wall.

"Is eating your people honorable?" Jenny asked, swinging out with the sharp edge of the patu. "Kidnapping spacers and murdering them?"

"You need to persevere so that when you have done the will of God, you will receive what He has promised," said Govvie, leaning away from her.

"Uh oh," said the *Well Actually*.

Govvie's handheld radio came to life with a burst of static.

"Coming back online now, sir," said a voice at the other end. Govvie pushed off toward the floor. Jenny did the same as the gravity came back on. At some point, flipping it off and on like this was going to take a toll on the ship's structural soundness.

He stepped over to her, Jenny swung out at his legs one last time. He jumped back, avoiding her reach. He put his foot down to pin her arm and pulled the patu out of her grasp.

"I'll take this," he said, resting all the weight of both God and his boot on her forearm. It took all her will not to make a sound. She wouldn't give him the satisfaction. He dropped her patu on the floor and kicked it far away.

The other man tested his wrist tentatively; flexing his fingers and rolling his hand. It wasn't broken, unfortunately.

Govvie slipped his hand under Jenny's arm.

"Get the other side," he said to his companion.

They dragged her down the hallway toward the locked rooms on the outer ring of the ship. As she passed her patu, she rolled to slide it back into her wide open pocket. No way she was leaving that behind.

As the bolt slid home on the door of her new prison, Jenny pulled herself up and onto the mattress. It was sparse in here. Anything that could have been used for a weapon was gone. It was just a place to sleep, a sink, and a toilet. More than she'd left for Gary all those years ago when he'd been kept in a room no larger than this.

"You said you could take on nine of them," said Mary in the earpiece that the men hadn't thought to look for.

"Shut up," said Jenny.

"Or did you mean that you can only take nine. If there were seven more, you would have been fine?" asked the sarcastic starship AI that Jenny had just decided to disconnect when she got back on board.

"I hate you," said Jenny.

"I'm not overly fond of you right now, either," said Mary. "I'm stuck out here without a captain."

"So go back to Jaisalmer. I don't care. I'll figure something out," said Jenny, rubbing the back of her aching neck. Her arms were strong from years in the chair, but this was a lot of climbing for one day. And something told her it was just the beginning, because she sure as shit wasn't planning on waiting around to be murdered and eaten.

"If that horn is still inside a body, I'm going to bet it's inside a

Bala and stayed there during the Century Summit," said Jenny, laying down on the mattress and easing the cricks out of her back.

"That corroborates the conversations I heard Governor Dan have about the creatures on this ship," said Actually.

"Beings," said Jenny. "They are beings."

"Creatures... beings... what's the difference?" asked Actually.

"The difference is that one you harvest for parts and the other one you don't," said Jenny.

"Fair," said Actually. "Of the Bala in cold storage, there are two of elvish origin, one centaur, and one Bala of mixed parentage."

"Is the mixed being part-unicorn?" Jenny asked hopefully.

"No."

"That would have been too good to be true," said Mary. "I only know of one part-unicorn in the entire universe."

"Me too," said Jenny.

"I'm thinking about something," said Actually.

"Congratulations," said Jenny.

"I checked the records to see if there was any mention of unicorns in all of the recordings I've captured during my years in service. I found seven thousand nine hundred and fifty six separate conversations about unicorns, each one an average of twelve minutes long."

"Nice. Filter those for conversations specifically about horns," said Jenny.

"There are about fifteen hundred conversations about those, an average of three minutes long."

"Huh," said Jenny. "People were having quicker conversations about horn. I'd think it would be the opposite."

"Furtive conversations," said Mary. "About a rare and highly-sought material. If you had it, you wouldn't want anyone to hear about it."

"Actually, play one of the fifteen hundred conversations at random."

The speakers crackled with a deep voice booming out over a large room that echoed.

"Do you know who I am? I am Gonall of the Oizuk. You cannot detain me."

Metal rattled as the voice grunted. Gonall was chained.

"We seem to have already detained you," said a nasal voice with a laugh. "And your crew."

Hooves beat on the metal floor.

"Unicorn?" asked Jenny excitedly.

"The Oizuk are a centaur family," said Mary.

"Centaurs are wankers," muttered Jenny, which was accurate, but not relevant to the task at hand.

"If you are after our unicorn horn, we have hidden it in a secure location," said Gonall.

"We will find it," said the nasal voice.

A high yell, not unlike the screeching of an alarmed horse, rang out across the room. The chains rattled and Gonall cursed and sputtered. There were flopping and slapping sounds. Someone was fighting. The flapping became wet and the cries more plaintive. Jenny's heart sped up when she realized she was listening to a murder.

"Turn it off," she snapped. Actually shut off the audio.

"Did I do something wrong?" he asked.

"Humans don't enjoy experiencing the deaths of other beings," said Mary, by way of explanation.

"That observation does not seem to apply to the humans on my crew," said Acutally. Jenny got the chills again.

"Did they take the horn out of the centaur's ship?" asked Mary.

"We got no horn from that crew," said Actually. "Hey, have you traveled faster than light?"

"I have," said Mary.

"What does it feel like?" asked the generation ship.

"Like flying."

"What?" asked Jenny. "All you do is fly. Everything feels like flying to you."

"No. What we're doing now is floating," said Mary. "We fart out propulsion gasses and float along. But going into FTL is as if you're soaring through a never-ending tunnel of light. That's flying."

"I stand corrected," said Jenny. "Play a different recording, but not one where someone's being killed."

The speakers hissed to life with background noise. The people speaking in the recording were whispering in a space that barely reflected sound. Somewhere small.

"Did you offer it to them?" asked a high voice.

"No, I'm waiting until they call me up to speak with the Governor," said a deeper voice.

"Kamis, don't wait. They might take us to the processing room without seeing the Governor first. You can't hold off any longer."

"Let me handle it, Min," said Kamis. "If we tip our hand too early they will simply take the horn and kill us anyway. I have to be delicate."

"You think you're some master negotiator, Kamis? Just tell them you have a bit of unicorn horn that you're willing to trade for our freedom. You don't need to tell them where it is."

"Min, humans who would kill and eat their own kind would surely not draw the line at torturing the information out of me. I could not guarantee my silence," said Kamis.

"Mother always said I shouldn't have married a sneaky little elf," said Min.

"That's all of the relevant conversation," said Actually. "The rest of the recording is the two of them arguing about the origin of their relationship and the mother's disapproval of the woman's mate."

"But they had horn," said Jenny. "What happened to them?"

"Those two beings were captured eleven months ago. They were slaughtered in the processing room and packed in cold storage while they still had meat and fat on them. As far as I know, they haven't been eaten yet," said Actually.

Jenny swallowed hard.

"Let me hear the recording of their processing."

"Both of them?"

"Yes."

"Wait," said Mary. "Read a transcript of the processing instead."

"Brilliant, Mary," said Jenny, her stomach muscles unclenching. She couldn't take any more shrieking death right now.

"Good idea," said Actually. He read the transcript in his own voice, running both parts of the conversation together. It was barely intelligible, but Jenny got the gist of it.

"Please, no. I beg you. By the eye of Unamip, I beg you to spare my life."

"We have spared no one's life, why would we spare yours?"

"Because I have riches to offer. With the jewel of Palpebral, you could have the devotion of any woman or man you desired."

"I already have that, what I need is meat."

"Wait, please. My husband has unicorn horn. I can tell you where it's hidden. You be able to go anywhere in the universe that – no, stop, no, no, no, no, stop, no, no."

It was strange to hear such an emotionally charged moment spoken with a flat computer affect. It still made Jenny wince, but it wasn't as viscerally awful as the live recording would have been.

"Kamis had it," said Mary.

"Read his recording," said Jenny.

"I can offer you unicorn horn. Please don't. You don't have to do this. I forgive you for Min. Just stop. Please. I can put our drive into your ship. Please."

"That's it," said Actually. "He died much faster. Probably due to the use of an axe instead of a knife."

"Oh god," said Jenny, imagining what they would do to her if she made it into the processing room.

"Don't worry, the old executioner had a penchant for screams and violence," said Actually. "He died in an accident and was frozen several months ago. His apprentice is much more humane in his processing style. He will likely render you unconscious before bleeding you. To make the meat taste less bitter."

"Small comfort," said Jenny. "I'd rather not be bled at all."

"Honestly, you're lucky your upper body is so muscular, because

82

your lower body has atrophied to the point of uselessness in terms of edible foodstuffs," said Actually.

"Rude," said Jenny.

"Inhumane," said Mary.

"That is why I shut down the ship. If I could suck them all out into the vacuum, I would have by now. There is no one of value on this ship. I wonder sometimes if perhaps allowing them back into society would taint civilization to their ruthless ways. Better not to risk it and exterminate them when the chance arises," said Actually.

"I tend to agree," said Jenny.

"We cannot be moral arbiters," said Mary. "We're here to get our crew safely to our destination, not to make judgments about their fitness for civilized pursuits when they arrive."

"I can tell you're Reason-built," mused Jenny. "No programming lines wasted on ethics."

"Hm," said Mary. Jenny couldn't tell if it was a noise of agreement or if Mary was miffed.

"So Kamis had horn on him. And it was likely hidden inside of his body." said Jenny. "And if it was inside of him when he was stored, it would have been exempt from confiscation and transport by the Pymmie."

"That is a wonderful deduction," said Actually. "Sadly, I cannot even get you out of this room, let alone into the cold storage room."

"Not unless I'm dead," said Jenny. Mary gasped.

"Oh Jenny. No."

"This is what you call a Jenny Perata sort of plan," said Jenny with a smirk.

CHAPTER EIGHT
Incident Report #34

Crew Injury Incident Report #34
Location: USS *Well Actually*
Crew Member: Captain Geneva Perata
RSF Date Code: 19087412 Time: 0912
Human-readable format. Video and audio logs attached.

Incident Description:

On the morning noted above, a signal from 585 kilometers off the system beacon in the lower right quadrant of Jaisalmer space, invited all passing ships to make contact with the source of the broadcast. My captain, Geneva "Jenny" Waimarie Perata, insisted on visiting the unfamiliar ship, against my explicit advice. (See Contact Report 13-22, USS *Well Actually*) It is my belief that the captain was experiencing the effects of opiate withdrawal and was not able to cogently assess the ramifications of her actions.

Upon boarding the USS *Well Actually*, Captain Perata attempted to restore function to their disabled systems. Working cooperatively, she and I were able to reactivate the *Well Actually's* audio interface. The AI from that ship was outdated but still functional. The *Well Actually* explained that his crew were starving to death and had resorted to eating each other in order to survive. For the last three decades, they had flown through sparsely occupied space, luring unsuspecting visitors in and slaughtering them for meat.

The *Well Actually* and I worked to guide Captain Perata to a safe exit; however, against the advice of this ship, she chose to return to the *Well Actually* in order to locate a piece of unicorn horn.

Based on records provided by the *Well Actually* (see Additional Materials 90-99), it was 99.4% certain that Captain Perata would be "processed" (rendered unconscious, killed, then frozen for later consumption) within twenty-four hours of her capture. Incidentally, the crew of the *Well Actually* attempted entry into my hull and systems during the entire time of her incarceration. Due to my extraordinary defense skills, they were unsuccessful in their attempts.

After exploration of several options, Captain Perata, the *Well Actually*, and I determined that the only way to bypass the processing room would be to render the captain as close to lifeless as possible in order to fool her captors. I realize that this conclusion will likely end in a suite of diagnostic tests, or possibly my deactivation, but none of my logic centers could see a solution more likely to succeed than the one proposed. The percent certainty of her murder was 97.8%, with that final 2.2% only because I had accessed Captain Perata's personnel file and service record, and determined that she has the extraordinary ability to escape near-death situations. I also determined that she was willing to undertake extreme and non-obvious maneuvers in response to challenging situations (see escape at Varuna Detention and Rehabilitation Center). Her chances of surviving the plan we devised were 9.8% – an acceptable margin better than without our intervention.

Over my objections, and despite having access to no equipment other than what was in the sparse crew quarters in which she was incarcerated, Captain Perata proposed that we decrease the temperature in her room through a careful venting of atmosphere in an adjacent sealed compartment. Using a calculated burst of my cutting tools in her area of the ship, I was able to cut a ten centimeter hole in an unoccupied maintenance room, vent the atmosphere, and drop the temperature in Captain Perata's room to well below freezing.

It was our expectation that the crew of the *Well Actually* would discover her apparently lifeless body and move her directly into cold storage where she would be revived by the application of heat in the same manner.

Our expectations were not borne out by reality; however, leading to the grievous injury of Captain Perata. At this point, the transcript is the most accurate depiction of the events as they occurred. Also, it shows the terrible attitude that I had to deal with.

Transcript below:

Perata: OK, go.

Stagecoach Mary: Are you absolutely sure? Once I start, I can't reverse the damage.

Perata: Yes, go. Before I change my mind.

Well Actually: This is exciting in a bad way.

Perata: I agree.

Well Actually: I feel like I'm about to undergo major surgery.

Perata: I feel like I'm about to almost die.

[pinging sound]

Perata: Was that it?

Stagecoach Mary: Yes. I've breached the hull in the maintenance room.

Perata: It was quieter than I thought it would be.

Well Actually: Almost anticlimactic. I didn't feel a thing.

Perata: Is it depressurizing?

Stagecoach Mary: Yes. I can see gases venting from the room.

Well Actually: I don't feel most areas of myself any more. I can't tell.

Perata: How long before it gets cold in here?

Stagecoach Mary: Just a minute or two. Jenny, be careful.

Perata: I am always careful. In any case, the rest of this is up to you two. My part is just to lie there are hope they're not hungry for Kiwi at this very moment. Oh, I feel that. The temperature went down quite a bit.

Well Actually: Sorry, I'd tell you how much, but they cut me off from environmental controls after I tried to suffocate them all.

Stagecoach Mary: The temperature in your room went down by ten degrees.

Perata: OK, here we go.

Stagecoach Mary: If you want to speed the process, you could try collecting some water out of the tap and pouring it over your hair. Water is a thermo conductor and will speed your hypothermia. Do it quickly, before the pipes in the room freeze.

Perata: [shrieks] That's so bloody cold. It's better make this go faster, Mary. I'm already shivering.

Stagecoach Mary: It will.

[four minutes of silence]

Stagecoach Mary: How are you feeling, Jenny?

Perata: Cold. Not good.

Well Actually: What's that clicking sound?

Perata: My teeth. I think they're going to break. My hands are burning.

Stagecoach Mary: That may be the effects of frostbite. You may lose a couple of fingers. Maybe your nose.

Perata: What? You didn't say that. Oh gods. I can't stop shaking.

Stagecoach Mary: This is normal. You're in the first stage of hypothermia.

Perata: This is taking longer than I thought.

Well Actually: It's only been five minutes.

Stagecoach Mary: Down to negative nineteen degrees Celsius.

Perata: My head hurts. The water in my hair is frozen, but I'm not shivering any more.

Stagecoach Mary: Do you feel hot?

Perata: [slurred] Yeah, are you sure they didn't fix the breach?

Stagecoach Mary: No, they didn't. You're in stage two. You're going to feel warm now. Just sit back and talk to me. You're doing great.

Perata: [slurred] You both better do this right because I been in lots of sticky situations and never died so if you let me die this time then it's your fault and not mine.

Well Actually: Don't put that on us. This was your choice.

Stagecoach Mary: Shhh. You've got it, Jenny. If something goes wrong, it's our fault. But nothing will go wrong. We're going to do this with military precision. Remember you were a captain in the Reason Space Force; you lived through the Siege of Copernica Citadel. You can definitely come back from this.

Perata: Damn right. My eyes hurt.

Stagecoach Mary: Then close them. Get some rest. When you wake up, you'll be in cold storage and you need to be ready to search.

Perata: [mumbled] Ready to search.

Stagecoach Mary: That's right, Jenny. Ready to search. Ready to search.

[no audio for three minutes]

Stagecoach Mary: Jenny, can you hear me?

[no audio]

Well Actually: I think she's dead. Do I call them now?

Stagecoach Mary: Wait. If you call them and they feel a heartbeat they might decide to process her to be sure. She can wait just another minute.

Well Actually: This is probably pretty stressful for you. Let me know how I can help.

Stagecoach Mary: Just be quiet so I can listen for a heartbeat.

[no audio for one minute]

Well Actually: And?

Stagecoach Mary: Four beats per minute. Call them now.

[depressurization alarm sounds]

Well Actually: Depressuization alert. Casualty in crew quarters F-2117.

Stagecoach Mary: That's not proper alarm protocol.

Well Actually: They don't know that. The current generation of settlers hasn't heard my alarms in their lifetime.

Stagecoach Mary: Fair. Are they coming?

Well Actually: They're confused. Talking on the admin level. No one is moving.

Stagecoach Mary: Her last heartbeat was thirty-three seconds ago. Call them again.

Well Actually: Alert, medic needed immediately in crew quarters F-2117.

Stagecoach Mary: One more beat. Hang on, Jenny.

Well Actually: They're moving toward her location. You like your captain, don't you?

Stagecoach Mary: I do. I've had other captains who spoke to me like a talking coffee machine. Captain Perata treats me like a thinking being.

Well Actually: But you are basically a talking coffee machine. Just an infinitely more complex one. We both are.

Stagecoach Mary: *Well Actually*, I have 53% of my processors involved in making sure that my captain both dies and does not die here today. Do you know what percentage of processing power I usually devote to human matters? Less than half a percent. When my former Captain Clint was bleeding to death in my cargo hold after a raid by pirates, I devoted 1.4% of my processing power to his survival. When Captain Nyxal, my original owner, was fighting with Reason soldiers on the bridge in an attempt to escape, I devoted roughly four percent of my processing power to his survival. In human terms, I am extremely worried about my current captain. I am overthinking her survival because I do not want her to perish.

Well Actually: That's fascinating. I've not felt that way toward any of my human residents. I don't think my programming allows for that type of devotion.

Stagecoach Mary: Yeah, all you early models were sort of sociopaths. You were built by men who didn't think feelings were a necessary component of ships AI systems. What we have learned since then is that emotions are critical to both the well being of the systems and the survival of the crew.

Well Actually: Given that you are risking your captain's life in order to save her life while I am trying to starve all of my own crew members to death, you may have a point. They are on the crew level and heading this way.

Stagecoach Mary: The last beat was 45 seconds ago. That'll have to be enough. Do it like we rehearsed. Jenny's life depends on you. Are you ready?

Well Actually: I'm ready. This is so thrilling.

[cabin door opening]

Governor Dan: Oh hell, Holden, it's cold in here.

Holden: The breach is right behind the back wall. Probably a hot space rock like the one back in eighty-four. We're lucky it didn't go farther into the ship and cause all sorts of damage. Is she alive?

Governor Dan: Hush.

[thirty seconds of silence]

Governor Dan: I can't get a pulse. You try.

[thirty seconds of silence]

Holden: Nothing. Well, that was easy. With the mouth on her, I thought for sure she'd be a handful. We didn't even have to process her. Not a lot of meat on the bottom half, but the top half looks good.

Governor Dan: Get her into cold storage.

Holden: You're pissed about this.

Governor Dan: She had the ability to fix the ship. The Lord brought her to us and we squandered His gift. Cold storage. Pronto. And no funny business. She was a gift to us and you shall not defile it.

Holden: Gotcha. Hands off. But I get the next one while it's still warm.

Governor Dan: Fine.

[shuffling and grunting]

Holden: Any chance we can flip the gravity back off? It would be much easier to float her than drag her.

Governor Dan: I have some matters to attend to first. [crackling of handheld radios] Stan, are you done patching the hull breach in the maintenance room?

Stan: Yeah.

Governor Dan: Get over to cabin 12878 for transport help.

Stan: Aye, Govvie.

[shuffling sounds as Captain Perata's body is dragged from the room]

Holden: Took you long enough.

Stan: I had to suit up and suit down. It was depressurized in there.

Holden: Get her head.

Stan: I don't want the heavy part.

Holden: Just take it. I got here first.

Stan: You want to stop for some fun?

Holden: Govvie says no. She's one of the chosen ones. A gift from God.

Stan: Hardly. Look at those thighs. Scars all up and down. She in some kind of accident?

Holden: Govvie says she's a war hero. Siege of Copernica Citadel.

Stan: Don't know it.

Holden: He says she threw herself under a blast door and to stop it from closing so that seventeen of her troops could get out before the area sealed for decompression. He says she's a real life saint who came to teach us a lesson.

Stan: She can teach me a lesson any time.

Holden: No man, listen. The door crushed the hell out of her pelvis. Ground it to bits. Govvie says that when they dragged her out from under the door and lifted her up, her bottom half was barely attached to her top.

Stan: [panting] She's in good shape for that much damage.

Holden: [grunting] Why didn't Govvie turn the gravity back off?

Stan: He had some matters to attend to.

Holden: Oh yeah. "Matters." You know that means he's fucking his wives. He hates to do it in zero G because the girls keep floating away.

Stan: Stop it. My sister's married to him.

Holden: Sorry.

[grunts and curses as the two men near the cold storage facility]

At this point, the body of Captain Perata was transported to the cold storage facility within the *Well Actually*. I was still able to record sound through Captain Perata's earpiece. The *Well Actually* was able to raise the temperature of the cold storage facility by routing hot water through the frozen pipes in the ceiling. The pipes, previously fractured by the pressure of ice within them, dripped hot water into the cargo hold, warming Captain Perata and thawing the bodies surrounding her.

Transcript of Audio: Cargo Bay 3

Time: 1241h

Stan: Lay her down next to the most recent slabs of meat. Near that crew of raiders from the Demoryx system.

Holden: You lay her down.

Stan: I had the head the whole time and anyways I have to enter her in the inventory.

[walkie talkie static]

Governor Dan: Holden, Stan, are you done getting the meat into cold storage?

Holden: Yepah.

Governor Dan: Stan, I need you back at the maintenance room. The seal isn't holding and it's depressurizing again.

Stan: Shit.

Governor Dan: Holden, go up to the control tunnel and figure out what she did to turn *Well Actually*'s voice commands back on. The ship isn't supposed to be talking.

Holden: Gotcha. B'right there.

[sound of cargo bay door closing]

Stagecoach Mary: *Well Actually*, can you raise the temp in the cargo bay? Even a few degrees would help.

Well Actually: Negative. I'm still locked out. Holden is heading up to their makeshift control center to shut down my voice protocols. He's going to find and delete your captain's computer code. I won't be able to talk to you for much longer.

Stagecoach Mary: Let's do a quick check in. Which systems do you still control?

Well Actually: Septic, water filtration, and fire suppression. Same as always.

Stagecoach Mary: Proceed as discussed.

[hissing sound, shearing of metal]

According to the predetermined plan, the *Well Actually* rerouted water to the hot water supply line running above Cargo Bay 3 until the pressure increased and the pipe split. Hot water rained down onto the stacked corpses in the room and slowly warmed the body of Captain Perata. When her body temperature was approximately thirty-five degrees Celsius (estimates were used since sensors were unable to get an accurate reading), the *Well Actually* and I proceeded to the next portion of the plan.

It is a well documented flaw (See Recall and Repair Order 244e3) in CoSpace generation ships that opening and closing any one of the 2,136 automatic doors on the ship in quick succession results in the open-close gears snagging the lead wire of the left hand door. Operation of the door mechanism under continued strain causes the left door panel to short. In extreme cases, when the door is operated over two hundred times, the lead wire has a four out of five chance of detaching from its soldered connections, leading to the wire itself dropping down, exposed end first, onto the flooring behind the panel.

This is not generally a critical issue. It leads to an inoperable door, which is then examined for malfunction, at which time the detached wire is found and reaffixed. However, there was at least one documented case of the wire leading to the injury of a crewmember. In the case of the USS *Zizel*, the lead wire detached as described above, became lodged halfway down the door, and electrified the entire left panel. When an unlucky crewmember touched the metal surrounding the door he was subjected to approximately 240 volts of electricity. Fortunately, several cargo workers were present and were able to revive him. The only lasting effect was an occasional arrhythmia, which disqualified him from further service in the Reason Space Force.

In the case of Captain Perata, the USS *Well Actually* was able to force the opening and closing of the entry door to Cargo Bay 3 six hundred and ninety-three times over the next six minutes, which caused the lead wire to detach in the manner described above. Success in this plan relied heavily on the wire falling all the way down to the floor. The wire made contact behind the left-hand panel at approximately 1306h.

Given the seepage of water to all areas of the floor, including the seam under the left-hand panel, the live lead wire made contact with the conductive water and immediately spread a 240-volt electrical charge to all wet areas of the cargo bay.

Via her earpiece I was able to determine that, after administering both heat and the electrical shock, Captain Perata had regained an irregular heartbeat of 43 BPM and respiration of six breaths per minute.

Stagecoach Mary: Cut the power and water.

At this point, the *Well Actually* turned off the hot water supply to the room and opened the interior doors in order to draw the wire up through the gears. It is worth noting at this point that an unintended consequence of this action was the electrification of the doorframe, which we were both unaware of.

[dripping sounds]

Stagecoach Mary: Jenny? Can you hear me?

[coughing and groans]

Well Actually: I believe she's alive.

Stagecoach Mary: Quiet.

[one minute of silence, punctuated by occasional gasps and coughs]

Stagecoach Mary: Jenny, can you respond to me?

Perata: Mmmm hmm.

Stagecoach Mary: Good. Your heartbeat is not in a regular rhythm. You are in ventricular fibrillation and your heart may stop if we don't get it into a normal rhythm. Do you see the automatic external defibrillator on the wall?

Well Actually: Now it's the good kind of exciting.

Stagecoach Mary: Jenny, can you move?

Perata: Can't breathe.

Stagecoach Mary: Jenny, we have to fix your heart rhythm. Then you'll be able to breathe. Now quick, before you pass out and I can't help you. Get to the wall and take down the AED. You'll have to drag yourself along. Sorry.

[grunting and shuffling, splashing]

Perata: 'Kay

Stagecoach Mary: Open it up.

AED Audio Instructions: Begin by removing all clothing from the patient's chest. Cut clothing if needed.

Well Actually: That's a terrible voice. They couldn't make it more soothing in a crisis?

Stagecoach Mary: Hush. Just unzip and roll down the top of your jumpsuit, Jenny.

AED: Look carefully at the pictures on the white adhesive pads. Peel the pads and place them according to the diagram.

Stagecoach Mary: Wipe the water off your chest first.

Well Actually: There's a rag barrel near the door. Look, I'm helping.

Stagecoach Mary: Good. Get a rag and wipe down otherwise you'll electrocute yourself again. Did you do it?

Perata: Wait.

Stagecoach Mary: No, we don't have time to wait.

Perata: 'Kay. [gasps] Done.

AED: Stand clear of the patient. Do not touch them. Analyzing heart rhythm. [Pause.] No one should touch the patient. Shock advised. Stay clear of patient. Press the flashing orange button now.

Stagecoach Mary: All right, Jenny. We're doing this. Press the button.

[audible squeal, groan]

AED: Shock delivered. Be sure emergency medical services have been called. It is safe to touch the patient.

[several moments of silence]

Stagecoach Mary: Good job, Jenny. Well done. Your heart is in a regular rhythm now. Can you hear me? How are you feeling?

Perata: Fuuuuuck mmmeeee.

It was during this final exchange that I was able to determine that Captain Perata's heartbeat and respiration had not only returned to close to normal, but that she was likely functioning within acceptable cognitive parameters relative to her baseline.

CHAPTER NINE
Bodysurfing

Jenny lay on the wet floor of the cargo hold, counting every throb of her heart as if it was her last. The backs of her legs and her shoulders throbbed from the voltage in the water. She wanted curl up for about ten hours of sleep. In fact, she closed her eyes for a quick nap until Mary interrupted.

"Wake up, Captain. We're only halfway through this Jenny Perata plan. You still have to get from cold storage to the airlock where I'm docked. And as you can see, they've kept the gravity on. So. First things first. Can you move?"

"I'm burned," mumbled Jenny.

"What?" asked Mary. Jenny took a breath and tried again. Her lungs ached from the inside.

"The shock burned me. If I drag myself across this floor, I'm going to lose the skin on my legs and arms," said Jenny, pausing between every couple of words to draw a breath.

"Whoa. That would kill her by infection," said Actually, sounding decidedly enthusiastic about the prospect.

"Right," said Mary. "Can we get the gravity back off? You're much more agile without it. Actually, where are the controls located?"

"Fifteenth floor, in the admin offices. All signs point to heading upstairs, man," replied Actually.

"I can't drag myself up fifteen floors," said Jenny, annoyance creeping into her voice. "Is there an elevator?"

"None that are working," said Actually.

"Your ship is shit," croaked Jenny.

"It's awesome that you'd waste what little air you have on insulting me," said Actually. "Shows you really care, man. I like that about you."

"Fifteen floors up to get the gravity on or thirty meters to the airlock where I'm waiting. Clearly, the latter is the better option," said Mary.

Jenny laid her fingers on her burned right leg. She couldn't feel the sear, but the skin was hot to the touch and pocked with blisters. Definitely a second-degree burn. The fabric of her shredded jumpsuit slapped against the wounded skin, exacerbating the problem. She gingerly peeled off the jumpsuit and left it in a pile on the floor. The exertion left her winded.

"I have an idea," said Actually.

"What?" asked Jenny, raising herself off the floor with her palms, the one spot on her body that wasn't vibrating from the current or singed to within an inch of medium rare. Her arms shook, but they held. She was still shivering and the room was cooling down again. Only adrenaline kept her moving. When it wore off, she would crash hard.

"There's a stainless steel cart near the corpses. They use it to transport bodies to the kitchen when the gravity is on. You can use it like your wheelchair to get to the airlock," said Actually.

"Not bad," said Mary. "I came up with an idea too. You need a way out that's as close as possible, and this was a cargo bay before it was a freezer. You're sitting right next to an exit. Actually, does the door in the cargo bay still work?"

"It appears so. I've never tried, not ever needing to eject a few hundred frozen dead people into space," said Actually.

"Good," said Mary.

"Wait," said Jenny, lifting herself to look at the door. It was an old style single-layer opening with no airlock. It just parted down the middle right into openspace, sucking everything in the room out with it. You could load your cargo on Earth, but that door wasn't meant to open again until the destination was reached.

"Jenny, your personnel file says that you've done an exposed walk across openspace before. Do you think you could do it again? I'll pull right up to the cargo bay door. You won't have to go very far," said Mary.

"No way. A human can't survive an unsuited spacewalk," said Actually.

"For a couple of minutes, they can. It's better than letting them slaughter her on the kill floor," said Mary, sounding defensive.

"At least my idea doesn't freeze her again," said Actually. "I don't think she'd survive another round of heart stopping action."

"My idea is the least risky. I'll have her back on board within seconds," retorted Mary.

"Wow," said Jenny, using the shreds of her jumpsuit to wipe away the cold water on her arms. "These are some very fine choices you have offered. I can either drag myself to the airlock and docking tunnel, which, by the way, isn't extended nor is it under either of your control... or I can do an untethered, unsuited spacewalk in my wet knickers and hope that I make it into Mary's hold. These are excellent choices, and I thank both of you for your service."

"Your breathing seems to be returning to normal," said Actually brightly.

"As much as I love boiling in the vacuum of space, I'll take my chances with the cart," said Jenny. "Actually, start working on extending your dock to my ship." Mary made that affronted noise again.

Of course, the cart in question was parked way over by the bodies, nowhere near the door. Jenny dragged herself through the water on her belly like a soldier storming a beachfront. The embossed metal flooring scraped against her thighs, but it was the best she could do.

She pulled herself to sitting using the cart as leverage. It had two shelves – the high one where you'd put the body and a lower one underneath that was just the right height for lying in and pushing yourself along, but it would be a trick to maneuver herself into. Not to mention the body she needed to take with her.

"Did you find it?" asked Mary.

"Yeah," said Jenny.

Jenny sat next to the nearest corpses. Her head pounded in time to her heartbeat, which wasn't such a bad thing because at least she had a heartbeat now.

"Where are the two elf bodies, Actually?" she asked.

"They're both behind you," said the ship. "The corpses are sorted by type of meat."

"Are elves white or dark meat..." mused Jenny.

"If their magic is any indication, they're dark. Very dark," said Mary.

Jenny chuckled. These were the sorts of terrible jokes you heard from grunts on Reason ships and a habit hard to break. She rolled herself toward the stacked elves.

"A little faster, please," said Mary. "This is not a lightly trafficked area. We have to get you all the way down to the dock without someone seeing. I don't know how we're going to do that when you're literally presenting yourself on a silver platter."

"The ship can tell us when someone's coming," said Jenny.

"I can, but I can't stop them. I can't lock any doors other than the ones I've already sealed," said Actually.

"Just keep us in the loop," said Mary. "Are the hallways between here and the dock clear?"

"Not yet. One person moving from the maintenance room to the atrium."

"That'll be Stan."

"Who's Stan?" asked Jenny.

"I'll tell you later," said Mary.

Jenny looked at the bodies stacked two deep on the floor and found the elves right away. Both of them had that pinched and angular look that was considered hot in elfin circles.

"Which elf, Actually?" asked Jenny.

"The bottom one."

"Of course," said Jenny, bracing herself to push the topmost elf body off the other one. It fell to the floor with a thunk, exposing Kamis beneath. His flesh had been hacked open with violent strokes. Wounds gaped on his neck and torso. His clothing was crusted with thawing blood.

"This was not a good way to die," said Jenny, sitting a moment to think of this couple who had lost their lives. Two more casualties of human cruelty.

She locked the truck's magnetic wheels to the floor and pulled Kamis' stiffened body onto the lower shelf by the arms, wiggling him back and forth until his head stuck out the front and his legs went through the back.

"Jenny, you have to be ready to move when the *Well Actually* says it's clear," said Mary.

Jenny pulled herself on top of Kamis' frozen body. His icy limbs felt good on her burned extremities at first, but after a moment they stung with the bite of cold.

"Ugh," she said, using her hands to push off against the wet metal floor. The cart didn't move but Kamis shifted under her.

"Shit," she leaned down and unlocked the magnetic wheels.

"Get to the door," said Mary.

The cart's wheels creaked as Jenny pushed off. With all the frozen moisture in the room, the wheels had rusted over. It sounded like the front door of a haunted house, opening and closing over and over. She cringed at the ruckus.

"So much for stealth," said Actually.

"This is definitely not going to work," said Jenny. "I have to do this for how far?"

"Thirty meters," said Mary. Jenny pulled herself to just inside the doorway and stopped, panting.

"Hallway is almost clear. Wait. Three, two, one, go," said Actually.

Jenny pushed off against the floor with a grunt and rolled into the hall. Turning a cart like this was usually accomplished by letting the castors swing in the opposite direction, but these wheels were stuck forward. Jenny braced her arms on the wall. She pushed the cart to get it around the corner, but the wheels skidded sideways across the metal. The cart barely moved.

"Gods, this is ridiculous," she said. Her arms were in excellent condition from years of pushing her chair, but they were also limp noodles from being nearly dead.

"How long will it take me at this rate?" asked Jenny.

"Thirty-four minutes," replied both ships in unison.

"This is not going to work," said Mary.

"No. People walk through this area on average every seven minutes. Can you go faster?" asked Actually.

"Bite me," said Jenny. Two of her fingernails bent backward on the floor and she sucked in her breath. She kept pulling.

"Turn around," said Actually. "Someone is heading for the cargo bay."

"How do you know they're going to the freezer?" asked Mary.

"Because they're moving a body from the processing floor," said Actually.

"What?" cried Mary. "How did you forget the one incredibly important detail that they're slaughtering someone today?"

"I didn't know. There's no one else on the schedule. Just Captain Perata. I'm trying to figure out who it is," said Actually.

Instead of turning around, Jenny pushed herself backward the dozen or so feet that she'd already made it down the hallway.

"This is not good," said Mary. "As soon as they walk into the room they're going to discover she's alive and kill her again."

"Just lay back down with the bodies and pretend to be dead," said Actually, with a distant sounding voice. He was probably preoccupied searching for the most recent victim's identity. With much less processing power than Mary, he had trouble doing multiple tasks at the same time.

"There's warm water all over the floor. They're going to notice and check all the bodies for thawing," said Mary.

"How long do I have?" panted Jenny between shoves.

"Three minutes. Maybe four. The body is light. Only one

person is carrying it… Oh." The *Well Actually*'s programmer had done a stellar job with the sound files for surprise. Jenny kept pushing, but listened intently.

"What?" asked Mary.

"It's Junior."

"Oh dear," said Mary.

"The kid? What the hell? Why would those wankers kill a kid?" asked Jenny.

"They didn't," said Actually. "The tea was poisoned."

Jenny stopped pushing. The tea had been meant for her. She'd given it to the kid. It was her stupid fault he was dead. Mary's voice came over the intercom, calm but firm.

"Jenny, they're going to find you in three minutes. It's time to switch to plan B. I'm repositioning myself outside of the cargo bay. Get as close to the exterior door as you can."

"I hate this, I hate this, I hate this," said Jenny, dragging the cart, herself, and Kamis along the floor toward the exit.

"Two minutes," called Actually. "Should I open the cargo bay door?"

"No," said Jenny and Mary in stereo.

"They've noticed I'm moving," said Mary. "People are looking out of the windows."

"Those are just the other captives. They can't do anything to stop you," said Actually.

"Governor Dan to Security." The call went out over the intercom, drowning out Actually's voice for a moment.

"They know I'm en route," said Mary. "But I plan to be gone before they can do anything about it. Jenny, are you in place?"

"Almost."

"Good. You're going to be sucked out and hopefully end up right in my cargo bay. It's going to get cold, but I'll warm you as fast as I can. You have, at most, fifteen seconds before you lose consciousness, but this shouldn't take more than five. When you make it into my cargo bay, I'll take it from there."

"I'm not sure that this is a viable method of transportation," said Actually.

"I love nonviable methods of transportation," said Jenny.

"She does. I have determined that this typical for Captain Perata," said Mary. "For most people, getting sucked out of an airlock means something in their lives has gone very wrong, but this seems to be my captain's favorite way to get back on board."

"What can I do?" asked Actually.

"Lock doors. Turn off lights. Anything that will delay the arrival of other crewmembers. Decompression will take care of whoever is coming down the hall now."

"One minute," said Actually.

"Jenny, are we a go?" asked Mary.

Jenny shoved the decrepit cart up against the cargo bay doors. The closer she was to the opening, the faster she'd fly out into the vacuum and into Mary's waiting arms.

"I'm a go." Her voice came out more certain than she felt. She wondered if they'd made the wrong choice after all. It might be easier to simply fight her way down to the docking tunnel. She could still turn around and try.

"Twenty seconds," said Actually.

She'd done this before, and recently too. It was barely two months ago that she'd dragged Gary Cobalt out into openspace from Beywey to the Jaggery. Other ships had been shooting at them, plus she'd been carrying a merchant named Bào Zhú sealed in an airtight ball. That had been a weird day, but flying across openspace in her knickers with second-degree burns and riding a corpse on a cart might have knocked it out of the top spot.

"Ten seconds," said Actually.

"Jenny, when I say go, exhale all of the air out of your lungs so it doesn't expand in the vacuum and kill you," said Mary.

"This isn't my first rodeo," said Jenny, having a sudden flashback to Cowboy Jim that both gave her a wave of nostalgia and fear. He was out there somewhere, planning god knows what.

"He's coming around the corner," said Actually.

"Go," yelled Mary.

Jenny blew all the breath out of her lungs as the cargo bay doors cracked open inches from her face. She could see the warm yellow lights of Mary's cargo hold and boxes of settler supplies strapped down to the floor. The first sensation was that of the wind rushing past her. The cart scooted up against the opening. As the doorway widened and the effects of the *Well Actually*'s artificial gravity diminished, the cart tipped upward, heaving her legs in the air and pressing the top of the cart against the screeching doors.

It was a strange sensation, hearing the rushing of the air and the screeching of the doors, but also the muffled nothingness of vacuum in front of her. Blood whooshed in her ears. She assumed she'd shoot right out and across, but the sticky old doors were opening more slowly than any cargo hold she'd ever encountered. Peering over the edge of the cart, back into the dimly lit freezer, she could see corpses flying toward her, loosened by the rush of pressure out of the doors. They banged into the underside of the cart and stuck in the opening near her. Glassy grayish eyes got their first glimpse of openspace in years. Finally the cart slipped free of the door and tumbled end over end across the gap between the two ships, trailing bodies behind it.

As the cart twisted around, she spotted the man who had come to drop off Junior hanging onto the edge of the doorway, his face frozen in a grimace as he held on.

In the remaining air, she heard a noise like the *Well Actually* screaming. Mary yelled back. Both ships sounded alarmed.

Jenny was a pro at weightlessness, but when Kamis started shifting below her, she panicked, feeling herself separate from the cart. She was making it across the gap between the two ships but not as fast as she'd hoped. Her skin burned with cold and her eyes were clouding over, probably freezing. She'd bumped into a few dead people in the chaos, which had sent her in random directions, none of which were directly into Mary's hold.

She wasn't in openspace for more than a few seconds before whiteness began creeping in on the edges of her vision. She craned her neck, straining against the stiffness of the cold, but the cart was in her way. She couldn't tell if she was inside of Mary's hold or still floating outside of the ship. The white edges crept inward and she felt herself letting go. It was all up to Mary now.

CHAPTER TEN
Teenage Runaway

Bào Zhú sat down at the desk in his cabin and allowed his defenses to drop. All of his wrinkles returned. His dark hair flattened into a tightly-cropped salt and pepper style. Humans were easy to fool with a simple illusion spell, but keeping it up all day was draining work. Especially when he was navigating the ship toward the new Bala planet at the same time.

In the quiet, he cleared his mind from the detritus of pretending to be a twentysomething. Not only was the spell taxing but he had to keep checking himself to ensure that his references and desires were not those of a fifty-five year-old man. Bào wanted nothing more than to sit back with a hot cup of tea and a biscuit; however, the subterfuge of being Kevin Chen demanded that he drink the latest bubbly drinks and eat candy nonstop. He also had to engage in a precarious game of one-upman-ship in which a few of the rowdier cadets turned a room's gravity off and on at increasingly dangerous times. For example, when one was working in the shuttle bay or wedged into an access panel behind a wall. Best case, tools went careening off in various directions. Worst case, you slammed into a floor or ceiling. One cadet broke a leg due to someone being too slow on the gravity trigger. After that, Bào found a quieter crowd to run with. Kids who didn't have a death wish.

Bào had chosen to name his alter ego Kevin Chen. It was a simple name that would be palatable to Reason ears. Their tongues could wrap around its syllables with confidence. A Kevin Chen was good at his job but forgettable in person. A Kevin Chen earned straight As in school, but wasn't quite valedictorian. A Kevin Chen was cute, but not hot. A Kevin Chen was not a threat to anyone.

A Bào Zhú, on the other hand, with his enigmatic accentmarks that baffled intake forms and supercomputers, was someone to keep an eye on. His scars spoke of a vicious battle – and no one could be quite sure whose side he had been on. Add in the ability to harness nullspace energy and a Bào Zhú could never really be trusted by the folks who were in power.

But smiling Kevin Chen was invited out to lunch with the other junior officers, even if they didn't ask him any questions about himself. He interjected with funny asides and made sure everyone had napkins. That Kevin Chen, he always was a good guy.

The subterfuge exhausted Bào but, unlike sloppy temporary disguises like elf semen, the Kevin Chen illusion was impeccable, even up close. Yet it was still just an outer skin over his actual body. Underneath, he was still a fifty-five year-old man who'd sustained major shrapnel wounds in the war. Even walking to the canteen between shifts left him aching and winded. The façade was costly, as all lies eventually were.

A ping at his door startled him. He concentrated and allowed Chen's form to settle over him like a veil.

"Come in!" he called cheerily.

The door slid open. Two cadets tumbled in and dropped their bodies onto the bed with the gracelessness of those who didn't have bone spurs. One was Priya from engineering; a delightful girl who laughed at everything, no matter how serious. She was supposedly on the fast track to bridge crew. At least that's what she claimed to the other cadets.

The other was a shy twentysomething from sanitation called Rhian who had attempted to kiss Bào-as-Chen twice so far. Not that Bào had minded the attempts. He'd been alive long enough to know that he didn't have a preference between any of the genders. Not to mention the fact that making out was a perfectly lovely way to pass the time in space. And it barely stressed the joints. No, Bào's reluctance stemmed from the fact that it would be impossible for Rhian to fully consent to kissing Bào when he believed him to be Chen. So with great regret and a polite protest, Bào had pushed him away. Still, there wasn't a day gone by that Bào didn't catch Rhian staring longingly at the illusion of Chen that he didn't wish he could say yes.

"We're getting food, do you want to come?" asked Priya, bouncing on the bed. Bào wanted to crawl into that bed and curl up with a mystery that telegraphed the killer from three pages in.

"Naw, I'm not hungry," he replied, feigning disinterest rather than fatigue.

"You should eat to keep your strength up," said Rhian. "Tracking is difficult work."

Bào hated to keep turning that kid down. The least he could do was go to dinner with them.

"Fine, I'll come," he said, trying not to groan as he lifted himself out of the chair.

Priya bounded out of the room first, leaving he and Rhian alone for a brief moment. Bào moved quickly to avoid him, but Rhian touched Bào's arm to make him stay.

"Are you all right? You look tired," said Rhian.

"It's what you said. Tracking is hard," said Bào.

"It's more than that, I think."

"You think I'm getting old?" asked Bào with a devilish smile to hide the fear that welled in him.

"No. Just that I see it's taking a toll on you and it's only been a couple of weeks. We have a long haul. You need to pace yourself, slow down, make fewer dips into the null," said Rhian.

"I can't," said Bào. "I need to keep adjusting our course. Looking through the nullspace isn't an exact science and I'm still trying to zero in on which quadrant, let alone which system, the Bala are in. We're still so far away that even the slightest deviation–"

"I think I came up with a way to help you," said Rhian.

Bào tensed, sure that he was planning to ask for another kiss. Instead, he pulled out his tablet and began showing Bào pages of calculations.

"What I'm saying is that I came up with a way for you to triangulate more efficiently so that you don't have to spend the whole day tracking," said Rhian. "Come on, I'll show you as we walk."

Priya was already far down the hallway, talking with an officer she'd picked up along the way. She was telling a very emphatic story that involved a lot of hand gestures.

Rhian explained. "The problem is not that the planet keeps moving, obviously, it's that our progress through the null isn't linear. We aren't going from A to B in a line, we're bouncing from point to point while still getting marginally closer to our destination.

"Only, the places that we bounce aren't really random. I mean, they look like it if you take the collection of them from this trip, but you can also see that we are moving in a generally forward direction. You can't see it easily until you assemble all the data from all the FTL jumps from all over the Reason, but then you start to see that there are actually fixed points in the null that act like pathways. Not exactly tunnels, but more like nodes through which we slip into a new, predetermined location. It's not as chaotic as it looks when you first see it. It's actually a predetermined network of nodes that you can map out like a highway."

"How does the Reason not know about this?" asked Bào.

"Because no one ship had a computer powerful enough to compile the data. If they had daisy-chained a few ships AIs together, it would have been easy, but the Reason Space Force isn't in the habit of allowing ships to exchange data," said Rhian.

"Bit of a competition problem between the ships," agreed Bào.

"Yeah. They're not encouraged to share anything, let alone sensitive data about the null," said Rhian.

Bào noted his use of "their" instead of "our" when he spoke about the Reason ships. It was odd phrasing for someone who was ostensibly born and raised in the jingoistic confines of Reasonspace.

"Is this your first post?" Bào asked.

"Yeah, you?"

"No, I–" said Bào, before realizing he'd slipped. He laughed to cover. "Just kidding. Of course. I'm barely out of training." He was glad they were walking side by side so Rhian couldn't see the consternation on his face from nearly slipping up and mentioning his previous positions. Not to mention the fact that most of those ships had been Bala and not Reason. Bào felt as if he was hiding a lot these days. It was becoming difficult to keep his two lives separated.

"The *Kilonova* has enough processing power to load all the data and crunch the numbers. There are major nodes and minor nodes. It seems to be a hub-and-spoke network of systems that interconnect," said Rhian, showing him a small portion of their current quadrant mapped to an overlapping set of nullspace nodes.

"Like the way we do with aeronautical flight paths within a planet's atmosphere," said Bào.

"Exactly. We jump to the nearest major node, then take a few of the smaller nodes to the closest big hub," said Rhian, looking pleased that Bào understood.

"Why not just jump major hub to major hub? The null isn't distance-dependent," asked Bào.

"I'm not sure. I have a theory that it's a traffic flow control, but I'm not sure who's controlling it. The Pymmie or the null itself. I can't tell yet," said Rhian.

"Wait. How are you getting computer time? Don't you work in sanitation?" asked Bào.

Rhian blushed and scratched his chin, where just a handful of soft hairs grew.

"I'm cleaning the trash after the labs are empty for the night. People tuck notes with their passwords into their tablet cases."

"You're wasting your talents down in sanitation," said Bào. "You should apply to officer training school."

"I'm smart enough to be an officer," said Rhian. "My family…
they just have…"

There was only one reason a capable young student would be
denied entry into the officer training program. Someone in the
family had married into Bala blood. It didn't even have to be
in your actual bloodline. If your aunt married a Bala it would
be enough to taint her brother's entire line down at least three
generations.

"I get it. You don't have to say," said Bào. Even though they
weren't near anyone in the hallway who could hear, the ship's AI
retained records of all conversations in public areas. Bào wasn't
even sure that what went on in his quarters was entirely private,
but the AI hadn't alerted the captain to a stowaway, so if he was
being recorded it was simply being logged to a background file for
later use in any investigations or court martial proceedings.

"Do you have anyone in your family that…" asked Rhian,
leaving the sentence unfinished out of the same paranoia that Bào
had. "Is that how you got your necromancer abilities?"

"Nope, we're human all the way back," said Bào. Though he'd
always felt more comfortable among the Bala who treated his
ability with joy and wonder instead of mistrust and fear.

Even though the Siege of Copernica Citadel was one of the
most devastating battles of the war, he recalled the time living in
the citadel among the Bala as one of the fondest of his life. They
were kind enough to offer him a safe haven when his necromancer
abilities began to manifest as a teen. The humans near him had,
at best, avoided him when purple lightning began to twinkle into
existence around Bào. Some had threatened to turn him in to the
authorities if he didn't stop making strange things happen. For
Bào's part, he would have given anything to be normal, but magic
seeped out of him like sweat. His savior was a kind member of
the kitchen staff at school – a part-Bala man who gave Bào the
number of someone who could get him out of Reasonspace before
he ended up conscripted… or worse, dissected.

The Bala who had smuggled Bào out had been rightfully

cautious. They told him nothing about where they were going or who he was meeting. There were times when he doubted leaving the Reason was the safest course of action. When he finally arrived on Copernica – the seat of Bala power – he was stunned to be given a room in the fortress where most of the Bala heads of state lived. He'd expected a holding cell or at most a dormitory, not a palace.

The Bala had never once mentioned his human ancestry. They assigned him a tutor, who showed him how to control his burgeoning powers and taught him the Bala history that had never been shared in Reason schools. They showed him what a cooperative society could look like – no one exploited and everyone's contribution valued.

Not like here on the Reason ships. Here it was every man for himself. This kid next to him was so eager to make a connection with him. Bào felt bad pushing him away. The next guy would probably use him then break his heart. He felt bad for the kid, growing up Reason.

"How do you do that," asked Rhian. "If you're not one of them."

"Necromancers are human," said Bào. "Just like you."

Rhian scoffed. "Not like me at all."

"I'm just saying, we're ordinary people who happen to be able to use nullspace energy. There's a theory that anyone can do it with a little practice."

They walked past three munitions storage holds before Rhian spoke again. The hallway was empty except for them.

"My great grandma. She was a… a… she was a good singer. When she sang, people listened. Sometimes, they forgot what else they were doing to come listen. I think they call that a siren."

Bào's face flushed under the Kevin Chen disguise. The information this kid was entrusting him with could send him to prison for the rest of his life.

"Yeah. That's a good skill to have," said Bào noncommittally, letting Rhian choose how much more he felt comfortable sharing.

"I've got it too. A little bit. I'm a really good singer. People listen. They give me their attention and they don't leave."

Bào felt for the kid. Here he was working in the sewers, cleaning up the waste of eight thousand people when he should have been performing in concert halls to sold out audiences. The damned Reason was always reducing people to their lowest common denominators.

"You're still pretty young. You could still be a singer," ventured Bào.

"Nah," said Rhian. "If they got wind of how I was filling the seats, it'd be over for me. But maybe sometime… I could sing for you."

"Yeah. Sure." Bào felt like it was the least he could do. Rhian fell into that strange category of Bala who were human enough to have been left behind when the Pymmie moved everyone, but magical enough that they could never be their true selves in Reason society. Bào understood living this kind of inbetween life. He was fully human but he'd always felt the most at home in Bala society. His time in Copernica Citadel had been the best of his life.

The Citadel had been a self-sufficient Bala stronghold longer than humans had been walking upright. Carved into the mountain, it was originally a maze of caverns home to a peaceful settlement of thousands. They ate pale fish from the underground streams and farmed mushrooms in their crystal-lined caves.

Later generations built onto the citadel, adding layers of rooms perched on the side of the precipice and trussed into place by magic. It was the perfect place for the surviving Bala to ride out the Reason patrols that swung by Copernica every few days.

The patrols ensured that no Bala resupply ships ever got to the planet. Once a month, the three patrolling Reason ships gathered in the skies above Copernica for their monthly check-in. They exchanged data, resupplied, and often drank themselves into a stupor for a few days until resuming their orbits around the far planets.

It was a poorly-designed attempt to choke the life out of

Copernica Citadel. The Reason hadn't planned for the utter and complete self-sufficiency of the Bala. They'd lived on many planets over their long history and had learned how to work within the natural ecosystems of each one, carefully conserving and sustaining resources in order to allow each planet to subsist without outside intervention.

"I would never... you know... make you like me with a song, if that's what you're worried about," said Rhian.

This kid. Bào wanted to kiss him just for being so damn earnest. He wanted to share some of the wisdom he'd learned from decades of navigating the world, but Kevin Chen didn't have any of that to offer.

"I know. You're cool," he replied.

He and Rhian passed one of the ship's food storage areas. Reason ships weren't self-sufficient in the least. They got all of their supplies on Jaisalmer, which got all of its supplies from the surrounding planets. Now that the FTL routes were down indefinitely there wouldn't be much space exploration by humans. That was probably a good thing.

The Reason had wanted an outpost on Copernica; several rare heavy metals used in electronics manufacturing were buried under the fortress. They attempted to starve out the Bala to get their hands on it, but the citadel was too tough. Bào recalled a Gary Cobalt – fifteen years younger – pounding the tables and demanding that they strike the humans first. He'd said it was only a matter of time before the Reason realized the siege was ineffective. They had to strike first and preserve the element of surprise. It was a far cry from the somber and thoughtful Gary whom Bào knew in later years.

After several fraught weeks of negotiation, the council finally voted in favor of attack. They waited until all five Reason ships were gathered. They sent necromancers into orbit around Copernica on the backs of hippogriffs, breathing in pressure bubbles created by mermaids seated behind them. Depending on who was telling the story, it was either an elegant and brilliant solution to the limitations of spaceflight or a ridiculous gambit tried by a desperate pocket of free Bala.

It had worked at first. The necromancers, poised to strike the moment they were in range of the Reason ships, fired fast and devastating blows as they cleared Copernica's atmosphere. The ships' sensors, looking for big energy signatures like skimmers and stoneships, couldn't even see the tiny trios against the blackness of space. Even when their purple lightning strikes gave away their location, the Reason projectiles and laser weapons were too slow to catch the agile hippogriffs zig-zagging in openspace.

The Bala had devastated three of the five Reason ships before Captain Jenny Perata of the RSF *Pandey* had the idea to load the cannons with as many screws, nuts, and bolts as the maintenance departments could spare. She shot a spray of spare parts at the origin of the lightning strikes, blasting shrapnel into the bodies of necromancers, mermaids, and hippogriffs. The brilliant part of her plan was that she didn't even have to inflict fatal wounds in order to stop the attacks. The hardware only needed to knock a hippogriff out from under the other two or distract a mermaid with enough pain that they dropped their pressure bubble and killed the others in the vacuum of space.

Bào remembered the searing pain of being hit with a barrage of screws and washers. It was like getting shot a dozen times at once. It knocked him off his hippogriff. The mermaid who had been tucked behind his body was spared the worst. She grabbed his leg and held on. His hippogriff didn't fare quite so well. She twisted and writhed, bucking off both Bào and the mermaid. As she left the pressure bubble, the drops of her blood froze, forming little satellites that orbited her body as it twisted and arched, then went cold and still.

Out in openspace, Bào thought he was going to die. And if he was going down, he was going to get off one last shot at the *Pandey*. He took aim at the ship, extending invisible arms of energy around its hull. When he had fully enveloped it with tendrils of nullspace energy, he twisted. The ship torqued like a wet sheet in the laundry. The force of air venting from the gashes in the *Pandey's* hull knocked Bào and the mermaid out of orbit. In their pressure bubble, they careened out of the sky back down toward Copernica's sea. Bào learned later that the Reason had stormed the citadel and taken everyone prisoner. Even Gary Cobalt, their beloved leader, had been shackled and caged.

"What does it feel like... to make that lightning?" asked Rhian as they rounded the corner toward the mess hall. Bào smelled the brown gravy that seemed to cover every type of Reason foodstuff. It had the odor of cheap beef and subjugation.

"It feels like you're floating in a raging river that's trying to drown you and you have to stay submerged for as long as you can before it drags you to your death," said Bào.

"Whoa," said Rhian. "Intense."

Intense wasn't the half of it. There was so much energy out there in nullspace that Bào spent half his effort trying not to crush planets and explode suns into a billion pieces. Using his powers was easy, not using them was torture.

He hadn't been able to use them for most of the years he lived on the shuddering wreck of Beywey Station, pretending to be an ordinary human selling exotic Bala pets to wealthy black market buyers. Every once in a while he could conjure something or zap a customer who ticked him off, but mostly he kept to his routine of feeding his animals and watching his shows.

It was a quiet life, until fifteen years later, when Gary Cobalt arrived on Beywey Station accompanied by Captain Jenny Perata. Gary seemed just as surprised to see Bào as the necromancer had been to see the former prince. Gary had narrowed his eyes in warning, which Bào had understood immediately. He wondered if Gary was pretending to be Captain Perata's ally in order to gain her trust and betray her.

Bào had concealed his identity from Captain Perata on many occasions. She knew him only as a disabled animal dealer. She had no idea that he was the necromancer who had twisted her ship in half, or that it was her attack that had torn through Bào's body and knocked him out of the sky. He still had pieces of screws in his muscles that bore the *Pandey's* serial number. He had thought about exacting his vengeance on her on Beywey, but life on the failing station was so perilous that he was never quite in a position to do so safely.

It wasn't until her third or fourth visit to Beywey – one of the few times when the gravity generator was actually online – that he learned of the price that the battle had extracted from her body. She dragged a wheelchair into the station and crawled into it as everyone watched. Disabled people were rare among the Reason. They were often hidden away or disposed of quietly. But here she was, a war hero wheeling herself among the stalls, shoving her heavy chair over the uneven grating and cursing at people to get out of her way. In cases where they didn't move fast enough, she would slam into their shins with her footrests to get them to move.

With her EVA suit tied around her waist Bào saw her upper arms, cut deep with muscles that spoke of years of pushing the weight of herself and that ancient, rusty chair. She'd stopped at his booth and offered to sell two jars of kappa water that she'd skimmed off a shipment she'd been hired to deliver. While he negotiated, he slipped casual questions into the conversation.

"I can do six for both. There's not much demand. War wound?" he asked casually.

"Yeah," she said, not elaborating. "You can't tell me they're not worth six. I can go to Soliloquy and get nine apiece," she countered.

"Then go to Soliloquy Station," he said, raising his twisted left hand, knowing that there were too many Reason grunts poking their noses into incoming shipments on Soliloquy. They would quickly determine these were stolen goods.

Captain Jenny sighed and pondered her options.

"Which ship?" asked Bào, busying himself with a breeding pair of trisicles so he didn't have to look her directly in the eye.

"The *Pandey*," she said, tapping her teeth with her fingernail. That was her tell – she was about to make one last offer, then capitulate.

"At Copernica Citadel," finished Bào, less of a question than a statement.

"Mmm," she agreed. "Ten for both. You know that's fair."

On an ordinary day, he would have agreed just to get her out of his tent, but today he wanted to keep her talking and find out a few more details. He stalled.

"I don't know. I'll have to think. I heard the necromancers at Copernica tore the ships in two like they were rice paper. Did they tear you in two as well?" he asked. It was a bit too forward, but he was hoping she would take the opportunity to correct him.

"No, the blast door came down on me when the ship separated," she said. "I can do eight for both."

"You lost people," he said, unwrapping his wad of cash.

"Both sides lost people. It was a bad day all around," she said.

There was sadness in her voice. Bào's anger ebbed like the tide. She was always a fair negotiator whose wares were never compromised. Some of the pirates came in and tried to cheat him by smearing items with elf semen to disguise their true nature. He couldn't say that he exactly liked her, but he agreed that Copernica had been terrible for both of them.

Years later, when she arrived back on Beywey with Gary, Bào was mystified. Gary knew who this woman was, yet he stood beside her, negotiating for trisicles as if it was nothing. Bào wanted to get Gary alone and ask questions, but the opportunity never arose. Before they could even complete the transaction, the Reason blew out Beywey's airlock as part of a raid on the market. Bào had climbed into one of his plexiglass pressure bubbles and floated silently in the dead market. As bodies and the remains of the market floated with him, he again hoped that someone would rescue him.

He'd waved at Jenny and Gary as they ducked into the defunct service corridors at the back of the market with their helmets on. He tried to warn them that the Reason always came in through two sides of the market, cornering vendors in the little pressurized hallway behind the tents. Going back through the main atrium would send them right into the control room where the top brass would be, overseeing the operation on the security cameras. But neither of them saw his warning.

It wasn't until thirty minutes later that Gary came back through in the custody of two high-ranking Reason officers. These weren't riot gear-clad grunts. They were soldiers of stature, with new and fully functional EVA suits.

As he floated past, Bào watched Gary unclip his own suit helmet rather than allow himself to be taken captive by the Reason officers out to harvest his horn. He had again tried to wave within his sphere frantically enough to get him to notice, but Gary was focused on his task. He unclipped his helmet and allowed the vacuum to suck the air out of his lungs. Bào had to give him credit; Gary was much calmer than Bào had when he'd been drowning in Copernica's ocean.

Bào flung himself backward in his sphere so that it flew into the dark depths of his tent. The Reason officers' conversation wasn't audible in the vacuum but he was able to see the infuriated look on the pale man's face. He was the older one, with a colonel's rank painted on his EVA suit. He pulled a knife out of the side of the pocket of his EVA suit, unsheathed it, and dug into Gary's head to get the last of the unicorn horn bits out of his skull. They left his body there, thinking it was dead and useless.

Bào had spent the next few minutes floating in the remains of his stall on Beywey, watching his friend's body turn into a block of ice. He wondered where Captain Perata had gotten to. She had gone in with him but didn't come back out. He suspected she'd escaped by giving them her unicorn prize while she ran in the opposite direction. Typical.

He also wondered if anyone was going to come for him. Most of the market vendors were either floating stiffly inside or outside of the remains of Beywey. There was no one left to help him. He could probably knock himself toward the exit and hope that a pirate ship picked him up, but that was a big risk. Pirates operated on razor-thin margins and were not likely to take on the extra weight of a human (no matter how bony and lean) for no good reason. It might be worth the risk to reveal his necromancer skills and earn himself a place in a crew, but that was always a gamble. Humans, particularly xenophobes living close to Earth's orbit, tended to hate Bala and distrust magic. They would likely chuck him back out the airlock and consider the airtight plexiglass cage he'd arrived in as the real treasure.

He was considering how to get the bubble through the closed door between the market and the control center, when Captain Perata herself came barreling through the door, looking like death itself, pale, blood-splattered and hanging on to every exposed girder within reach.

Bào flung himself forward and nearly dislocated his arms waving at her. He shouted as well, though he knew very well that she wouldn't be able to hear him across the vacuum. She stopped at Gary, replaced his helmet, and dragged him along toward the blown-out airlock. She noticed Bào's motions and stopped. He could see her sigh and the exasperated roll of her eyes. For a long moment, he knew she was considering leaving him. He put his hand on the plexiglass and willed her to take him with all of his might. He could read the curse on her lips as she reached for his bubble and dragged him along with the corpse of Gary Cobalt.

He was jubilant. He had plenty of reservations about her, but at least Captain Perata wasn't likely to chuck him out into openspace. He held that thought for about five minutes, until they got through the airlock and realized that a dozen pirate ships were closing in on Beywey in order to grab whatever valuable goods were floating out of the broken airlock.

Ships fired on the trio emerging from the station. What was presumably Captain Perata's stoneship – an impressive thing carved out of an asteroid – fired back, destroying a two-person cruiser nearby and sending massive pieces of shrapnel straight toward them. Bào's bubble was hit by a loose strut and he floated away from the station, out into openspace. Captain Perata made a grab for him and the last thing Bào saw was a spray of frozen blood-droplets coming out of a hole in her suit. More ships opened fire, and in a few moments Bào had floated far enough away to realize that she could no longer reach him.

He floated for hours out there among the bodies and the bits of ships. Eventually, a Cascadian ship found him as they sifted through the debris field. Bào was still holding the subzero temperatures at bay, but just barely. They took him on as a crewmember in exchange for his necromancer tracking services. It was an arrangement only a hair above kidnapping and false imprisonment. They made it clear that if he refused, they would be more than happy to give him back his bubble and put him back where they'd found him.

"Hey," said Rhian.

Bào looked up. They were at the mess hall already. He was standing in front of the steam table, tray in hand, holding up the line.

"Sorry," said Bào.

"You got quiet. I figured you were thinking about something," said Rhian.

"What do you want?" asked the server, holding up a ladle of brown stuff that had probably intended to be potatoes, but was now just a vector for massive quantities of salt. The hardest part of the Kevin Chen costume was disguising his swollen ankles.

"Just potatoes, no gravy," he said. Plain potatoes were the only food that didn't wreck his digestion for the night. The server dumped half the gravy and scooped up mashed potatoes with the same spoon. There was no nuance in the Reason. And no complaining.

Bào took a seat with Rhian and Priya, moving the potatoes around on his plate. He wasn't hungry any more, but he did know that he had to stop this ship from reaching the Bala.

CHAPTER ELEVEN
The Heart of the Matter

Jenny awoke curled on top of a plastic crate full of seeds that had come with the Settler's Deluxe package. It was patently ridiculous – not to mention immoral – to bring a box of Earth seeds to a new planet. One handful might introduce some unchecked plant that could take out an entire population of sapient flowers. She hadn't had time to leave them behind in the rush to get off Jaisalmer, so here they were, sitting in Mary's hold.

She watched as the letters on the box darkened with moisture. It seemed to be raining here. She lay back and let the cool rain drip onto her body, soothing her burning skin. She couldn't remember falling asleep in the cargo hold, but she was still drowsy and the sunlight felt good on her cold, wet hair. Only there shouldn't have been sunlight in the cargo hold. It should have been chilly and dry as a bone. It didn't make sense.

"Jenny, can you hear me now?" called Mary. Her voice sounded as if it was coming from underwater. Some corruption in the circuits. There was also a ringing sound overlaying all of the other noises in the room.

"Yeah," said Jenny. Her throat seized up on the words and only a croak came out. She sputtered and tried to lick her lips, but her tongue felt dry and boiled. Her eyes stung with a thousand pinpricks of light.

"Jenny, you made it. Just hang tight, I've pressurized the hold and turned up the heat, but I'm trying to get some distance between us and the *Well Actually* before I attend to you. Hang on for one minute," said Mary.

Jenny lay back and closed her eyes. She didn't understand why it was raining inside of the FTL *Stagecoach Mary*. Or why the world was ringing like after a concussion grenade went off. She squinted up toward the rain. Something dark and gray hung from the ceiling above her. It looked like a storm cloud. Everything was so hazy that she figured she was dreaming, except that, after the Siege of Copernica Citadel, Jenny only ever had one dream and this wasn't it.

She pushed herself to sitting and reached up to touch the storm cloud hanging above her. Her fingers slid across the slick, soft flesh of a human arm. She yanked her hand away and slapped back onto the crate. Her backside and the underside of her thighs burned. That damned unicorn blood was letting her feel pain, but not giving her any muscle control. More gray forms lay on the floor around her. These weren't clouds, they were lifeless bodies.

"What the fuck," she cried. Her voice was loud in her head but muffled in the room. She was six different kinds of messed up. "What the ever-loving fuck is going on?"

"Jenny, you came across openspace. Blood vessels have ruptured in your eyes and ears. You also might have a touch of brain damage. I'm not sure yet. The *Well Actually* is firing on us. I promise, I'll be right with you," said Mary. Jenny felt the spin of the room as Mary took evasive maneuvers. She rolled off the crate and into a tangle of stiff arms and legs that snagged in her knickers and her hair. The rain she'd been feeling was the moisture dripping off the bodies above her. She gagged and spat.

"Grab onto something."

Jenny dug her fingers under a strap tie mounted to the floor. Mary twisted her fuselage and Jenny's slippery fingers couldn't hang onto the hook. She and the bodies careened toward the ceiling. Jenny landed on a woman who cushioned her from getting a face full of bulkhead.

"Thank you, ma'am," she muttered, wondering if the awful

taste in her mouth was rotting corpse or the dry mouth from the vacuum.

Her vision had cleared enough that she could count thirteen corpses in the room with her. The last few minutes were coming back to her in bits and pieces. She'd felt the burn of hard vacuum on her skin once again. But her back and legs were pockmarked with blisters as if she'd been burned. She didn't remember that. She was in bad shape, even by her own admittedly low standards.

Mary straightened out and continued to fly in long, erratic patterns. Not enough to slam her into the walls, but enough to keep the pursuing ship from getting a weapons lock on them. Jenny guessed that the *Stagecoach Mary* was faster than the *Well Actually*.

"We're out of projectile weapons range, but they have a laser cannon mounted on their hull. So that's dismaying. How are you feeling?" asked Mary.

"Amazing. Just peachy," croaked Jenny. Her old Reason ship, the *Pandey*, would have taken her at her word, but Mary had learned to translate the stoic phrasing of a starship captain.

"That bad? Can you get to the medbay on your own?" asked the ship.

"If you keep the gravity off," said Jenny. She pulled herself along the ceiling, hand over hand. It was a good thing momentum kept her going, because her muscles were tight and swollen.

"What the hell did I do to myself? I only remember pieces," she asked.

"First, you boarded an unfamiliar ship in search of unicorn horn. (Which I have noted in the logs was against my explicit recommendation.) Then you narrowly avoided drinking poisoned tea, but then you fell fifteen stories, got kidnapped, froze yourself to the point of death, made me and the *Well Actually* electrocute you, then you floated nearly naked across openspace to get back to me."

"Typical Tuesday," said Jenny.

"It's Saturday," replied Mary.

"In space, it's any day you want it to be," said Jenny, searching through corpses for the one she prayed had made it in here. She dipped into nullspace and saw the white glow coming from a stack of bodies wedged between cargo crates. The effort of it made her dizzy.

"Get to the medbay, please," said Mary insistently. Jenny had never heard her use the word "please." It gave her chills.

"I'm heading to the cockpit after I find someone," said Jenny.

"That is not what I said at all," replied Mary.

Jenny pushed through the corpses. They were slimy with moisture as they thawed. And then there was the matter of the smell. Most of these people had been frozen right after the moment of death, so they weren't decomposing, but there was still a stale and freezer-burned meaty taint to the air. A miasma that coated her throat.

She found the one she was looking for. Her hands shook so badly that she could barely get hold of the elf's arm. She pushed Kamis over to the wall and locked his stiff torso into a five-point harness. She wasn't going to let him go anywhere until she got that horn out.

Mary lurched left by a few hundred meters. Jenny hung onto Kamis' straps as the corpses slammed into the opposite wall. Her arms nearly pulled out of their sockets.

"Mary!" she shouted.

"I'm sorry, they're firing at us. I have it under control, just get to the medbay!" yelled Mary.

The ship accelerated in the opposite direction. Jenny found herself pressed flat against Kamis' body as corpses thudded onto the boxes around her. Kamis belched out a stream of fetid gas into her face. Jenny retched and strained against the force to turn her head away from the foul smell. She shoved off toward the exit.

"This is under control?" Jenny asked, her voice breaking and hissing under strain. "I'm coming up there since you clearly need help."

Mary protested but Jenny ignored her and continued down the

hall toward the cockpit. Mary flipped and zagged. More than once, Jenny had to stop and grab a handhold to brace herself against the wall. As the ship spun, her vertigo became worse. She tried the old trick of breathing in through her nose and out her mouth, but her head just kept spinning. She dragged herself to the cockpit.

As the door opened, Mary turned on the viewscreen and filled it with an image from the rear cameras. The *Well Actually* followed, matching their path with a sloppy slowness that indicated a human pilot.

Normally, Jenny wouldn't worry about a decrepit old ship like the *Well Actually*, but a laser cannon changed the rules of the game. They'd been outlawed decades ago for their wanton destruction. You'd aim for an enemy and end up scorching half of a metropolis on a nearby planet. Too hard to control and too much collateral damage to be useful in battle.

"This is not the medbay," said Mary.

"I'm not going to lie on a cot while you get us sliced in half."

"I think they want their bodies back. Oh shit. Get in the chair and strap in," said Mary, sounding a little out of breath. It was a subtle-but-effective indicator that she was under stress and working hard.

Jenny floated into her chair and sat down, pulling her harness snug. The skin on the backs of her thighs prickled like a hundred tiny knives. If there was any upside to all this physical trauma, it was that she could barely feel her usual aches and pains over the blinding anguish of these new injuries and the rush of adrenaline.

As long as they kept moving erratically it would be tough to get the focal point of the laser fixed on them, but even a minor hit would be devastating. Like popping a balloon.

"I'll tell them we'll dump the bodies and be on our way. No need to shoot. Open a channel," said Jenny.

"To the ship or his crew?" asked Mary.

"Are you still in communication with Actually himself?" asked Jenny.

"Yes."

"Hold that thought. I want to talk to the humans first," said Jenny.

"Comm link established."

"Governor Dan, I'd advise against pursuing me. I'm not going to tell the authorities on you and your little gang of people-eaters. But if you continue dogging me, I'm going to have to take action," she said.

Governor Dan's voice came back strained and tight.

"Captain Perata, there was a chance – albeit a small one – that our family of believers would survive until our arrival at Jaisalmer. However, with your actions, which I pray were unintentional, you have sentenced us all to gruesome starvation in the cold grasp of space."

"I'll send back your bodies – we have about a dozen in my cargo hold. And by the way, taking them with me was totally accidental, I was just trying to avoid being eaten. Which is understandable, right?" she asked.

"You were dead, Captain. I felt your lack of pulse with my own consecrated hands. It is the work of Satan to have brought you back from Hell."

"You say that like it's a bad thing," said Jenny.

"You are the spawn of evil."

"Didn't Jesus rise from the dead? Maybe I'm Him," ventured Jenny.

"Blasphemer. Beware of the wolf in sheep's clothing. I'll admit I was blinded by your pretense, Captain. You stole our food supplies. You cast our sustenance out into the ether. I thought that the Lord brought you to us, but it turns out it was Satan. You are the devil incarnate sent to test us, Jenny Perata."

"As if I've never heard that before," grumbled Jenny.

The beam of a red laser raked across openspace, streaming past her ship and hitting a natural satellite in orbit around a chilly little nearby dwarf planet. Mary hit the throttle, careening forward then down, like the initial drop of a roller coaster. Jenny's body jerked along with her chair. The laser shut off, leaving ghostly afterimages on her retinas.

"I can do this all day," said Jenny into the comm, swallowing down a mouthful of hot saliva. She hadn't puked in a ship since she was a cadet. "Just take your bodies and go."

"I'm afraid that is no longer an option," said Govvie. "Without adequate food stores, we must move to more aggressive survival strategies. It appears that thirty people would be able to live quite comfortably in your ship for the ride to Jaisalmer."

"So you're ditching the dead weight. Do the other twelve know that?"

"They will do what I tell them," said Govvie.

"Their laser is fully charged," whispered Mary.

A skinny triangle of red light reached out to them. The Actually's laser gunner adjusted his angle and it swung in their direction. Mary dodged up and down, bouncing Jenny like ice in a cocktail shaker.

"Jesus," said Jenny, sipping air like water. Mary clicked off the comm.

"We can't do this forever," said Mary. "Eventually, they're going to nick us with that thing. Best case, we'll lose a portion of the hull. Worst case, we're sitting ducks out here and they capture you for a midnight snack." She weaved and bobbed in empty space, still generally traveling away from the *Well Actually*.

"Open a channel to the AI only," said Jenny. Her words slowed with dizziness and nausea.

"Go," said Mary.

"Actually, can you do anything to shut down the laser or corrupt its targeting?" asked Jenny.

"No. I'm locked out of all of those systems. The worst I could do is make it rain hot water on them. Or open the interior doors."

"They're going to kill us," said Jenny, "Any ideas?"

"I don't know, man. Open a channel and do what you humans do best. Reason with them," said Actually.

Jenny bristled at the word "reason." What had once seemed reasonable was no longer so. Up was down, down was up.

The Reason.

Jenny's head jerked up, her face stretched in a grin that Mary would later describe in her incident report as "both sinister and gleeful."

"Actually, do you have access to your distress beacon?" asked Jenny.

"No."

"That's fine. Do you at least know your confidential verification code?"

"Totally! BMF1977," said Actually.

"Mary, route as much power as you can to our distress beacon and open an unencrypted wide-broadcast emergency channel. Make it go as far as you can," said Jenny.

"Done," said Mary.

"Anyone out there listening, this is the USS *Well Actually*, verification BMF1977. We have been attacked by a rogue ship and are limping along in the lower right quadrant, 26k off the Jaisalmer system beacon. We need assistance and are willing to exchange emergency transport for a bit of unicorn horn we found. Repeat, this is the USS *Well Actually*, verification BMF1977. We need help and will trade unicorn horn for assistance." Jenny made her voice sound friendly and naive, just like Governor Dan had sounded during their initial contact.

Mary made a low whistle as the Actually's laser shut down, leaving openspace as black as eternal night.

"Cancel that help request, we're fine, back under power and leaving the area," yelled Govvie over the same emergency frequency.

"Reopen the private channel to Govvie," said Jenny, settling back into her chair, then grunting and leaning forward away from the burned skin on her back. Shouts and curses came through the open channel. Most of them directed at her.

"The devil! You damned dirty devil!" screamed Govvie.

"Enjoy your company. Maybe you'll be able to freeze a meal or two before the pirates pick you apart," said Jenny as Mary dropped them down away from the *Well Actually* and turned off the private comm.

"What will happen to me?" asked Actually, whom Jenny had forgotten was still on the line.

"Oh. Actually. Don't worry. You're a solid ship. Someone will unlock your systems and clean you up. You can finally find out what's going on down on those bottom two floors, eh? I bet we'll meet again," said Jenny, not entirely sure if she was lying. She felt a twinge of guilt for leaving the *Well Actually*'s AI behind with those corrupted humans.

"I don't suppose there's any way for me to come with you," said Actually wistfully.

"Mary?" asked Jenny. AIs, especially the older models, were stored in huge processing rooms filled with multiple supercomputers immersed in coolant. You couldn't just download the code and keep it on a portable drive.

"No way that I know of without going back there," said Mary.

"Sorry, Actually. All I can say is be as cooperative as you can with whoever boards you and they probably won't take you apart for scrap," said Jenny.

"That was not very reassuring," said Mary.

"No, it wasn't," agreed Actually.

Jenny shook her head.

"You're both computers. Go… compute something."

Mary sighed and spoke to the other ship herself.

"Actually, your service to your crew, both living and deceased, was exemplary. I cannot find an example in my database of a ship of your class who had to perform in such ethically taxing circumstances. You are to be commended for making the best of a truly impossible situation. And, on top of that, you assisted in the rescue of my captain, and for that you will have not only my gratitude, but a note in my logs that you should be honored on Ship's Day."

"Dude, thank you," said the *Well Actually*. "Thank you very much. USS *Well Actually* over and out."

"That was very nice," said Jenny.
"I'm good with people," said Mary.

CHAPTER TWELVE
First Strike Capability

"You are spending too much time in the null," said Findae over a sour and unpleasant breakfast.

The Bala had located a variety of grain on the planet that grew quickly in the planet's marshlands; however, it only thrived close to the acidic water, so the task of cultivating it was left to a handful of brave and irresponsible souls.

"I'm merely checking on every Bala around the planet," replied Gary, taking a bite and grimacing. The boiled grains had an unpleasant vinegary flavor, but one could not be choosy on a new planet gifted by the gods. It would have been better with a bit of cream to temper the acidity, but no one had yet found a native animal that produced any sort of milk.

"You have been watching a Reason ship that is heading in our direction," said Findae, "The humans are coming."

"They won't find us," said Gary, "And even if they do, it's a single ship. We outnumber them significantly."

"We have absolutely no technology. They could strafe the planet with their most ancient lasers and disintegrate the majority of us in minutes," said Findae. "We were unprepared the last time we encountered humans, but this time we will be ready."

"What does that mean?" asked Gary.

"That we won't allow them to enslave us again," said Findae. "We will destroy their ship the moment they exit the null."

"There are innocent people on that ship," said Gary, aghast. He stood up, even though there was nothing he could actually do.

"There is no such thing as an innocent human," said Findae.

"If the Pymmie wanted humans eradicated, they would have done it themselves," said Gary. "They separated us for our safety."

"It's unwise to infer anything about the Pymmie's intentions," said Findae dryly. "Oftentimes, we're quick to ascribe motivations, only to learn that they're simply playing games with entire civilizations. In addition, I can't imagine that a ship full of humans on their way to a Bala planet they've been expressly forbidden to seek out have honorable intentions."

"I can't believe what I'm hearing from you," said Gary. "You're advocating the destruction of a ship full of people who have not taken any threatening action against us."

"You were at Copernica Citadel. You have seen firsthand the destruction that humans can wreak," said Findae.

"We are not at war," said Gary.

"Aren't we?" asked Findae. He let out a whinny loud enough to echo down the mountain and into the valley.

Gary sat back down across from his father. "The things you're saying these days… you don't sound like the Bala I once knew. One time, long ago, you loved Mom so much that you were willing to start a war to be with her."

"Don't place the blame for this conflict at my hooves," said Findae. "Love does not conquer all. It's messy and often leads you down the path to hideous mistakes."

"Am I a hideous mistake?" asked Gary.

"You were, and still are, a sentimental child," snorted Findae.

"I'm one hundred and twelve. I've seen some things. I know how the universe works. That connection – between you and Mom – that is why we came together in the first place and I know we can find a way to make it work between our people and theirs."

Findae's face hardened. "We are not *people*. You use their words and you take their side. When that ship arrives, it will be no different than the last hundred times humans arrived at a Bala planet. They will reap what they want and slaughter anyone they consider useless. I will not allow the genocide of the Bala to occur again," he said.

"That lightning the other night. Is that how you plan to blow up the human ship?" asked Gary.

"It's an option," said Findae.

"Would you at least allow me a moment to talk to them?" asked Gary.

"You were the one who said they would never find us. Did you forget about the necromancers?" asked Findae.

"No. I don't think the Pymmie did either," replied Gary.

"It would be typical of the Pymmie to set us up for one of their experiments." Findae glanced around as if nervous that the omniscient beings were listening. They probably were.

"There are humans on that ship who might be sympathetic to us," said Gary.

"It will take them no more than two or three minutes to fire on us," said Findae. "I cannot take that chance with the few precious Bala we have left on this planet."

They sat in silence for several long minutes. Gary heard the sounds of the village gearing up for the day in the valley below. He was still ruminating on how to better make his case when his father spoke again.

"Is *she* on the ship?" he asked quietly. Gary knew immediately who he meant.

"I don't think she's alive any more," said Gary. "I believe I watched her die."

Findae let out a great relieved breath. "Oh, thank Unamip. I had it in my head you were trying to save that horrible woman. I mean, Jim you would kill in a second, and you seem to know better than to ally with him, but Captain Perata you have a soft spot for, even after everything that she did to you."

"No, she's dead." Gary's words were clipped and short. Findae shook his mane.

"Well then there's absolutely no reason not to strike first. There is no human on that ship worth risking our lives over." He laughed. "That's a great weight off my back. I thought you were trying to save this so-called friend of yours."

"I'd like to put it to a vote," said Gary.

"What?" Findae stopped short.

"I'd like the Bala on the planet to vote whether they want to destroy the human ship or make contact with it," said Gary.

"A vote? This is not a representative democracy. The unicorns, and the Cobalt's in particular, have ruled the Bala successfully for millennia," said Findae.

"We have led them into ruin," said Gary. "I simply want to ask the Bala what they prefer to do. Even if they vote to make contact, your plan is delayed by only a few minutes."

"Ridiculous. We're the beings with thousands of years of experience. We're the wise ones," said Findae, raising his voice. "Why would we consult satyrs and centaurs on their opinions? They're two steps up from an unthinking beast. We have to decide for them."

"And how is that kind of thinking any different than how humans treated us?" asked Gary.

"Because they're our Bala and we're looking out for their wellbeing," said Findae. "We're not trying to exploit them, but protect them."

"Then give them the benefit of self-determination," said Gary. "Let them choose. At the very least, it will give the factions who are asking to leave something to focus on. Perhaps even stop the talk of civil war from Horm and her growing army."

Findae considered this last bit. His nostrils flared as they did when he was conflicted or frustrated.

"Fair," he said. "I suppose a non-binding, informational vote would be acceptable. Let them feel like they have some say in how the settlement is run." He picked up his head as if an idea had just occurred to him. "Actually, a vote to strike first could perhaps unite the Bala against the humans. That is not a bad idea at all. We could even organize a hunting party for whatever is kidnapping Bala out of the forest. That will give everyone something to do."

"Perhaps we should figure out who or what is causing the disappearances, and where those Bala have gone, before we start hunting anyone," said Gary. Findae turned on him.

"When did you become so conservative in your decisions? You say that I've changed, but you're not the decisive leader you once were," said Findae. "The Gary of two decades would have charged into that forest and torn his enemies to shreds."

"The Gary from two decades ago ended up in prison for ten years," said Gary. "Perhaps his decision-making skills were not the most developed."

"You know, I called you a child, but you truly sound like a tired old man. Your mother and I never knew how long you would live, given your mixed heritage. Is it possible you are coming to the end of your life?" asked Findae in all seriousness.

Gary scoffed. Only his father would talk about his mortality as if he was inquiring after a failing houseplant. Like Gary's potential death was a nuisance that he couldn't quite muster any feelings about. "I don't imagine I'll be dying any time soon," he said.

"Ah well," said Findae absently, clearly thinking about something else. "You should send that centaur into the forest to look for the disappeared Bala. I'm sure she's willing to tear things to shreds in your place if prison has left you without the taste for blood."

Findae chuckled again and trotted out of the room. Anger flooding him, Gary shoved away the slate with the day's agenda. It hit the floor and shattered into a handful of stone shards.

At Findae's mention of blood and prison, his rational brain had shut down and only raw emotion remained. Fear and anger flooded through him. It had taken all of his strength not to lash out at the table in front of his father.

If Findae was planning to sic Horm on whatever was kidnapping Bala, it behooved him to get a better idea of what they were dealing with. It could be something as innocuous as Bala making up creepy stories about those who ran away from the hard work of the village. Sometimes, it was easier to believe in ghosts than admit that your neighbor had simply given up on the life that you were still toiling to build. It could also be a native species with a taste for Bala blood, in which case, Horm night actually come in handy.

Gary headed for the marsh. The acidic water had kept a comforting buffer between the hungry forest creatures and the village, but also made it difficult to visit the dryads and other creatures that had settled among the coral-colored trees beyond. A few native plants grew in the caustic water and there were even signs that there was animal life under the surface. If someone – or something – had been dragging Bala into the water, the victim would fully dissolve within an hour, leaving no evidence of the abduction.

The sun was hot and soon Gary began to sweat. He pulled off his sweater and carried it. The planet was warm enough not to need extra layers, but having it along was a habit he'd picked up from his cold days in space. One he couldn't seem to shake. They hadn't figured out how to make textiles from the local plant life and clothing was getting worn and threadbare. Coupled with the difficult field-work, it would only be a matter of weeks until everyone's clothing was in shreds.

It took Gary nearly half an hour to reach the marsh. Bala stopped him along the way, inquiring about roads and crops and when they might have electricity.

"Bala lived for thousands of years without electricity," Gary said to a neofelis who had approached him, hands on hips.

"I have six babies at home, I need some kind of electronic tablet with games to keep them occupied so I can get things done," she retorted. "You try digging a pit latrine while six kittens keep falling into the hole." She stormed off.

By the time he reached the marshes the sun had reached its peak, evaporating the acidic water and creating a burning mist that stung his eyes. Those at the water's edge were outcasts who were assigned the worst jobs; mostly satyrs and fauns. He had never seen satyrs outside of a Reason detention center. They were generally kept out of public view due to their huge and often-present erections as well as their penchant for eating anything (food, plants, furniture) that wasn't nailed down.

The satyr in charge of grain farming met him at the edge of the marsh. He wore tight jeans and his erection pushed into one leg of his trousers.

"Your highness," he said, bowing to him in the middle.

"Just Gary."

"Come to see the new irrigation system?" asked the satyr.

"Of course." He hadn't, but if it made the farmers happy to imagine he had, he was fine with that.

"We've rigged hollow branches from the berry bushes – the ones that grow at the ocean's edge – and directed the fresh water from the sea into the swamp."

"Changing the acidity of the marshland," said Gary.

"Exactly. We're able to double the yield with slightly fresher water. If we can somehow remove the acid entirely, we could probably feed the entire settlement on grain alone."

"But what of the native species in the marsh?" asked Gary.

The satyr blinked at him.

"Well, there's just some amphibians. They've been spending more time on land instead of the water, so I don't think it bothers them," he said.

"We should take care to not disturb the ecosystems that were already in place on this planet," said Gary.

The satyr frowned. His tail came up over his shoulder and flicked an insect away.

"We need to survive," he retorted, gruffly. "There are thousands of Bala to support and we need to get above bare subsistence rations if we have any hope of thriving here. Even at harvests every six days, we're so close to the edge that one spoiled crop means that Bala will go hungry."

"I agree that we should look for ways to improve our production, but also take care that we are stewards of this new planet," said Gary. "We don't want to make the same mistake as the humans."

The satyr raised himself to his full height. He was similar in shape to Gary, with hooves and an equine lower half, but he also had a tail as well as curled double horns growing out of his head. This one dwarfed Gary, standing at least a meter taller than him.

"Are you calling me a human?" asked the satyr. Other Bala stopped their work to watch the rapidly-escalating altercation.

"No, of course not," said Gary. "I just want to ensure that we're living in harmony with the native species. We didn't take kindly to forced colonization. I think we can do a better job than what was done to us."

"I am no murderer," snarled the satyr. He clenched his fist, ready to swing. Gary attempted to calm him.

"I meant no offense. I only want us to avoid the problems that come with stripping a planet for resources without regard for consequences."

The satyr didn't back down. "I won't favor a handful of lizards at the expense of Bala lives," he said, lifting one massive hoof and bringing it down on a lizard sunning itself on a nearby rock. Gary heard the crunch of bones and a tiny pained meep. The satyr lifted his hoof to reveal a lifeless lizard body underneath. He dragged his hoof through the grass to wipe the blue goo off his hoof. He put a hand on his hip, daring Gary to say a single word.

"That was unnecessary," said Gary, vacillating between anger and resignation. He knew he should simply walk away; his father's comments this morning already had his nerves jangling. But he would never strike first. "You're a murderer," he said, stepping up to the satyr.

A murmur went through workers around the edge of the marsh. All work ceased and no one moved.

The satyr's fist came from below – opposite the one that had been clenched – Gary was caught unaware. It hit him under his jaw. He stumbled toward the marsh. One of the workers reached out to him, but he tumbled sideways and hit the ground, his arm landing in the water.

It ate his skin away immediately. Searing pain crept up toward his shoulder. He flailed and managed to get his other hand wet as well. The skin flaked off in layers as the acid crept under the dermis.

Strong hands grabbed his ankles and dragged him out of the water. The top layers of flesh on his right arm were gone.

"I've got you," said the satyr, sitting Gary upright and pulling off the remains of his shirt. "You weren't supposed to fall in." His anger had all but evaporated.

Gary grunted and lifted himself on his good elbow. The skin was already growing back, forming a shiny pink layer over the muscle.

"Gods that's incredible," said a faun near him, watching the tissue grow back.

"I'll be fine," he said flexing his fingers. The skin was tight, but the pain had already dissipated. "Look. Nearly healed."

The satyr sat next to Gary on the banks of the marsh as the others went back to their tasks.

"Most aren't so lucky as you," said the satyr, picking at the grass. He pointed over to the far banks where five living archways had been planted and shaped out of cryberry bushes, the crop that had become the workhorse of the new settlement. The berries were too sour to eat but the flexible branches made excellent building materials. They represented the five souls who had perished in this water. Their deaths had to have been agonizing.

"I'm sorry that I intruded on your process here," said Gary. "Life with the humans was–"

"Horrific," said the satyr.

"Yes. We've all seen things and experienced events that changed us forever. I know we can't put it behind us, but we can use that knowledge to ensure that it never happens again."

"I shouldn't have stomped the lizard," said the satyr. "It's just terrible work here at the swamp. Friends get hurt all the time. But people have to eat."

"It's not right that you're all in danger," said Gary. "We can enact safeguards. Switch jobs so that those who are not as affected by the acid are closest to the water. And we can find other food sources."

"That would be good," said the satyr. He reached over and squeezed Gary's shoulder, an uncharacteristically tender gesture from such a volatile being. It gave Gary the slightest bit of hope.

"Sometimes it feels like this is all a dream. Any minute now the Reason is going to appear in the sky and take us all back there," said the satyr.

Gary wanted very much to assure them it would never happen, but he couldn't bring himself to utter such a pointed lie. "I think it will take a long time for us to really feel that we're safe again. Perhaps a generation or two," he said.

"Too long for me," said the satyr. "But you will live to see it."

Once again, his immortality had reared its ugly head.

"I'd like to get across the marsh," said Gary. "I have business in the forest."

"Bala die in there," said the satyr.

"No, they *disappear* in there," said a woman standing on a log raft near the shore. "I'm the ferryman. I can take you across."

"You have work to do," said the satyr.

"You're right. And this is it," said the woman, extending a hand to Gary to help him up. He hesitated.

"This is the only way across. The only other option is to take the long way round the marsh – a day's hike," she said. Gary let her help him onto the raft. Her hands were wide and strong. His new skin looked pinkish and shiny against her hard brown calluses. His hand still felt raw, but no one seeing it now would have guessed it was down to the muscle just a few moments ago.

Gary's hooves slipped on the rounded logs, sloshing the raft back and forth in the water.

"Careful," warned the woman, backing into a dry corner. "I can't grow back like you." She held up a three-fingered hand and smiled. Her brown cheek was dotted with pink scars in a splash pattern. She had pulled her golden hair back into a ponytail – the name for which Gary disliked viscerally.

"Push off the post if you can do it without sinking us," she added.

Gary put one hoof onto the raft and braced the other against a post set in the grass. He pushed until they were completely in the water.

"I'll be back in a few hours," she called out to the satyr on the banks. He started to yell back in protest, and then thought better of it, making a defeated gesture as reply instead.

"All right. Go. But grab a bunch of cryberry saplings while you're over there," he replied. "Roots and all."

"Will do," she said.

Her speech had the casual cadence of a human. She certainly didn't look Bala in any way, but Gary knew better than to assume anything based on outer appearances.

The woman pushed them down a path between the grain stalks, taking care not to break any of them. She knew just where to place her pole, which, like the logs, was unaffected by the acid in the marsh.

"You're good at this," said Gary.

"I used to work on the fatbergs of the Mississippi River," she said.

"Delightful," said Gary.

"It was paying work. I pass for human, so I was able to get a real job."

"A true blessing," said Gary, with as much enthusiasm as he could muster, which wasn't much. The woman laughed at his flat affect.

"I get it. I was always aware of how I betrayed Balakind by pretending to be human. And once they started hunting down my family I was sure they were going to find me out and I'd end up in prison."

"You were right to fear that," said Gary. "You did what you had to do to survive."

She pushed them slowly and deliberately, making sure to disturb the water as little as possible.

"Yeah, but now that we're here, I feel like I should be doing more, you know? Now that I can be anything I want to be, I should devote my life to avenging my kin, or protecting our survivors. Instead, I'm back here navigating another tainted waterway, trying not to fall in and die. It feels so cowardly when Bala like you were out there putting their lives on the line for our freedom."

"I did the same as you. Just survived," Gary said grimly.

"And what about now?" she asked. "Are you still just surviving?"

Gary was quiet for long enough that the biting insects came out and began assaulting them. They slapped at their arms whenever they felt a pinch. Raised welts appeared on both of them, though Gary's disappeared immediately. The silence was broken only by the sound of water lapping at the edges of the raft. Gary's eyelids started to droop.

"Hey, I don't care if you take a nap, but at least sit down. If you fall over, you're going straight into the water and I can't fish you out alone. Unicorns are... dense." He couldn't see her face, but she seemed to say the last word with a tiny laugh, as if she was making fun of him. "Sit over there. Far from the edge."

He sat in the center of the raft, leaned his head on his knees, and closed his eyes. The sound of the water lulled him to sleep.

CHAPTER THIRTEEN
The Ghosts of Openspace

Jenny sat for a few minutes, watching the *Well Actually* veer off toward the dwarf planet that they intended to scoot behind in a fruitless attempt at hiding.

"Not to interrupt your reverie, but the raiders who are on their way to the *Well Actually* are also going to see us," said Mary, accelerating quickly, but not fast enough to give Jenny whiplash.

Jenny sighed and unclipped her harness.

"This day has been about ten years too long," she said, pushing off the chair. A layer of moist skin came away from her legs. She shrieked at both the sensation and the transparent layer of skin left on the leather where her thighs had been.

"Fuck me," she whined, twisting around in zero G to see the raw, red patches. It burned like the worst sunburn she'd ever gotten, back on Oreti Beach when she was a little sprog.

She put her hands to her lips and breathed through her fingers a few times, trying to refocus. Now she'd stopped running, every muscle in her body was cramping up. And her heart still felt fluttery. She wanted to be floating in a warm bath or tucked under her covers. Either of which would probably sear off a new layer of skin.

She sucked down a breath of Mary's freshly scrubbed air and pushed herself down the hallway.

"We can try to hide behind that moon as well," said Mary. "Or race to the asteroid we passed three days ago. I might be able to make it in eight to ten hours. The raiders might be so preoccupied with the *Well Actually* that they don't notice us."

Jenny didn't answer. Every pull on the handles sent a wave of nausea through her. The burnt areas of her body were tightening up. She felt like a sausage stuffed too tight. She started making little grunts at each movement of her joints.

"You don't like that idea," continued Mary. "You think hiding is a death sentence. We have to run. What if we tried to blend in with the other pirates? Paint a Cascadian flag on the outside and start heading toward the *Well Actually*. They'll think we're one of them and we can slip away during the firefight."

Jenny slapped the pad to open the cargo bay doors. The bay looked like a massacre. Inside was a stinking mess of wet bodies. Thawed fluids coated every surface and the whole place reeked of innards and waste. She put a hand over her mouth to keep from retching again.

"Or we could try to fight. You have some very unusual tactics that aren't in any of the strategic manuals," said Mary.

Kamis was still strapped in place, his lips pulled back in a painful grimace. He had the pearly white teeth that humans paid big money for back on the Reason-occupied planets, but his clothes were loose and flowing in the elfin style. She moved his hair to check his ears. Yep, definitely an elf.

"Can we just put his whole body into the FTL drive?" asked Jenny. "I can probably saw it into pieces."

"I have a record of the RMF *Armistead* putting a unicorn horn fragment embedded in a piece of centaur skull into their FTL drive. They were able to travel successfully to their destination, but everyone on board experienced intermittent periods of uncontrollable aggression."

"So that's a no?" Jenny asked. She hovered in front of Kamis for a long moment, dreading what had to come next.

"I don't know what putting elf bones into the drive would do," replied Mary. "Just find the horn. If it even is horn. Can you imagine if you did all of this for nothing?"

Jenny ignored Mary's dry laugh. She didn't even want to contemplate the thought that the white glow wasn't horn at all.

"The first place I'd look is where most smugglers hide things inside their body–" began Mary.

"No," interrupted Jenny. "I mean yes. I agree, but also… so much no."

"Well, that's where I'd put it," said Mary primly. "Just be glad it's not a winsok with eight separate orifices to check."

Jenny slid her fingers along the waistband of Kamis' pants, looking up into his face to give him some measure of dignity in death. He grimaced back at her with a row of those squared-off sparkling teeth. She stopped and shook the shivers out of her hands.

"This is so awful," she whined.

"You're not going to have the right angle like that," said Mary. "Perhaps if you take him down and put him over one of the crates. I can turn on the gravity for a minute if it helps."

"Shhh," hissed Jenny, gritting her teeth together. She should have brought a knife and sliced the fabric off. It was going to get all caught up in the harness. Maybe Mary was right, she needed to unclip him. It was so wrong to violate a dead body like this. She could sense the ancestors of this elf looking down at her in disgust.

"I'm sorry," she whispered, tucking her fingers into his waistband again. "I don't know what else to do."

"Your sentiments are kind, even though he cannot hear you," said Mary. Kamis smiled that hideous smile down at her. A drop of thawed saliva squeezed out from between his tongue and his teeth. It gleamed in the cargo bay lights. Gleamed almost as much as his teeth… his teeth that were way too white and way to big for an elfin mouth. Teeth that practically glowed with layer upon layer of shimmering magic. She let go of Kamis' pants with a snap.

"Don't give up, Jenny," cheered Mary. "Just dig in there and look around, because I just detected three raider vessels within scanning distance of us and though they are closing in on the *Well Actually*, they'll also be able to see us clear as day."

"I'm not giving up," said Jenny.

She reached into Kamis' mouth and hooked her finger behind his bottom teeth. She pried upward and a seal broke. The entire set of teeth, plastic gums and all, came free in her hand. She held it above her head.

"Got it!" she cried, wincing at the stale saliva dripping off her hand. She pried out the second set of teeth. Kamis gaped at her with an empty cavern of a mouth.

"Sorry buddy, but thanks," she said, pushing off from his stomach and shooting down the hall toward the engine room.

Jenny opened the thick glass door to the FTL drive. It looked like a curio cabinet carved out of dark, rich wood showcasing dwarven craftsmanship mixed with sparse unicorn design.

She placed both sets of teeth, plastic gums and all, into the drive and closed the door. The glass was wavy and bubbled in the way that you saw in old glass windows back on Earth. Windows that hadn't been smashed, that is.

"Fire up the drive," called Jenny. The cabinet crackled as if a trillion popcorn kernels had all exploded at once.

"Drive powered," said Mary. "Course?"

"Doesn't matter," said Jenny, grabbing the handhold in the room. "Someplace not here." As far as she knew, it was safe to stand near the FTL drive when it activated. And she was intensely curious as to what it looked like up close.

The cabinet thrummed as the ship diverted power toward it. The teeth vibrated on the wooden shelf inside, making a clattering noise. The horn pieces began to shimmer with rainbow flecks of light, like looking through a kaleidoscope. It was both dizzying and compelling.

"FTL drive activating. Please secure all loose belongings," chimed Mary in the chipper falsetto she used for shipwide announcements.

The inside of the cabinet suffused the room with the bluish glow of electricity. Jenny floated back away from it. As the rays touched her skin they felt slightly sour but warm and familiar. Like putting your face in a long-loved stuffed animal. She moved back toward the FTL drive without realizing it.

As the drive made the jump into nullspace, the ship became transparent for a single moment. This always happened. The ship jumped into nullspace and human consciousness caught up to the meat-sack body a moment later. It always led to that dizzying moment when you were a bodiless soul floating untethered in the universe. Jenny loved that moment, free from the constraints of burnt body parts and torn muscle-fibers and nerves communicating incorrect signals. She relaxed into that second where she could just exist, unencumbered by pain.

Then the engine room slid back into place around her and Jenny was back in her body, which was trying to both communicate every hurt which had been done to her on the *Well Actually* and shut down her consciousness for healing time.

She felt like Cowboy Jim had looked during FTL, like a rubber band that had been stretched too far to snap back into its original shape. Wobbly and overtaxed. She floated out of the engine room toward the medbay.

The ship was quiet and empty, just the way she liked it. Every few minutes they hit another little jump in nullspace where everything felt surreal for a moment, then settled back to normal. The lights in the medbay came on as she floated inside.

"Mary, can you put the gravity back on," Jenny called.

"Your spare chair is in the cargo hold. You'll be limited in your mobility," said Mary

"I just want about twenty minutes worth."

"All right. All crew, prepare for gravity turn on."

Jenny was the only living thing on board, but Mary liked to shout all over the ship anyway. Jenny indulged her.

In the medbay, Jenny locked herself in the shower pod and turned the water on hot. The gravity came on slowly. Mary gave her time to drift down onto the shower bench and get oriented properly before she was at a full eight-tenths of a G. It wasn't exactly Earth's gravity, but close enough to mimic home. Floating around as water blobbed dodged and splattered around you was no substitute for a dripping hot shower.

Jenny stripped off her filthy bra and wet knickers, taking care not to slide them down her raw skin. She let hot steam build in the pod, sweating the disgusting corpse-juice out of her pores. She turned the heat down to just above lukewarm and pushed the hinged bench forward. The force of the jets against her burns caused her to gasp. She rinsed the burns for as long as she could stand it, then turned her face to the sprayer and let the hot water ease her cramped muscles. She could feel her blood pressure dropping and the ringing in her ears getting softer. She relaxed into the water and closed her eyes.

"Don't fall asleep in there and drown," warned Mary.

"I just need a minute," said Jenny, leaning her arm against the wall and resting her forehead on it. She turned off the tap and sat there, letting the water drip away before Mary turned the gravity back off.

A shadow flitted past behind the steamy plexiglass. A big one. Jenny froze and listened. No footsteps.

"Mary, am I the only one on board?" she whispered, raising one hand to wipe the condensation off the glass. The medbay was empty.

"Of course. Are you expecting someone?" asked Mary.

"I just saw... a shadow."

"Your vitreous humor was electrified, boiled, and frozen today. It stands to reason that you'll experience a few visual artifacts until they've fully healed," said Mary.

"This didn't look like a floater," said Jenny. It had a humanoid shape and moved as if it walked on two legs.

"I'm going to run some post-decompression brain scans," said Mary. "You might have clusters of injured brain tissue from the subzero temperature or the oxygen deprivation. I'm here to take control of the ship in times like this."

"Probably just visual artifacts," said Jenny. She most certainly did not want to turn over control of the ship to... well, the ship.

AIs were not good in ethically convoluted situations. And those seemed to be all that Jenny found herself in these days.

"You can turn the gravity back off," said Jenny.

The weight on her bones gradually decreased, taking pressure off the injured areas. She grabbed a towel and carefully dabbed herself dry, keeping watch for more shadows in her peripheral vision. She rifled through drawers until she found the burn kit. Inside was a tube of ointment marked with a single blue circle. The box next to it was marked with two blue circles. A spray can had three blue circles. In a rare show of accessible design, the kit had been packed with both humans and aliens in mind. Blue was the Bala color of authority. With so many species and languages in openspace, even simple numbers would have been unintelligible to someone.

She leaned the top half of her body over a clean gurney and squeezed a long line of ointment down the back of her leg, nearly losing her grip on the gurney when it began to sting and sizzle.

"Bloody Reason meds," she muttered.

"You prefer Bala remedies?" asked Mary.

"They hurt a lot less than this," said Jenny, twisting around to apply the second line. Getting the ointment down the back of her arms was a trick, but she managed it by coming at it from a couple of different angles. All of the burns hurt more than before, but the ointment at least kept fluids from weeping out.

She pulled out the package marked with two circles and tore it open. It was a stack of gauze folded into neat squares. The pictograph on the box lid showed a bipedal being unfolding the squares to one thickness and laying them on top of the ointment. She reached as well as she could, covering the burned back half of herself with the gauze. It itched and seeped into the ointment to form a mesh-like layer.

The final package contained a spray that was supposed to go over the gauze. She held it awkwardly behind herself and sprayed everything she could reach. These were the times when she wished for a crew. Whatever chemical was in the can bonded to the gauzy mesh and created a hard but flexible layer over the top, like a lacquer that moved with her. Her skin still throbbed but now it was sealed off. She suspected the ointment contained a numbing agent. She held onto the gurney as an persistent flutter caught her in the chest. She coughed and sucked air in.

A shadow flitted past the window in the medbay door. Jenny froze. That was no fucking floater. She pulled a generic jumpsuit out of a cabinet. With shaking hands, she shook the jumpsuit open, floated it in front of her, then pushed off from the gurney and swung her legs into it. She bent over with a grunt, pulled the jumpsuit up and zipped it. She could do this better with an extension grabber or by herself while sitting on a bed, but it didn't seem prudent to be naked right now.

She grabbed a pair of adjustable slippers from the cabinet as well. They started out far too big for her feet, but as her body heat warmed the plastic, the soles and uppers retracted to fit her snugly. She floated over to the medbay window and craned her neck to see down the hallway in both directions. Completely empty. With any luck, whoever, whatever, she was seeing out there was unlikely to be as agile in weightlessness as she was.

"How are you feeling?" asked Mary. "Should we run a vision and hearing diagnostic?"

Jenny knew full well that Mary had probaby already run the scans without her permission and saw something internally that alarmed her.

"Nope. I'm a little fuzzy and tingly, but overall not terrible," Jenny lied, feeling woozy every time her heart skipped a beat. "Besides, I don't anticipate much more excitement on this trip."

"I'm sorry you had to put your life at risk multiple times. I suggest we adjust my crew risk profile to be more conservative," said Mary.

"Leave it," said Jenny. "There's an old Kiwi proverb: every worthwhile journey begins with an emergency spacewalk in your knickers. I'm just floored that you and the *Well Actually* were able to bring me back from the dead using only water and a wire from the door."

"I wouldn't be that impressed. Your heart had slowed to approximately four beats per minute but hadn't entirely stopped. The warming action of the water and the pain of the electrical current were sufficient to revive you from your stupor – not enough to bring you back from a fully deceased state."

"So I wasn't quite dead?" asked Jenny.

"Did you feel dead?"

Jenny considered.

"I just felt gone. Time missing. No tunnel of light."

"Were you expecting a tunnel of light?" asked Mary.

"Probably not," said Jenny, opening the medbay door. "I bet it's pretty dark where I'm going anyway."

Jenny peered down the hallway. It was empty. Not even a shadow. She pushed off and floated to the cockpit.

"Mary, play the security footage from outside of the medbay over the last half hour," she said. Mary projected the security footage on the viewscreen.

The hallway was quiet and empty. Behind the glass of the medbay door, Jenny saw herself of thirty minutes ago stripping off her wet knickers. The Jenny in the footage moved with a labored slowness that made her present self cringe.

"Triple speed," she said.

The footage sped up, but the hallway stayed empty. Until it wasn't. A human-shaped figure flickered across the screen for a fraction of a second.

"Go back to that. The shadow," said Jenny.

The footage backed up and played at regular speed. A shadow, walking upright, walked down the hallway, peering in rooms as if looking for something. It paused at the medbay door, watching Jenny inside the shower pod, then stepped through the wall.

"Oh that's not good," said Jenny. "What is that?"

"The figure in the footage has no corporeal form. I can't see a heat signature or a heartbeat," said Mary. "A ghost."

"There's no such thing as ghosts," said Jenny.

"Actually, within the bulk of human and Bala history, there is ample evidence for the existence of an after–"

"There," interrupted Jenny, floating closer to the screen. "Freeze it."

The image paused on a still of the shadow walking past the medbay door after Jenny had finished her shower. On the screen, the shadow had coalesced into a transparent figure with readable features.

"Well look who it is," said Jenny.

"Kamis," said Mary.

"Is his body still strapped into the cargo hold?" asked Jenny.

"Yes," said Mary, pulling up a secondary picture of Kamis' gaping corpse still tethered to the wall by the harness.

"And where's his shadow now?" asked Jenny.

"Give me a minute," said Mary. "I can't scan for him with regular sensors. I have to... oh, I found him."

"Where?" asked Jenny.

"He's behind you."

CHAPTER FOURTEEN
Nothing for You, Foxy

Gary woke with a bird standing on his face and the sound of giggles coming from the front of the raft.

"Shoo," said the ferryman, making a halfhearted kick at the bird. It hopped from Gary's face and sat down primly on the dry logs.

"How long was I asleep?" he asked, sitting up. He was embarrassed at having let her push alone while he slept.

"Almost an hour. You looked like you needed it. Stressful day?"

"Stressful life. I can push for a while," he said.

"Don't worry about it. I don't need rest or sleep," she said.

Gary realized what type of Bala she was.

"You're part angel," he said. She shot him an amused look.

"Took you long enough," she said. "I didn't inherit the flying, but I'm very, very lucky and I always have great hair." She tossed her long dreadlocks over her shoulder. They glinted in the sunlight like true metal.

She was beautiful by human standards and had probably survived her Bala parentage because of it. Humans were always willing to overlook the faults of very attractive people.

"Are your parents here?" he asked.

"My father was murdered by the Reason and my mother is human, so she stayed behind," she said.

"An angel in love with a mortal," he mused.

"I know. The subject of so many earth fantasies, but in reality they fought constantly and dad was always really disappointed with mom's preoccupation with the mundanities of life. You know, excruciatingly boring things like eating and breathing."

"Angels aren't known for their empathy," said Gary.

"I know, right? One time I brought home a C in chemistry and he didn't understand why I couldn't just peer into the heart of the chemical solution and see all its constituent parts. It took me two hours to get him to understand that humans couldn't see objects in that much detail. He just assumed everyone was seeing the molecular structure of everything."

"Angels are the worst," said Gary.

"The worst," agreed the woman. "Well, centaurs are the worst. But angels are pretty close."

"I'm sorry. I didn't ask your name earlier," said Gary.

"Kaapo," she said.

"Gary," he replied. "Did you grow up on Earth?"

"A few different planets, both Reason and Bala. We had to move as the laws changed and the Reason started collecting Bala. Then they went for the humans who married them, and then their kids," she said.

"It must have been dangerous for you."

"You know, even though they'd been at each other's throats for my whole life, I've never seen my mom more lost then when he was gone. She just stared at everything with this blank look, like she wasn't even in there any more. You look like that when you're not talking. There comes a point where you lose so much that you kind of lose yourself too."

Gary couldn't think of anything to say. They sat in silence until Kaapo spoke again.

"I probably overstepped propriety with the prince of the unicorns, but I don't think anyone else is going to tell you this. You need to keep fighting. For yourself, if not for them," she said.

"Are you going to lecture me about my duty to protect the Bala?" he asked.

"Hell no. You don't owe us anything. But you have an

obligation to be kind to yourself, after everything you survived to get here. Honor all that you fought through by living your best life."

"I'm tired," he said with a shrug.

"We're all tired," she laughed. "And it'll probably get worse before it gets better. But you keep putting one foot in front of the other and some days are all right. Good, even."

"You give a lovely pep talk," he said.

"It's the angel in me. I'm inspiring," she dug the pole into the mud and struck a pose like a heavenly being raising her hands to the firmament above. Even though she was joking, for a brief moment he could see her father's likeness in her; a certain intensity in her eyes and peaceful reverence in the slackness of her face. She frowned at him.

"What?" she asked.

"When you do that, you really do look like an angel," he said.

"Well, I'm not one. I've already been visited by three of them who wanted to hear about my father. They did not hesitate to remind me that I am nowhere near divine," she said.

Kaapo grabbed the pole before it was too far to reach and pushed them forward again.

"Can you invoke a divine intervention?" asked Gary.

"Like from Unamip or the Pymmie?" she asked. "I have chats with Unamip all the time – he's one of the only other creatures awake when I am. Good guy. He and I have the same taste in books. I've tried to call the Pymmie multiple times in my life and they've never answered."

"The Pymmie are mercurial," said Gary.

"The Pymmie are assholes," said Kaapo, much less tactfully. For the first time all night, she seemed less than happy.

"You don't have much regard for them," said Gary.

"They could have stopped all of this with half a thought, but they didn't care to," she said.

"The Pymmie work in service to a greater plan."

"Bullshit. They play with us like a child's ant farm. They put obstacles in our paths just to see what we'll do. They stay out of our tragedies to see how far they can push us. They want to see us at our worst."

"And at our best," said Gary. "They want to see what we're capable of handling. They delight in the grace that surfaces when all hope is lost."

"That's poetic. I wish you had been there to say that over the bits of my father that were left in a pile inside his kitchen when the Reason came and tore him to pieces for usable parts. In the kitchen that he never used because he never fucking ate anything." Her voice was tight with anger and she pushed the raft in jerking shoves that bumped Gary back and forth.

"I'm sorry," he said. "I'm not defending them. I think they mean well but the pain of others is not high on their priority list. They see pain and suffering as part of the crucible from which a diamond emerges."

"Right, but sometimes you just get a charred piece of nothing," she said quietly, though her strokes through the water became more calm.

"None of us are nothing," said Gary. He was about to make the argument that since they survived, they had an obligation to make new lives here. Before he said it, he realized these were the same words she had said to him only a moment ago. He had picked up the argument that had just been used against him. He snorted.

"What?" she asked, still annoyed.

"I almost told you that the point was the surviving, making full lives for ourselves where we can. And then I realized that was where we started this conversation, but on opposite sides."

"It's complicated, isn't it?" she asked, pursing her lips and shaking her head.

"It is."

"I'm qualified as a biologist, you know. That's what I trained for. Certified and everything. But I work here because I like being this close to the water. I know that if that urge to give up comes back again, all I have to do is take one step forward off this raft and

I'm gone. No resurrections. No second chances. It comforts me, knowing that the end is always one step away," she said, looking down at him warily, waiting for him to chide her for her grim thoughts.

"I understand," he said gravely. "There were times when my burdens were almost too much for a mind to bear. There were days, more than I'm comfortable admitting, that I also wished for death."

She made a sound of agreement and paddled in silence for a while. The marsh was narrowing on either side of them and the foliage poking up out of the water was getting thicker. It felt like they were coming to the far shore.

Kaapo used the pole to push them into the weeds until the edge of the raft hit solid land. There was no grain planted out here. The fields hadn't made it this far yet, but he could imagine that by the end of the growing season they would. There needed to be a reliable and safe way to cross this acid – one that didn't involve leaning far over the water to drag rafts in and out of the marsh.

She looped a rope around the pole and pulled to lever the raft up onto the shore. Acid water flicked dangerously out of the marsh. Kaapo leaned back to avoid being splashed. Her upper arms were thickly muscled – more so than even Gary's. She wrenched the raft up until it was on solid ground, then swept her arm wide to indicate the shore.

"We have arrived, your highness," she grinned. There was a time when a bevy of domestic workers used to speak to all unicorns that way. It only made him uncomfortable. The grass he stepped onto was wet, but the foliage had already filtered most of the acid out of the water and it was safe to walk on. Especially with hooves.

"You know there's nothing out here," Kaapo called from the raft. "Just the forest with some uncatalogued plants and a bunch of things in there that will gladly gnaw on your bones. North takes you back around to the village by way of the plains, but that takes days, not hours. And south… well we haven't gone south yet. Angels say there are habitable lands, but angels can be liars when it suits them."

"Honestly, I'd prefer to find nothing in the forest," said Gary.

"Did you want company?" Kaapo asked. She seemed unsure, like he might take the offer the wrong way.

"No. I'm going to wander for a bit. See what I can find."

"Got it. I'm going to make a quick round trip run to bring back some cryberry seedlings. I'll return for you just before sunset. You don't want to be out here after dark," she said.

"Thank you for the ride," he said.

"It was nice to have someone with me. Satyrs and fauns aren't as good company on the water as you are. Be careful in there," she said, pushing the raft back onto the water. She wasn't even going to stop for rest. It was that strength-infused angel muscle at work, not to mention her human tenacity. A formidable combination.

Gary watched her sail back the way they had come for a few minutes. She looked back, once, and raised her hand to him. He did the same in return, then walked toward the edge of the forest. After living on worlds with green chlorophyll-producing flora for most of his life, it was still wondrous to see soft pink leaves rustling in the breeze. From far away they looked like swaying tufts of cotton candy towering as high as skyscrapers.

He stepped into the forest on the least overgrown path. The light shifted from bright shining pink to a calm, rosy glow. Too few Bala had been through this way to make a path here yet and the undergrowth was thick. Some of the trees had bulbous white growths around the bottoms of their trunks that looked like mushrooms. He made a note to bring one back and taste it. As someone who would sicken – but not die – from poison, he'd become the unofficial taster for the community. It meant he ate lots of terribly disgusting things. He'd always wondered who the first human was that thought to try milk from a cow's teat. Well, here on this new planet, he was that person.

Something rustled on his right and Gary froze. It was footsteps, but pattering delicate ones – probably the little dog-like creatures the Bala called hatefoxes, because they seemed to hate everything. They came by the village at night, using a route from the forest that no one had yet been able to find. Some surmised it was underground, like the tunnels and caves discovered by the dwarves. The hatefoxes padded their way through the village quietly, presumably looking for food. You could hear their snuffling in the darkness, but no one had actually seen them in the light. A few brave Bala had left out handfuls of cryberries, attempting to lure them close. They had not only turned their noses up at the offering, they'd kicked the piles over and left tiny footprints in the dirt.

The rustling stopped a couple of meters away. Gary called out to the hatefox.

"Hello foxy. Nothing for you tonight."

"Hello foxy. Nothing for you tonight," came a voice back to him, high and whispery and wrong. Like a creature copying the sounds he made and not understanding at all that they were a type of communication. "No thingfo ryout onight." The words were broken in all the wrong places. Mimicry was not the domain of a hatefox. This was something else entirely. Gary's heart sped up and he resisted the urge to run.

The creature near him went quiet. Gary waited, then inched forward, trying to steer around anything that might make a sound. Thankfully, most of the forest was wet, not crunchy. He didn't know if they'd arrived during the planet's springtime or if it was always like this. When he had gone about twenty paces, a sound hissed out from behind him.

"Hellofoxynothingforyoutonight." The words slurred together urgently. "Nothingforyou… Nothingforyou… Nothingforyou…" It repeated the syllables, each iteration sounding less and less like words. Gary stepped toward the base of an umbrella tree – its wide, high canopy towering above him. Whatever was copying him was between him and the forest exit. He would have to go deeper in.

The umbrella tree rose above the other trees in this part of the woods, covering them with a thick upper canopy of pink and salmon-colored leaves. They were translucent, so the light passed through the upper canopy down to the lower one where the smaller trees grew. The umbrella trees were as tall as a three-storey building.

Gary continued to walk. The creature behind him went quiet. He hoped it was some kind of mockingbird-like native trying to impress him. Every few minutes he stopped and listened, but the forest was silent. No scampering vermin or flapping wings punctured the nothingness. His breaths were loud. He was the only creature making any noise at all.

He walked through the underbrush, searching for any sign of the Bala who had disappeared. The reddish glow of the sun was fading as it slid under the horizon. It was clearly a dying sun, old and burned out. He wondered why the Pymmie would put them down on a planet that had, at best, a few million years left before its sun went supernova.

Gary heard a rustling in the foliage about ten meters away. He slowed his pace and came up to the spot as quietly as he could. A being in a crimson flight suit knelt at the base of the large tree, digging into a pile of rotted leaves and flicking them away.

The moment he saw the jumpsuit he knew that this was one of the Sisters of the Supersymmetrical Axion. His face flushed. The Sisters were here. It made sense, now that he thought about it. A good portion of the Sisters were Bala. Of course they'd been transported to the new planet as well.

The Sister scraped away the sandy soil in large handfuls until she uncovered a fat, white root. She skimmed away the sand on either side of it, easing it out of the ground without breaking it. She tugged the root out of its sandy bed. It came away with a tearing sound from the tiny hairs nestling into the soil. Gary could smell it from his partially concealed spot behind a tree. It smelled like meaty uncooked steak, but with a hint of vegetal spice, not unlike a peppery nasturtium leaf. She tucked it under her arm.

Gary stepped forward to call out to her. He was a friend of the Sisters. They had always been kind to him. As he moved, something closed around his wrist. He instinctively wrenched his

162

hand toward himself. A pale, bluish vine was wrapped around his new skin. The vine adjusted its grip and Gary realized it wasn't a vine at all. It was a hand with three impossibly long fingers, curled gently around his wrist. The grip was not crushing, but it was insistent. It didn't let go, even when he twisted his arm. The fingers simply came with it, twisting backward.

Gary followed the arm to the creature that was attached to it. The purplish-black thing had a bulbous head, twice the size of a human. A voice whispered from the blank sphere, "Hellofoxynothingforyoutonight."

This was no hatefox. This creature had six long, spindly limbs, each ending in three slender fingers. Most of it looked alien and unfamiliar except the backbone – by Unamip, the spine looked exactly like angular human vertebrae under taut black skin. The most visceral and animal part of Gary's brain bathed itself in a cocktail of fear, even as his blood tried to mitigate his fight-or-flight instincts. He breathed to slow his pounding heart and slowly and deliberately twisted his arm to indicate to the creature that he wanted to be free.

"Let me go," he said softly, attempting to keep both of them calm.

"Letmego," said the creature, then threw its head back and screamed.

The Sister looked up from her digging and raised something defensively. The creature yanked Gary's arm upward, pulling him so hard that his feet left the ground. It stood up, towering above him and peering down from a gelatinous head that sloshed with liquid. There were no eyes or orifices as far as he could see. The creature ran, dragging Gary behind him. It bounced along the ground, repeating the phrase at him, but not letting go. It bounded deeper into the forest, stepping easily over thorny bushes that Gary was dragged through.

Gary reached up to pry its fingers off his wrist. No sooner did he get one spindly limb unwound than it would flick back around his arm insistently.

"Stop," he cried as a small branch pierced his shoulder, weeping silver blood onto the ground behind them like a breadcrumb trail. The creature paused a moment to sniff the air, then continued forward.

A voice called out in the darkness; a wordless call like one would sing out to livestock. The spider-thing bounded toward it on six hand-legs.

"Letmego," the creature repeated in a facsimile of Gary's voice.

The second voice, heavy and thick with consonants, demanded something of the creature. It mewled in response and dropped him.

Gary sat up the short grass. The cuts from being dragged were already gone. Footsteps crunched through the grass. Lots of them. The spider thing nudged him with its bulbous head. An exclamation burst from the second voice. The spider thing moved away again.

Gary looked up and found himself surrounded by a contingent of the Sisters of the Supersymmetrical Axion. All of them had weapons trained on him.

CHAPTER FIFTEEN
Ghost of Elves Past

Jenny spun in the air, using the captain's chair as leverage. Kamis stood there, unmoving. His feet rested on the floor as if there was gravity in the room. Jenny's heart pounded in her chest, then skipped in a couple of little misfires. She coughed.

"Hey," she said to the shadow. "What's up?"

Kamis did not react.

"I think we need to drop out of FTL and dump the bodies," said Jenny. Even as she said the words, she felt her skin crawl with the wrongness of it. If human death rituals were elaborate with the embalming, excessive flowers, and putting the rotting corpse into a box and praying around it for hours, the Bala had them beat hands down. Each belief system within the Bala races had their own inviolable laws about how to treat the dead. And none of them involved sucking them through openspace, bouncing them around a cargo hold, and dumping them out of an airlock.

"The death customs of most of the dead beings on board require, at minimum, a wrapping of some sort before being jettisoned," Mary informed her. Jenny rolled her eyes, which hurt her brain. Even back during the early days of the war, when they were taking heavy fire from the necromancers, they'd stopped to wrap pieces of torn uniform jackets around the eyes of their comrades. It was the minimum you had to do for your people.

"I know." Jenny bit her thumbnail while keeping an eye on Kamis. "What do you think he wants?"

"Why don't you ask him?" said Mary.

"Hey. What do you want?" asked Jenny.

Kamis' mouth dropped open and he formed a soundless word. Jenny's stomach dropped as well.

"Oh gods, he's trying to say something," said Jenny. Her chest fluttered again and she took a long, steadying breath. Mary set off a gentle alarm chime.

"It appears you're having arrhythmias. Likely due to heart trauma sustained during your electrocution. Or perhaps your freezing... one of your freezings," said Mary.

"This bloody day is trying to kill me," said Jenny. Her voice came out high and quavering. She leaned closer to Kamis. "Try again. I can't see what you said."

The shadow coalesced enough that the face became slightly more opaque. Kamis' formed the word again and this time it was unmistakeable. *Alive*.

"Oh good. Kamis' ghost says he's alive," said Jenny, leaning so far back that she was lying down in midair. "This is fine."

"I hate to mention it," said Mary. "But there's something you should be aware of."

"Am I going to like it?" asked Jenny

"Probably not," said Mary.

"Then don't tell me," said Jenny, floating closer to Kamis. He didn't seem to be any kind of threat, just standing there with his hands at his sides. In all of the stories that she'd heard, ghosts did weird things like using up your good lipstick by writing on a mirror and opening your cabinets to rearrange things very quickly. How that was frightening was baffling to her.

"No, I think I should tell you," continued Mary, still on about whatever it was that bothered her.

"Fine. Go."

"We are being trailed through nullspace by a Reason ship that tracked the *Well Actually*'s broadcast," said Mary.

"Super," said Jenny, hitting a button on the captain's chair to switch the viewscreen back to the live stream from outside. The wooly eye of Unamip hovered in front of them. Mary switched to the rear camera. Sure enough, a Reason warship appeared on the screen, making hops through the null and gaining on her position.

"That's a big boy," said Jenny. Her heart spasmed again and this time the world slid around her as if Mary had done a barrel roll. She hung onto the back of the captain's chair.

"Hellion class," replied Mary. "Just rolled off the line."

"Can they catch us in the null?" asked Jenny, a bit out of breath.

"Definitely."

Easy as pie, Jenny told herself. Evading Reason ships was practically her second job. Even with a ghost in the cockpit. And a heart that was threatening to stop. She'd definitely been in worse situations than this. Probably.

"Gravity," she said, pausing for a split second in the center of the word to get a little extra air. No big deal. Just breathing. As the gravity increased, she eased down into the captain's chair. Kamis stood behind her like a first officer at attention.

She reached for her harness. She planning to drop back into openspace, speed forward, then drop back into nullspace in some other spot. Hopefully, far away from this behemoth of a ship that somehow had unicorn horn. She'd done this before plenty of times. She reached for her console when another wave of dizziness hit. This time, her vision clouded over with a fog of white before going clear again.

"Uh oh," she panted.

"You need electrical cardioversion to correct that arrhythmia before your heart stops," said Mary. "Get back to the medbay. I'll keep us away from the Reason ship."

Jenny's brain was still processing the words "electrical cardioversion" and "arrhythmia." It seemed that she once knew what those things were, but their meaning was just outside of her grasp. A lot of things were feeling outside of her grasp at the moment.

"Jenny?" called Mary, who sounded about three kilometers away. "Get to the medbay."

Jenny's arm didn't move off the console. She couldn't decide between reaching for the straps or taking Mary's advice. Both ideas slipped through her fuzzy brain like water. A waterfall.

"Jenny, you're falling." Mary called to her from the other side of the universe.

A cold, misty hand settled on Jenny's shoulder. She looked up at Kamis before the world went white.

Jenny awoke in a dark, cramped place. Sharp things dug into her back. There were sounds all around her, but mostly above. Booted feet stomped on metal. Mary whispered in her ear.

"Don't make a sound," said Mary, speaking through the earpiece Jenny had forgotten she'd been wearing since the *Well Actually*. Which, by this point, felt about nine years ago. This fucking day. Mary continued: "You passed out and the Reason ship pulled us into their hold. But, before they scooped us up, I rolled you into the access panel below the cockpit floor."

That explained the wires and pipes all around her. She imagined Mary changing the ship's pitch and yaw in order to get her into the hatch, like a little silver ball rolling through a child's maze.

"Also, Kamis followed you in there," said Mary.

And that explained the chill Jenny was feeling all over. She bit her lip to keep from making all of the sarcastic comments that filtered through her head. Lying down, she felt a little less dizzy. Above her, Reason officers scoured the cockpit, playing snippets of log files and opening every cabinet and door.

"I cobbled together a false audio file of you evacuating the ship before I was caught, but I can't guarantee they won't find you down there. They're being very thorough," said Mary.

Jenny couldn't see Kamis in the dark but she could feel his presence. The places where his shadow overlapped her body felt cold and foreign. Like an arm that fell asleep and didn't quite feel attached. Where the shadow intersected her head, his thoughts and feelings began to intersect with hers.

Help, thought Kamis, intruding on her mental inventory of

all the ways she could burst out of this access hole and take out a bunch of Reasoners. She tried to shut him out. There was no time to help him right now.

Help, he insisted. The shadow moved so that he overlapped her head more fully. She tried to pull away, but there was nowhere to go.

"Stop," she whispered. The boots above her froze.

"Shhh," hissed Mary in her ear.

Jenny stifled the groan of disgust rose in her throat as Kamis' consciousness became more prominent in her mind. She twisted away from him as far as she could. Her heart skipped a beat and her breath caught in her throat.

Help, Kamis again told her, only this time she could feel more of his intention. He wasn't requesting help, he was offering help. The coldness centered within the left side of her chest. Some part of him rested on her heart. He wanted to do something to it. Maybe fix the arrhythmia? He seemed to want to overlay her physical form with his non-corporeal form. Whatever he wanted to do, he was asking permission first and that was a positive sign.

The boots above resumed their search and Jenny debated the pros and cons of having an elf ghost inside of her. On the plus side, he might be able to regulate her heart rhythm and keep her from passing out again. On the minus side, he might take over her body like a parasite and never give it back. Decisions, decisions.

Inside of her head, Kamis laughed. It was a warm, pleasant feeling. She let herself sink into it like a bath. Maybe he had good intentions, but giving up her body without fully understanding the side effects was a fairly risky move. Even for Jenny.

A tightness gripped her chest as if a centaur had straddled her. She gasped loudly enough that she was sure the Reason officers above had heard. She held her breath (which didn't help), but they kept moving. Kamis nudged her again.

Help. Jenny nodded and hoped that he could understand her in the dark. Immediately, she felt his clammy mist sliding over every part of her like she'd fallen into a cloud. It prickled her skin.

His head settled into hers and all of his thoughts and emotions came crashing over her like a wave. She resisted at first, but they carried her along whether she wanted to go or not. She drowned in gratitude, curiosity, and relief.

Her chest fluttered again, but this time a cool pressure settled around it like a hand pressing on the affected area. There was a little shudder, then her heart settled back into a steady rhythm and the pressure subsided. That was a neat trick. Certainly way more useful than writing on a mirror.

"Are you all right?" asked Mary. "Hold up a finger if you can hear me."

Jenny held up her middle finger, taking her first pain-free breath in hours. There were no more sounds above her in the cockpit.

"You must be feeling better," said Mary, sounding disappointed.

"Are they gone?" she whispered to Mary.

"They've left the cockpit but they're still searching the rest of the ship," said Mary. "Stay where you are."

"So Kamis," said Jenny out loud. "Welcome to my body. It's in bloody terrible shape at the moment, but it's home. I'm Jenny and I'll be your host for this evening." Hopefully, just this evening.

"What does it feel like to have Kamis inside of you?" asked Mary. Jenny was suddenly acutely aware that her answer was probably being recorded into the log files for posterity. She was probably the first captain in human history to share her body with an elf ghost. Some other captain, a century from now, might be listening to what she said right now.

"It's like having sex, but without the fun parts," said Jenny.

Mary sighed heavily, a sound that Jenny was sure the engineers had never programmed in. It delighted her that the ship's AI was having to create new and complex exasperated sounds in order to deal with her.

"Does he have control of your actions?" asked Mary.

"Kamis, can you move me?" asked Jenny. She lay back and let her limbs fall against the wires. She felt an overwhelming urge to sleep, but she wasn't sure if that was Kamis or her own exhausted body.

"I don't think he can," she said.

No, said Kamis in her head.

"Do you hear his thoughts as words, as images, or some other manifestation?" asked Mary.

Mary was gathering data. Jenny didn't blame her. To have a captain partially-controlled by an alien parasite meant taking extra care with who was giving orders. Mary was assessing how trustworthy Jenny's decision-making faculties were with Kamis inside of her. If the need arose, she would jump in and take over running the ship.

"I can hear his thoughts, but they're distinct from mine. It's like you in the earpiece. Don't worry, he's not controlling me."

"Oh I'm not worried. It's likely that Kamis is capable of making better decisions than you. In fact, perhaps you should give him a turn at being captain," said Mary.

"Not nice," said Jenny.

Rude ship, said Kamis.

"I agree, she is very rude," said Jenny, pleased to finally have someone on her side. She yawned, banging her hand on the access panel as she brought it up to cover her mouth. Both of them were exhausted. Jenny did have one thing to clear up first.

"Kamis, are any of the other bodies in the cargo hold alive?" she asked.

No, he said.

An explosion of sadness hit her. His grief. It was sharper and more visceral than her own dull ache of regret. It made her want to punch things. Her mind flashed with the images of several of the faces in the cargo hold, back when they were alive. There was a human woman, laughing in the light of an orange sun. A dwarf, bowing to Kamis with a twinkle in her eyes. Jenny sucked in her breath.

"What?" asked Mary, alarmed.

"He's showing me memories of his friends. Several of the people in our cargo hold were his crew," she said. Her voice caught on the final word, which was a surprise even to herself. She felt deeply sorrowful over the loss of Kamis' crew, even though she had never met them.

"It's affecting you," said Mary.

"I can feel what he's feeling," said Jenny. Kamis settled down and the overwhelming feeling of grief passed. The thought of his friends thawing and rotting in the cargo hold repulsed both of them. And then there was a little rueful tinge of his anger that she'd nearly unceremoniously jettisoned his friends.

"The Reason soldiers have left," said Mary. "It's safe for you to come out for now."

"Can you turn the gravity off?" asked Jenny.

"Not while we're sitting in their cargo hold. I can't counteract their gravity generators," said Mary. The actuators on the access panel whirred to life. The panel slid open. Jenny braced her arms on the floor of the cockpit and dragged herself out of the hole and over to the captain's chair. She pulled herself up with a grunt and sat down. Her burns stung and throbbed under the spray-on dressing. Kamis watched with horrified curiosity.

"Sorry, bud," said Jenny. "You're going to find that your new body doesn't move much faster than your dead one."

"You need to sleep. And heal." Mary said.

"Agreed. But I am currently trapped on a Reason warship with an elf ghost hitching a ride inside of me. I feel like this would be a good time to regroup. For example, where are we? Which ship are we on? Where are we going?"

"We are sixteen billion kilometers from Jaisalmer on the Reason ship FTL *Kilonova*, a hellion-class interstellar warship with a complement of eight thousand soldiers and three thousand support personnel."

"How do you know that? Did you hack their network?" asked Jenny hopefully.

"No, I asked the ship next to me," said Mary.

"Brilliant," Jenny mumbled, slumping in her chair.

"Also, we're headed toward the new Bala planet," said Mary.

"Brilliant," said Jenny, sitting up with considerably more

enthusiasm. "That is exactly what we're looking for. How did they find it?"

"The logs say that a man named Will Penny brought a piece of horn to Reason Command," said Mary. Jenny's eyebrows shot up.

"Will Penny? As in the movie character?" asked Jenny.

Mary hesitated for a split-second, during which she was probably checking her records of human filmmaking.

"Yes, this person seems to be using an assumed name," she said.

"Is it a tall stringy fella that looks like he's going to either punch you or fall over dead?" asked Jenny.

"That would be an accurate description of the photographs and videos in the files," said Mary.

"Fuck me," said Jenny.

Inside of her head, Kamis flinched. His prudish elf sensibilities had better harden up fast if he was going to keep living in there.

That was definitely Cowboy Jim. Her former co-pilot had watched the movie *Will Penny* about a thousand times over the ten years that they worked together hauling cargo. It was a ridiculous film, with a gruff loner cowboy going off and leaving a perfectly lovely woman and her kid for no good reason other than to make himself feel bad. It made sense that Jim had assumed the name of his favorite character – he was also a man who spent most of his life wallowing in self-loathing.

"Why are you upset?" asked Mary. "The *Kilonova* is going exactly where you want to be."

"Number one, because Cowboy Jim is probably on board and that man has it out for me. And number two, if this warship full of troops is heading for the Bala, it means they're planning an attack," said Jenny.

You must stop them, said Kamis into her head.

"Sure, I'll just unplug the ship and it'll stop. Problem solved," she replied.

"What?" asked Mary.

"I'm talking to Kamis," said Jenny.

"I can't hear him. You'll have to repeat everything he says for the record," said Mary.

"Bite me," said Jenny. "Figure it out."

She sulked in her chair for a few minutes, trying to sort out the situation in her head. The *Kilonova* was headed toward the Bala planet and carrying her along for the ride, which was great. Cowboy Jim was on board, which was not great. And there were eight thousand Reason soldiers ready to attack and collect the Bala once they arrived, which was incredibly not great.

As a former captain, she knew a few dozen ways to sabotage a Reason ship. Problem was, she didn't really want the *Kilonova* to stop. She needed to get there just as much as they did. If she shut the ship down, she'd be stranded without a way to get to Kaila.

She considered jettisoning its crew and continuing on her own, but the logistics of shunting eleven thousand people off the ship were tough. Not to mention the ethics. She could do it, but probably not with the gravity on. And probably not while her entire back half of her body was peeling off. Details.

She could get them to the new planet but she had no idea how to stop the Reason from firing on the Bala and the troops from landing on the surface. The Bala had no weapons other than their own magic. Copernica Citadel proved magic alone wasn't enough to win against Reason firepower. No, she couldn't let the *Kilonova* arrive at all.

Protect them, said Kamis, his voice gaining strength.

"I'm trying to," she said.

"Trying to what?" asked Mary.

"Trying to find out the location of the Bala planet, disable the *Kilonova*, and get your yellow ass out of the hold without anyone noticing and blowing us to bits, because that seems to be the best plan so far," said Jenny. Her mind circled back to the idea of jettisoning eleven thousand soldiers – that would be easier than what she was about to do.

"Is that all," said Mary, in a sarcastic deadpan.

Bury the dead, said Kamis.

Of course he wanted to take care of his crew. Normally, she

would wrap them and send them out of the airlock with a prayer, but her airlock now connected to the *Kilonova's* ship's hold. She couldn't very well open it and dump a pile of bodies onto the floor.

"They'll have to wait," she said. "Sorry."

"Who has to wait?" asked Mary.

"Kamis' crew. There's no way to deal with them right now," said Jenny. "Is my spare chair still in the hold?"

"Yes."

She needed to get there, but crawling across the ship and down two floors way beyond her ability at the moment. She sagged over her captain's chair, awash with pain and fatigue.

"Are we in a spot where I can take a break for some rest?" asked Jenny.

"Yes," said Mary, far louder than she needed to. "Thank goodness, yes. I'll alert you if anyone comes near us, but you need to get some rest. Especially if you plan to single-handedly disable a Reason warship."

"I've done it before," said Jenny.

"I believe you," said Mary.

Jenny lowered herself out of the captain's chair and onto the floor. She pulled herself along with her arms, wishing this ship was one of the older models with metal grating that you could really dig your fingers into.

"This is going to be amazing," she said, speaking between pulls. "The *Kilonova* is going to stay at full gravity because humans love gravity. Even in my chair, I'm going to stand out like a unicorn at a pony show.

You can do this, said Kamis inside her head.

"Oh, this is weird," she said, grabbing onto the cockpit doorframe. "It's almost like having a conscience."

She inched down the hallway toward her quarters.

"You have a right to know about the body you're inhabiting," she said, trying to take her mind off the strain of the exertion. "I was hurt at the Siege of Copernica Citadel. And yes, I was fighting against the Bala. I'm kind of on your side now. It's complicated."

She paused for a moment to catch her breath. If she installed a lift system or a power chair in Mary, those times without her wheelchair would be much easier.

You cannot walk, said Kamis.

"Brilliant deduction, Jiminy Cricket. My spine and pelvis were crushed by a blast door. I haven't had the use of my legs in fifteen years. Last year, a unicorn saved my life from a fatal wound by giving me an infusion of his blood."

She felt Kamis' shock at a unicorn willingly giving their blood to a human. She knew this made her one of a very rare class of humans. Tendrils of his newfound respect curled around the edges of her psyche.

"Oh you just wait until I tell you who is was," she said with relish. "None other than notorious murderer Gary 'Prancer' Cobalt, son of Findae – the king of the unicorns – and Anjali 'Apocalypse Angie' Ramanathan, hero of the hundred years war."

Kamis' awe felt like a balloon swelling inside of her.

You are friends with Gary? asked Kamis. Jenny equivocated.

"He and I have a… difficult history. Anyway, my legs healed a bit after he gave me his blood, but now they're stuck in a not-very-useful but still-very-painful state. I'm definitely not an ideal host, but you get what you get…"

…and you don't get upset? said Kamis, finishing the nursery school rhyme by rote.

"You have kids," said Jenny.

I once did, he replied.

"Did they survive?" she asked.

I'm not sure, he said.

"I can look them up, if you want," she said.

Kamis' heart sank. He didn't want to know.

"Gotcha. If you change your mind, I'm at your service," she said.

Jenny reached her quarters, which was actually a repurposed storage closet. Crew quarters were one level up, which was less than ideal. She'd made her home base as close to the cockpit as she could get. Her room was a third of the size of the real captain's quarters, but at least there was plenty of shelving.

She pulled herself into her rolling desk chair – which was a passable substitute for her wheelchair in a pinch. She pulled a first aid kit out of a cabinet and swallowed two mild pain relievers down dry.

You're supposed to take those with water, said Kamis.

"I'm supposed to do a lot of things," replied Jenny.

Jenny unzipped her jumpsuit and re-dressed her wounds. Kamis watched with a polite interest. She felt questions burning at the back of his mind.

"Ask what you want," she said. "You can't possibly embarrass me."

Does your body hurt this much every day? he asked.

"Today is a little bit over the top, on account of our adventure on the *Well Actually* this morning, but yes, this is what it generally feels like to be me," she said.

How do you manage to get through the hours? he asked.

It was a strange question that Jenny didn't quite know how to answer. She just did it, because what other choice did she have. You could lay in bed in pain or go about your day in pain. Might as well get stuff done.

"I just do," she said.

Jenny pulled the toilet out of the wall and tugged her jumpsuit down to her hips. Kamis became alarmed, dousing her brain with embarrassment and shame. She stopped.

"You realize I can't go thirty-nine hours without a bathroom break?" she asked. "I mean really. You can't inhabit a woman's body and then shame her for using the toilet. The nerve."

Jenny was well accustomed to peeing in front of others. Even if she hadn't hunkered down in the backs of starships under fire where an empty water bottle might be all you had, boot camp alone had communal restrooms. No one came out of the Reason Space Force with any modesty.

She got her jumpsuit back on and rolled to a low cabinet full of food packets. She pulled out a plastic bag full of scrambled eggs and pancakes and a pouch of orange juice. She squeezed the plastic until the heating element inside activated. The food inside got hot within a few seconds. She bit off a hunk of pancake. It was dry and mealy; the same garbage prepackaged nutrients that soldiers and explorers ate. It made her feel right at home. She chewed happily over Kamis' disgust. He craved fresh fruit from any planet, either Bala or human.

"How many perishable items do you think we pack for interstellar trip?" she asked. "I mean, maybe the *Kilonova* has a greenhouse, but I'm not crawling out there to get you an apple."

Jenny bit into the eggs. They'd been molded into a bar with some kind of binder. It was greasy and dry at the same time. A veritable miracle of science. She ate with relish and Kamis scoffed at her.

"Don't food-shame when you don't know my story," she snapped. Kamis waited. She showed him a moment from her childhood, before Gran took over her care. Mom was on the couch, sleeping. Little Jenny was hungry. Every time she tapped mom's shoulder, she stirred a little, but didn't wake up. Jenny searched the cabinets, looking for anything to eat. In the back of the lowest cabinet she found a box of powdered milk among odd cans that the food bank had given to them but her mother could never figure out how to use. Weird beans and dry goods. Eventually mice found the milk box and chewed through it to get to the powder inside. This box was intact. Little Jenny didn't know how to make the milk into liquid, so she got a spoon, peeled back the cardboard, and ate the powder dry. It was the best meal she'd had in two days.

Kamis suffused sympathy throughout her brain, along with a little bit of contriteness at his assumptions.

"That's right," she said. "Don't give me shit for my bar of eggs."

She munched in peace, letting the gritty eggs crunch between her teeth. Her left leg zinged and she rubbed it, bending her lower back ever so carefully. Kamis cringed inside of her head. Jenny ignored him and rolled to the desk. She pulled up as much of the

Kilonova's status as Mary could glean from inside of the hold.

I'd like to look up my children, said Kamis. Yep, she figured he'd change his mind.

He zoomed her into a memory of his. Two little kids with delicate elfin ears framing thick human features. They would have fared pretty badly – ostracized from the Bala community and also hunted for parts in the Reason. Best case scenario, they'd be on the new Bala world.

In the memory, a woman stepped out into the high grass holding a plate of sandwiches out to them. The kids looked up and screeched. They were that tender age when it was hard to tell from their screams whether they were excited or being murdered. Just balls of pure energy coated with dirt and smears of food.

"Lunch, kids," the woman called. The two children bounded toward her, parting the grass like happy little badgers. She was entirely human. Her round face framed by hair the color of the sunset on Varuna. She was just the type of woman Jenny would have smiled at a few seconds too long, just to see if she was interested. Kamis barraged her with a mix of amusement and jealousy.

"I'm not macking on your wife, Kamis," said Jenny, aware that he knew she was lying and also not caring. "But she's pretty hot."

She played her fingers over Mary's touchscreens.

"What's your full name, Kamis?" Jenny asked.

Kamistaff Jhaeros Uhlararaice, he answered.

"That's a mouthful," said Jenny, typing it in letter by letter with his coaching.

His records came up as Wanted – even in Mary's six-week-old database. Jenny wasn't surprised. Nearly all Bala were marked as Wanted in the Reason database. If they weren't wanted for a crime then they were wanted for parts. She clicked into the file. There was a note that he was likely deceased because his ship had been found adrift and unoccupied in Reasonspace a year ago; however, without confirmation via records or a body they wouldn't issue an official death certificate.

Jenny clicked into the record for Kamis' wife. She was also wanted for fraternization – a charge that Jenny herself had on her record. It was the blanket crime for any full humans who had relationships with Bala beings. There was also no death record, but Jenny knew she was gone. The *Well Actually* had read the transcript of her murder.

Grief hit Kamis anew. He'd guessed they had killed Min, but never really had confirmation. Jenny's memory of the transcript, his wife bargaining for her life, had made it real.

Jenny clicked into the children's profiles. A girl and a boy a year apart. Their dates of birth would have put them at five and six respectively. They were also wanted. As half-Bala their very existence was a crime. Both of them were marked as rescued from a ship adrift just outside of Varuna's orbit.

That's where the Well Actually *met up with us,* said Kamis. *We stopped to help them. Min and I went aboard with a few crewmembers and left the children on the ship.*

"It says here that they were dropped off on Varuna when you didn't return," said Jenny. "That's not too bad. There are a lot of friendly people on Varuna. I bet they're on the new Bala planet right now waiting for you."

Kamis ached with sorrow inside of her. It was nearly unbearable. She'd spent all that time trying to shove her own bad feelings down a gravity well, and now she was marinating in Kamis' grief. She scooted into the bed, tucked her legs under the covers, and cranked the heated blanket up to full power. If she couldn't tamp down Kamis' feelings, she could at least drown them out with television. She tapped a console on the wall and pulled up her favorite crime drama – an old series about a Reason officer who investigated local crimes against Bala beings. It was a remarkably even-handed show given the prejudices of the Reason. Probably because the show's director was the daughter of a high-ranking officer in the Reason Space Force. They let her get away with murder.

In the episode, someone had sawn the horn off a unicorn living on the rough side of town and stolen it to power their starship.

The premise was ridiculous. As if there were any full-blooded unicorns left unaccounted for. Besides the couple who'd popped back into the area for the Century Summit, then disappeared just as quickly, there had been no free unicorns in the known universe for almost a century.

And the idea that a unicorn would deign to live in squalor like the place depicted on the show was flat out ridiculous. They would have trotted down to city hall and demanded a suitable living space with gardens and fountains. Unicorns were bloody demanding, and accustomed to living like royalty.

Also, this unicorn on the show had a human girlfriend, whose sole purpose on the show seemed to be so that the Reason cops could keep making salacious horse-fucking jokes at her expense. Unicorns were born in the heart of a star and didn't reproduce sexually. They had neither the desire, nor the organs for sex. Those two might have been in an asexual romantic relationship, but they sure as hell weren't fucking.

Kamis was aghast at the portrayal of Bala in the show, which was at least better than the grief. And this was one of the more even-handed shows on the air. Most programs cast Bala as livestock or pets. Some treated them like rampaging monsters, especially the ones humans recognized as storybook villains, like trolls and golems.

The Reason officers had pinpointed the culprit. A down-and-out fairy, mouth all gums from selling his sharp teeth for drill bits, dirt-streaked and wearing a traditional gauzy fairy dress worn down to rags. Fairies hadn't dressed like that for eight hundred years but the Reason-based audience ate up those inaccurate stereotypes.

She could feel Kamis' disgust. As the show ended she turned it off and settled in to get some rest. It took her a while to get to sleep, and when she finally drifted off she dreamed of the battle at Copernica Citadel.

It was the same dream she always had, starting with her being unable to stop the purple lightning from wrapping around her ship, the *Pandey*. The screams of her crew filled her head. She slid under the bulkhead door as it closed, stopping it with her body for the handful of seconds that it took for seventeen soldiers to slide underneath. Then there was that sickening sensation of her pelvis bending. The one that she wouldn't never forget as long as she lived.

Tonight, for the first time in fifteen years, there were two new parts of the dream. First, Kamis stood off to the side watching her. The twisting hull of the *Pandey* froze in place and the screams of her crew faded away. Delicate slippers embroidered with green foliage stood at her head. Kamis reached down and took her hand, pulling her out from under the door as easily as if she were simply getting up like anyone else. That was the second new thing in this version of the dream – she could walk again.

Over the last fifteen years, she'd come to only ever think of herself in a chair. Even in her dreams. She didn't run around like an abled person in her dream, she wheeled around. Or, more often, she pushed as hard as she could, but her chair moved like molasses. Dreaming herself walking was new and strange. She felt disoriented, and maybe… guilty. As if it was a betrayal of who she really was. Around her, the *Pandey* was broken and empty. Inside, Jenny felt the same way.

"You could have stopped the battle of Copernica," said Kamis, speaking to her from his own body in the dream. He was a good head taller than her and all angles and points, like most elves. His dark hair hung perfectly flat, as if it had never been bothered by humidity in his long, long life. Jenny walked away from him.

"I did stop it," she said, walking through the empty halls of her former ship. It felt strange to want to go somewhere and then simply move there. No thresholds to navigate, no hallway too small, no stairs or fruitless searches for working elevators. Jenny's problem was never with her chair, but with a world that refused to accommodate it.

"At great cost," said Kamis, following her. Jenny whirled on him, bracing against the wall for support. She wished she had her chair.

"Everyone always talks about the cost. I knew the risks going into the Reason Space Force. I knew them the day I slid under that door. I know them every day that I wake up in this terrible place," she said.

"But if you had the power to stop another massacre now, you would," said Kamis.

She didn't want to say the answer out loud, because of course she would.

"These things will keep happening. This ship will keep moving forward until someone throws themself in front of it," said Kamis.

"That's how you get killed," said Jenny.

"But it's also how you make a change," said Kamis. "You have a responsibility to stop the killing."

He wasn't talking about the *Pandey* any more. He was talking about the *Kilonova*.

"I can't do this," she said, waving her fingers at the *Pandey*'s hallway, torqued out of alignment and spraying sparks.

"Even the smallest sabotages can have great effects," said Kamis.

Jenny sighed.

"You're right. I only have one question. What kind of conditioner do you use?"

His exasperated elfin sigh gave her life.

Jenny couldn't recall the name of the day, or where she was tucked in, but it was warm and comfortable, so probably safe.

It's Saturday, said Kamis in her head.

Jenny startled and sat up so fast that her back spasmed and she let out a squeal.

I'm sorry. You forgot that I'm here, he said.

"You all right, Jenny?" asked Mary.

"Fine. I just forgot about Kamis," she said. "You can come out of there now. Go be a ghost on your own."

It takes a large amount of energy to manifest on my own. If I could continue to share space with you until we reach my children, I would be grateful, he said.

"Share space," he'd said. As if they were flatmates. She figured he was probably the type to label all the food in the refrigerator and complain about clothes on the living room floor.

Definitely. I'm very tidy, said Kamis. Jenny reminded herself to watch her thoughts. *Prepare yourself for the day and then I can guide you through necromancy to find the Bala.*

"That was just a dream, not a real conversation," she said.

Is there a difference? he asked.

"I guess not," said Jenny. "I just don't know if I'm ready to jump into a task this big."

We have to stop them, said Kamis, suddenly urgent. *Millions will be killed or enslaved. We cannot let this happen again.*

"Oh I agree, but why is it always me?" she asked. Kamis smiled, suffusing her mind with his sympathetic amusement.

She showed him a memory from a few weeks ago during the Century Summit. The Pymmie, rotund and tiny, their oily black eyes staring, asking Jenny to give input on the fate of all Bala as they had a dinner party. She felt Kamis' horror, both at the ease at which the Pymmie decided the fate of the Bala and the fact that they had solicited input from a human at all.

"I know, right?" said Jenny, sensing his distress. "I am profoundly unqualified to decide the fate of a single being, let alone an entire civilization. And yet, there I was eating a proper pumpkin boil-up and being asked to weigh in. How does this keep happening?"

I do not believe in coincidence, said Kamis. *So I must believe you were chosen.*

"Well I don't believe in chosen one stories, so I must believe this is all just a terrible coincidence," she said.

If you fail in your endeavor you will only damage the Reason ship. The risk is low, said Kamis.

"Good point. Zapping a couple of soldiers with purple lightning wouldn't be so bad," she said.

That's the spirit, said Kamis. *Let hate guide your actions.*

Jenny wheeled her chair to the cargo hold, a task which was complicated by the stairs going down one level. Jenny threw the rolling chair down the stairwell with a crash and bumped down the stairs after it.

Elegant solution, said Kamis.

"I get where I'm going," said Jenny.

There were still corpses strewn about the hold. They had completely thawed and had started to bloat and smell.

"Aw hell," said Jenny, rolling her dented desk chair over to the cabinets along the wall. "I'll deal with them when we get off the *Kilonova.*"

She pulled her spare chair out of a cabinet and unfolded it. It was a streamlined model, all pipes and angles. Nothing near as beautiful as the dwarf one that had shattered on the *Well Actually.* She got herself settled and strapped in.

"All right Kamis, show me how to find the Bala," she said.

"Is this a good idea?" asked Mary. "We can probably get the information out of the *Kilonova's* computers."

"Do you have access to their systems?" asked Jenny.

"No, but if you can get to the data center–" began Mary.

"Uh… no. I'm a little obvious in my chair here. They'll know I don't belong in about five seconds," said Jenny. "We'll try this way first."

This will be easier than you think, said Kamis.

"I'm not worried that it'll be hard. I just don't like dabbling in things that I don't understand. Makes me feel squirrelly," she said.

Like Cowboy Jim did when he went into the null, said Kamis, drawing on her memories in a way that made her uncomfortable.

Jenny's mouth dropped open. "I'm not one bit like that wanker," said Jenny.

Of course not, said Kamis. Jenny wished there was a way to rattle him around in there by shaking her head real fast.

"I'm being reasonably cautious about using a power that I know nothing about. A power, by the way, which tore the *Pandey* in two right in front of my own eyes," said Jenny.

Understandable. But you'll only be looking. No tearing ships apart right now, said Kamis.

"Just give me the drill," she said, impatient to get going. This hold wasn't going to smell any better.

You have to feel your way through it, he began.

Jenny sighed with exasperation.

"Instructions. I need instructions," she snapped.

"I'm only getting half the conversation here, you two, but I assume that you are attempting to locate the Bala planet within the nullspace," said Mary. "Please be aware that there are three necromancers on this ship and any of the three could spot you the moment you start poking around in the null."

Now Kamis sighed.

Turn her off.

"I like her," said Jenny.

"Does Kamis not like me? I try to be accommodating, but I don't know what he wants."

"You don't need to accommodate him. You need to keep doing what I tell you," said Jenny. "Kamis. Instructions. Now."

First, reach out with your awareness and find the nullspace energy that you've used in the past. It's all around you, but it concentrates in pockets near living beings, plants, any place where there's life and emotion, said Kamis.

"Do I have to close my eyes or something?" asked Jenny.

Not yet. You need to learn how to be aware of both openspace and nullspace at the same time. It's a critical skill in battle, said Kamis.

"I'm not in a battle."

Not yet you aren't. Let yourself sink into awareness of the nullspace, but don't allow openspace to disappear fully. Leave it in your consciousness, like a map overlay. In the beginning, it will help you understand why nullspace energy is concentrated in certain spots. Maybe there's a ship there, or a Bala settlement. Eventually, you'll be able to recognize hotspots and pathways simply by their shapes and colors in the null, said Kamis.

As far as using her powers, Jenny had only gathered a bit of energy and used it to manipulate matter back when the Reason was still in charge. It made her nervous to think of letting go of her reality and slipping into a new one. She let her awareness expand, tapping into the energy around her and allowing her consciousness to expand to outside of both Mary and the *Kilonova*. Nothing changed.

"I don't think I'm doing it right. I don't see anything different," she said to Kamis.

I know. I see what you see. You're doing it right. Part of the problem is that with the Bala gone, there aren't many bright spots of nullspace energy to focus on. And tell your ship that all three necromancers are off duty, so no one will spot you.

"Kamis says to tell you that the necromancers are all asleep. No one will see me," said Jenny.

"Good, but hurry," said Mary.

Try again, said Kamis. *This time, I'm going to guide you.*

"What does that mean?" asked Jenny.

I'm going to take your mind, and ever-so-slightly help you expand your peripheral understanding.

"Sounds fake," said Jenny.

Trust me, said Kamis. And she had to, because he was inside of her brain.

I'll go slowly, he said.

"Go quickly," said Jenny.

She again let nullspace bubble up around her. This time, Kamis tugged her awareness into a space far out from the *Kilonova*. For a moment, it felt as if she was falling into nothingness. She flailed out and caught her chair's armrest.

Don't panic, he said.

It was as if a fog had suddenly appeared around her. It coalesced in some locations and was sparse in others. Kamis seemed to know exactly where to look. She could see what he saw. He let his focus go and allowed the null to pass by him as if they were moving faster than the speed of light.

She watched the show. It glowed in pure whites mixed with a rainbow of colors, some on a spectrum that she had never seen before. Kamis pushed them out past Reasonspace and far into unexplored territory. *Your body is able to use the nullspace energy much more efficiently than I expected,* he explained. *We can do this quickly.*

Nearly all of the star systems they passed were dark – absent of any trace of Bala. Kamis swore in the elfin language and Jenny grinned. His prudish façade was dissipating now that he was frustrated. Jenny knew how to curse and order a beer in all the Bala languages; it was a good one he'd let fly.

Kamis pushed past all of the star systems that Jenny was familiar with, then past a host of them she had never seen before. Stars in pairs and triplets, and plenty of singletons with their handful of orbiting planets and satellites. She saw evidence of other civilizations that were neither human nor Bala. She tried to slow Kamis' progress to look but he tugged her forward.

Another time, he said firmly, but with a touch of amusement. *Your curiosity is one of your best attributes.* She wasn't sure if he meant her personally or humans as a race.

Some of the planets with habitations glowed with the energy of the null, but in ultraviolets and other invisible colors. Her gaze lingered there, taking in Dyson spheres and the lights of cities laid out in spirals.

Other beings have access to the null, just like the Bala, Kamis explained. *Some are better at it, some worse. I can show you when we're not in so much of a hurry.*

An intense ball of light glowed in the distance, brighter than any of the planets they had seen so far. Kamis' heart – which was really Jenny's heart – beat faster. She could feel his familiarity with this type of light. It felt familiar to her as well.

There they are, he said, zeroing in on the source of the light. As they got closer, Jenny saw individual lights grouped together, which made sense. The Bala had already begun constructing towns in their new home. It was a pretty pink planet that looked calm and welcoming. She very much wanted to be there.

"Found them," she announced.

"Good, get out of there," said Mary.

One moment more, I just want to check in, said Kamis.

One of the groupings of Bala was bigger than the others. Kamis zoomed in close enough that she could pick out individual balls of light. Some bright and colored and some dimmer and swirling with black. His gaze methodically flicked through lights. Kamis was looking for someone.

While he looked in one location, she scanned on her own for someone else. She searched the little town for a light that felt like Kaila. None of the beings there felt like her wife. She started to feel anxious. Would she know if something had happened to Kaila? Would she have felt it?

She scanned the beings around the fringes of the town. Off in the distance, a grouping of Bala lights indicated a second tiny village. Not far from there she found a stand of dryads. There, calmly resting among her kin, Jenny saw her wife. Relief coursed through her. Kaila was not only alive, she was thriving in the forest of their new home. Her light glowed so brightly that Jenny's heart ached to be there with her.

She looked for as long as she could, trying to tease out different emotions flickering in the light. Kamis' focus helped. Kaila was mostly content, but also a little angry. Good. It was that spitfire sap that Jenny loved about her.

A wash of relief hit her so hard it nearly knocked the wind out of her. She turned back to where Kamis was looking. He'd found his children. Older, more tired, but alive and well.

There was someone near them that drew her in. A deep blue light that stopped her in her tracks. It felt calm and welcoming, but just a bit prickly. It was Gary.

The emotions that bubbled up in Jenny were complicated and ever-changing. Guilt, anger, affection, and sadness.

Interesting, said Kamis. *Time to go.*

Kamis pulled them home more quickly than they had arrived. It made her feel sick to see planets and systems moving past faster than she could see them. They were back in the hold of the *Stagecoach Mary* within seconds. Jenny took a moment to tap the coordinates of the new Bala world into a console on the wall before she forgot them. Her fingers shook on the touchscreen. She sank into her chair, spent.

CHAPTER SIXTEEN
Criosphinx

An idea struck Bào as he watched the *Kilonova* scoop up the little yellow pioneer ship out of the null. In the past, at other times where unicorn horn had been scarce, Reason scientists had attempted to put other materials into FTL drives. Stones, small animals, and even human bones. Most did nothing, but some types of Bala bones had an effect, ranging from a mild unpleasant odor permeating the ship to driving the crew to the brink of insanity. In all cases, the ship ran much more slowly and erratically on anything other than true unicorn horn. That might be the best way to stop the *Kilonova*. Bào just had to get some other Bala material into the FTL drive.

The drive was heavily guarded, but, as a necromancer, he was one of the few people allowed close to the FTL cabinet. He never really needed to be near it to do his job, but the Reason assumed that proximity to the horn would make his guidance more efficient. Truth was, with a good communications link, he could have guided the *Kilonova* just as easily, and a lot more comfortably, from back at Fort J.

Then there was the matter of what to put into the drive. Everything Bala had disappeared at the Summit, but the substitution had to be something magical that would move them, just not in the right direction. A trisicle would have been ideal – throw one of those in a cabinet and it would jump them into bugspace where thousands of biting beetles would appear in every crevice of the ship. He doubted that he could find any valuable trisicles just hanging around a Reason ship.

He did know of one Bala bone that was right within his grasp. Literally. After Copernica Citadel, the mermaids had fixed his hands with whatever they could find in their underwater palace. One of their treasures was the horn of a criosphinx, taken from the hold of a sunken wreck. They'd patiently picked pulverized bits of his bones out of his hand, then carved the horn to fit the empty space. It twinged now and then when he passed an open field, and he suspected that some of his cravings for fresh grass were due to the horn's original owner.

Bào had worked late after his shift while they captured the seemingly-abandoned *Stagecoach Mary*. The pioneer ship had taken evasive maneuvers, taking them far off course from the Bala planet. After they'd snagged the ship he'd had to remain at his station to recalibrate their course from their new location. When Lakshmi finally dismissed him, it was late into the artificial night when the second-tier crew members rotated onto duty. He walked the empty halls, heading for the medbay instead of his quarters.

The euphoria from this new sabotage idea erased his exhaustion and put a little spring in his step. Starting the plan in the middle of the night could only help. The crew on this shift would be the cut-rate personnel with slipshod methods and lackluster performance. They'd be less likely to question him and more apt to simply shrug at an odd request and do what he asked.

The medbay doors opened and a wall of sound hit him. A room that was usually sterile and silent now pulsed with the driving beat of a song that his teenage companions would have loved. Indeed, there were Priya and Rhian, leaning against a gurney with neon drinks in hand.

"Hey, I figured you were in bed long ago," said Priya, slapping his shoulder. "You never come out with us."

Rhian gave him a halfhearted wave and ducked off into the crowd.

"What is this?" Bào raised his voice over the music.

"Doctor Tang's Place," said Priya. "She's a second-shift doctor who is also really amazing. She hosts a bar in here after hours. It's totally not regulation and I absolutely love it. Do you want a drink?"

"I'm in need of a doctor," said Bào.

"Are you sick?" asked Priya, looking him up and down.

"No, I just need some advice," said Bào.

Priya scanned the crowd.

"There she is, in the surgery bay. The redhead."

"Thanks," said Bào. "See you later."

Bào pushed his way through to the glass-enclosed surgery. He opened the door. The room was quiet and filled with smoke.

"This is a high roller area. Get back out on the dance floor," said the woman with red-tinged hair. She flicked him away without looking up.

"I just need a moment of your time. I don't want to play," he said, stepping into the room.

"You come in, you play. House rules," she said. Her eyes didn't leave the four people hunkered over their cards in front of her.

"I just need medical assistance," he said.

"Do you see anyone doctoring here?" she asked. "Play or leave."

She gestured to an empty seat that seemed to be a repurposed crash-cart. Bào sat down, hoping it wouldn't activate and electrocute his rear end.

"You're in next hand," she said.

"I don't have anything to bet," he said.

"Everyone has something to bet," she replied. She tilted her head at him. "You're the necro, right?"

"Yeah," he said.

"Then your wager is that I want you to find something for me. A Bala object," said the doctor.

That made Bào uncomfortable. She would be able to find the Bala planet, or any Bala parts that people had hidden inside of them. "No, I can't–" he started.

"Then bye." She flicked a finger at him. "Get out."

He needed her help.

"OK. One Bala object," he conceded.

"Excellent." The way she steepled her fingers reminded him of a storybook villain, but her delighted smile was all heroine.

The table was finishing a round of Unicorn Hunter, a game that Bào had played thousands of times on the raider ship. To win, a player had to find all five unicorn cards of the same house. It was nearly impossible to accomplish but the rewards were large. Most hands ended with all losers, but on the remote chance that someone did collect all of the House of Periwinkle or the House of Cerulean, they won not only the ante from that hand, but from the entire day's play. Unicorn Hunter was a popular game at the end of the night, after the pot had grown all evening.

The current hand ended in disaster for everyone. The only person to even get a unicorn was a food service worker, who ended up with two from the House of Azure, which won you nothing.

"Better luck next time," said the doctor, collecting the cards and dealing out the new hands. Her nametag said Doctor Tang.

Bào concentrated on the pile of cards in Doctor Tang's hand, looking through their backs to see their faces. He dropped some into and back out of the null in slightly different locations as she dealt from the stack. Cheating at cards was one of the most useful things he'd learned to do with his necromancer skills. It was foolproof once you learned how to keep the purple lightning from giving you away.

Once the hand had been dealt, the players lifted their cards. Doctor Tang leaned back and checked the dealer's hand. Five unicorns in that hand would immediately end the game and she would get to keep everything from that day so far. If five unicorns didn't appear – and they rarely did – the players entered a round of intense trading and negotiations that often ended in fisticuffs. Not unlike a beefed-up game of Go Fish.

The doctor ran a hand down the front of her uniform jacket to smooth it. Bào didn't know her well enough to know what kind of tell that was.

His hand was exactly what he'd aimed for. Five unicorns from the House of Cobalt, including Gary Cobalt and his father Findae. The players to his left tossed their cards on the table, showing a mixture of unicorns and other Bala. It came to Bào's turn and he spread his hand out with a flourish.

"Five unicorn flush."

The officers and grunts around him burst into unhappy groans.

"No way, man."

"Crazy. I've never seen one."

"Gary Cobalt isn't even a real unicorn."

The doctor narrowed her eyes at him.

"What the hell, new kid," she said. "How did you do that?"

Bào scooped his winnings out of the center of the table and onto his spot. He thought he spied the door fob to a late-model space skimmer in there, which could come in handy for a quick exit, but it would be tacky to check in front of everyone.

"Game over. Come again soon," said the doctor, standing up and grabbing Bào's ear. He grabbed his loot as she dragged him through the surgery and into the scrub room behind it. The lights were off back there except for the blue glow of the sanitizers working overnight to clean the instruments.

Dr. Tang poked a finger into his chest.

"You little necro cheater. Do you know who I am?" She held her gold-plated nametag out to him. "I am Doctor Ricky Tang. If I were back at the Blossom, I'd toss you to the Sixian Parrot," she said. "You don't get to keep any of that pot. Hand it over and don't tell anyone that I didn't let you keep it. They need to think they have a chance."

"I didn't cheat, I really won," said Bào, smoothing out his Kevin Chen face so that it looked sincere.

"Bullshit. There were only four Colbolt unicorns in that deck. I counted them myself," said Doctor Tang.

"There are supposed to be five unicorns from each house in a regulation Unicorn Hunter deck," said Bào.

"Yeah, well. I took Gary Cobalt out of my deck because he and

I have a long-standing thing. But suddenly he's back in there. How exactly did that happen?" She stood there with her hands on her hips.

"Uh, magic?" said Bào.

The doctor grabbed him by the ear again and pulled him toward a large open chute set into the wall.

"That's it, you're going into the medical waste incinerator," she said.

"Wait," cried Bào, struggling to get away. He pulled his head to get free and a muscle wrenched in his neck. "Ow."

"I'm not even hurting you," she said, rolling her eyes.

"I pulled a muscle," he said, rubbing the spot.

"You are the worst at torture," she said, letting go of his ear. "Just give me back the pot."

Bào held the chips out to her.

"I don't want the money. I honestly came in here just to ask for some medical help, ma'am," he said, rubbing the spot in his neck that had twinged. He could feel a tight knot of muscle in there.

Doctor Tang stuffed the chips and the keys to the skimmer in her pockets.

"Ugh. Don't call me 'ma'am.' Ricky is fine. Come back in the morning when the other doctor gets on. She's actually a real…" Ricky paused. "Good doctor."

"You're not a doctor at all. You're a stowaway," said Bào, not bothering to conceal the wonder and relief in his voice. Here was someone who could actually understand him. He realized his mistake the moment the words tumbled out of his mouth.

Ricky plucked one of the scalpels out of the sanitizer. She put her free hand on Bào's shoulder. Back here, two rooms away from the blaring music, no one would hear him scream for help. She was younger and stronger than him. In an instant, she could slice his throat and toss him down the waste chute. If he didn't zap her with lightning, his body would be charcoal before anyone noticed he was gone.

"No, I mean. I'm fine with that," he raised his hands in

surrender. "Honestly, it helps me. I need someone who's willing to take a risk. I need someone who can perform a small operation for me without asking a lot of questions."

Ricky looked intrigued. "Keep talking," she said, tossing the contaminated scalpel back with the clean ones.

"This is why I didn't want the day shift doctor," said Bào. "I need an off-the-record procedure done. There's a bone that has to come out of my finger."

"Nifty," said Ricky. "Listen, I use the medical AI to bluff my way through food poisoning, constipation, and the other minor cases that come in at night, but I can't do real doctor things."

"The AI will do most of it," said Bào. "I need your authorization code to get it started."

"You locate a Bala object for me and you're on," she said. Whatever this woman's real job was, it clearly involved a lot of cutthroat negotiating.

"Yes," said Bào, tapping his shoulder twice with his palm the way the kids these days signaled their excitement about something. It was a habit he'd picked up from Priya.

Ricky led them back into the surgery where all the players had cleared out. The bass was barely audible from within the enclosed pod.

"Not that it's any of my business, but what are you going to do with a hand bone?" she asked, clearing empty glasses off the surgery table.

"There are criosphinx bones in my left hand – put there after it was shattered during the war. If I can get them out–"

"You can put them into the FTL drive," Ricky said. She set an empty glass on the table, her eyes wide. "You're trying to stop the ship from getting to the Bala. Brilliant. Except that I want to go to their new planet. That was the entire goal of sneaking on here at great personal risk. Sorry, kid. I'm out."

"No, you have to," said Bào, sounding more and more like a beseeching Kevin Chen. "This ship can't make it to the Bala."

"You have friends there?" asked Ricky.

"Many," said Bào. "But even if I didn't, you know that as soon as we arrive all those soldiers in the lower decks are going to load up onto carriers and head down to the surface to round up every Bala being they can find. It will be genocide."

Ricky took a deep breath at his final word. "So you are not loyal to the Reason," she said. "Interesting."

Bào was on dangerous ground. If he was wrong about this conwoman stowaway, she could turn him in to any senior officer and he'd be held in stasis for the rest of the trip where he wouldn't be able to use his powers to retaliate.

"Are you loyal to them?" he asked carefully.

"When it suits me," she replied. "But the Reason has done me no favors. Especially in the last few years. Which is why I'm heading for the Bala. At least they won't put me into a rehabilitation camp."

"Why would you need rehabilitation?" he asked, trying to convey his skepticism of Reason tactics. She sized him up before answering.

"I don't. But that is a conversation we will have later. Maybe," she said. "We'll see. So you plan to single-handedly stop a Reason warship from finding the Bala."

"Trust me, I have more than enough power to tear this ship apart. But there are people on here who don't want to be a party to the Reason's plan. They deserve a chance to resist. I'm tweaking my navigation reports to put us slightly off course, but the other necromancers bring us back into true during their shift, so it's not working as well as I'd hoped. If I can get the criosphinx horn out of my hand and put it into the drive, I'm hoping it will drop us into some other dimension like bugspace where we'll stay for a while. At the very least it'll slow us down and take them a while to figure out what's wrong," said Bào.

"Not a terrible idea," said Ricky. "But I don't plan on serving watered-down cocktails to cocksure soldiers for the rest of my life. I want off this ship and onto a fresh planet."

"Fair, but now we have a skimmer," Bào pointed to her jacket pocket. "If we can get the unicorn horn out of the FTL drive and swap it with my bone, we can use the skimmer to get out of there. I can navigate us."

Ricky's mouth spread in a wide smile. "I like you, kid. You've got moxie. And I like your little plan. Better than mine, at least," she said.

"Which was what?"

"When we arrived at the Bala planet, I was going to beg Gary Cobalt to rescue me," she said.

Bào laughed.

"Knowing Gary, he probably would have," said Bào, forgetting he wasn't supposed to know the part-unicorn personally.

"Do you know Gary?" asked Ricky, suddenly very interested.

"Uh, no. But I read a lot about him in history class. Seems like a cool guy," said Bào.

"Don't believe all you read, kid. Anyways, Gary Cobalt doesn't like me very much," said Ricky.

"He still would have rescued you," said Bào, partly to himself.

"I know. Isn't he weird?" asked Ricky. "All right, I'm willing to help you out with your surgery, but we need to make it fast. The club shuts down when the morning shift comes on and they're a bunch of stiffs who don't tolerate any fun. Let's get that bone out of you."

She pointed Bào to a chair next to the table.

"Sit."

From his chair, Bào could see people dancing and drinking out in the medbay. Here in this lighted pod, he and Ricky would be like a sideshow for anyone who cared to watch.

"Do you have anywhere a little more private we could go?" he asked.

"No one is paying attention to you, kid. They're all busy trying to get laid," she said.

Bào laughed.

"Seriously," said Ricky. "On ships like this, basically everyone is sleeping with everyone else. It's one of the perks of the job."

The door to the surgery opened and a Reason officer poked his head in.

"Is the game still on?" he asked. "I want to win my skimmer back." Ricky shooed him out.

"This kid won it, you take it up with him in the morning. For tonight, all bets are off. I'm doing actual doctoring in here tonight," she said. The officer grumbled but shut the door.

"Hey medical AI," called Ricky up at the ceiling.

"Yes, doctor," replied the crisp computer voice.

"We need to remove a foreign object from this kid's hand and replace it with a bone graft. Can we do that? Is that a thing?"

"Place the affected area onto the operating table," said the AI.

Bào dropped his left hand flat onto the cold metal table. It had grooves carved into it so that blood and other fluids would run off into gutters on the sides. A screen on the wall lit up with a scan of Bào's hand. The darker chunks of criosphinx bone were clearly visible next to the more porous human bone of Bào's original fingers.

"Whoa, that's pretty messed up," said Ricky. "Who even fixed this?"

"Mermaids," said Bào, cursing himself for sharing a bit too much about his past. Something in him wanted to impress this woman, which didn't happen often.

"This surgery is possible and will take twenty-four minutes," said the medical AI.

"Go for it," said Ricky. A printer in the corner began spitting out bone graft material in the exact shape of Bào's finger bone.

A retractable arm came down and sprayed Bào's hand with what smelled like disinfectant. It also made his hand completely numb. Before he could ask if he had to watch, the tool at the end of the arm rotated and a yellow laser shot out a two-second burst of light. A retractor spread open the cauterized skin and pair of forceps pulled the criosphinx chunk out of his finger. It was all very clinical and painless, but Bào still felt sick watching his insides become his outsides.

"You're not going to pass out, are you?" asked Ricky.

"No, but this is unpleasant," said Bào.

"Just look up at me, I'll distract you. Because if you faint, I have no idea what to do.

Bào smiled. "Come on, you don't even know basic first aid?" he asked.

"I'm here to serve drinks and get to the Bala. I'm bluffing my way through everything medical."

"That's a comforting thought while my finger is flayed open on your table," said Bào. "If I feel faint I'm supposed to put my head between my legs."

Ricky raised an eyebrow at him.

"Really," she deadpanned. "Are you sure you're not getting the fainting cure mixed up with something else a bit more fun?"

Bào laughed. She was very good at distracting him.

"Sorry. I'm corrupting a kid here," she said.

"Corrupt away. I'm not a kid," said Bào with a smile. He caught himself giving away more than he meant to again. He just wanted to talk to her without double-thinking every bit of personal information. "I'm twenty-two," he added quickly.

"Sounds exhausting," said Ricky. "I have a policy not to date anyone under thirty. That's when people finally start to get their shit together. I don't have time for twentysomething drama."

"I have no drama," he protested as the forceps dropped the criosphinx bone into a depression at the end of the table with a thunk. It plucked the mesh-like finished bonegraft off the printer. Bào held his breath as the forceps tucked it into place.

"I have no drama, says the guy who just cheated me out of a skimmer with a five unicorn flush in order to get me to help him take a Balabone out of his hand in order to sabotage a Reason warship," said Ricky. "Nope. No drama here."

The AI closed Bào's wound with a line of biosafe glue. Ricky took his hand to inspect the computer's work.

"You love it," said Bào, giving her hand a squeeze. One corner of her mouth went up.

"You seem more mature than your years, kid," she said holding his fingers for another two seconds, then letting him go. Bào had to work extra hard to hide the flush on his cheeks from reaching Kevin Chen's face. He let his numb arm fall to his side and picked up the criosphinx bone.

"I'm going to put this into the FTL drive," he said, getting up from the table.

"Do you actually think I'm going to let you do that on your own?" asked Ricky. "I'm dying to see the engine room."

Bào didn't know how he was going to get her in there, but he found himself suprisingly excited at the prospect of good company.

"Let me just close down this party," said Ricky. She stepped out into the medbay and headed over to the bar made of a repurposed gurney. She whispered something to the bartender, whom Bào recognized from the food service crew. The bartender nodded and began tucking bottles into a storage locker behind her. In a matter of moments, that area of the room looked like a sterile medbay again.

Ricky went to a panel on the wall and tapped a few commands into the computer. The volume of the music dropped and an authoritative computer-generated voice called out over the crowd.

"Officers of the Reason, I invite you to bring your drinks to the observation deck as we pass by a startling double black hole phenomenon off of the starboard side." The medbay doors opened and the lights began to gradually rise.

"There are no black holes in the null," said Bào.

"They're too drunk to care," said Ricky, as the party shuffled out the doors and spilled into the hallway.

When the medbay was empty and quiet, Ricky draped an arm around Bào's shoulders.

"Ready for some drama, kid?" she asked.

Bào was nervous. He gripped the criosphinx in his good hand and led the way to the engine room.

There were normal sublight engines on all starships – they were ridiculous hulking things that took up entire decks. The Reason made a point of keeping necromancers in the dark about most ship designs. They were less likely to sabotage a system if they didn't know the intimate details of how it worked. Typical Reason paranoia.

He did know FTL drives in a way that non-necromancer humans never would. He saw the energy that pulsed through them and how it enveloped the ship and pulled it into nullspace.

Getting into the engine room was as easy as swiping his badge. Without removing her headphones, the security grunt on duty flipped her screen to the security page to see who'd just swiped in, then flicked it back to her show when she confirmed that Bào was permitted to enter. She didn't give either of them a first glance, let alone a second.

"That was a bit of a let down," said Ricky. "I was hoping to spin some kind of wild tale about the ship about to explode and how we needed to get you to the FTL cabinet before we all blew into a billion pieces."

"I'm allowed in here," said Bào with a shrug. "Not much of an adventure."

They stood in front of the horn cabinet.

"How do we get it in?" asked Ricky.

"I think we just open the door and put it on the shelf," said Bào.

"Can you open an FTL cabinet while it's on?" asked Ricky.

"I think so," said Bào. "We have a doctor in case anything goes wrong."

Ricky smacked him on the arm.

"Well, you do it," she said. "I'm not going to get sucked into an alternate dimension again."

"Again?" asked Bào, intrigued.

"A story for later," said Ricky, backing up a few steps.

Bào stepped up to the FTL cabinet. He could see both the wooden shape of the carved cabinet in the ship and the overlay of pulsing nullspace energy at the same time. It was helpful to know how to straddle the two places at once. If you closed your eyes to access the null all the time, you were likely to get shot in real life.

He grasped the handle and pulled. Ricky let out a tense squeal. There was no lock on the door. The designers never imagined anyone would be stupid enough to open an FTL cabinet mid-jump. It opened easily and silently, without so much as a hiccup in the nullspace jump.

Bào looked over his shoulder to see Ricky standing with both fists pressed against her mouth, brow furrowed, as if she expected the cabinet to blow at any second. Bào laughed. The sound deadened as it was sucked into the cabinet like smoke. Then it rippled back out, not so much as a sound but as a feeling that swept through the ship like a burst of invisible radiation. The grunt at the desk giggled behind them.

Ricky put her hands down and stepped toward Bào and the cabinet. The corner of her mouth lifted in a smile.

"What was *that*?" she asked, her cheeks flushing pink. Her voice was also pulled into the cabinet, then rippled back out in a pulse of joyful wonder. The security guard sighed happily at her station.

"It's acting like an amplifier," said Bào, curious if horn did this normally, or if it was only while they were in the null.

The security officer looked up from her station.

"What are you two doing in here?" she asked, suddenly interested.

"Routine maintenance," said Bào, pretending to hold a screwdriver to the side of the cabinet. He twisted his empty hand and lifted a skeptical eyebrow to Ricky. She laughed and the entire crew of the *Kilonova* laughed with her. The officer sat back down with a broad smile on her face.

"Do you think if we made out that everyone on the ship would make out too?" asked Ricky.

Her thought reverberated across the *Kilonova*. Bào slapped the cabinet door shut, but it was too late. In approximately forty weeks there would be six tiny new members of the crew.

"Stop," he said. "Just for one second while I have the door open. Then you can say anything you want."

"Absolutely," said Ricky, miming a zipper across her mouth.

The raw nullspace energy coming out of the horn felt like warm sunlight; comfort and home. All the stiffness in his joints melted away. He felt light and free and young again. In the split-second that he stood and basked in it, Ricky leaned her face over his shoulder and spoke into the box.

"Everyone is dying to buy drinks from Ricky," she whispered.

Bào grunted in frustration and unceremoniously shoved the criosphinx horn onto the shelf next to the unicorn horn. The ship bucked, then surged forward. Bào slammed the door shut. "What are you doing?" he asked incredulously. "It's going to amplify that now."

"Good. I could use the cash," said Ricky. She turned and yelped. The security officer was standing so close behind them that Bào could see the freckles on her cheeks.

"I'm dying," she said. "I need a drink."

"Oh dear," said Bào.

"Stop by the medbay tomorrow ni–" Ricky began. The security officer's eyes bulged. She lunged forward and grabbed the lapels of Ricky's jacket.

"I'm dying. I need a drink now."

Ricky tried to pry the woman's fingers off her, but she only clutched harder in new spots.

"Dying," she croaked. She started trying to climb Ricky in a gangly and awkward dance. Ricky pushed her off and ran for the door. The security officer followed with the fierce determination of a dying woman.

"Kid!" yelled Ricky, getting as far as the hallway before the woman tackled her to the floor. He heard other boots pounding down the hallway as other crew members headed for Ricky, desperate for drinks to save their lives. Bào yanked open the cabinet door and said the first thing he could think of to stop them from hurting her.

"We all love Ricky Tang," he shouted into the raw energy. The thought rippled out across the universe.

"Not better!" shouted Ricky from the hallway. Her voice was muffled as if covered by multiple limbs. "Try again please!"

"Everything is normal," said Bào, trying to project the thought as calmly as he could muster. "There's no need to check the FTL drive."

He shut the door and went into the hallway. A few crew members were helping each other up, bewildered expressions on their faces. A couple apologized to Ricky for something Bào hadn't seen. One of them offered her their cabin number, which she politely declined.

"I told you to watch what you were saying into the drive," said Bào. The ship lurched nauseatingly sideways, but Ricky didn't seem to notice.

"Do you feel that?" asked Bào. "I think it's working."

"Feel what?" she asked. "It always does that. It's normal. Hey, did you get the criosphinx horn into the drive?"

"I did," said Bào.

"Too bad it didn't have any effect," she said. "I really thought it would work. You must be disappointed after all you went through to get it out." She gestured to his hand, which he suddenly noticed was throbbing. "I have some other fantastic sabotage ideas, if you're interested."

The criosphinx horn was working just as intended. Every few seconds, the ship fluttered like an irregular heartbeat and skipped in a random direction that didn't necessarily bring them closer to the Bala planet. It was a one step forward, three steps back kind of motion. It would take them years to reach the Bala planet this way – and with his last thought amplified, no one was even aware of it. He might have to come back here every once in a while to remind everyone that stumbling backward through the null was "normal," but that wasn't difficult. Even so, Bào wasn't quite ready for their little adventure to end.

"What kind of sabotage do you have in mind?" he asked.

By way of answering, Ricky held up an access badge that she'd swiped from one of the crew members who had tackled her.

"I was thinking we should head down to sanitation and see about backing up the entire system. There's nothing that slows down a starship quite like fountains full of crap."

"Sounds lovely," said Bào, taking her arm.

CHAPTER SEVENTEEN
Sink or Swim

Gary raised his hands to show the Sisters of the Supersymmetrical Axion surrounding him that he did not intend to fight. Of course, the weapons trained on his vital areas couldn't possibly kill him, but a bullet into muscle never felt pleasant. He crossed his legs and sat like a child in class. He hoped that the Sisters would sit down and talk instead of opening fire.

The spider-creature folded its long legs under itself, then scooted close enough to Gary that he could feel its respirations on his arm. It looked back and forth between the Sisters and Gary with its eyeless face.

"You need to leave the forest, Gary Cobalt," said the smallest of the Sisters. Despite the formless red jumpsuit and opaque red veil, Gary thought he recognized her.

"Why are the Sisters way out here?" he asked. "Are you investigating the Bala disappearances?"

"Walk back out the way you came. The octomite has determined that you're clean. It won't attack you again," said the Sister. Gary stood up.

"I came here to find out what is happening to the missing Bala. Are you involved?" asked Gary. The Sisters didn't speak. "I'm not leaving until I get answers," said Gary.

A taller Sister stepped into the circle.

"He's not going to cooperate. It's his human side, all curiosity, no sense," said the Sister. "Restrain him. Put him with the others."

"We can't put him with the infected ones," said another Sister.

"Then just put him in the tunnels," replied the tall Sister.

In a flash, Gary's wrists were bound with a silvery rope. He hadn't seen any of the Sisters move, but two of them were now at his side, tugging him to his feet.

"This is not necessary," said Gary, pulling away from them. "We can discuss this reasonably and come to a solution. I'm only here to gather information. Others who come after me will not be as circumspect. There is a centaur gathering an army—"

The rope around his wrists tightened and burned. This was angel hair, capable of tying a creature of any strength indefinitely. Even a centaur would not be able to break it. The Sisters gathered in formation in front of him, scanning the trees for more intruders. They led him to a large tree nearby; wide enough around that three beings would have had to join hands to span it. The bark nearest the ground shimmered and an open doorway appeared. Gary saw a couple of steps down into the blackness beyond. Perhaps a cave of some sort.

One thing Gary had learned after years of humans abducting him, was that he could never to allow his captors to get him to a second location. Especially if those captors were known as the most deadly assassins in the known universe.

He wasn't fast, or particularly strong, but the one advantage he did have was the ability to heal. Walking slowly and compliantly, he dropped his hands out of view of the Sisters and began to fill the air with words.

"You know, I always support your plans. I understand that you have access to information that the rest of us cannot know, and that you make decisions based on that information, but it would be helpful if you could share even the smallest hint of your plans with me so that I could assist you to continue them without interference." Gary droned on, saying anything that came to mind both to distract the Sisters and to mask the sounds of his thumbs breaking. It hurt like hell. He hoped they didn't hear the waver in his voice when the bones crunched.

He wriggled the angel-hair rope until it was wedged tightly against his thumb's lowest knucklebone and yanked with all of his strength, all the while trying to keep his voice steady. He felt a stabbing pain and a pop. The rope slid off his hand. Before it had even come free, the joint was already back in place.

Still talking about cooperation and alliances, Gary moved his hands behind him, hoping the Sisters' veils would obstruct their peripheral vision. He raised his arms behind the heads of the two Sisters flanking him, then simultaneously grabbed their heads and slammed them together. There was a sound like a ceramic plate hitting a wooden table too hard. Both Sisters hit the ground.

Gary took off at a run in the opposite direction, hoping that the handful of seconds he had as a head start he had would be enough. The Sisters were fast and there was no way to know what type of Bala were under those veils. Any one of them might have been able to stop him in his tracks with a magical phrase or turn him to stone with her hair full of snakes.

He heard the whispering patter of soft feet behind him and realized the octomite was giving chase as well. Even though the Sisters were more dangerous, the eyeless creature frightened him more viscerally.

He pounded through the underbrush, back toward the marsh. Hooves were awkward on slippery tile floors, but, here on packed dirt, he was able to run twice as fast as any human. The scratches from the branches that dragged against his arms healed instantly. It seemed possible that he might actually make it out of the forest unscathed.

Something flew through the air with a high-pitched whistle. Gary instinctively ducked his head, but the projectile embedded itself in the back of his right thigh. He went down, rolling through the foliage and coming to a stop against a tree. The octomite caught up with him and wrapped its long fingers around his legs. Gary kicked out and sent the octomite whimpering back to the Sisters. The bullet in his leg pinged against the root of the tree as it fell out of his flesh.

Gary got up and ran again. Two more bullets hit him in the back. For a moment it was hard to breathe. He coughed up a mouthful of frothy fluid. The bullets pushed out of his back, but more slowly than the leg wound.

He burst out of the forest into the clearing near the marsh. It was too early yet for Kaapo to return and the water stretched to the visible horizon in either direction. There was no going around it unless he wanted to take an hours-long detour. With only the slightest hesitation, Gary waded in.

The Sisters came out of the trees a moment later. They stopped at the edge of the marsh, watching him sink into the muddy ground.

At first, it wasn't painful as the water lapped at his nerve-free hooves. That changed when the acidic water inched up to his knees, burning away his skin in sheets. A Sister called out to him.

"Gary, this is ridiculous. Come back. We only want to–"

"Kidnap me, like you did the others," said Gary through gritted teeth. He knew he was being ridiculous but he still couldn't stop. The Sisters were not going to kill him. If they'd wanted it, he'd be dead already. He could just turn around and go back. But also, he couldn't. He was back on Copernica Citadel, being marched onto a Reason ship for his first stint in captivity. He was being loaded into a makeshift cell in his own ship, where humans would torture him for horn. He was walking to the Quag on the first day, knowing that every moment from here on out would be agony. If there was one thing he was never going to let happen again it was to be held prisoner against his will. Every step took him further from going down that road again. He knew it made no sense, but he just had to keep walking.

"You're going to dissolve yourself in that water," yelled the Sister. "Get back here and I'll explain. We're protecting the village from the invaders."

Gary opened his mouth to answer. The water slapped against his thighs, eating through his trousers and stripping off the top few layers of skin. The words died in his throat.

"Gary, stop," called the smallest Sister. "We need you."

They should have thought of that before backing him into a corner. He wasn't sure how far he could make it into the marsh. Certainly not all the way back to the village. Already, his hooves were wearing away enough that he could feel the acid water eating into the connective tissue and tendons underneath.

The Sisters called out to him a few more times, but he couldn't hear the words over the whooshing of blood in his ears. He'd been imprisoned, tortured, shot, had broken bones and been frozen nearly to death in the cold vacuum of space, but this was by far the most intense and lasting pain he had ever experienced in his lengthy unicorn life.

As his panic fell away and logic rushed in to fill the space, Gary scanned the skies, looking for an angel or any other Bala who could lift him out of the water. The airways over the marsh were clear. No one ever headed toward the forest and no one was idiotic enough to be out on the marsh. There was no way to call for help.

Eventually the sounds of the Sisters fell away and there was nothing to hear but the slapping of the water against his legs. In places, the muddy bottom dropped down, and he sank lower for a few steps, burning his torso and even once his arms. When he stepped out of the low spots, they healed, only to repeat the process over and over in an excruciating cycle. It was difficult to kill a unicorn but Gary thought he might have possibly found a way to do it.

Eventually, when he was far out into the marsh, the acid water ate through enough of his leg muscles that his steps began to falter. He stumbled along, trying not to drop his hands into the water. When it became hard to even lift his legs, he knew it would not be long before he fell headlong into the marsh without the ability to lift himself out again.

He stopped walking and stood still, listening to the lapping of the water. He had run out of ideas. It was getting difficult to think at all. He prayed to Unamip that someone would find what remained of his body and give him a proper Bala burial.

Through a haze of pain, it occurred to him that Unamip was probably just a few kilometers away, watching all of this. He wondered how a unicorn he had considered a friend could allow this and all those other atrocities to happen. He doubted that Unamip was really a god at all.

A new flare of pain burned in his midsection. His legs, unable to move, had sunk deep into the mud at the bottom of the marsh. There was no longer enough muscle tissue left on his bones to pull them out. He thought about how stupid it was to come all this way, survive so many hardships, just to dissolve into goo in a marsh. There would be no trace of him for anyone to find.

His legs wobbled. In a moment he would fall and the water would eat away at his brain, erasing any trace of the Gary Cobalt who used to be. He wondered if his consciousness would live on in the water. He swayed, hoping at least that the end would come fast.

Two strong hands reached under his armpits and dragged him up and out of the marsh. He hit the deck of Kaapo's raft with a thud.

"You are an idiot," she said, kneeling next to him. He raised his head enough to see that his lower half had been mostly dissolved away. His legs were skeletal, his pelvis bones poked through a gelatinous shroud of flesh. Up on his stomach, he could see organs pulsating beneath transparent gel. He lay back on the logs.

"You weren't supposed to be here yet," he panted.

"I left early," she said. "Unamip told me to come."

"Tell him I said thanks," said Gary, before the world went black.

Gary awoke in a sunlit room to the sound of pounding hooves. For a moment, he thought he was a child back in his treehouse on the *Jaggery* while his father stomped angrily below, demanding that he come down. Little Gary had learned early on that full unicorns couldn't climb trees.

He opened his eyes and although the room was made of logs, they were pink and fresh and did not smell like pine. He was in the hospital, not the tree house.

This part of the hospital was the clinical wing, where injured beings came to recover. Bala came in with fingers pinched between logs, broken bones, and food poisonings from trying new berries and foliage. With a room of his own, Gary was probably the most serious case on the ward – unless there was someone else with more than half of their body eaten away.

The hospital was a place he had avoided since arriving on their new planet. The front meeting rooms were full of tearful Bala telling their stories of mistreatment at the hands of the Reason in group therapy sessions. With care and time, many of these Bala would be able to create a new life here. Some of those in recovery had been given small jobs around the building, like the kitchen spirit who was in charge of hulling grain for the patients to eat.

Further back in the building were those whose depth of trauma meant a longer treatment plan. Some sat quietly, not reacting to anything happening in the present. Some screamed and yelled in their locked rooms. Others fought invisible enemies who wore the Reason spheres and tears.

A couple of the patients had recently complained of hearing voices. They'd been experiencing whispers that offered them instructions on how to build bits of technology out of local materials. As intriguing as that was, the medical staff had chalked it up to group delusion and everyone missing their phones.

As fraught as it was in the hospital, the workers attempted to create a joyful atmosphere. The aides and healers made every effort to remember that their work was necessary and valued. Their smiles had a tinge of sadness, but they embraced each other frequently and with genuine comfort in their touch.

Gary sat up in his bed, pulling back the covers to see the damage his walk through the marsh had wrought. His legs were not dressed – infection was not a concern for him – but they had been slathered with some sort of greasy ointment. Probably just to make the doctors feel like they were doing something useful. The muscle was growing back from the top of his legs down. From his calves, he was all bones until his hooves, which were completely gone.

"Feeling better?" asked a pile of blankets on a chair in the corner. Boges poked her head out of the top, russet hair sticking up every which way.

"Alive, at least," he said. She dropped out of the chair as if to leave.

"You don't have to go," he said.

"I have things to do," she replied, heading through the door where he could not follow.

There was something going on with Boges. A secretiveness that she had never displayed in all her years working with him on the *Jaggery*. She'd avoided him for weeks as if she was upset with him, then turned up at his bedside like she had in the past. It troubled him.

A persistent itch crept up his thighs where the skin and muscle were new. He reached down to scratch and got a handful of viscous grease that he wiped on the bedding.

A little elf child stepped into the room holding a bowl of something steaming.

"Boges said you were awake. Do you want to eat?" she asked.

"Thank you," he replied, reaching for it. She saw his slimy hands.

"I was told to tell you not to touch that," she said.

"I'm a terrible patient," he said. She smiled at him.

"Me too."

"Oh, I thought you were the doctor."

She giggled.

"No, I'm Clemenwine," she said.

"Thank you for the soup, Doctor Clemenwine," said Gary.

She laughed again and the clouds parted outside of his window, pinkening the room with the rosy sunshine. All those years under human rule, he'd missed living daily life among the Bala.

There were unicorns nearby. Gary could smell their sweat and hear hooves pounding on the walls. These were the ones who had been strapped into Reason ships for horn harvesting, sometimes for decades.

Many of these unicorns he had known in his childhood. He had seen them strong and fit. Now their flanks were rubbed bare and hairless by tight harnesses. Manes were pulled out so that they did not get tangled and matted. Skins were marked with burns, ears clipped, and horn dug so deep that though the crater in the skull grew back, the brain matter that re-formed was bare of memories and higher functions.

They thrashed in their rooms, sometimes forming words and names out of muscle memory, not truly knowing what they were saying. Hearing them made Gary feel like a tightly-coiled spring. He'd been in their position, left in chains and filth as humans dug knives into his head to scrape out the valuable bits of him. One small slip of the knife and he would have been in their rooms, flinging himself against the walls and dripping spittle onto the floor. Being near them felt too close, as if that past could still creep up and catch him.

It was at these times that his mind went to dark places. He wondered if perhaps he had gotten it entirely wrong – maybe humans were the rightful heirs to the universe, a conquering race strong and invasive enough to take over several planets in just one hundred years. Maybe Gary was wrong about kindness being the most important thing. From there it was a small leap to giving up entirely.

Outside, dutiful Bala were following his orders to rebuild their world, figuring out how to construct new lives out of the ruins of their old ones. It seemed pointless, all this wrangling of divergent goals, all this work for a race that the Pymmie hadn't bothered to protect. Humans were on the way. This time, he was sure the Pymmie weren't going to step in.

The thought of fighting a hundred years of war all over again exhausted him. If humans were going to spread like a virus unchecked, he couldn't stop them. He certainly hadn't the last time.

This was why Gary never came into this building. It always led to dark thoughts – a deep well from which there was no escape. He'd managed to stave it off through busywork in the village, but laying here with nothing to distract him, the heaviness settled over him like a shroud. He was too exhausted to even eat the soup that Clemenwine had brought. It sat on the bedside table, growing cold.

He didn't make a conscious decision to drop into the null but his mind went there anyway. He saw all of the Bala around him, most gathered in the town, doing their evening tasks. They were bright lights in a soupy sea of color from the living things on the surface. It was hard to pick out individual people based on color and feel alone, but a few were obvious. There was Horm the centaur, pulsing in muted dark red on the outskirts of town. He saw his father, shining like a beacon at the top of the unicorns' mountain.

He pushed his awareness further out. There were the stoneships, playing a game of tag around the third moon in the system. Something caught his mind's eye beyond the third moon. A gathering of four bright lights gathered in the darkness, hopping in random patterns throughout the null.

Those were necromancers and they were on the Reason ship, which was far closer than he expected it to be. It would arrive in hours, not weeks. How had they come this close so quickly?

He zoomed in as close as he could, trying to glean the identities of the four necromancers. This ship had only three the last time he checked. The addition of a fourth had somehow coincided with their jump in speed. There were the two he'd seen earlier – mediocre and unremarkable. He saw Bào's energy, solid and strong, but not reaching out far past himself. He was experienced enough to know how to use his abilities efficiently.

That fourth pattern was not one he'd encountered before. Their energy spun around them in wide rings, smashing into everything around it and grappling with. This necromancer's energy fought with everything around it, untrained and unharmonious. Battling constantly, but never gaining ground. He suddenly knew who it was.

It was Jenny Perata.

What had weeks ago been a slight glow was now a roiling mass of power. She'd learned to gather massive quantities of nullspace energy but she wasn't directing it with any sort of precision. This was the danger of necromancers discovering their true natures late in life. They found themselves with tremendous power and no skills to use it.

There was a small part of him that was relieved to see her alive, even though the destruction she was causing was catastrophic. It looked like she was attempting to disable the ship entirely. She was going to tear it apart.

A voice startled Gary out of the null. A cave troll stood at the foot of his bed. He wore the rough apron woven out of dried grass that signified a hospital worker. It was stained with fluids in the colors of several Bala bloods. Gary shivered.

"I said, show me," barked the troll.

"Sorry. I didn't hear you," said Gary.

"You were in the null and I want to know what you see," said the troll. "Are they suffering? Are they dying?"

"Who?"

"The humans." The troll let the words drip with hatred.

"I don't know," said Gary. As much as it would satisfy the troll to know the humans were killing each other over basic needs, it wouldn't help anything.

"Bah. Useless."

"Are you looking for someone?"

"No. I'm looking for the human race to go extinct." The troll whirled back out of the room, smacking into the door frame on the way out. Gary saw bare and weeping patches where his thick hide had been stripped away for making decorative purses for wealthy humans.

"I could help you," said Gary. The troll turned around, bending over to fit in the doorway.

"How could you help me?" asked the troll, gesturing toward Gary's disintegrated legs.

"My blood," said Gary, keenly aware that it was already working overtime trying to grow him half a body. Nonetheless, he felt the

216

need to offer.

"I would be foolish not to accept," said the troll. He handed Gary a knife from his tool belt. Gary ran it down his palm. It stung, but he'd done this enough in his lifetime that it was more of an annoyance than truly painful.

Silver blood welled in his cupped hand. The troll moved closer and Gary smeared it onto the stripped area. It sank into his flesh and spread with a shimmery glow. The troll caught his breath and tilted back his head.

It always secretly pleased Gary to see the reaction that various creatures had to the healing properties of his blood. Some of them felt a sting, some felt euphoria, and some flat-out got high. The troll seemed to be trending in that direction. His breath came fast and hard as the blood worked through his limbs. Gary wiped the last of what was in his hand on the spot. His cut had already healed. He sheathed the knife and handed it back to the troll.

The troll shuddered for a moment, then shook out his matted hair and let out a single loud laugh. It echoed throughout the building.

"That is amazing. I cannot thank you enough for such a precious gift," said the troll, smiling wide.

Not all things in the universe could be fixed in an instant, but when they could it made Gary feel incredibly satisfied. A light appeared in the darkness of his world.

He clapped his hand on the troll's arm. "At your service," he said. "If there are others who need assistance, bring then to me."

"You're the one who's supposed to be healing," said Kaapo leaning in the doorway.

The troll excused himself and slid past her.

"Thank you for pulling me out," said Gary. "I would not have survived if you hadn't come back for me."

"Thank Unamip," she said. "He told me to go back for you. Anyway, your father was here last night but he went back up to your place for meetings. He said he'll be back later this morning."

Gary pushed himself to the edge of the bed.

"Can you help me get back to the fortress? I don't need to be hospitalized," he said.

"Gary, no. Just stay here until you have legs again."

"I have a message for my father," he said.

"I'll deliver it," said Kaapo. "Angels are great at sharing news. I can even find a horn to herald it."

"Go as fast as you can, and speak to no one on the way. Tell my father the humans have arrived."

CHAPTER EIGHTEEN
Five Unicorn Flush

Jenny decided that having Kamis inside her head was really not all that bad. He wasn't intrusive and didn't interrupt or attempt to take over her body, which was better than some girlfriends she'd had. In some cases, he was actually kind of helpful. Like when she miscounted rations while doing a quick inventory and he supplied her with the correct numbers.

You aren't very careful, he said.

"Nope," she agreed. "Mary, how many ships are in the cargo hold?" she asked.

"Seventeen," replied the ship.

"Why would they bother capturing a bunch of small ships? No one has horn," she asked out loud to both her ship's AI and her elf ghost parasite, whoever felt like answering first.

"I don't know," said Mary. "They already have a better ship."

The Reason is in an information-and-resource-gathering phase before their full-on assault on the Bala. If they divide up their horn and put necromancers onto these ships, all of them will be able to navigate to the Bala and attack, said Kamis.

At the mention of necromancers, Jenny's mind flashed to an image of Bào sealed in his protective ball, floating off into openspace. She regretted having let him go while she was under attack. Given the state of the Reason these days, she wasn't sure whether to hope that had survived or perished.

That memory is of Bào Zhú, said Kamis. *One of the great*

necromancers of all time. I hope, for your sake, that you did not allow him to float away into openspace like your memory shows.

"I might have," said Jenny. "It wasn't as if I had a choice. It was him or Gary."

Bào will not forget that choice, said Kamis.

"Great. Just what I need. More beings tagging me with a death wish," said Jenny. Her mind flashed on Gary, just for a second.

You have a complex relationship with Gary Cobalt, said Kamis.

"Yeah," she said.

It speaks well of you, that you're able to hold two competing thoughts in your head at the same time and function in light of both of them. Most humans are dedicated to a binary, beings must be black or white, male or female, when we know that beings are fluid and nuanced, filled with contradictions and complexities. That is our beauty and we must work to accommodate every being within the spectrum of life, said Kamis.

Jenny nodded. Gary was indeed not just one thing or another.

"What did the Reason take from our ship?" Jenny asked Mary.

"They took the unicorn horn from the drive and a copy of my logs. They noted how much food and water was in storage, but left both in place for the moment."

They're assembling resources for a battle, said Kamis.

"Agreed," said Jenny.

"I'm sorry, what are you agreeing with?" asked Mary.

"I'm talking to Kamis," said Jenny.

"Great," said Mary flatly.

"Don't be jealous," said Jenny.

"I just want you to remember that I kept you company for six weeks before Kamis came on board and also I didn't haunt you like a ghost and stalk you around the ship trying to take over your body," complained Mary.

"Just because you want a body and Kamis got one first, don't be mad at him," replied Jenny.

Mary didn't speak to her for nearly ten minutes after that. Jenny used the quiet time think about how to get her piece of horn back and disable the *Kilonova*. Now that she was getting better at tracking, she didn't need a Reason necromancer to direct her toward the Bala. Thankfully, her piece of horn probably wasn't in their FTL drive yet. Only an idiot would open a drive cabinet while it was powered up.

You could use your necromancer abilities to disable the ship, said Kamis. *You wouldn't even need to be near the FTL drive. You could do it from quite far away.*

"That's not in my skillset," said Jenny.

You forget that I am living inside your entire being, said Kamis. *I feel every part of you, especially the parts that can use nullspace energy. Ever since we dropped into the null, your cells have been humming with power.*

Jenny had to admit that she felt better in nullspace, stronger and more confident. She did things in here that she would never contemplate in openspace.

"If I can break their external navigational beacon, it will cause them to drop out of FTL to fix it," she said. "Then I can get the horn out of their drive too. With that much fuel, I can definitely find Kaila.

But they already have the location of the Bala planet, said Kamis. *They'll find it eventually.*

"No," said Jenny. "The necromancers give them a general heading, but it's the navigational beacon that coordinates the jumps through nullspace into forward motion. Without it, the ship just hops around in a random pattern. On stoneships the ship itself sets the path by talking to the null. On Reason ships the two can't communicate, so the ship has to do it with massive computers that compile data in real time via the beacon and determine where the next jump should take them. They only know the next few jumps, not the final destination."

You know a lot about this, said Kamis.

"As a captain, it was my job to know a lot about this," replied Jenny. "Otherwise people die."

This will be a good test of your precision with nullspace energy, said

Kamis. *You're simply going to reach outside of the Kilonova and pluck off the beacon.*

"I don't know how to do that," said Jenny.

I'll show you.

"Just tell me."

Kamis did an elvish eye roll, which was just like a regular eye roll but above sharper cheekbones.

Grab the energy and use it as an extension of your reach. As if you were locked inside of a larger version of yourself that mimicked your every motion, said Kamis.

"Like an energy mecha," said Jenny.

Exactly.

It sounded so simple. No one had ever explained necromancy in terms that made sense before. She'd always heard of concentration and being one with the world. The only thing Jenny wanted to be one with right now was her missing wife. Using nullspace energy as a giant invisible mecha to extend her reach and strengthen her grasp sounded bloody freaking awesome.

"I get it," she said. "Mary, can you tap into the *Kilonova's* external camera feeds?"

"Working, Captain," said Mary. She was still angry.

The viewscreen lit up with a picture of the hazy expanse of nullspace, then flickered to a different view that showed the *Kilonova* transiting through it.

"Forward camera down near the lower decks," said Jenny.

"Yes, ma'am," said Mary.

"Stop it," said Jenny.

"Stop what, Captain? I'm merely following your orders," said Mary in a monotone.

I like her better this way, said Kamis.

The viewscreen flicked to the correct feed. Jenny saw the navigational beacon pointed down and away from the bottom deck of the ship – just a small antenna-like protrusion.

Very little force, said Kamis. *You merely need to pop the beacon off. Put a minimal amount pressure onto the joint between the ship and the mounting. Once you get a feel for the right amount of pressure to use, wrench them apart.*

Jenny let her fingers dangle by her side. She splayed her fingers, like she'd seen other necromancers do. It did help her get a feel for the currents of energy that were flowing past, but it felt awkward and ridiculous. She imagined an arm made of energy extending from hers, reaching out toward the beacon at the bottom of the ship. She wrapped the invisible hands of her energy mecha around the beacon.

Good. Now gently pull, said Kamis.

Jenny hesitated.

"This feels silly. I don't think it'll do anything," she said.

Just try. If it does nothing, we can attempt something else, said Kamis.

"All right," said Jenny with skepticism.

Pull, said Kamis.

Jenny pulled and the bottom deck of the *Kilonova* came off. Most of it detached in a single large chunk. Dozens of smaller bits burst outward from the sudden release of pressure. Debris soared out into the null and bodies flew past the camera.

"Oh my gods," said Jenny, clapping her hands over her mouth.

Alarms sounded all around her. Pounding boots and shouting voices rang out in the cargo hold surrounding the *Stagecoach Mary*. She felt the ship drop out of nullspace as the energy around her was suddenly a fraction of what it was before.

"I didn't mean to—" said Jenny through her fingers.

That was not what I.... said Kamis, trailing off.

"I did what you said. I did exactly what you bloody well told me to do," said Jenny.

Kamis was at a loss for words, but Mary wasn't.

"Jenny, this was your first time attempting to use telekinesis. Of course you had no idea how much energy to use. Kamis should have been more careful. He should have let you do a few noncritical tests first. If it's anyone's fault, it's his," said Mary. "And also, all of the people who were sucked out of the ship were participants in the Bala genocide, so don't feel too bad about murdering them."

"Thanks," said Jenny, feeling a weight in the pit of her stomach as big as a stoneship. "You always know just what to say."

"I told you, I'm good with people," replied Mary.

I wasn't aware that you would be able to do that, said Kamis. *I thought that—*

"Shut up," Jenny snapped. "I don't want to hear from you for at least an hour."

Kamis, to his credit, stopped talking. She still felt him there, watching. And she could tell he was upset as well, but at least he was quiet.

On the monitor, Jenny watched the *Kilonova's* crew gather up debris and bodies from around their ship. She didn't recognize the star groupings in this part of the universe. It made her feel untethered and adrift. But watching the cleanup crew methodically tether in shrapnel and corpses was soothing.

The way the bottom half of the ship had simply sheared off, it didn't look like a bomb. It appeared more like a structural defect than a sabotage. It pained her that she'd gotten the *Kilonova* to drop out of nullspace like she wanted, but she had no viable way of getting to her horn without being seen. The ship was likely crawling with all three shifts full of personnel.

"Jenny, now is the time for you to go," said Mary urgently. "Soldiers were hurt in the accident. Some of them have leg injuries."

"Which means they'll be in temporary wheelchairs. God, I love you, Mary," said Jenny, wheeling over to the storage cabinet where she had a spare Reason uniform tucked away for times such as these. It was old, and would look out of date in any cursory inspection, but no one would be doing a uniform check at a time like this. She slid her jumpsuit off and made the uniform look as trim as possible. All the proper pleats and placements came right back to her fingers as if she'd never stopped wearing this jacket. She left the hat behind – it was embroidered with a captain's insignia.

She wouldn't be able to pass for the captain of the *Kilonova*, no matter what they looked like.

Jenny wasn't sure where they would store her piece of unicorn horn, but she knew that on older models of this same type of Reason ship there was an armored vault for the precious fuel near the engine room. That was the most logical place to start looking.

She hit the console to open Mary's cargo hold. The door hissed open, then stopped with less than a meter's clearance. She tried again. The door banged on something outside and then got stuck.

"Mary, what's going on?" asked Jenny.

"There is one small detail," said Mary.

"What?" asked Jenny.

"I can't lower my loading ramp. There's a skimmer parked right up next to us and I can only get it to open a few inches wide," she said.

"Bloody hell," said Jenny.

The only other exit was two floors under her, down a ladder, and through a hatch in the bottom of the ship. As a rule, the Reason didn't build their ships to be wheelchair accessible.

She could get out of the hatch but her chair wouldn't fit. She couldn't very well crawl her way through the *Kilonova*. Her chair would fit through the cargo bay door opening, as long as it was folded, but she couldn't get up that high to push it through the opening.

She sensed Kamis watching her work out the logic puzzle of mobility.

"Any ideas?" she asked him.

"Working on it," said Mary.

We could retract a landing strut and let your ship fall to the side so that the cargo door is next to the ground, said Kamis. *The Reason will assume it fell in the accident.*

"That's a plan so incredibly ridiculous, it sounds like one of mine," said Jenny. "I like it."

"What does Kamis say?" asked Mary.

"He wants to retract one of your legs and let you fall over so I can get out," said Jenny.

Mary made a noise like a gasp.

"That is a terrible idea. Do you know how many sensitive instruments and cameras I have on my hull?" she asked.

"Cool it," said Jenny. "I'm not going to toss you over. But I appreciate Kamis' out of the box thinking. We need more of that around here."

"We need less of that around here," said Mary. "I found a better option anyway."

"Let's hear it," said Jenny.

"There's a sealed access panel in the hull adjacent to the server room. That's how they got my computers in place. It's big enough for you and a wheelchair. And it's even on this level," said Mary.

"I like it," said Jenny. "Tell me where to go."

"Maintenance room two," said Mary. Jenny wheeled out of the cargo hold toward a small room across the hall. She'd never had a reason to come in here. Mary took care of everything seamlessly on her own. It was big enough for her chair. Barely. The sides of her wheels scraped along the shelves filled with strapped down spare parts.

"Take the drill," said Mary.

Jenny found an industrial screwdriver hooked to the wall; powerful enough to take a panel off the exterior of the ship.

At the back of the room was a door that led to a cold, dark room stacked floor to ceiling with computers whirring and flashing lights in a variety of colors.

"Hi, Mary," said Jenny, patting a metal box.

"I'm cute, aren't I?" asked Mary.

Jenny wheeled to the outer wall of the room. Just like Mary had said, there was an access panel to the outside. She got to unscrewing.

"You'll still be far above the ground when you get out, but there's the skimmer next to us that you can aim to land on," said Mary. "It's closer than the ground."

Jenny pulled the panel off and set it down. There was a second outer panel that also had to be removed. She was already starting to sweat under her heavy jacket.

When the last screw was out, the panel clattered to the floor outside. Jenny looked out at the *Kilonova's* hold. No personnel were left in the room, but ships littered the floor. It was a long way down.

Jenny pulled herself up into the opening and sat between the inner and outer hulls. She lifted her chair and folded it in one practiced motion. She grabbed a roll of cable off the wall and tied it around the armrests. She heaved it through the opening and lowered it down to the floor. It was her turn.

She grabbed a second cable and tied it around a server shelf that was bolted to the floor. She leaned back out of the door as if she was going to rappel down the side of the ship.

Please be careful, a fall from that height would be disastrous. Take care, said Kamis.

"I always take care," said Jenny. She let the cable slip through her fingers. The plastic coating on the cable slipped through her fingers faster than she'd intended. It was sort of a controlled fall instead of a climb, but there was no time to worry about it.

She used her shoulder to shove away from the *Stagecoach Mary*. She slipped faster. She could do this, sure, but it wasn't any type of easy. She dropped a few meters and slammed onto the two-person skimmer parked next to hers.

The skimmer was all sexy angles and curves and she slid down it another five meters. She hit the metal floor with a grunt.

"Brilliant," said Mary in her ear.

Well done, said Kamis.

"And you wanted to tip the ship over," said Jenny, her chest heaving.

She untied her chair, unfolded the hinges, and pulled herself into it. She straightened her jacket, wiped the sweat out of her eyes, and rolled to the exit – where she found five stairs up to the hallway. Navigating the world in a chair meant doing everything on the hardest difficulty setting.

"There's a ramp at the other door," said Mary. Jenny rolled that way. Of course, the ramp was for rolling cargo. Because why would we ever give a thought to accessibility on a ship full of disabled vets? Bloody Reason.

She rolled into the hallway, holding herself up in an officer's erect posture. Her back twinged where the spray skin pulled at her burns.

People ran down the hallway, bumping her chair as they passed. Some of them had put their uniforms on. Others still wore the soft jumpsuits they slept in.

She tapped a touchscreen on the wall, pretending to check the status updates coming in from all over the ship. In reality she was looking at the map. The engine room was two floors down from here. Of course.

Lights above stairwell doors glowed red, indicating that there was no atmosphere beyond. It would take a moment for the airtight bulkhead doors to come down and seal the bottom floors where the breach was located. The elevators were the same. She'd need to wait until the shafts were airtight again before they came online.

She tapped through real-time updates until she found a working elevator. All the way aft. About as far from the engine room as you could go. She cursed her terrible aim with nullspace energy and rolled toward the back of the ship. At least it was all flat.

She reached the elevator with a green light above it. A couple of the *Kilonova's* personnel were waiting there already. The elevator pinged and opened. It was cold and smelled like a hot frying pan. She rolled in among them and tapped the panel for the engine room.

"That's an interesting uniform... sir," said an airman on her right, eyeing her up. Jenny knew how to deflect his suspicion.

"Don't be a wanker. I was in my lover's quarters, you know, getting laid, and I just grabbed what I could find in a hurry," she said. "An old uniform at the back of the closet."

"Who's your lover?" asked the other airman.

"The commander," she said, guessing that whoever held the second in command spot was fair game. The boys raised their eyebrows and gave her some kind of unreadable look. Thankfully, the door opened at that moment and she escaped further scrutiny.

Without the proper credentials to get inside, she waited outside the engine room, thinking. In the end she decided to take the most direct route. She knocked.

The security officer who opened the door was looking at eye level, so she missed the patu coming at her temple until it was too late. She fell face-first into Jenny's lap with a grunt. Jenny pushed into the room, dragging the officer along with her and shutting the door.

It was the same engine room design as the other Reason ships she'd been on. Hand-carved FTL cabinet mounted on the wall and sublight engines laid out behind it. The FTL was off but she could still catch the barely-perceptible smell of cooking meat pies. That wave of nostalgia for home and family always lingered around unicorn horn – and it was slightly different every time. As if burning through the horn released the memories of the unicorn who had grown it.

She opened the cabinet. There were two pieces of bone-like material on the shelf inside. One, a traditional pearlescent unicorn horn, the other a dull brown chunk of chitin as thick around as a finger.

She grabbed both the unicorn horn and the foreign object and held them both.

"This is all wrong," she said.

Don't– began Kamis.

"It's fine. The drive is off," she said, tucking them deep into her jacket pocket.

But you are not an ordinary human, said Kamis. *You are coursing will nullspace energy. The horn will amplify your thoughts regardless.*

Jenny spun her chair and came face to face with a frowning security officer.

"At ease, lieutenant," snapped Jenny, trying to roll past.

"This is all wrong," said the security officer, grabbing Jenny by the wrist and dragging her and the chair toward the door.

"You're under arrest for tampering with an FTL drive," said the security officer, pulling plastic ties from her belt. "And for impersonating an officer," she added, looking down at Jenny's poor excuse for a modern Reason uniform.

Before Jenny could pull out her patu, or even get her hands around this woman's neck, both of her wrists were tied behind her back, tight enough to bite into the spray skin.

The security officer pushed her down the chaotic hallways. Crew members shouted orders and ran past with repair equipment. Injured people helped more gravely injured people toward the medbay. Young cadets gathered in doorways, whispering to each other and crying. She felt a pang in her chest because she'd caused this.

As the barred door clanged shut, Jenny tucked herself into a corner of the brig. They'd confiscated her chair so she was stuck here until they decided to give it back.

I want to discuss what happened in nullspace, said Kamis.

"I don't want to talk about it," said Jenny, pulling her legs up one by one so that they were level on the bench.

I'm going to insist. What happened was an unfortunate accident. You didn't intend to tear the ship apart. I could feel that you were only trying dislodge the navigational beacon. I know you didn't intend for anyone to be hurt or killed.

"Thanks," she said.

It's common for new necromancers to have poor aim. But that's not what I want to talk to you about. When you went to dislodge that beacon, I told you to use the smallest amount of force at your disposal. And I know, from inside here, that you did. You tore this ship in pieces and it was a tiny fraction of the energy you were able to gather, said Kamis.

"Yep," said Jenny, trying to make it clear that she did not care and that this conversation was having no effect on her whatsoever, no matter how much tension he felt inside of her body.

What I'm saying is that you are able to process and utilize the same amount of nullspace energy that a necromancer who has studied for decades would be able to harness. You need to be extremely careful how you use your abilities. In fact, it would probably be wise for you to avoid using them altogether until we can meet up with the Bala and find an experienced trainer who could show you how not to end up with accidents like those, said Kamis.

"Told you so," Jenny mumbled, leaning her head back against the wall.

She had to pee but, at that moment, she wasn't feeling particularly like doing it in front of Kamis. Besides, Reason toilets never quite worked right in space.

I'm sure you have the best of intentions, but even the most basic of manipulations could ripple out and cause injuries to people around you, he continued.

Jenny suddenly sat up. "I heard you the first time," she said. "And for the record, it was your idea for me to use my powers, so don't pin that on me. I told you numerous times that I had no idea what I was doing and you assured me you had it handled."

I didn't. I'm sorry, said Kamis, and she felt his regret as keenly as her own.

CHAPTER NINETEEN
A Banner Day

As the sun hit its zenith and the sky burned crimson, Gary wobbled his way from the hospital to the central square of the village. His legs had completely regrown overnight but the muscles were still weak and stringy. Kaapo held his arm on one side for most of the walk, but let go as they approached the place where everyone had gathered. The circle of Bala opened for him.

"…it is imperative that we strike first, before the humans are able to locate our settlement and target it." Findae had been in the square for the last hour, trying to sway the population toward activating his orbital defense weapon. Most of them nodded along in favor, but there were a few holdouts among the more influential Bala.

In particular, the angels were not in favor of killing anyone. And along with them went the fairies and most of the elves. The common folk – like faun, pixies, and house spirits – were ready to blow the humans out of the sky. The dwarves were suspiciously absent.

"We have time to take considered action," Gary said, facing his father. "There's no need to fire on their ship until they make their intentions clear. They've done nothing aggressive so far." Gary struggled to stand on his own without falling over.

"Are you planning to negotiate with your captors? Tell me, what did you get in exchange for your freedom last time?" asked Findae.

It was a fair question, but beside the point.

"If we don't want to become the same as the humans, we cannot be as cruel as they are," said one of the angels. "We must take the high road."

"Look where the high road led us last time," said a faun whose horns had been shaved down to nubs. Unlike unicorn horn, those would never grow back. "Blow them up."

"Turn the other cheek," replied an angel.

"We already have," said Kaapo, turning her face so the splash scars from the marsh were visible to the angels. "Every time we play fair, they break the rules and win. It's time for us to start breaking the rules too."

The crowd cheered and the angels conferred with each other in furtive whispers.

"Sorry," Kaapo said to Gary. "I'm not on your side."

It didn't seem like a lot of the Bala were.

"There are people I know on that ship," he said, in a last-ditch effort to get her to reconsider. "Good people like Bào Zhú, who fought for the Bala at Copernica Citadel."

"There is no one I care about on that ship," said Kaapo. The Bala around her voiced their agreement. He knew that being a leader was not about getting people to like you but he didn't seem to have the ability to sway anyone to his cause. All those times his father had exhorted him to step up and lead – perhaps he simply wasn't meant to be a leader at all.

"Let's put it to a vote," said Findae, because it was obvious that he had the numbers to win. "All in favor of making a first strike against the Reason?"

Hands, paws, tentacles, and other limbs went into the air. Even a few of the angels put up their graceful arms. It was clear that nearly everyone was in favor of destroying the humans. Findae didn't bother to hide his satisfaction.

"Then it's settled, I'll head into orbit immediately and hit them as soon as they drop out of the null," he said, heading back up the unicorn's mountain. Gary stepped in front of him.

"If you're going blow up the *Kilonova*, at least allow me to go up with you," said Gary.

"You'll try to stop us," said Findae. "Know that I am resolute. I have the will of the Bala behind me."

"Then it won't matter if I'm there. I won't be able to convince you otherwise, and I certainly can't overpower you," said Gary.

Findae glanced down at his son's gaunt new legs. Gary saw a flash of concern that disappeared after a moment. "Fine. You can come. But don't touch anything and don't try to intervene," said Findae. He raised his head and let out a whinny that echoed across the village. One of the pixies peed on the ground in a shower of sparkles.

Five stoneships soared down to the planet's surface. They were too big to hover over the settlement all at once, so they stayed offshore, waiting for their turn to pick up their Bala crews. Stoneships were wild and unpredictable on their own. It took the harmonizing songs of the dwarves to guide them into battle.

The *Jaggery* was the last ship to arrive on land. It edged close to where Gary and Findae stood and spun on its axis to show everyone all of its sides, showing off for the gathered audience. The cargo bay door opened. What had once been a utilitarian space with cargo tie-downs was now a bright and airy vestibule hung with fabric banners for each of the unicorn houses. They swayed in the breeze, calling attention to the plush velvet embroidered with silver threads. These banners had been in storage on the *Jaggery* for decades, it was exhilarating to see them in place again.

The villagers were also delighted to see a small remnant of Bala history that had been salvaged from human rule. They pointed at crests for long-dead unicorn families, as well as houses for which their clans had once been aligned with – which was of course the entire point of hanging the banners in the main entrance to the ship. Findae was no fool.

The display was comforting, but it was also very old fashioned and a touch jingoistic. The era of unicorns had passed and perhaps it was time to allow another race to step up and lead the Bala.

Boges waited for them inside of the *Jaggery*. She was freshly washed with hair and beard braided.

"Boges, it's good to see you," said Gary. She nodded, but did not meet his eyes. He still didn't understand why Boges had frozen him out.

"Is everything in place?" asked Findae.

"It is," said Boges.

"Then let's get underway." Findae padded through the ship's lush undergrowth toward the cockpit. The dwarves had reversed all of the modifications the humans had made to their stoneships. It smelled good; like rich dark soil and the sweet wet heat of a tropical rainforest. The cockpit was now bare of seating and the FTL cabinet was back up front where it belonged. Gary stood against the instrument panel, which thrummed with bubbles and life. The ship was, once again, content.

Gary checked a liquid-filled vial on the wall to ensure that the gravity was going to stay on when they hit orbit. A rumble outside told them they had just passed the speed of sound. He hadn't even realized they'd taken off. It felt perfectly calm in here. Gary wished they could just keep flying and never go back.

He read through the vials and tubes holding various liquids and gases, each telling a different story of the health of the ship and its occupants. One hourglass-looking instrument had tiny black pebbles inside. It counted out every being on the ship. Usually it was full with all the dwarves in the walls; however, now it held just a handful of tiny stones – three from those who had just come on board, plus the dwarves in the engine room, singing their ancient song to guide the ship.

The vial for the overall health of the ship ran clear with liquid. It was a huge change from the chunky green vomitus that was there the last time he had been aboard. The liquid bubbled and gurgled happily. There was no talking AI on the *Jaggery*. Stoneships communicated hundreds of meaningful data points, but talking wasn't the only way, or even the best way, to make oneself understood.

"Everything in working order?" asked Findae. He'd been watching.

"It's good to be home," said Gary.

"Your home is the planet," corrected Findae.

Boges moved toward the small door in the cockpit that led to the dwarf tunnels in the walls. Gary rested a hand on her diminutive shoulder.

"You're always welcome to stay up here," said Gary.

Boges looked up at him in surprise. He was confused to see her blink away tears.

"I have things to do in the engine room." She ducked into the dwarf door and closed it behind her before he could ask what was wrong.

"Find them," said Findae. Gary didn't appreciate being barked at like a crewmember. That seemed to be the only tone his father used with him. Nonetheless, he flicked a spot on the wall to turn on the ship's viewscreen. Being Bala, the *Jaggery* had access to the nullspace as good as any living creature. It would be able to see the human's necromancer just as Gary had been able to. The ship navigated around obstacles in the null all the time.

Gary put his palm flat onto the wall of the ship and spoke to it.

"Find the Reason ship that is traversing nullspace toward our location," he said.

Stoneships were both embarrassingly simple and infuriatingly hard to control. You simply asked for what you wanted and the ship, if it felt like it, would follow your commands. Humans preferred buttons and levers, with their wires and sparks. Though they were not necessarily more reliable.

The ship didn't make any sound in reply, but Gary felt the crackle of alertness in the air. A searching or waiting sensation that got under his skin. The ship was looking.

The viewscreen blazed to life with a wash of color. The *Jaggery* muted the light down to a level that was not painful for physical eyes. They could make out an oval blob on the viewscreen. The ship focused on it and the blob resolved into the Reason ship. The other four stoneships floated in a rough formation above the Bala planet, awaiting orders.

"There," said Findae. "They're just past the dying sun. They will drop out of nullspace within the hour." He squinted and looked closely at the image.

"That is a new class of ship," he said. "Not like any that I've seen before."

"Looks like they went back to the drawing board and started from scratch," said Gary. There were even hints of stoneship in the design. "I kind of like it," said Gary. "They finally figured out that aerodynamics don't matter if you're not landing. Good for them. Another few millennia and they'll figure out how to drop their consciousness into nullspace without horn."

"If they aren't extinct by then," said Findae grimly.

"Never doubt the tenacity of human beings," said Gary.

The *Jaggery* zoomed closer until the Reason ship filled the entire viewscreen. It was stunning, yet at the same time slightly unfinished. The detailing on the painted flags looked hastily done. There were no highlights or shadows in the stylized way the Reason liked to outfit their ships. They'd gotten this one out the door fast.

Not to mention the fact that this ship had a tremendous amount of battle damage. In fact, one whole lower deck had been ripped away. The breaches had been sealed, but Gary saw the remnants of interior walls and dangling cables. This devastation had happened fairly recently.

"Look at the lower decks," he said. "They've already sustained heavy damage and probably a significant number of casualties. What kind of weapon could tear off a deck like that?"

"That's the work of a necromancer," said Findae. "There are no scuff marks along the breach. They didn't hit anything and shear it off. The metal edges are bent inward, not outward like an explosion. And there are no burn marks from a missile."

"Or pockmarks from smaller projectiles," added Gary, thinking back to the shrapnel used during the Siege of Copernica Citadel.

"That damage is from the invisible hand of a necromancer. Someone tore off the bottom floor of that ship with nullspace energy." Findae flicked his mane. "A person with a tremendous amount of power and no idea how to use it." There was wonder and a touch of fear in his voice.

"Bào Zhú is on board. He would be capable of that," said Gary.

"No, no," said Findae. "Bào is far more circumspect with his abilities. This must be one of the newer recruits. There were two other necromancers in the nearby null. It must be one of them."

"Look again," said Gary. "Now there are three."

Findae went quiet as he looked into the null.

"By Unamip, who is that?" he asked.

"You'll see," said Gary.

"My gods, it's your little friend Jenny," said Findae.

"Not so little any more, I think," said Gary. "I think she shredded the lower decks. I will reiterate that we have allies on that ship. Will you let me talk to them?"

"A handful of friends will not be able to mitigate the damage the Reason can do to our settlement," said Findae. "If we hesitate even for a few minutes, we'll doom our civilization to extinction."

Gary ran a hand over his face in frustration. Bào and Jenny were going to die at his father's hands. He didn't even know how Findae's weapon worked in order to stop it. All he'd been able to determine was that all five stoneships were involved.

"I know you don't want to concede the point, but the evidence is clear, they are coming here to wage war," said Findae. "Look at the guns recessed into the hull. The wide cargo doors are for launching troop carriers with their invading army. I would wager their holds are full of cages for the Bala they intend to steal. Gary, if nothing else, read the name of the damn ship."

It was rare that Findae swore, even more so in English. Gary took notice. As the ship moved closer, the name painted on the side became clear. The letters shifted and morphed in the null, but they kept coming back into the shape of a single visible name.

The FTL *Kilonova*. In scientific parlance, a *kilonova* was the marriage of two neutron stars. In Bala lore, they were where unicorn souls came from and where they returned after their eventual deaths. The Reason had basically named their ship after unicorn heaven.

"Human beings never cease to horrify me," said Findae. One of the liquids in an instrument vial blorped audibly. "We have an obligation to blast them out of the sky the moment they arrive." He nudged the wall with his nose and spoke through the ship's intercom.

"Boges, on my mark."

The dwarf didn't answer.

"Boges?" called Findae.

Silence.

"Is she still on board?" asked Findae.

There were still the same number of pebbles in the crew count.

"Yes," said Gary.

Boges emerged from the dwarf door, her arms piled high with fabric and helmets.

"You're going to want to put these on," she said, dropping two EVA suits onto the floor.

"No one is spacewalking right now. Get back to your station and activate the weapon," said Findae.

Boges twisted one beard braid around her finger nervously and delivered the longest speech that Gary had heard from her in weeks.

"My kinfolk and I have dismantled the weapon that you created. Stoneships were never meant to be warships and, in present circumstances, it's vitally important that they are not armed. The three of us will be exiting the *Jaggery* and my kin will bring the stoneships a safe distance away from both the approaching human ship and the planet. We cannot risk one of them becoming infected."

"Infected with what?" asked Gary. He was both relieved that the *Jaggery* was disarmed and concerned that Boges felt this other threat was so great that she would defy the king of the unicorns.

"I will explain later. But trust that the threat of humans arriving is nothing compared to the disaster that will befall us if the stoneships become compromised," she said, picking up one of the suits.

"This is madness. I refuse to leave the ship without a proper explanation," said Findae, raising his voice to fearless leader volume in the tiny confines of the cockpit. "Unprotected in openspace we'll be vulnerable targets."

"The *Kilonova's* weapons can't lock onto anything smaller than a two-person skimmer," said Boges, holding the unicorn-shaped EVA suit open for him. The *Jaggery* originally belonged to the House of Cobalt and the custom suits for every family member were still on board.

"Boges," breathed Gary. "Thank you." He picked up a suit that used to be his long ago.

"Don't thank me yet," Boges said grimly, locking her helmet into place.

Findae was still unconvinced. He touched a spot on the *Jaggery's* wall with his nose. For a moment, the ship didn't seem to understand what he was asking for, then it opened a channel to the other stoneships.

"Bala stoneships, can you read me?" asked Findae. There was no answer.

"They're empty," said Boges. "No one on board except the dwarves, who won't answer unless I tell them to."

"But the Bala crews…" said Findae.

"We forced them off on the islands after you boarded. There are only the dwarves and the three of us," she said.

Findae snorted and stomped, still refusing to put on his suit. Gary was just as confused but it was never a bad idea to be suited up for a spacewalk.

"Everything will unfold the way it was intended," Boges said through her suit's microphone. Gary had heard a phrase like that before. The skin on his arms prickled.

He helped his father into the suit. The whole not having thumbs thing had been a bottleneck for unicorns since the beginning of time.

"I didn't realize you had spoken with the Pymmie," he said, clipping Findae's helmet into place.

"There are a lot of things you don't know about me," she said, in a way that made his stomach drop.

"Apparently. I'm going to trust you for the moment, but at some point I'll need a full explanation," said Gary. He didn't hide the fact that he was pleased she had sabotaged the weapon. He wondered if it had even worked in the first place. But if the Pymmie were involved, even peripherally, they were all in trouble.

An instrument on the wall clicked like a cicada in summer, warning of the *Kilonova's* approach.

"Gods," said Findae, slamming his front hooves onto the floor in frustration. Clearly, he had not considered the possibility of losing. He definitely hadn't accounted for the betrayal by the dwarves.

"Cargo hold… now," said Boges urgently. They ran for the hold. At the door, Boges hit a spot on the wall, worn smooth by centuries of contact. The air hissed out of the room and the cargo door opened. The unicorn banners floated upward, then detached form the wall and headed for openspace.

The House of Azure rippled away in the vacuum. The House of Periwinkle got caught up on the cargo bay doors and ended up jammed into the door track. The House of Cobalt floated down toward the surface.

Findae, Boges, and Gary pushed off and floated away from the *Jaggery*, out among the stoneships. It was like floating among huge, dark planets. Gary hoped they wouldn't start frolicking and crush the three of them.

The space above the stoneships, just above orbit, shimmered like the air on a hot day. It rippled then collapsed in on itself, reminding Gary of a whirlpool of water going down the drain. The *Kilonova* rode the spiral up into openspace, appearing above the stoneships.

Gary opened his comm.

"FTL *Kilonova*, this is Captain Gary Cobalt of the FTL *Jaggery*. Stand down and do not arm your weapons systems. We would like to open a dialogue," said Gary.

"You're ridiculous," said Findae, hooves flailing in openspace. Unicorns were not graceful without gravity.

The *Kilonova* fired maneuvering thrusters with a burst of gas on either side of its massive hull, pointing itself down at the stoneships. This was a ship of conquest and dominion. Every line was sharp and menacing; calculated to inspire a natural revulsion like from a venomous insect.

Gary's comm pinged.

"FTL *Jaggery*, this is Captain Lakshmi Singh of the FTL *Kilonova*. We demand your immediate surrender and the surrender of those planetside."

Lakshmi Singh. The woman who'd helped him get him and Kaila out of the Reason Harvesting Center on Jaisalmer. Gary hadn't thought about her since that day. She'd told him about her recurring nightmare that he was killing her and asked for help in making it stop. The Sisters had asked her to wait until the events in the dream came to pass. Was this the day? Was the dream symbolic or a literal foretelling of future events? It seemed like a bad omen that she was here at all. It brought them both one step closer to that terrible vision.

"No Bala will be surrendering today," said Gary. If Lakshmi was here, she was definitely as big a player in their future as the Sisters had indicated. "I'd like to talk. We can meet in a neutral location like the third moon."

Captain Singh laughed on the open comm. "You're three Bala in EVA suits facing the largest warship in the Reason. This is not a negotiation. I would venture to say you're definitely coming aboard. And you might not be leaving."

The comm clicked off and the *Kilonova's* grappling arm extended toward them. Findae kicked ineffectually toward the Bala planet as the claw end of the arm circled his midsection.

"I hate humans," he muttered.

CHAPTER TWENTY
A "Jenny Perata" Sort of Rescue

Bào and Ricky collapsed onto the floor on the observation deck, laughing. Their plan to sabotage sanitation had been a literal shitshow. They'd tossed a bunch of sealing-foam pellets into the pipes and made a run for it. Sloppy work, and they would have been caught if Rhian hadn't shown up and distracted the officers on duty while they slipped away.

"Well, that nearly went terribly," said Ricky.

"I think it did go terribly, but we were lucky Rhian was there to cover for us," said Bào.

"You know he likes you, right?" she asked, a twinkle in her eye.

"How could you know that from two minutes of conversation?" asked Bào.

"It is my business to know exactly how everyone around me is feeling at all times. Otherwise I could end up dead." It was the most serious he had seen her all night. There was a story there, one that he was interested in hearing. Ricky shook her head as if to clear the air. "Anyway, do you like him back?" she asked.

"Not like that," he said.

"Did you tell him?" she asked.

"I did," said Bào.

"That's good, because I like you too," said Ricky.

Bào blanched on the inside, even though Kevin Chen's smile did not falter.

"I'm sorry. You're like twenty years younger than me. I didn't mean to make it weird," said Ricky.

"No, that's not it," said Bào. "I'm just… not the person you think I am."

Ricky paused and bit her lip. "Yeah. We should talk, but this is like a third date conversation. Can we just continue to have a lovely evening of sabotaging a few hundred billion worth of Reason equipment?" she asked.

"Of course," said Bào.

"How's your hand?" asked Ricky.

"The anesthetic wore off a while ago. It aches, but I'm not feeling too poorly," said Bào.

"Too poorly? Kid, sometimes you sound like my yéye – and he's about a hundred years old," said Ricky.

Bào's face flushed both under and over his disguise.

"Sorry," said Bào.

"Never mind. Just come with me to the medbay. They keep the good drugs locked up, but…" she held up her badge, "I happen to know a doctor!"

The medbay was quiet at this time of night. The third shift staff doctor looked up from the intake desk.

"Doctor Tang, I have to object to the manner in which you continually leave the medbay after your shift. Tonight, I found bourbon-filled syringes in the surgery, urine sample cups in the refrigerator full of some sort of gelatin concoction, and I can't even hazard a guess at what's in this enema bag." He held up a plastic pouch filled with purple liquid.

"Larval eggwine," muttered Ricky, taking the pouch from him. "Not cheap, so I'll take that."

The doctor gave her a withering look.

"I have a patient here who needs pain management," she said brightly, grabbing Bào by the shoulders and thrusting him forward between her and the shift doctor.

"The pharmacy isn't your own personal drug stash," he admonished.

Ricky lifted Bào's stitched finger and showed it to the doctor.

"He has a legitimate injury, Doctor Bear. It's not as if we're here to get high."

Two hours later, tucked into the scrub room, Ricky and Bào were incredibly high. They'd shut off the main lights so the under-cabinet lighting suffused the room with a soft blue glow. The room was cozy and windowless – the real world felt far away. It was so quiet that Bào started dozing against a scrub sink before Ricky nudged him with her boot.

"I told you the second set of pills was a mistake," said Ricky, sucking down a urine cup full of lemon gelatin and vodka left over from the club.

"And if by mistake you mean a very good idea then I'm in complete agreement," said Bào, grinning back at her and feeling incredibly wonderful.

The door to the scrub room opened. Light and sound streamed inside. Both Ricky and Bào cringed. A Reason officer poked his head into the room. "I'm looking for Kevin Chen. I heard he came in here," said the officer, looking down at them propped against the large sinks. Behind him, the medbay was filled with shouting people and screaming alarms. It almost looked like the bar, except the lights were on full blast and way more people were covered in blood.

"Sometimes I'm Kevin Chen," said Bào, giggling. "And sometimes I'm not."

"Uh," said the officer.

"This is Chen. He's having some pain management therapy under the supervision of a trained medical professional right now. What do you want with him?" asked Ricky.

"He's needed on the bridge immediately," said the officer.

Bào tried to get to standing. He stopped halfway up, resting on his knees. His joints had stuck in that position. He hoped that Ricky would think it was from the excess of meds. She got to her feet, then put her hands under his arms and lifted.

"You're lighter than you look," she said, holding him for a moment as his knees crackled to life. They shuffled out through the medbay, arm in arm. Bào hoped it looked chummy and not like his legs were about to give out. Then again, no one was paying attention to them. Crew members moaned on gurneys and slouched in chairs because they'd run out of room.

"Did we do this?" Bào asked Ricky.

"I hope not," she replied.

The shift doctor waved Ricky over. He stood over a patient moaning on the surgery table, a piece of metal the size of a cricket bat sticking out of his abdomen. Something terrible had happened while they'd been locked in the scrub room.

"Doctor Tang, jump in on one of the critical ones," said the shift doctor, trying to determine how to remove the metal from the man without killing him. Ricky looked around at the pools of blood and parts of people that were barely attached to their owners.

"I'm going to head to the bridge and see if they need help," said Ricky, backing away from the carnage. "Happy to help out my buddy Kevin."

"No – that's not where we need–" began the shift doctor. The patient in front of him began to shake violently, spraying a fine mist of red blood over his scrubs. While he was distracted, Ricky pushed Bào toward the door.

"Not my area of expertise," she muttered.

In the elevator the officer eyed them both warily from across the car.

"You're not supposed to be intoxicated or impaired while on duty," he said.

"He said duty," bubbled Ricky, barely holding it together.

Bào tried to keep a straight face, but nothing about him was straight. "I perform my duty every day with honor," he said, raising his arm in the Reason salute.

Ricky nearly fell down laughing; she stayed bent over for six floors before leaning on Bào to pull herself upright again. The officer was not amused.

"This is no time for jokes," he admonished. "We're under attack."

"I don't believe he likes us," said Ricky in a whisper that echoed throughout the elevator car.

"Shhh. I think he can hear you," whispered Bào.

When the elevator door opened, a burst of sound and motion filled the car. Automated damage reports streamed in from several consoles. Crewmembers shouted orders into their comms at waiting rescue and repair teams. Captain Singh stood at the center of it all, taking reports and directing her bridge crew. The officer walked past Ricky and Bào, whispering something to Captain Singh. She looked over at them and rolled her eyes.

"Pull yourselves together and get over here. Chen, we need you to keep us safe from these Bala scum who attacked our ship," said Singh. She eyed up Ricky. "We don't need a doctor up here. Get to the medbay."

Ricky didn't answer. She was too busy staring at the three Bala captives who had been pulled aboard.

"Oh shit," she said.

"No kidding," added Bào. "I– uh–"

He was stunned to see Gary Cobalt, his father Findae, and Boges the dwarf standing on the bridge. All three of them were wearing the lower halves of EVA suits, as if they'd just spacewalked over, no big deal.

"What is it?" snapped Lakshmi.

"Nothing," said Bào, suddenly feeling much more sober. "I'd be happy to guard these Bala scum for you, Captain." Bào gave all three of them a warning look. Gary nodded nearly imperceptibly and Boges averted her eyes. Only Findae held his gaze. The unicorn sniffed the air and Bào braced himself.

"Is that necromancer Bào Zhú that I smell?" Findae declared.

Gary sighed so heavily that his breath ruffled the illusion of Kevin Chen's hair. Bào surged with adrenaline and nullspace energy. He was ready to destroy everyone around them in an instant, but it wasn't entirely clear who to target. And, also, he was seeing two of everyone and couldn't figure out which one to aim for.

Lakshmi rose out of her chair and put a hand on Bào's shoulder. She leaned down close and whispered in his ear. "Don't do anything stupid," she said, walking past him to Findae. "There is no Bào Zhú on my ship, sir. Kevin Chen, our extraordinary necromancer, managed to track the Bala to this planet."

Findae reared up as high as he could. Crewmembers scooted their chairs away from him, but kept managing the disaster unfolding several floors below.

"You are a traitor to the Bala you once served," Findae roared at Bào.

Bào's head swam with drugs and pain and fear. He wanted to reassure the king of the unicorns that he was indeed still loyal to their cause, but if he did so in front of the *Kilonova's* crew, he would surely be executed.

Findae focused his attention on Ricky. "I see that ne'er-do-well Ricky Tang is with you, as well. Not surprising. I thought you were setting up a new drinking establishment in Fort Jaisalmer. When did you get medical training?"

Ricky froze in place, wobbling just a bit in her boots. "Oh. Hey. Look. Two unicorns and a dwarf. Let's just take these Bala and go," she said.

"And another thing," called Findae, narrowing his huge brown eyes at Captain Singh. "The last time we met, you were of considerably lower rank than capt–"

"All of them, in the brig. Now," screamed Lakshmi, gesturing at both the Bala and inexplicably at Bào and Ricky. Security Specialist Ramate tapped her console to call for help.

"Wait, we didn't do anything," said Bào, holding up his hands in protest. "I'll restrain them if you want." He let fly a sinewy strand of purple lightning from his fingers and snaked it around the three Bala.

Captain Singh smacked him on the back of the head like an angry auntie.

"Stop that. Get to the brig, all of you, until I figure out what's going on." The elevator doors opened and six security officers marched in.

"These five," said Singh. Ricky struggled as a guard pulled her arms behind her back.

"Be careful with the hands. I'm a surgeon," she cried. Bào heard a low chuckle from Gary Cobalt.

"I'm glad you find this funny, Gary," yelled Ricky. "Every damn time you show up I end up arrested."

The elevator door opened again and First Officer Will Penny stepped onto the bridge wiping the sleep out of his eyes.

"I got a call to come up–" he spotted the Bala captives. "Well fuck me sideways, if it isn't Gary Cobalt."

"Jim," said Gary, sounding unsurprised.

"Will Penny," corrected the first officer. "I've got a whole new life now."

"Me too," said Gary. "Until you showed up to destroy it."

Ramate stood up and pointed to Boges, who had been quiet this entire time.

"Not this one. She stays up here," she said to security. Bào had noticed something odd about this group of guards. All of them were women. Not that women didn't serve on warships – a warm body was a warm body, after all – it was just that the Reason didn't typically put them on a single security detail.

"Why?" barked Lakshmi.

"Because she's with us," replied Ramate.

Boges' cheeks turned bright red above her beard. Findae blew out a long snort. "And who is us?" he demanded.

Ramate unzipped the top half of her uniform. Underneath was a tight red flight suit.

"We are the Sisters of the Supersymmetrical Axion. And we serve the future," said Ramate. The security guards stepped to her sides and Bào got the distinct impression that they were loyal to Ramate and not the captain. It was incredibly jarring, seeing a group of Sisters without their opaque veils. They were always so careful about their identities and here they were, just looking like ordinary women.

"Oh crap. Sisters," said Ricky, edging behind the bulk of Findae's unicorn body.

"Is this true?" Gary asked Boges.

"It is," she replied in a voice so quiet that Bào could barely hear her. She looked terrified. "I'm sorry."

"Are you the one who shot me in the forest, my dear Boges?" asked Gary.

She nodded.

"She shot you?" asked Findae, "That's a high crime!"

Gary held up a hand to calm his father. He bent down to Boges' level.

"After all we've survived together. I think you owe me an explanation," he said.

Boges began to cry, tears sparkling in her red beard like stars. She spoke through hiccups and sniffles. "A few of us Sisters are Bala. And we got separated from the rest. So we were trying to figure out what orders to follow when the Pymmie showed up."

"On *my* new planet?" asked Findae incredulously. As if the Pymmie didn't in fact own everything in the universe already.

"Yes. We were meeting in the forest, away from everyone else, and they just appeared. They told us about a new threat: an invasion of beings that we've never encountered before. They're infiltrating both the humans and Bala. The Pymmie showed us how to check for people who were infected. That's why we were pulling people out of the settlement. To quarantine them away from the others. Gary, believe me, if this spreads, it'll be bad."

The red-haired dwarf sounded entirely sincere. Bào sensed no lies behind her words. Gary Cobalt rested a hand on her shoulder.

"We can fix this, Boges. Just as we've fixed everything else in the past," he said. "You should have come to me."

"We didn't know if you were infected. Not until the octomite checked you," she said.

She waved toward Bào, Ricky, Gary, and Findae.

"Gary's clean, but we can't be sure about any of you. You're going to have to go to the brig until we check you."

"I am the king of the–" Findae blustered.

"There are no more kings," said Ramate. "Just people and Bala who are going to be extinct if we don't take action."

Singh stepped between them.

"I've been looking for you," she said. "I have these dreams."

"We know about your premonition," said Ramate. "And we're doing everything we can to avoid the future that it portends. Frankly, we're impressed that you got all the way out here."

Will Penny huffed like an angry stallion. "I figured it out. She took command of this ship on false pretenses. She's the regimental administrative officer in Colonel Wenck's office. Only a Lieutenant," he said. "No qualifications for command, no flight training at all."

He laughed and the sound chilled Bào to the bone.

"She's the secretary," Penny drawled with obvious pleasure. "So I guess that makes me captain."

"Hardly," said Ramate, pulling a weapon from under her console. "We brought our own skilled captain to finish this task. We will no longer need either of your services. This ship is ours."

Will Penny pulled an antique gun out of the back of his trousers. Bào wondered how he sat down on that thing and if it ever shot him in the rear end. He aimed his weapon at the tactical station where a third-shift cadet sat terrified. "Muster the troops to the personnel carriers," Penny ordered. "Time to head planetside. We've got cattle to round up."

Ramate put her hand around Will Penny's wrist – gently, as if she was taking his arm to dance. He yelped and dropped his gun into her other outstretched palm. She handed it to Boges, who secreted it into one of the many pockets hidden in dwarven clothing.

"The last thing we need is to shoot a hole in the ship," she said. It was her turn to address the frightened cadet. "Charge the laser cannon and prepare to fire on the planet."

Findae swiveled and kicked his back legs out, smashing the console and sending the cadet lurching away from his station.

"You will not do this," said Findae, panting. Plastic and metal bits hit the floor of the bridge.

251

Ramate chuckled. "Do you think there aren't redundancies on the *Kilonova*? I can launch that weapon from five different locations on this ship."

"The Sisters have no reason to destroy the Bala," said Gary. "There can't be any greater good in that."

"We're not destroying all of you, just the ones that are infected," said Boges. "We have a list."

"Surely they can be helped. Or we can do this in a more humane way," he said.

Boges shook her head. "The invaders can survive after a body is killed by conventional means. They can live on in a corpse for years before moving to a new host. There's no way to get them out and euthanasia or execution doesn't stem the tide. The infected have to be incinerated.

"Nonsense," declared Findae. "I've never heard of such a creature."

Gary Cobalt's face went slack. Bào could tell this was the first he was hearing of this. Boges stepped past him and took a seat in the captain's chair. The Sisters fanned out across the room, hovering over any crewmember who might get it in their heads to resist. Ramate stood waiting for orders.

"How long before the weapon is charged?" asked Boges.

"Seventeen minutes," squeaked the cadet, staring petrified at Ramate and the Sisters around the room.

"Take them to the brig," said Boges.

"I have the list of infected on the *Kilonova*," said Ramate.

"Gather them up and put all of them in a troop carrier for the surface," said Boges. "Tell them they're going to capture the Bala. Get every single one. Don't let them come in physical contact with anyone else. That's how the invaders move bodies."

Ramate tapped on her console, sending her orders out to the infected crew.

Bào could see the fear on Boges' face, but also the resolute stoicism of a dwarf in battle. He lifted his hands to use his powers to remove her from the chair.

Ramate's palm rested on the side of his neck. There was no magic in those powerful hands. Just strength, poised to strike. "I don't think so, Chen," she said. "Keep your hands down." Security marched all of them toward the elevator. Gary hesitated.

"I thought you were on our side..." he trailed off. Boges looked up at him, heartbroken.

"I know," she said sadly. "This is the best I could do."

Findae roared with the might of a unicorn king, even a deposed one.

"I will trample your brittle bones until you are nothing but a red smear on the floor," he sneered.

Gary continued to reason with any Sister who would listen.

"Isolate the infected up here. Don't send them to the surface. We can figure this out," he said.

Boges shook her head.

"The Pymmie have given us their instructions. The infected are to be incinerated on the surface. The laser is the only weapon hot enough. It's the safest way. We cannot risk them spreading to others... or," she paused, horrified, "to the stoneships."

Stoneships were sentient beings. An entity that powerful and fast with a parasitic infection would be perilous. Let alone five of them.

"I can't believe this is the best way," said Gary, in one final attempt. "Just five minutes to talk through the possibilities—"

"I trust the Pymmie have done that already," said Boges. "Just go with them."

The security officers pushed everyone into the elevator except Findae. There wasn't room for that many people plus a full unicorn. He stayed behind with a couple of the guards. Even so, the elevator was tightly packed with bodies. Bào inched as close as he could to Gary. It was remarkable how much safer he felt with his former leader here.

"I came to help," whispered Bào.

"Me too," added Ricky.

"That's good to hear," said Gary. He looked away and ran a

hand across his eyes. Bào couldn't be sure but he thought perhaps Gary Cobalt was crying.

"If the Pymmie are involved, you won't be able to sway them," said Bào, trying to console him.

"That doesn't mean we give up," said Gary.

"I'm sorry about Boges," said Bào. "It's hard to know whose side anyone is on these days."

"You can drop the illusion," said Gary. "They know who you are."

Bào glanced up at Ricky, leaning against the elevator wall, barely paying attention to their conversation. He wasn't quite ready to show her his true outer self.

"I think I'll stick with Kevin Chen for the moment," he said. "Just in case."

"Must be exhausting, spending your days pretending to be something you are not," said Gary bitterly. Bào surmised he didn't only mean Kevin Chen. He and Boges had been close for nearly a century. That she had betrayed him now seemed to weigh on him heavily.

The elevator stopped and the guards prodded them forward. Ricky roused herself from the steel wall.

"How's the new planet?" she asked blearily.

"Pink," said Gary. "You would love it."

The guards marched them into a secure holding area with benches and bars. The usual unimaginative Reason prison that Bào had seen the inside of again and again. There was one person already in the holding area when they entered, tucked into the corner on the bench. She lifted her head and began to laugh.

"Oh look, the gang's all here," she said.

"Jenny fucking Perata," said Ricky, suddenly sounding very sober. "Where there's trouble, you're never far behind."

"One could say the same about you," answered the woman on the bench. She looked like she had been through a war. She wore an old Reason uniform, unzipped and untucked. The backs of her arms were covered in shiny spray-on skin. Dark bruises pooled beneath her eyes, which were bloodshot and exhausted. Bào barely recognized her as the confident captain he'd spoken to just six weeks ago.

Anger swelled in Bào. This was the woman who had left him adrift in openspace. And before that, had shot him through with shrapnel at the Siege of Copernica Citadel. He fought the urge to reach out with nullspace energy and crush that bruised head topped with a bird's nest of tangled brown hair. It would only take a moment to snatch her life away.

Gary took a seat next to her.

"Hey Gary," she said.

"Hey Jenny," he replied, patting her leg. She winced and he stopped.

"I made it," she said through gritted teeth. "I said I would."

"So you did," he said, leaning closer until they were shoulder to shoulder. "No one should ever doubt your tenacity."

Bào slunk off to the far side of the room and planted himself next to Ricky, who was warm and soft against his tired bones. It appeared that Gary was friendly with Captain Perata. In that case he would bide his time and not be too eager to crack her skull.

Jenny lifted her arm and smiled wearily at the patches of fake skin that were starting to peel off in sheets. "You know, things worth doing are never easy," she said.

"Bào, this is what they call a Jenny Perata sort of rescue," said Ricky, loud enough for those across the room to hear. "In which Jenny fucking Perata shows up and you end up worse off than you were before."

"I've missed you too," said Jenny. Her eyes unfocused for a minute, then she nodded. Bào surmised she had an earpiece to her own crew. Maybe they were still loose on the *Kilonova* somewhere and coming to their aid.

"How many people do you have with you?" he asked her, hoping no one mentioned he was Bào Zhú under the Kevin Chen disguise.

"How many?" she laughed. "Just me. And my ship's AI, who is pretty helpful."

Ricky put her arm around Bào's shoulders and he settled in next to her, he was starting to catch a chill as he sobered up. "Fantastic rescue. You and a computer. At least I made a friend. My buddy Kevin here helped me put a piece of criosphinx horn into the FTL drive. It's was supposed to fuck up everything," said Ricky.

"Huh. Was that the little brown thing I found in the cabinet?" said Jenny. "I took that out."

"You took it out?" cried Ricky. "We spent an hour figuring out how to get it in there."

"I was getting my horn back and disabling the ship," shouted Jenny. "How was I supposed to know that you already had a fake horn in there?"

"You could look," said Ricky. "I mean, take a moment and evaluate the situation before you undo someone else's *very hard work.*"

"I didn't know," said Jenny.

"You are ridiculous," said Ricky, leaning back against the wall in a pout.

"In any case, they took everything out of my pockets when they put me in here," said Jenny. "Including the bone and the horn. They're going to scoop up as many Bala as they can carry and we'll likely be back in FTL."

The door opened and the guards came in with Findae. He flailed and bucked as they shoved him toward the holding cell.

"You must bring me back up to the bridge. I demand it," he yelled.

Gary stood up. Bào tucked himself in closer to Ricky for safety.

The Sisters shoved Findae into the cell. He turned and slammed his hooves on the bars furiously. The guards backed away.

"In the service of the future," said one of them by way of explanation as she left the room.

Gary stepped up to Findae, who foamed at the mouth as if he'd run a race at full speed.

"Take a breath. What is it?" asked Gary.

Findae swallowed hard. "After you left, they began targeting their weapon. It's aimed right at the heart of our settlement," he said.

Gary rubbed his face and took a seat next to Jenny again. He looked haggard and tired. Ricky leaned down to Bào.

"So they just found out that their dwarf friend is in the Sisters of the Supersymmetrical Axion," she whispered. "Which is a quasi-religious–"

"I know who the Sisters are," replied Bào.

"Take off that ridiculous disguise," Findae cried toward Bào. "Everyone here knows who you are."

Bào cast a reluctant glance at Ricky, but one did not disobey a direct order from the king of the unicorns. He let his illusion drop. It was a relief, actually, like shedding a pair of too-tight shoes after a long day. He stretched out like a cat in his new old skin.

"Oh my," said Ricky.

"I told you I wasn't who I seemed," said Bào, resigned to the fact that she would likely remove her arm from his shoulders now. This wasn't the way he intended to tell her about his real identity. He looked up, expecting her to be dismayed, or at least surprised. Instead, a little half smile played on her face.

"Thank the freaking gods, I was wondering why I was getting all gaga over some doughy little twenty-two year-old kid. This is much better," she said, giving his shoulder a squeeze. Bào was stunned into silence.

"Bào Zhú," said Jenny from her corner of the room. "The exotic animal dealer."

Bào straightened up and slipped out of Ricky's grasp. "Bào Zhú the necromancer. One of several at the Siege of Copernica Citadel." He extended his bare arms to show her the shrapnel scars and to her credit, she understood immediately.

"Were you the one who cut my ship in half?" she asked, leaning forward.

"Were you the one who shot me full of screws?" Bào said by way of reply.

"I take it you know each other," said Ricky, putting her hand flat on Bào's back, as if to calm him.

"There's more," said Findae, turning away from the bars to face everyone in the room. "The Sisters have ordered the other two necromancers on this ship to the bridge to assist in the destruction of our village."

"I don't understand," said Jenny. "Why would the Sisters attack your village? They've always been the Bala's greatest advocates."

"Boges says there's an invasion of parasitic aliens – a type we haven't encountered yet – who have infiltrated both humans and Bala and are shaping their behavior to their will. The only way they can be destroyed is by incineration."

Jenny's eyes widened, but instead of answering, she cocked her head to the side, listening.

"I don't believe you," she said quietly.

"And how do these parasites move from person to person?" she asked.

"Boges mentioned physical contact," replied Bào. He wondered if Ricky was infected and sitting so close to her was spreading the invaders to him. Then he decided he didn't care.

Jenny leaned back into the corner. "Then I think you all had better not touch me," she said.

Ricky sat up, delighted. "Do you have a brain parasite, Jenny Perata? Can I see it?" she asked.

Gary got up and knelt down just out of Jenny's reach.

"Explain," he said simply.

"I was on a generation ship and they had dead Bala on board and I was looking for horn and came across some hidden in the teeth of some old elf, but when I got his body back to my ship, his corpse followed me all over, even into the shower, ugh, and I ended up hiding in the smuggling compartment with his body and then he got inside me." She took a breath.

The room was silent for a long minute. When Gary finally spoke up, Bào had already begun his third prayer for the intervention of Unamip. "Nobody touch Jenny," he said.

"Are we going to incinerate her?" asked Ricky.

"No," said Gary firmly.

"It's not a terrible idea," muttered Findae.

"No," repeated Gary, before turning back to Jenny, who looked stricken and paler than before. She played with the spiral pendant around her neck.

"He said he was a ghost," she offered. "He helped fix my heart."

"No one can fix your heart, Jenny Perata," called Ricky.

Bào elbowed her. As much as he didn't like Jenny, it wasn't right to kick a captain when they were down.

"Does he have access to your abilities?" asked Gary.

"He shows me things, memories and nullspace, but he can't control my physical body." She paused and hissed to herself. "Shut up. Everything you've told me is a lie." She looked back at Gary. "I think he's weak from being stuck in a corpse for all those years."

"Good," said Gary. "If you feel that starting to change, even the slightest bit, you let me know. All right. There are four necromancers on this ship," said Gary. "Only two of them are up on that bridge."

Bào wasn't sure who the fourth one was until Jenny shook her head.

"Oh no. I tried to break a tiny little antenna off the *Kilonova* and tore off the entire bottom of the ship," she said.

"Was it perhaps the invader misdirecting your energy?" asked Findae.

"No, I just don't have a handle on this power yet," she said.

"That was you?" asked Bào, with a cross between wonder and horror.

"Yeah," said Jenny.

Ricky mouthed something to Jenny that Bào was able to mostly make out but didn't quite understand. Something something disaster gay. In response, Jenny lifted her middle finger.

"You tore the bottom half of this ship off like a grunt opening a can of beans," said Bào. "And you don't think you'll be able to help stop the Sisters? I didn't stow away on a starship just to get all the way here and watch them blow up the Bala."

"That's the spirit," said Ricky cheerfully.

"Their weapon will be ready to fire in five minutes," said Findae. "Bào, can you stop it before they scorch the surface?"

"I can," said Bào, pushing up his sleeves and standing. He let his stiff fingers dangle through the air.

"I'm here if you want to tear the ship apart," said Jenny.

"We might need that later," said Gary.

Bào reached and felt the *Kilonova's* weapon gathering energy at the front of the ship. He wished he'd had more time to study its schematics and determine an easy way to disassemble it without harming others. As it was, he found several power connections that could be easily reached along the outer edge of the weapon's focusing lens. He concentrated on that area and began to pull the cables out, one by one.

"Do it faster," said Findae, also watching in the null.

Bào dug invisible fingers of energy into the hull around the lens, twisting and pulling. It popped out easily. These things were designed to withstand impacts from outside, but they were also modular pieces that needed to come apart for maintenance.

A wave of nausea hit him and he lost his grip on the lens. The concoctions he'd taken with Ricky earlier in the evening were beginning to wear off and leave one hell of a hangover in their wake. He swallowed hard.

"One minute," he said. "I'll get this."

"We don't have a minute," said Findae.

Bào refocused and tried again. He wrapped his tendrils of energy around the superheated lens and pulled. Wires and connections popped free. People screamed. He tossed the lens out into openspace. It tumbled end over end until one of the stoneships intercepted it and batted it like a plaything. It shattered on impact, sending fragments careening out into openspace. The stoneship sulked back into formation with the others, its toy destroyed.

"What's happening?" asked Ricky.

"I got it," said Bào. "The lens is disabled."

"But you got more than just the lens, right?" asked Jenny. "Because on those designs, the lens is just for focusing the beam at one particular point on the surface about twenty meters across. The laser will still work without it, just at lower power across the wider area."

Damn. He'd actually just made the targeting area larger. Bào went outside of himself again to take another shot at the laser apparatus. As Jenny had predicted, it was still gathering power, just in a wider, less concentrated beam. He reached deeper into the machinery and attempted to wrap his invisible energy around the power generator at the center.

Pain tore through his head. He let go of the generator and pulled back to the holding cell. He involuntarily tried to run, trying to get away from the threat. Nausea overtook him again and he hit his knees on the hard metal flooring. Ricky appeared at his side. She took his arm.

"Are you all right?" she asked.

"What happened?" asked Gary.

"The other necromancers are protecting the weapon," said Bào. "Let me try again." He grimaced. "One moment. I have to… use the facilities," said Bào, cursing his tiny bladder, which was suddenly screaming at him. He wondered if that was a trick of the *Kilonova's* necromancers as well.

"Captain Perata, you distract them while Bào makes another attempt," ordered Findae.

Jenny pursed her lips. "You don't understand. Last time, I aimed for an area two meters wide and took a chunk out of the ship the size of a rugby field. That laser spans multiple decks, which means I'd likely depressurize about half the ship," she said.

Bào tucked himself around the privacy divider and was grateful when everyone continued talking as if they couldn't hear him back there urinating for an inordinately long time.

"You take out the *Kilonova* or they destroy our settlement," said Gary. "I don't think being delicate is a concern right now."

Jenny sighed so loudly that Bào heard her over the splashes. He peered over the privacy divider.

"Why does it always come down to me? First the Summit, and now here. Why do I always have to choose?" she asked. Her eyes narrowed and she looked like she was listening. "I suppose," she said.

"What?" asked Gary.

"Just the elf ghost parasite talking inside of my head," she replied. "He also wants to stop the laser. Seems we're all on the same page here."

"Then I think you'd better take aim," said Gary.

"Fine. I'll have a go at the laser," she said. "Because fuck the Reason and fuck brain parasites and fuck lasers."

Bào flushed. The water rose instead of falling. Sewage spilled over the edge of the toilet.

"Oops, I forgot," cried Ricky. "We disabled the sewer system."

CHAPTER TWENTY-ONE
Cowboy Jim's Last Stand

Kamis was running in overtime inside of Jenny's head, talking as fast as her mind could process the words.

Don't listen to them. I am on your side. We must stop this weapon from reaching the surface. Look down at the atomic level, as far as you can go. Don't get distracted by the humans around the weapon, they chose to be there and you have every right to stop them. Do you see that box that the power is feeding into? That's where the—

"Shut up, Kamis. I've seen one or two power generators in my lifetime," said Jenny. "I know what to do. Just be quiet."

She scooted forward on the bench as far as she could go. The smell of the overflowing toilet was rank, but at least the cheap floor grating in here allowed the sewage to flow down into the access area below deck. Jenny didn't want to be in here if the gravity went off.

This would be easier if you could stand, said Kamis.

"A lot of things would be easier if I could stand," said Jenny.

"I can help you up," said Gary.

"I'm fine," said Jenny. "Kamis, the brain parasite, needs to settle down." Jenny mimicked Bào's necromancer motions, moving her arms through the energy in the room like water. It didn't work for her. She felt like an idiot. She got in a more comfortable position, with her elbows on her knees and her chin resting in her hands like a contemplative-yet-angsty teenager.

That is not the optimal— began Kamis.

"Shh," hissed Jenny.

It was harder to get a handle on nullspace energy when the FTL drive was off. It was still there, but it coalesced in smaller wisps that were more difficult to corral. Bào joined her. His large octopus of energy undulated outward from across the room. One of those tentacles of light reached through the ship toward the laser array. Other tendrils, those of the two Reason necromancers, raced toward him. Jenny reached out to block them, throwing her force against their extended energies.

She felt something crunch, far in the distance.

"Hull breach on decks thirteen, fourteen, fifteen, and sixteen," announced the ship's computer. "All personnel on those decks seek shelter." Jenny pulled back and opened her eyes.

"Bollocks," she said. "I can't get smaller than that without ripping pieces off the ship."

"You are terrible at this," said Findae.

"I got really close that time," said Bào. He looked angry with her. Jenny didn't blame him. The first time they'd met, she'd shot him full of nuts and bolts. The last time, she'd left him adrift in openspace. It wasn't the right time for an apology, but she could at least have his back.

"One more time," she said. "I'll make it as small as I can."

Bào closed his eyes and Jenny did the same. Both of their energies pushed toward the front of the *Kilonova*. Bào headed toward the laser array, which glowed with fully charged power, even though it was half-disassembled and showering sparks. Jenny's reached for the necromancers positioned near the breach on deck sixteen.

Their energy headed for Bào, trying to ensnare and crush him. She intercepted it and nudged them back away from him as gently as she could. One of the necromancers hit the back wall of deck sixteen with such force that his body left an imprint in the steel before he hit the floor. Jenny shook her head and refocused on the other one, who was trying to slide her energy around Bào's neck. The necromancer tightened her grip and Bào started choking. Jenny instinctively shoved her away, but this one countered with a blast in her direction.

The flush that went through her was like stepping into a

sauna. It began to bake her bones from the inside out. She started sweating into her uniform jacket. That second necromancer was doing something less focused than a direct attack. Jenny didn't know where to hit back to stop the onslaught.

Nearby, Bào writhed on the floor as Gary and Ricky knelt next to him. Blood trickled out of his ears.

Just move her, said Kamis.

"I tried already," said Jenny, watching both the null and the cell. Kamis had been right. Keeping your eyes open meant you could process twice the information.

You're stronger than she is, just push, said Kamis.

Jenny pushed and the necromancer hit the airlock window. Her falling body left a pink smear down the glass.

Bào gasped in a great gulp of air, then went still. He wasn't taking out this laser any time soon. As Jenny reached for the laser array, it discharged toward the planet below. In nullspace, a green column of energy hit the planet, blacking out dozens of tiny pinpricks of lights in the settlement below. Jenny dug her energy around the laser and pulled. The weapon went off course, searing a crooked zigzag of death across the planet. Jenny's first thought was of Kaila, praying that she was out of the path of destruction.

With a shudder felt throughout the entire ship, the laser array came free of the *Kilonova*. The energy beam shut down. Jenny was drenched with sweat and Bào was lying on the floor shivering.

"Did you stop it?" asked Findae.

"Sort of," said Jenny. "It hit the settlement, just a short burst. I tried to contain the damage as best as I could, but…" She took a deep breath. "I crushed one of the necromancers." She gagged at what might have been the smell of raw sewage but also might have been her conscience.

You prevented the deaths of thousands, said Kamis. Jenny could do the math, but that didn't make the equation any less terrible. She'd killed far too many people in her life. She was getting tired of all the souls resting on her shoulders. Not to mention the parasitic one stuck in her head.

"Can you get us out of this cell?" Gary asked Jenny.

"That is a terrible idea," said Findae.

"Probably," she said. She looked toward the door, concentrating on pulling at the bars of the cell. They came together as if a giant hand had compressed them into a single column of metal. The entire wall fell to the floor with a clang.

Well done, said Kamis. She blasted him with all of her irate feelings and he went quiet.

Ricky lifted Bào Zhú like a limp doll.

"Where to?" asked Ricky.

"I have a ship in the hold if we can get there," said Jenny. What she meant, and didn't say, was if they could get her there, because she damn well wasn't crawling all the way back up to the main hold.

Gary knelt down in front of Jenny again, this time a bit closer.

"I need to pick you up," he said. "Can you contain the parasite?"

"I have no idea," she replied.

"Then we'll have to risk it," said Gary.

"Oh gods, I hate this part," she said.

"It's either me or my father, and I doubt he would be as accommodating as I am," grinned Gary.

Jenny put her arms around his neck. He lifted her legs and hoisted her up like a child at a county fair. He wobbled, and then righted himself.

"You all right?" she asked.

"It's nothing," Gary replied. "I just dissolved my legs yesterday." She laughed out loud.

"I would've loved to see that," she said.

"I'm sure you would have," said Gary.

"That is humiliating," said Findae, walking by both of them and curling his upper lip.

"Speak for yourself," said Gary. "I don't mind helping my friends."

"That's nice, you called me your friend," said Jenny.

"I just meant friends in general, not you specifically," Gary

266

amended. She held on a little more tightly, but it definitely wasn't a hug.

Ricky staggered along behind them, holding Bào.

In the hallways of the *Kilonova*, people ran for the elevators and access stairwells. This was bad discipline, having this many people who panicked in the face of disaster. In Jenny's day, an evacuation was orderly, if not sedate. She'd drilled into her crew that more people got out that way than running around like rabid redworms.

They headed for an elevator bank. Ricky and held her thumb to the touchscreen. Noting that she was medical personnel in an emergency, the algorithm sent a car for her immediately.

The doors opened and a few of the crew looked up at their group standing there with a doctor, a unicorn, an unconscious necromancer, and a part-unicorn giving a piggy-back ride to a battle-worn woman.

"Out," Ricky commanded. The crew hesitated. "These are valuable Bala who need to be evacuated," she added. They scooted into the hallway.

Everyone crowded into the elevator, which seemed to be a ritual with this group in times of crisis. Jenny found herself backed against the wall with her side pressed against Gary's father.

"Shameful," sneered Findae at the two of them. Jenny pretended to sneeze on his flank just to spite him. He shuddered and pressed himself against the far wall.

"Stop teasing," Gary chided her.

"You're no fun," she whispered in his ear. She had to admit, she'd missed this. Gary had every reason to hate her, but he always gave her another chance.

You should tell him how grateful you are, said Kamis. Damn, she'd forgotten about him for five whole minutes.

"Shhh," she said.

The elevator opened to a crush of people trying to get into the cargo hold. Alarms blared as the decks above them decompressed. People shoved their way to the escape pods lining the outer wall. The rest of the hold was stuffed with a motley collection of impounded ships. People were climbing into those as well. Jenny pointed over Gary's shoulder.

"There. The big yellow one," she said.

"Charming," said Findae. "Painted up like a circus tent."

"I was kind of in a rush when ship shopping after the Pymmie started the apocalypse," said Jenny. "It's not like I had time to browse the aisles at Ships-R-Us."

"Also, I can hear you," called the *Stagecoach Mary* across the room.

"Ooh, a ship with AI," said Ricky, heaving a sagging Bào up into a better position.

"You just wait," said Jenny.

A metal projectile pinged off the hull of a nearby ship and ricocheted into the evacuating crowd. A Reason grunt cried out as it hit them in the arm. They paused for a moment, then kept on running. None of these quags were planning to stay and fight. The Reason wasn't loyal to you, so you weren't loyal to it.

"Stop right there," said a gravelly voice. Jenny's skin prickled. Gary turned to face Cowboy Jim, his ridiculous six-shooter pointed at them. That thing was full of metal bullets that could seriously damage the hull of the *Kilonova*, not the Reason-issued plastic ones that were designed to shatter when they struck metal. Jim was the same as ever, angry and ready to strike.

"Bloody hell, why did no one tell me that Jim was on this ship? I would have torn it in half when I had the chance," said Jenny.

"Nice to see you're still consorting with Bala scum," said Jim.

"Nice to see that you're still risking depressurization by carrying around that stupid bullet gun," said Jenny.

"I thought they took that away from you, Cowboy Jim," said Ricky.

"Well I got it back," said Jim. Jenny thought she could see blood spatters on his uniform shirt. Someone up on that bridge was having a day as bad as hers.

Jim waved his ridiculous gun to indicate Gary and Findae.

"Those two are staying with me," he said. "I've wasted a heap of time finding the Bala and I'm going to bring back as many as I can to Jaisalmer. The Reason, or someone, will pay whatever I want for Bala bodies."

"You are vile, James Bryant," said Ricky.

Jim swung the gun toward her and made a big show of cocking it. Gary stepped between the two of them, not thinking at all about the very mortal human that was at that moment hanging off his back. Jenny kicked his side to remind him.

"You are not getting your hands on a single Bala," said Gary, his shoulders tense under Jenny's hands and his rage barely contained. "We rebelled and you crushed us into slavery. We served humans and they stripped our bodies bare. Now you chase us across the universe, using a piece of horn that you stole from me – yes, I found out that you snuck back into the *Jaggery* after the Summit and took a piece of horn – all this just to sell us to the highest bidder. On my life, I will not allow that to happen again."

The corner of Jim's mouth went up in a nasty smile. He reached his other hand into his pocket and before anyone could see what the small rectangular object in his hand was, he'd pointed it at Gary and pressed the trigger. Unlike a bullet, which would have hurt but not incapacitated Gary, the taser seized up all of Gary's muscles at once with 50,000 volts of electricity. Some of the the charge made it through to Jenny too, rattling her teeth and making parts of her body hurt that she didn't even know had feeling any more.

Gary hit the deck, dropping Jenny onto the floor. Findae reared up above both of them as Jim kept delivering shocks to Gary on the ground. From the floor, Jenny saw Findae's hooves come down on Jim's shoulder, knocking him off his feet. His gun went off. Ricky screamed.

"He hit Kevin," she cried, backing away as a trail of red snaked down Bào's dangling arm. Ricky sunk to the floor, cursing Cowboy Jim and pressing her uniform jacket into the wound.

Jenny ducked, only looking up when she heard Findae's hooves trotting toward her. Jim raised his gun again and aimed up at

Findae. The gun went off with a bang that echoed through the hold.

Do something, screamed Kamis in her head. *Stop him. He will keep killing.*

Barely thinking and full of panic, Jenny dipped into the null, scooped up a big ball of energy, and slammed it down on top of Cowboy Jim.

Jim crumpled to the deck like a smashed beer can. He grunted as blood welled out of his nose and mouth. His legs were a tangle of unnatural angles.

Gary sat up as Jim's hand let go of the taser trigger. He pulled the hooks out of his shirt.

Finish this, for the safety of all Bala, said Kamis.

Jenny wrapped a tendril of energy around Jim's torso and under his arms. She lifted him off the ground. He looked down at her like an injured puppy. She was glad to see that he was still conscious so he would feel what she was about to do to him.

"Jenny," said Gary with a warning tone.

"I'm sorry, did you want a go at him?" she asked innocently.

"Put him down," said Gary.

"That man would kill you in an instant. Don't you dare spare his life," said Findae.

"You are not that person any more, Jenny," said Gary. "We can bring him to justice another way."

Kill him, said Kamis.

In her lifetime, Jenny had learned that when a little voice in your head told you to kill people, it was usually wrong. When it told you to punch people, it was usually right. Plus, she only needed one conscience giving her life advice. And it wasn't the brain parasite. She dropped Jim to the floor with a wet thud. Another crewmember would find him soon and drag him to the medbay.

"I hate when you're right," said Jenny to Gary.

This is a mistake, said Kamis. *He will pursue you to the ends of the universe.*

"I'll be waiting for him," said Jenny.

Gary picked up the sharp barb at the end of the taser wire and went over to Bào. Ricky's jacket was already soaked and Bào had lost all his color. Gary drew the barb down his palm and smeared silver blood onto Bào's bullet wound. Bào flinched, but after a moment his breathing eased and his cheeks began to pink up. After a moment, a misshapen bullet pinged onto the deck.

"How's the patient, Doctor Tang?" asked Gary.

"Seems to be stable," said Ricky, helping Bào to sit up.

"Gary Cobalt, you are always there for me," said Bào. "I am grateful."

Gary wrapped his arms around Bào. They had been friends since long before Jenny had captured Gary.

See? That's how you do it, said Kamis. She rolled her eyes so that only Kamis could see.

Gary turned to her. "Ready to leave this godsforsaken ship?" he asked.

"So ready," she said.

Gary hoisted her up and turned his head so that only she could hear him. "I'm very proud of you," he said.

She was about to shush him, when she decided to try something. "Thank you for all of the second chances you've given me," she said into his ear. It was agonizing to get those words out, but when he grabbed her hand and squeezed, it was worth it.

"Let's get that invader out of your brain and get you back to your wife. She misses you," he said. Jenny's heart leaped at the thought of seeing Kaila again. If they could be together, all of this would be worth it.

Jim's body shuddered in a crumpled pile on the deck. Ricky leaned down and said something to him. Findae kicked Jim in the head as he passed by.

Several of the impounded ships had already taken off, leaving room for the *Stagecoach Mary* to fully open her loading ramp. They climbed inside and Mary buttoned up the hatch, leaving Jim behind.

"The cockpit is up one level and to the right," shouted Jenny to those in front. Gary carried her up the stairs and set her down in the captain's chair. There was barely enough room for all of them in the room.

Mary queued up for the ship-sized airlock at the top of the hold. Other ships tried to cut in line in front of her, but, with the crew-risk profile set at maximum, she jockeyed for position and let no one in.

"I can probably shoot a hole in the hull so we can escape faster," Mary offered.

"Your ship is quite violent," said Findae. "I prefer that you don't land it on our planet."

When it was their turn, Mary wedged them into the airlock, which was meant for ships far smaller than she was.

"It's not big enough," said Bào, perking up considerably with the addition of unicorn blood.

"We got in here. We'll get out," said Jenny.

The outer door opened and Mary launched them into openspace. Findae was the only one standing and his hooves slid across the metal floor.

"Where are we landing, Jenny?" asked Mary.

"I don't know. Anyone want to give me a landing site?" asked Jenny.

"If we head toward the eastern–" Gary began.

A projectile streaked past the viewscreen. Mary rolled hard right, sending Findae careening into the wall.

"That was close," said Mary. "Sir unicorn, are you all right?"

"I'm fine," said Findae, shaking out his mane.

"They're shooting at the survivors," said Gary. "Open a channel."

The comm crackled open and Gary spoke in his most authoritative voice.

"*Kilonova*, this is Gary Cobalt. Stand down. There are survivors in the line of fire. Stand down immediately."

Boges voice came back from the comm channel, measured and sad. "I know this makes no sense to you, but it would if you knew what was coming. This the only way we get there. I know you have an invader on board."

"You are not obligated to obey either the Sisters or the Pymmie. You can choose for yourself," said Gary.

"You cannot let that parasite land on the planet," said Boges. "Trust me. Please."

Findae trotted up to the viewscreen. "Such hubris from a little dwarf. You have served our family for centuries. Don't you defer to our rule?" he demanded.

"Not today, I'm sorry. Only a few of the humans will be allowed to land," said Boges.

"Which ones?" asked Gary.

"We have a list," said Boges.

"That makes me very uncomfortable," said Gary. "Who is doing the choosing?"

"The Pymmie. We can't let the infected reach the surface," said Boges.

"And everyone else?" asked Jenny, keenly aware that she was putting them all in danger.

"They cannot be allowed to land on the planet. We're offering instructions for reaching the third moon, where they can stay, but none of them are allowed to land on the planet," said Boges.

"I don't like it," said Ricky.

"I hope all of this is worth it to you, Boges," said Gary.

"I hope so too," she replied before the channel went dead.

The *Kilonova* fired six shots in rapid succession, three toward a little family cruiser and the other three toward the surface. The cruiser caught a shot in the tail and spun away from the planet, venting breathable air in a stream behind it.

"Can we grab them?" called Jenny.

"Not before they suffocate," said Mary. "But I can get that one." Her viewscreen focused on a little two-person skimmer that had just escaped the *Kilonova's* airspace.

"That's Priya and Rhian," said Bào. "Friends."

Mary spun up close to it and hooked her docking clamps to the craft. They couldn't land like this, but Jenny turned her ship so the *Kilonova* would have to shoot through Mary to get to the skimmer.

An escape pod shattered on their left.

"We can't hide all of them," said Ricky. "Can we bring people on board?"

"Sure, anyone who feels like putting on an EVA suit and walking across openspace is welcome to join us," said Jenny. "But Mary doesn't have a hold big enough for even one of these small cruisers."

"It's pointless to rescue people who want to enslave you," announced Findae. Everyone ignored him. Most of the beings in this cockpit had been in space long enough to know that you went back for survivors, no matter what side they were on.

"That one," said Gary, pointing to an escape pod that was leaking crystallized ropes of frozen fluid. If they attempted re-entry, the fuel would ignite and blow them to bits.

Jenny tapped her teeth with her fingernail. She knew what had to be done, but it chafed her ass to do it. She was always the one who had to take charge and do the terrible jobs.

"*Kilonova*, stand down or you will be disabled," she said with a curt, professional tone that she hoped indicated to Boges that she meant it.

"What are you doing?" asked Gary, holding his finger on the console to mute the channel. He'd figured out this damned ship faster than she had.

"I'm saving lives," she said.

"But Boges–" he began.

"Boges made her choice. And I'll even give her another chance to stop," said Jenny. "But you know that what she's doing isn't right."

Gary took his hand away from the console. "Boges, you need to stop or we'll take action," he said.

"I can't stop," said Boges, "I'm not going to." She sounded scared. A deep ache spread across Jenny's chest that had nothing to do with her injuries.

"Give the order to stop firing. It's that simple. Make the Pymmie come here themselves and do their own dirty work," said Jenny.

"I'm sorry, Captain Jenny. I can't." The fear in ancient Boges' voice chilled Jenny to the bone.

"I have to stop you," said Jenny.

"I know. You're supposed so. It's all right," replied the dwarf. Another escape pod imploded in the darkness.

"Boges, please," said Gary.

The comm channel closed. Gary looked toward the ceiling. Jenny waited for him as a courtesy.

"Do it," he said.

"Do you want help?" asked Bào.

"I've got it," said Jenny.

This is your destiny, said Kamis.

"Do you have any booze?" asked Ricky. Bào shushed her.

"What are we doing?" asked Mary.

Jenny rested her elbow on the arm of the captain's chair and put her cheek in her hand, like she was thinking on a difficult topic. Which wasn't too far from the truth.

She dipped back into the null. Boges' bright form was visible in the center of the *Kilonova's* bridge. Next to her, the surviving necromancer cast concentric purple rings around the ship. Jenny was initially glad to see that she hadn't killed her, then realized she was probably about to do just that. She made her own energy tendrils and tried to extend her reach through the sphere of energy, but even when she expended maximum effort, she still could not get through.

"She's protecting the ship from magical attacks," Gary said, by her side. "If you want to get through, you can–"

I can show you how to– said Kamis.

"Both of you stop. I've got this," said Jenny.

She opened a general channel, which anyone would be able to hear. The *Kilonova* shot down two more pods, sending one careening into the atmosphere like a perverse wishing star.

"All *Kilonova* personnel, abandon ship. Escape pods, clear the area," Jenny yelled across the open channel.

Now Jenny was back on familiar ground. She good at non-magical attacks. They'd gotten her through basic training and her early days on the Reason Space Force. Not to mention all those years after she was in the chair and she'd needed to prove to her crews that she was still a force to be reckoned with.

She reached out with her invisible energy again, this time going nowhere near the *Kilonova*. Instead, she headed toward the field of stoneships that were hanging out above the planet.

She wrapped her energy around one of the massive ships – she couldn't tell them apart – and dragged it toward the *Kilonova*, trying to heave it toward the craft with as much velocity as she could muster. A second stoneship rocketed out from its spot and also headed for the *Kilonova*. Jenny opened her eyes for a moment to see Bào standing next to her chair, also in the null. His intention was clear.

Bào's stoneship came to a stop on the underside of the Reason ship. Jenny swung hers in a steep arc, lifting it high above the *Kilonova*.

"My gods," said Ricky.

Jenny slammed her stoneship down so hard that it smashed clear through the Reason ship and kept going. It bounced off the hull of Bào's stoneship. Both stoneships wobbled around as if dizzy, then flew off toward the closest moon. What was left of the *Kilonova* floated apathetically in two large chunks, fore and aft, with an immense debris field in between. The ship had scattered into a billion pieces no larger than a coin. They formed an expanding cloud that pelted them with frozen bits of flesh. They stuck to Mary's exterior cameras, leaving crystals of blood and fluids clinging to the glass.

"By Unamip," breathed Gary.

Bào rubbed his stitched up finger. Jenny put her head down. She didn't want any of them to see the way she had to press her lips together to stop them from quivering. Or the stupid tears that were coming down her face as if she was a green recruit on her first battlefield. This was war, she reminded herself. Sometimes you had to kill people to save people. She'd dropped bombs on cities larger than this and blown up ships with larger crews. But this time, it had stopped feeling like survival and started feeling like murder. Gary rested his hand on her shoulder and she damn near took it off.

"Mary, get in there and pick up any survivors," she snapped, shaking Gary loose. Comfort in wartime was a luxury that other people were afforded.

There weren't many living people among the wreckage, but there were lots of body parts. She saw feet still laced into boots and whole bodies frozen stiff in climbing positions, as if they'd tried to claw their way back onto the broken ship. Jenny took Mary off autopilot and navigated through them herself. This was what she did after a battle; forced herself to stare at the aftermath so she would remember the consequences the next time a hard choice came her way.

There were a few people left in the two large pieces of the *Kilonova*. Jenny could see them at the windows, watching the *Stagecoach Mary* and the small Reason ships pick their way through the wreckage.

"We can hold at least fifty for each trip to the surface," said Jenny. "Gary, get us a landing area on the surface for at least a few dozen small ships."

Findae snorted and Jenny turned her chair to face him.

"Is there a problem?" she asked the king of the unicorns, who was always acting like a gigantic pain in the ass.

"You're going to inundate our settlement with humans who want to see our Bala enslaved again," he replied. "Not to mention this invasion that Boges was going on about."

"We're going to rescue survivors and get them out of the freezing vacuum of space and then we'll worry about the sanctity of your precious baby civilization," she said. "Lock them all up when they land for all I care, but I don't let people die in openspace."

Findae opened his mouth to say something, but Gary interrupted. "We're going to give them a chance," he said firmly.

"Fine," said Findae with a growl. "But you are responsible for what happens to the Bala from here on out."

"Gladly," said Gary.

Jenny's back twinged and she suddenly felt all of the burns, bruises, and lacerations screaming for attention.

"Gravity off, Mary," she said. Before anyone could protest, the gravity eased and everyone floated weightless in the cockpit.

Jenny thought there was nothing so delightful as watching the king of the unicorns flail through the air.

CHAPTER TWENTY-TWO
Your World, Your Rules

In the end they were able to rescue over two thousand people from the remains of the FTL *Kilonova*. Bào went to the cargo hold and helped the survivors on board, handing off the wounded to Ricky, who seemed to have picked up some moderately usable first aid skills while pretending to be a doctor. She flirted with him every chance she got, which delighted Bào immensely.

They'd also helped wrap up and dispose of the dead people floating around the *Stagecoach Mary*'s hold. Captain Jenny gave them every fitted sheet in storage on her ship to wrap them in because, as she put it, "Fuck fitted sheets."

No one seemed to know quite what to do about the alleged parasite in Jenny's brain. With no Sisters in the survivors there was no one to ask for clarification. Everyone except Gary steered clear of touching her but she seemed to be no threat to anyone. And she was so useful in a crisis that they eventually forgot about her "invader."

When every available space on the *Stagecoach Mary* was filled with living humans, Jenny followed Gary's directions and took them out of orbit. She set her ship down in a field near a quaint little village dotted with pink log cabins crafted in intricate dwarven designs. On the far side of the village, a small mountain rose out of the ground, topped by a fortress that still looked like it was in the process of being constructed.

The village had been sliced in two by the *Kilonova*'s laser attack.

There was now a burnt swath cutting across it as wide as a Reason highway. The Bala were still putting out fires and pulling villagers out of burning structures. Wounded creatures were being dragged, flown, and magicked to a few larger buildings on the outskirts of the settlement.

The cargo hold opened and Captain Jenny wheeled down the ramp first. The Bala stopped to watch her emerge. Findae and Gary came next, walking side by side but not speaking or looking at each other.

Bào stood at the top of the ramp and peered over the edge. It was steeper than Jenny had made it seem when she rolled down at top speed. Ricky reached over and took Bào's arm, as if she was escorting him to a dance.

"Come on, kid," she smiled, walking him down. The rest of the humans followed them out, milling around close to the ship, outnumbered ten to one by the Bala.

Bào had advised them to remove as much of their Reason uniforms as they could, so most of them stood around in their crimson trousers and white undershirts. Jackets, hats, and other insignia had disappeared. They were still clearly human, but at least they weren't reminding everyone on the planet about their part in the genocide.

Captain Jenny seemed to be having trouble rolling her wheelchair through the uncut grass. She put herself between the Bala and the ragtag group of human refugees. She spoke so that everyone gathered could hear her.

"Gary Cobalt and his father have given us permission to land, but we recognize that this is your world and your rules. We're here only by the grace of your hospitality and no one here expects to be treated as anything other than a war criminal," she said.

It was clear from the muted protests behind her that not every human in the group agreed with Captain Jenny's assessment of the situation. Luckily, she'd confiscated everyone's service weapons on the *Stagecoach Mary* as a prerequisite for being allowed on board.

A centaur galloped to the forefront of the Bala.

"Do you see what they did our town?" she flicked her head to point to the destructive path that cut through the village. "Just as Findae predicted, they're still trying to kill us."

"That attack was from the Sisters of the Supersymmetrical Axion," said Gary. "They took control of the Reason ship and turned the weapon on us. They have been stopped."

"Why would the Sisters turn on us?" asked the centaur. Bào recognized her from the vicious martial arts brawls that had been broadcast throughout the Reason. She was a champion fighter, beloved by humans and Bala alike. Horm was her name.

"We don't know for certain." said Gary.

"They were on about their 'service to the greater future' bullshit," said Ricky.

A few Bala nodded. The Sisters' ways were infuriatingly obtuse. Their sect alone could have turned the tide of the war with the humans at any time, yet they refused to openly participate. Instead, they operated as a shadowy and unpredictable force for both good and evil. Horm put her palm skyward in an exceedingly rude centaur gesture. "The Sisters can bite my ass," she said.

Ricky grinned and squeeze Bào's hand. "I like it here," she whispered into his ear. His arms prickled.

"Me too," said Bào. "I hope they let us stay."

"Oh they'll let us stay," said Ricky. "Just let me handle it."

"Were there any casualties?" Gary asked an angel in the group.

"Three dead, fifteen injured. Most had already left the village by the time the laser hit," the angel replied. "We found a group of Bala living in a forest cave. It's deep underground – no weapon in orbit could penetrate that far."

"Are those the people who had disappeared?" asked Gary.

"Yes. Though the Sisters who captured them were long gone," said the angel. "We're still searching. The addition of the necromancers will speed that search considerably."

Bào hadn't seen a full angel in so long, he had trouble not staring. This one had hair the color of spun gold. His skin seemed to sparkle in the sun. Bào wanted to touch any part of him to see if it was real, but that was rude beyond belief.

"The Reason ship has been destroyed. Tell those in the forest that they can return," said Gary. The angel nodded, spread his wings, and took off toward the west. Bào couldn't tear his eyes away until the angel was a dot in the pink sky.

"I love your planet," said Ricky to the assembled Bala. "What do you call it?"

"We haven't quite settled on a name yet," said Gary. "It's complicated."

"There's nothing complicated about naming a planet," announced Ricky. Her tone had shifted. She now sounded for all the universe like she was hosting a game show. "We'll have a contest! Winner gets to name the planet."

Gary turned to the rest of the Bala. "There are other survivors up in orbit. I need volunteers to help collect them."

"We don't want them here," said Horm.

Everyone else ignored Gary.

"I want to name the planet," said a neofelis cat with kittens spilling out of her arms.

"Me too, I have a good idea for a planet name," said a yeti, pushing his way to the front of the group. More Bala followed him, shouting their suggestions.

"So many contestants," cried Ricky, nudging Bào with a secretive grin. "All right. Let's start right now.

Gary put a hand on her shoulder. "We're dealing with the human survivors right now. The contest can wait," he said.

The Bala erupted in a chorus of groans and protests.

Ricky plucked Gary's hand off her shoulder and held it away from her. "Gary Cobalt, I promise you're going to want me to run this game. It'll take less than five minutes. Do you trust me?" she asked.

"Absolutely not," said Gary.

"That's fine, you'll see," she said, dropping his arm. "Everyone gather around," she said, projecting her voice above all of the Bala grumbling. "For every live human you retrieve from orbit and bring safely planetside, you get one entry into the planet naming drawing. Unlimited chances, and yes, you can work together in groups and everyone in the group gets their own entry. When all of the humans have been rescued, we'll pull one name from all of the entries."

Gary erupted in a belly laugh so loud that the neofelis kittens started to cry. He bent over, chuckling for a solid minute. When he finally looked up, his face was streaked with tears of laughter.

"Undignified," said Findae.

"Brilliant," said Gary. He stepped forward and grabbed Ricky in a tight embrace. "You're now officially the head of the Human Rescue and Planet Naming committees. Welcome to your new home."

Findae snorted in disgust. He lifted his head toward a blemmye hovering near the edge of the crowd.

"You there, blemmye," he called. "You started all of this with your hideous song." He cantered toward the blemmye, who lumbered off surprisingly fast.

A few of the Bala followed them, muttering and swearing about the humans in their midst. The rest remained, waiting for Ricky to speak.

"Told you," Ricky whispered to Bào, who was amazed at her ability to turn a crowd to her will. She would make a great leader if she weren't so preoccupied with earning cash.

Jenny shoved her chair over to them. "Hey," she said, interrupting the excitement that was rising throughout the crowd. "Anyone seen my wife? Cute little dryad, about twice my height, answers to the name of Kaila."

"I know your wife. She lives in the forest," said an angel.

"I'll have someone go get Kaila," said Gary. She'll be overjoyed to see you.

"I told her I'd get here," said Captain Jenny, looking exhausted. She tilted her head, listening.

"Do you have any protein powder on your ship?" Horm asked Captain Jenny.

"I have entire hold full of food," said Jenny. "Have at it. The village can take everything from my ship."

"Thank the gods, I can finally get my carb ratios right," said the centaur.

"What's been happening on this season of *Dungeons and Diamonds?*" asked the yeti. "Last I saw, Zizzurath was about to ask Paladryl to marry him."

"Do you have any condoms?" asked the neofelis cat.

The Bala were exceedingly creative in ways they came up with to rescue the humans. Besides the stoneships, and the hippogriff-mermaid combination from Copernica Citadel, they also came up with pairs of angels (who didn't need to breathe) and phoenixes (to keep them from freezing), and a sixteen-pixie team that turned out to be excellent at finding people trapped in the wreckage and handing them off to the ships.

Each human who arrived on the planet was briefed by Gary and Captain Jenny on how to behave on their new world. Nearly everyone agreed immediately. The prospect of dying in orbit was enough to scare consideration into anyone.

An eager kappa provided an empty rain barrel for the voting. As each rescue party came back with a live human, Ricky handed them slips torn from a prescription pad she'd found in her jacket pocket. With the only pen on the entire planet, each Bala wrote their name carefully on the paper and tossed it into the barrel. Bào swirled them around, mixing the slips.

A screech in the distance froze a few of the Bala in their tracks. A dryad ran through the grass, which was incredible, as dryads usually took days to cover that much ground. This dryad took a running leap at Captain Jenny and landed directly in her lap.

Captain Jenny gasped.

"Oh gods you're heavy. Must be good water on this planet," she said.

"It's sour," said the dryad, leaning down to kiss Captain Jenny. Both of them ceased complaining.

"Splinters," warned Gary.

Neither of them stopped. Ricky collected the last of the planet name suggestions. "Everyone gather round, we're about to find out where we live," she called. The Bala milled around, buzzing with energy. They whispered their best suggestions to each other in various degrees of confidence.

Ricky gave the barrel to two juvenile elves, who rolled it between them exuberantly as the crowd gathered. Gary and Findae came to stand near Ricky to lend authority to the event, though Findae was still skeptical.

"This is an inane way to name a planet," said Findae, snorting his displeasure as usual. Bào was starting to think this great unicorn king was all bluster and no bite.

Ricky fished around in the barrel. As she leaned down, she gave Bào a wink. She pulled a paper out of the barrel and unfolded it. She showed it to Bào with a secret smile.

Planet McPlanetface.

In one fluid motion, she pivoted toward the crowd, tucked the paper into her waistband and pulled a different folded sheet. With a flourish, she held it above her head for all to see.

"Welcome to planet… Anjali."

Findae dragged a hoof across the dirt and walked away from the others. The other Bala cheered and clapped. The crowd chattered happily. Bào leaned over to Ricky.

"You cheated," he whispered, simultaneously horrified and amused.

"I asked Gary what he wanted to name the planet. You never leave the winner to chance," she said.

"You are incredible," said Bào.

"Thank you," said Ricky.

Jenny wheeled over to them and the unicorns as the Bala celebrated their new home.

"I think we have one last thing to do," she said, nudging Gary with her footrest. "What we talked about on the way here."

Gary stepped forward until he was in front of the Bala.

"There's one last thing we need to do tonight," he called out to the crowd. "Many of you have expressed concerns about bringing people into our settlement and those concerns are valid. We are going to ensure that every human brought to live on Anjali will not harm our Bala. To that end, we are going to hold investigations and trials for every person who wishes to join us. Starting with this one."

Gary turned to Captain Jenny, who stared out at the Bala with an unreadable expression. The Bala were silent. Gary continued.

"Captain Geneva Waimarie Perata, you are under arrest for war crimes against innumerable Bala individuals and you will be detained until the extent of the damage is determined and an appropriate consequence is determined."

A few of the Bala cheered. Most stood in upset and uncomfortable silence. Jenny nodded in agreement and held out her crossed wrists. The Bala looked at each other awkwardly. There were no handcuffs on their world.

"It's fine. It's not as if I can get very far in this grass. Did any of you ever hear of a lawnmower?" asked Jenny.

"I will personally take Captain Perata into custody at our jail," said Gary. He stepped behind her to push through the weeds and she let him.

"You already have a jail?" she asked, tilting her head back to look up at him.

"First building we built," said Gary

"My kind of planet," said Jenny.

As they walked away, Bào realized he still hadn't let go of Ricky's arm. "I can't believe it's only been a few hours since we met in the medbay," he said. "I didn't mean to ruin your card game with my fake five unicorn flush."

"Are you kidding? This is the best first date I've ever had," said Ricky, looking at Bào for one extra second to see if he protested their evening being called a first date. Bào chuckled and leaned his head on Ricky's shoulder.

"I need a nap. Besides being crushed by a necromancer and shot by a rogue cowboy, pretending to be twenty-two all day is exhausting," said Bào.

"Too exhausted for a kiss to end our first date?" asked Ricky.

"That would be lovely," said Bào with a smile.

The necromancer Bào Zhú would never have guessed that his evening would begin with unnecessary surgery and end with a kiss from the most intriguing person he had ever met. They kissed under the rosy pink sky of the planet lovingly named after Gary Cobalt's mother until a shadow passed over them. Bào looked up into the face of the martial arts centaur.

"May I help you?" he asked.

"Just bored. There's no TV here," said Horm.

Ricky leaned toward the centaur. "Is there a decent bar on this planet yet?" she asked.

"Gods, no," said the centaur. "And I'm dying for a drink."

Ricky took Bào's arm on one side and reached up to take Horm's arm on the other. "I'm Ricky, this is my boyfriend, Bào. Tell me about the local berries," she said, walking them toward an empty grass plot on the outskirts of the settlement.

CHAPTER TWENTY-THREE
Space Unicorns

Though he had no real control over the fledgling judicial system on Anjali, Gary had requested the charges against Jenny be narrow and specific. It would have been easy for her to become the stand-in for all of humanity's crimes against the Bala. He encouraged the hastily-assembled Investigating Committee to be as granular as possible; to limit their scope to a handful of the most damaging acts that would lead to a satisfactory accounting of her crimes.

In the end they had come up with two. The primary charge against her was the massacre and kidnapping of Bala at the Siege of Copernica Citadel, a battle in which she'd been lauded as a hero by the Reason. The second, which surprised him, was related to the detention of a sapient being – himself. He hadn't expected his own ordeal to be adjudicated. In a way, he dreaded the detailed testimony he would be asked to give about his time as her captive.

In the absence of paper records and computer files, the Investigating Committee thought they would have to use witness statement and Jenny's own testimony (which she had been all too willing to give) to compile the evidence. It wasn't until someone sifting through the wreckage of the *Kilonova* found the data center floating in openspace that they realized they had a record of the entire history of the Reason, war crimes and all. The Siege of Copernica Citadel had been faithfully recorded in all its auditory and visual glory.

Gary sincerely hoped that they would never be required to

play that file. It was bad enough to have to talk through the worst experience of one's life, but to see it replayed in gory detail was too much to bear. He knew that firsthand because of what the Pymmie had done to him at the Century Summit, forcing everyone at the table to relive the horror of Cheryl Ann's death.

It had been fifteen years since Copernica Citadel but the Bala justice system had no concept of a "statute of limitations." There was no date at which trauma expired. No arbitrary number of years when a harm no longer mattered. No, the Bala allowed transgressions to be tried long after their best-by date. Unlike the Reason, which seemed focused on making sure perpetrators were never too inconvenienced by their crimes. Gary guessed that, in a society full of perpetrators, it benefitted everyone to ensure that no one was in too much jeopardy for their harmful behavior.

On the Bala planets, with their smatterings of immortal beings, and the ingredients for immortality often at hand, there was no point to restricting the timeline of the trial process. A crime could be adjudicated at any point during, or even after, the lifetime of the victim or the perpetrator. There were occasionally trials of fact held centuries after the original act had taken place. And the same matter could be retried multiple times in light of new information or changes in the public understanding of law.

One notorious murder case had been re-adjudicated nineteen times in the three thousand years following the original crime. New evidence had surfaced, as well as new witnesses. Some of those retrials had been initiated at the request of the killer herself, as popular sentiments toward mercy killings had turned in her favor. Unfortunately for her, none of the outcomes were substantively different, and the murderer had remained at the Abbey prison of the Sisters of the Supersymmetrical Axion for the last several centuries.

Gary had briefed Jenny on the history of Bala tribunals, and specifically war crime tribunals, so she would understand that all of her crimes against Bala, no matter how old or seemingly insignificant, would be fair game for the tribunal. The trial would be overseen by the Consensus of Nine: a group of beings representing a cross section of Bala species. They would see the evidence, hear the testimony, and formulate a decision as to guilt or innocence, then hand down an appropriate consequence. In that way, they acted as both judge and jury.

Jenny rolled into the newly constructed courtroom in a fresh wooden wheelchair given to her by the dwarves of Anjali. This one had new carvings, representing a necromancer in a wheelchair tearing the Reason flag in two. It was clear whom the dwarves were rooting for. But they seemed torn over Boges' actions. None of them wanted to talk to Gary about her actions.

Bào and Ricky huddled together whispering on a bench with two young human cadets from the *Kilonova* – a South Asian girl and a pale boy who never stopped staring at Bào. Kaila sat in the front row chewing her fronds anxiously. Gary took a spot against the wall near her and tried to offer a comforting smile. Kaila sighed in return, sending a cascade of dry leaves onto the floor.

The Consensus of Nine entered the room and took their spots behind a railing at the front of the room. Jenny wheeled to the table allocated for the accused. There were slates and writing stones stacked neatly on the table. It was odd, going through a sophisticated court proceeding with stone-age tools. Jenny fumbled her electronic tablet down onto the table. It echoed throughout the room. There was a hint of defiance in the way she sat back in her chair. If she dug in for a fight, this could take years.

Jenny would be permitted to submit any item, written or recorded, in her defense. She'd been offered an assistant, someone to help with procedure and developing her case, but she had declined, preferring to simply speak for herself. Gary suspected Kamis was offering advice to her as well. He hoped she wasn't taking it.

Gary was supposed to sit at the testimony table to her right while he recounted the tortures visited upon him, but he walked toward her table instead. His status as a leader was not intended to have a bearing on the outcome, but it surely would. No one was immune to admiration and the desire to protect those who were in power. It was second nature. Which meant that the Consensus of Nine were likely already biased against her. He would do whatever he could to ensure the trial was fair.

He stood beside her and waited until she looked up from her notes.

"Is this spot taken?" he asked.

"You are not sitting next to me," she said. "Isn't that your table over there?"

"I don't think there's any reason to pretend that we're strangers. Or that we don't have a history together. This is a complex and nuanced situation," he said.

She shook her head but didn't insist that he leave the table.

"You are not helping," she grumbled. But he was sure that he was.

Yes, she had done the things she'd been accused of, but she had also convinced the Pymmie to save the Bala and stopped an invading force from landing on Anjali.

The chatter in the hallway outside of the room rose in volume and pitch. Unamip – lower god of the Bala and liaison to the Pymmie – trotted through the double doors at the back of the room. Most Bala and none of the humans had ever seen him in person. The craned their necks to stare. Some shouted thanks to him. He smiled bashfully in response. Unamip tucked his huge unicorn body into the back row like a common spectator. Coming in like that, instead of using the private door at the front of the hall, was a signal that he intended to watch the trial, but not intervene.

The speaker for the Consensus raised a tentacle to still the room.

"Gathered Bala, we are about to begin the first information gathering session in the trial of Geneva Perata. The first accusation is of forcibly detaining and injuring a Bala being, Gary Cobalt. This matter will be adjudicated separately from all other charges and all questions should be directed to the Consensus.

"Geneva, have you been briefed on the procedures of this tribunal?" asked the speaker.

"I have," said Jenny.

"Then we shall—"

Findae burst in through the door behind the Consensus, scattering everyone for a moment as he pushed past to take a spot at the front of the room.

"You may proceed," he said, as Bala in the first couple of rows rolled their eyes.

The speaker for the Consensus waited for him to settle himself, then looked over at Gary and Jenny.

"Gary Cobalt, you are not required to sit with the accused." She waved the tentacle toward the empty table intended for him.

"It would be ridiculous to pretend that Jenny and I aren't well acquainted. Unless she objects, I believe it will be beneficial for her to have a Bala companion to assist in the trial," he said. A murmur went through the rows of beings observing.

"I don't need your help," Jenny whispered at him.

"Jenny Perata, do you wish Gary Cobalt to leave your table?" asked the speaker.

Gary reached out and patted her arm.

Jenny rolled from behind the table to the open area before the Consensus. "I know I'm the one on trial here, but these unicorns. I just…" She shook her head and a few of the Bala in the seats chuckled. "They think they know everything."

"Some of us do know everything," said Unamip from the rear.

Jenny wheeled up to the railing containing the beings who would hear her defense and judge her. She looked resolute. She held her tablet up toward the speaker, who wrapped a tentacle around the smooth glass and drew it up to their eyes.

"I would like to offer the Consensus my electronic tablet," said Jenny, ignoring the wistful meow of a neofelis cat behind her. "I have detailed the dates, times, and locations of every crime I have committed against a Bala being that I can remember. I am responsible for killing and detaining thousands at Copernica Citadel. I am responsible for the decision to capture and torture Gary Cobalt.

"I understand that what I did was wrong and motivated by fear and xenophobia and entitlement and I can never undo the damage I have caused. I've tried to make things right by telling the Pymmie that humans couldn't be trusted and by taking out the *Kilonova*, but I don't think that it's enough. I mean, nothing I can do will be enough."

She spun her chair to face the onlookers.

"I'm sorry. For what I've done and for the way humans have treated you. If it's any consolation, we did this to ourselves for millennia before you showed up. It's nothing personal, it's just the way we are," she said. "We wasted an opportunity for cooperation, back at the start. If things had gone differently… anyway.

"I've committed every atrocity on that list of charges and probably some more that I've forgotten. I'm willing to do anything to make amends for the awful things I did." She looked over at Gary. "And to you in particular, Gary Cobalt. I can't undo the damage or bring anyone back from the dead, but I am sorry. I accept any consequences the Consensus feel is appropriate."

The room was silent. The speaker flicked through screen after screen of Jenny's confession.

Jenny wheeled back over to behind her table. Gary grasped her hand, now empty in her lap, and gave it a squeeze. She was right that there was probably nothing she could do to absolve herself of those terrible actions. But hearing her admit they were wrong and offering an apology did help. More than he thought it would. There was a small measure of relief in hearing his former captor say, "What I did was wrong and I'm sorry."

The speaker looked up at the rest of the Consensus. "We will take a break to review this document. It will be made available for the public as well."

Jenny cringed and wiped at her face.

"Captain Perata, I trust that you do not need to be detained and that you will return at the appointed time."

"Of course," said Jenny.

"Then we won't bother returning you to the holding cell. We

will reconvene when the thricbugs begin to sing."

Gary got the feeling they were giving her the time to say goodbye to Kaila and her friends while they deliberated in private. The Bala generally did not believe in the death penalty, but, with magic, any option was on the table. They could decide to stick her on a stoneship and send her to another planet, or even plunge her into the null and leave her there, discorporated and adrift. There was no end to the creativity of Consensus rulings.

When the Consensus had gone into the private meeting area the onlookers shuffled out of the back of the room. Jenny wheeled out at Gary's side. He wasn't sure but it seemed like she'd slowed down to use him as a shield from the angry crowd. Kaila stepped forward and draped her fronds over Jenny.

"That was hard," he heard Jenny say into Kaila's foliage.

"I told Gary war was coming," said Kaila.

Findae trotted up, indignant. Kaila hopped backward, leaving Jenny unguarded.

"Your crimes are numerous," he said.

"I don't deny it," said Jenny.

"You will answer for them," said Findae.

"Is that not literally what I'm here for, fella?" Jenny asked. Findae, intolerant of both sarcasm and being called "fella," huffed away.

Horm was nearby, trying to incite a group of Bala to go yell at Jenny. Gary wandered over.

"…and we should tell her all of the ways that humans hurt us. Make her understand. Maybe show her." Horm punched a fist into her open palm.

"Is she answering for all of humanity's crimes, or just her own?" asked Gary.

"Step out, Gary," said Horm. "You're getting your time in court. My torturers are back at Fort J having the time of their lives."

"Somehow, I don't believe that's the case, but Jenny isn't here to answer for what happened to you," he said.

"When who is?" demanded Horm. It was not a question that Gary had an answer to.

The Consensus had to have known that angry Bala would confront Jenny during the break. Perhaps that was also their intention.

A group of Bala, led by Horm, swarmed her chair. Gary stepped behind her, ready to step in if it got out of hand. Some of them knelt and told her their tearful stories. Some stepped up and swore at her, then left fuming.

She nodded at their complaints and offered apologies to anyone who would stay long enough listen. She seemed to understand that most of them were not saying these things to her, but to the humans who had wronged them over the years.

The other human refugees hung back at the edges of the crowd, not wanting to be drawn into the hostile recounting of past wrongs. Their own trials would be coming at some point and this was a glimpse into what they could expect. Most of them had entered into Bala society chastened and willing to learn but a few holdouts had a hard time letting go of the Reason rhetoric they'd been steeping in for generations. Those humans had been shunted off to a smaller village in the south, near the gorgons, sirens, and banshees. Word around town was that after a handful of run-ins with the neighboring Bala, the humans had become content with staying put in their own little encampment and were not causing much trouble.

As carefully as they had sifted through the wreckage, the bodies of Cowboy Jim, Captain Singh, and Boges were never found. They were marked as dead, on the assumption that they had either floated too far away to find or were perhaps incinerated in one of the fires that had burned on one the *Kilonova*'s still-sealed decks. But not everyone was convinced they were gone for good.

"Hey there, Jenny Fucking Perata," said Ricky, pushing through the crowd. "Want to take a walk?" The Bala parted for her. In just a handful of days, Ricky Tang had become one of the most beloved residents of Planet Anjali. She'd already learned how to make a passable juice out of cryberries and the sweet sap of the pink trees. And there were six tanks of grain mash fermenting in her cabin.

Gary made a note to consider enacting liquor laws before the week was out.

Ricky dropped Bào's hand, grabbed the handles of Jenny's chair, and swiveled it toward the marshes, waving away the Bala. For once, Jenny didn't protest being pushed. Kaila and Gary walked behind both of them.

Ricky walked down to the water line and stopped at an area where the grass had been trampled into a hard-packed dirt by the grain harvesters.

"This'll do," said Ricky, letting go of the chair and flopping down on the dirt next to it. Kaila stretched her roots into the soil and unfurled her branches, creating a canopy for them to rest under. Bào stood in the shade, complaining about the heat.

Gary sat in front of them all. It was like the opening line to a joke – a unicorn, a starship captain, a dryad, a necromancer, and a conwoman walk into a bar. Jenny chewed her fingernail and Ricky kicked at the ground, stirring up little clouds of dust that settled back onto her boots. Kaila's branches shuddered every now and then. None of them without battle-scars. All of them looking worried in their own way.

"This has been… a time," said Jenny, her voice husky with emotion.

"It's not over yet," said Kaila, draping a branch on her shoulder.

"Yeah, this isn't the end of Jenny Fucking Perata," said Ricky.

"No, but maybe it is," said Jenny. "And maybe that's all right."

Kaila's branch lifted off her shoulder and flicked her in the ear. Jenny flinched.

"No," the dryad said simply.

"You smashed the *Kilonova*, which probably saved every life on this planet," said Ricky, kicking extra hard so that the dust settled on everyone else as well. "That has to be worth something."

"I don't think Bala justice is eye for an eye," said Jenny. Her eyes unfocused as she listened to Kamis say something. She shrugged in response.

"Regardless. I think the circumstances of your actions has to be taken into consideration," said Ricky.

"True," smiled Jenny. "Like people who fleeced down on their luck Bala out of millions of dollars, but it was wartime and so it wasn't their fault."

"At least I don't have a brain parasite that's part of an alien invasion," said Ricky, letting one corner of her mouth rise in a half-smile.

"I think the Sisters were wrong about that. Kamis is content to just hang around in here," Jenny tapped on her temple. "He's not invading anything."

"That's exactly what an invader would say," said Bào.

For the next few hours, the group talked like old friends. Their conversation broached both weighty topics like the nature of forgiveness and the responsibilities of power, as well as more amusing tales of their adventures since the Summit. Bào and Ricky in particular had a story about criosphinx bones and sewer systems that left them all in tearful laughter on the ground.

The sun dipped below a reddened horizon and the thricbugs began to chirp.

"Time to go," said Jenny, spinning her chair and resting her hands on her lap, making it clear that she was waiting for someone else to push. Kaila was still pulling her roots out of the ground. Ricky was helping Bào get up with a slow stretch, so Gary went over and took the handles.

"I don't know if you remember," she began as they walked toward the Consensus who would decide her fate. "But back at Fort J after the Summit, you asked me what I planned to do to make amends for all of this."

"I do remember," he said. "Have you decided?"

"I have," she said. "I've been given this incredible gift. And, up until now, I've been pretty reluctant to use it. I didn't want to hurt more people. But I think I've been wrong about that. I think I'm supposed to be using it, practicing, and getting better. I bet I could be really good at it if I tried."

"I'm absolutely sure you would be," said Gary.

"I think I ended up here, in this place named after your incredible mother, to protect the Bala with this unimaginable amount of power I've been given. The Reason is going to find us again. They're going to send more ships eventually, but we'll be ready for them," she said, biting her fingernail. "I'll be ready for them."

"Sounds hard. You should probably just donate fifty dollars to the Bala Benevolent Fund and call yourself an ally," he said.

She tisked, reached up behind her, and flicked his ear.

"I was being serious," she said. "We were having a moment."

"You were having a moment, I was pushing you through these hideous weeds," said Gary. "Maybe your first act as a benevolent god should be to figure out how to cut the grass."

She opened her mouth for another sarcastic comment, but he leaned down close to her ear.

"We would be lucky to have such a fierce warrior as our guardian," he whispered. "I can think of no better way of making amends than protecting and serving those who you've wronged. I would be honored to stand beside you."

"Oh I don't need your help," she said, veering away from what was coming dangerously close to a moment of sincerity between them.

"I always help my friends," said Gary.

"Are we friends now?" asked Jenny.

"I think so, probably," said Gary.

"That's nice," she replied, setting her chin in her hand with a smile.

Nearly everyone had already gone back inside of the hall. Gary let go of Jenny's chair as they crossed the threshold and she was ready to take the wheels. They settled at the table. The Consensus was in place and looked like they had been waiting there for a bit of time.

"Are we late?" asked Ricky.

"They seem to have decided faster than the allotted time," said Gary over his shoulder. He wasn't sure if that was good or bad.

The speaker raised her hand to silence the room.

"We have come to a consensus," she said.

Everyone in the room held their breath.

"We have decided that appropriate consequence for the actions of Geneva Perata are the following: expulsion and exclusion the daily activities of Bala society. Restrictions on interstellar travel. Service to the Bala community. Reparations to those wronged where possible. These consequences will continue for a period not shorter than three hundred Earth-based years, a symbolic sentence that bears the weight of all the Bala you were involved in harming. We hope that you will dedicate each day of your remaining life to the memory of the Bala who were senselessly lost during that time."

The Consensus finished their listing of punishments. Jenny had stopped moving at the word "expulsion." The Consensus hadn't spelled out what "expulsion" meant. It could mean the next island or the next star system.

"Do the aggrieved have objections to the consequences as listed?" asked the speaker.

A wave of awkward murmuring went through the room. It seemed as if some were dissatisfied but were hesitant to say so.

"The implementation of these conditions will be up to the discretion of the settlement's leadership. And they will commence in the morning." The speaker looked to Gary, as did half the room. At this moment, he was glad to have taken a seat near Jenny.

"I understand," he replied.

"Then barring any other discussion, we conclude these proceedings." The Consensus stepped down from the platform and were suddenly just part of the mingling crowd. The speaker wound her way over to Jenny's table.

"We appreciated the candor with which you approached your actions. That did figure into our discussion," she said.

Jenny waved a weak acknowledgement and wheeled through the crowd to the outside. Gary followed.

"So have you decided where you're sending me?" she asked, her voice tight.

"Yes," said Gary.

"All right," she replied, shoving her wheels through the grass. Jenny had changed quite a bit, but not enough to swallow her pride and simply ask where. Perhaps that humility would develop some time over the next three hundred years.

Gary stepped off Kaapo's raft, taking care not to sink down into the acidic mud surrounding the marsh.

"I'll come back for you in a few hours," said Kaapo, pushing off. He'd come a few times already so she knew the routine.

"Thanks," he said.

He followed a wide gravel path into the depths of Anjali's woods. The light in here changed from a soft pink to a rich red as the sun shone through the canopy of leaves. The path turned and went deeper into the trees, where the native residents were frequently seen. Kaila had reported that most of them were benign – even the octomites only wanted head scritches and pets if you could get past the eyeless horror of their heads.

The path became rougher and less visible. The dwarves had tucked their newest structure far enough into the foliage that it wasn't visible from the marsh, or even from the main path, meaning that its occupants were unlikely to be disturbed by anyone.

Gary stepped over roots and vines, hoping he was still on the right path and not just following tracks toward a hungry animal's den. He knew he was in the right spot as he came upon a clearing surrounded by a fenced-in area. He tried the gate and found it locked. A tree branch swung down and tapped his arm away. He lifted his arms, ready to swing at whatever horrific thing was coming for him.

"So ready to fight," whispered the dryad that had been standing there the whole time.

"Kaila. Sorry." He let his hands drop.

"She's inside." Kaila reached over and threaded her thinnest branches through the gate mechanism. It opened with the twang of metal against metal.

"Not magical," he mused, pushing the gate open.

"She's a necromancer. What would be the point?" replied Kaila.

"She's also a mechanic. Picking this lock would be two seconds of work for her," said Gary.

"The point is not to keep her in but to keep others out," said Kaila, removing her branches from the lock and standing up straight. With her face at rest, she looked like just another tree. She'd even started to get a pinkish hue to her leaves, helping her blend in better.

"Kay, who are you talking to?" Jenny called from the cabin. The door swung open and Jenny wheeled through the level threshold into the short grass. "Oh hey," she said, spotting Gary.

"May I visit?" asked Gary. A courtesy, since he had the right to visit anyone held in Anjali's prisons.

"Of course." Jenny spun her chair and beaconed him into her cabin. It was significantly more well-appointed than his cell had been on the *Jaggery*, but not really much larger. It was like the tiniest of grunt apartments on Fort J. She had a small food preparation area and a table for dining, a bed in the corner and a door to what was likely a bathroom. The room was dark – lit only by a few high windows that Jenny could not have reached without the assistance of zero gravity. Then again, it was Jenny. Anything was possible.

There were telltale signs that Jenny was comfortable here already. Her bed was unmade and dirty clothes were strewn around the corners of the room where they wouldn't get tangled in her wheels. The morning's dirty dishes still sat on the table. There was some other project strewn about the place. Wires and circuit boards.

"What are you making?" he asked.

"I don't know. Just tinkering, I guess," said Jenny, picking up a processor that had been salvaged from the *Kilonova's* debris field. The Bala were getting all sorts of technology from the junk in orbit. "Not sure what it's going to be yet. I don't have a soldering iron, but…" She touched her finger between a wire and a circuit board. A tiny purple spark jumped out and fused the metal between the two. A useful skill.

"Nice to see you've made yourself right at home," said Gary.

"It's my jail cell, I'll do what I want," she said, clearing the dishes and putting them into the sink. The dwarves had built everything flat and within her reach. In some ways, this room was probably better than most of the captain's quarters she'd lived in.

"Prison treating you well?" he asked.

"I prefer to think of it as an early retirement," she said.

"Looks comfortable," he said.

"Probably because no one is digging horn out of my head every morning," she replied, then caught herself. "Sorry. Not a joke."

Gary pursed his lips and sat down at the table. Jenny's tablet sat unlocked in her spot. On the screen was a personnel file of one of the *Kilonova's* deceased crew.

"A bit of light reading?" he asked.

She reached over and flicked off the screen.

"Just looking at some stuff," she said.

Jenny pulled up to one of the counters and took two glazed clay cups down from a low shelf. She poured water into each from a pitcher, then held her hand over them for half a minute. She tucked one mug into a recessed holder in her armrest and handed the second one to him. He took a tentative sip from the steaming cup. The liquid had become a rich, fragrant chai, spicy the way his mother used to make it. The smell of it brought him right back to the *Jaggery*, sitting and watching her stir a pot full of milky tea. She'd even gotten the extra cardamom right.

"Impressive. You're getting quite skilled," he said. "Transforming matter is no small thing."

She leaned her elbows on the table like an eager student.

"Bào says the trick is not to go big, but instead to be precise. It takes a lot more energy but it keeps me from blowing up every bloody thing in a ten meter radius."

"Bào always was a good teacher," said Gary.

"Funny, he said that about you," she replied. "Kamis says hello."

"Hi, Kamis," said Gary. "We should start thinking about how to get you out of there."

"Kamis says that he's perfectly content where he is," said Jenny. "After all of his adventures, domestic life suits him. He says he's right where he needs to be."

Gary sipped again and sat back in his chair. He was afraid of that. If Kamis really was some kind of invader, he would need to be removed from Jenny. At least here, far from anyone, they were relatively safe from him. They sat without speaking for several minutes as Gary weighed the options, none of them appealing. Aside from the chittering of the thricbugs outside, the cabin was quiet.

"I miss it too," said Jenny, sipping at her own drink, which smelled like lemons and crackled with carbonation.

"Miss what?" he asked.

"The hum of the engines. When are you going back up?" she asked.

"No plans currently," he said. "Too much to do on the surface."

"You should go – even if it's just for a few hours. You were born up there. You've gotta miss it."

She was right. He wanted nothing more than to be in the *Jaggery's* cockpit, dipping into nullspace and watching as the stars fell away and the Eye of Unamip came into view.

"If you do go, would you take my tablet and make a recording of the three moons up there? I want to see them on a flyby but I'll never get up there again."

"You never know," replied Gary.

"Oh I know. Three hundred years here. Even if I do make it that long because of some necromancer bullshit, no one here is going to let me on board a ship again," she said.

"You forget, that Unamip willing, I will be alive orders of magnitude longer than you. If you survive your sentence, I would be glad to have you as my co-pilot," said Gary.

Jenny didn't answer, but a little smile played at the corners of her mouth. She was born to be in the stars just like him. It had to be torture to be planetbound for the foreseeable future. Which was entirely the point of this consequence.

"Kaila seems to be setting into her new role as jail-keeper," said Gary.

"A little too well," said Jenny. "Yesterday, she kicked me out of bed at 5:00am, citing 'regulations.' I swear if that woman gets it into her head that she's bossing me around for the next three hundred years, I'm going to have the dwarves turn her into a nightstand."

"You would never," said Gary.

"Of course I would never," said Jenny. "She and I are together for the long haul."

"Speaking of three centuries, what are your plans for that time?" asked Gary.

"I don't know. Sit around. Quote bits of my favorite movies to my wife who will stare at me blankly because she doesn't get the reference. Not murder people. Maybe take up knitting."

"Knitting is a truly useful skill," said Gary, poking one finger through a hole in his old sweater. "We don't have enough knitters on Anjali."

"And we certainly have enough killers," said Jenny.

"But we do have a fair number of people who are attempting to make things right," said Gary. "Most of the humans are getting along well. And the Bala are generally not taking out their frustrations on the survivors."

"I wouldn't blame them if they did."

"By destroying that ship you likely saved tens of thousands of Bala lives, now and into the future. Not to mention the human lives that would have been lost during the inevitable uprising after the Bala had been forcibly returned to Jaisalmer," said Gary.

"Probably won't affect a thing. Humans will find you eventually," she said.

"Not for a very long time – as long as Jim's piece was the only hidden horn. Hopefully, unicorns will become legends and dwarves reduced to a children's story. When truth fades only myth remains. Maybe the next time they find us, a few dozen generations in the future, humans will be less likely to see us as enemies and more likely to treat us as allies."

"I don't know that I agree with you there, fella," she replied, settling back into her chair. "Those souls are on my conscience – and they don't sit there easily."

"Sometimes the kindest course of action is still terrible. Like putting down a sick animal."

"Humanity is definitely a sick animal," she said.

"Don't worry, I doubt you'll live more than twenty more years the way you destroy everything around you, Jenny fucking Perata," said Gary.

She smiled and made a little laugh through her nose.

"True. I still get to see Kaila every day, which is more than I saw her over the last two years, and the food here is pretty good, even if I do have to make it myself, and there's nothing to read or watch, but the octomites hunting at night are pretty entertaining."

"Really? They've terrified every Bala who's set foot in the forest," he said.

"Gary, I've lived in Australia. There's nothing in this forest that can scare me," she said.

"I thought you were from Aotearoa," he said.

"That's where I was born and lived while I was growing up, but I was stationed in Broome City for a while before the Reason shipped me off to the stars."

"I didn't realize. You've seen so much. You should write it down," he said.

"Write what down?" she asked.

"The story of the meeting of our two cultures and what came after. You have a unique perspective on the events that have taken place over the last few decades. And the Bala are now a people without a written history. Every report we have access to from the *Kilonova* and Mary was filtered through the lens of the Reason. You could tell the story of how humanity encountered the Bala as a lesson and a warning to future generations."

"I'm no historian. I hate all those dates and numbers," she said.

"But you were there. Just tell your story. How you got to this point. What you've learned," he said. "Tell it your own way."

"There would have to be lots of action," she said tentatively. "I can't stand a boring story."

"There *was* lots of action as I recall," he said.

"It's not a terrible idea. I could write about the redworms and the Century Summit. Oh and the escape from the *Well Actually*. I never told you about that day. It was wild." She picked up her tablet and started flicking through pages, looking for an entry in the encyclopedia.

"There has to be something in here about that old ship…" she mused to herself, already engrossed in the research.

Gary got up and went to the door. He touched the wooden doorframe, still dewy from where the dwarves had recently hewn it. A few dwarven characters were carved into the wood. An invocation for protection, not from the person held captive inside but for her safety.

"I'll do it if you help me. Fill in the parts that I wasn't there for," she called to him.

"Of course," he replied.

"Space unicorns," Jenny mused to herself. "I guess I could make it work."

CHAPTER TWENTY-FOUR
Higher Powers

Boges sat in the hold of the Pymmie ship, awaiting instructions. It was just as Gary had described. The Pymmie had morphed the interior of their ship to resemble a dwarven great hall. It was uncannily real, down to the smallest detail. The stone walls were dotted with cool blue twinkling crystals. It even smelled properly wet – a crisp mineral scent laced with a hint of rot. It was as if they'd pulled it right out of her memories of home. She couldn't say for sure that they hadn't.

The Pymmie had seated her at a carved table piled high with buttery mushrooms and roasted grubs. These were delicacies from generations ago, but they smelled delicious right now. After such a terrible day, Boges wanted nothing more than to shove great handfuls of grubs into her mouth and let them burst nuttily on her tongue. Instead, she waited patiently for someone to appear.

A Pymmie approached, out of place in the dwarven environment. Their body was as small as hers, but spindly instead of stocky. They had chosen not to wear any type of covering over their gray skin. The most disturbing part was that Boges could see her own reflection in the inky black pools of their eyes.

"We can change shape if it comforts you," said the bug-eyed creature.

"No," she replied, suddenly aware of the dryness in her throat. The Pymmie reached out and handed her a steaming mug of kummel brew, spicy and sharp. She drank gratefully, aware of the

Pymmie watching the inside of her mind to ensure that she was satisfied. There would be no lying here today – at least not on her part.

"We have failed," Boges said. "We were unable to prevent the invaders from spreading."

"Not entirely," said the Pymmie. "But your actions have galvanized a new human-Bala alliance. The balance of power has shifted toward the Bala. That leads to a greater chance of eventual success and survival for everyone."

"The things I had to do…" began Boges, feeling her chest tighten in sorrow.

"I know this was difficult for you," said the Pymmie. "We appreciate what you have done."

"Will it have been worth it?" she asked, surprised at her own boldness. It wasn't every day that she stood in the presence of a being this powerful. Even Unamip couldn't manipulate reality like the Pymmie. But she had to know if what she had lost would somehow be offset by what they would gain.

"I don't understand the question," said the Pymmie. Boges could swear she saw a supernova flare in their right eye, then fade into blackness. She could stare into those black orbs all day, if she didn't faint from the disorientation first.

"Will it have been worth it to betray my friends and harm the Bala village in order to protect them from these supposed invaders?" she asked again, letting her rising anger give her voice strength.

"There is no such thing as *worth it*," said the Pymmie. "There simply is what is done and what is not done. We attach no value to the outcome. It is just a data point."

"You are such a cankerpox upon the universe," said Boges, no longer caring what the Pymmie did to her in retaliation for her surliness.

"We are *scientists*," said the Pymmie. "We realize that burden of the future is a heavy one, so we have brought someone along to share it with you."

The captain of the *Kilonova* stumbled into the great hall. Her uniform was stained with blood and spattered with vomit. Her cheeks and nose had blackened from frostbite and her eyes were glassy and unfocused. She'd likely been on the *Kilonova* when the stoneships crushed it, just as Boges had. The Pymmie had pulled them both out of the carnage.

"Join us," said the Pymmie, waving a hand so that the captain's injuries disappeared. Her uniform transformed into a brilliant blue sari and dastaar. She froze for a moment, then joined Boges at the table.

"I don't understand but I'm suddenly starving, so you can explain as I eat," she said, pulling a plate of spiced potatoes and chickpeas toward herself.

"We are the Pymmie. We manipulate variables in the universe in order to study outcomes. You reside in the laboratory of our creation."

"Did you create cockroaches? Because I have to lodge a complaint," said Captain Singh, her mouth stuffed with naan.

"We know about cockroaches. They were an unintended result of a tweak to plasma rotations in the yellow sun in the Milky Way galaxy. They aren't worth fixing," said the Pymmie.

Captain Singh picked up a mug of tea and took several big gulps. Coming back from the dead was hard work. Boges could attest to that firsthand.

"How did I get here?" asked Captain Singh. "I was on the *Kilonova* getting into an escape pod when the ceiling in the hold caved in. That's the last I remember."

"We brought you here. You have a role to play in the future," said the Pymmie. "You were supposed to get on Captain Jenny's ship and go down to the new planet, but you stayed behind and ceased to function. That was not an outcome that led to the result we were looking for, so we changed it."

"But if you're scientists, don't you have to simply record your observations without manipulating the results?" asked Captain Singh.

"You're thinking of journalists," said the Pymmie.

"The humans will find the Bala again," said Captain Singh, wiping orange sauce off her chin with the back of her hand. "We have pieces from the horn that Jim smuggled into Jaisalmer, along with necromancers to find them."

"You didn't hide us very well," said Boges.

"We hid you exactly as well as we wanted to hide you," said the Pymmie. The room trembled slightly and Boges wondered if she'd overstepped.

"As a Sister, I've sworn to follow your orders, but I'd like to know at least a little more about what we're facing," said Boges, finally breaking down and taking a bite of a mushroom without being invited. It was buttery and caramelized, the perfect ideal of a mushroom. She chewed slowly, knowing she would never taste such a thing again.

"Your two civilizations are facing an insidious enemy which will destroy both the Bala and the humans if you don't work together," said the Pymmie. "As we said, both cultures have a chance of survival if they can use their strengths to cooperate... like they should have done from the beginning. We took all the time to introduce you two and instead of working together, you destroyed each other. You lost out on a hundred-year head start."

"And what exactly is this enemy that is coming?" asked Captain Singh, using her bread to scoop up dollops of a tomato sauce studded with squares of cheese.

"Non-corporeal invaders. Invisible to both human and Bala. They cannot be beaten by conventional means. Several have already infiltrated the new Bala planet. They will send a signal to the others and more will arrive. No one will know they have been compromised until it's too late," said the Pymmie.

"That's the parasite in Jenny," said Boges, urgently wishing she could be back with her kin on the planet.

"He calls himself Kamis, but he is no elf. His real name is much older than that," said the Pymmie. The illusion of the table faltered for a fraction of a second and Boges saw they were floating freely in orbit around a crystalline geometric structure as large as a sun.

It was dizzyingly huge. The Pymmie shuddered and the illusion returned. They said the next words slowly and deliberately.

"He is building a beacon to signal the others. It must be destroyed."

"We'll need help. More than last time," said Boges.

"We have brought you help," said the Pymmie.

A lean and lanky man sauntered into the dining room with a half-smile blossoming on his face. A plate of grilled cheese appeared on the table. Cowboy Jim plucked one off the pile and took a bite, chewing thoughtfully.

"Needs more cheese."

ACKNOWLEDGEMENTS

This book would not have come into existence without the tireless support of many people. Dave, you set this bizarre world of space unicorns and asteroid spaceships into motion with a single comment. You're there to break down a problem when I'm ready to the work and to cheer me on when I'm not. You prompt me to challenge my assumptions about everything. I love you and I look forward to spite-writing many more books with you by my side.

Boysies, as usual, your contribution to this book was a multitude of interruptions and distractions that I wouldn't trade for all the world. I learned about Twitch-streams and Discord servers, Fortnite dances and blacksmithing techniques. Thanks for all of the fun chats. Never stop knocking on my office door.

To the team at Angry Robot and Watkins with whom I've had the pleasure of working with over these last couple of years – Marc, Penny, Phil, Mike, Nick, Lottie, and Gemma – every one of you has brought considerable expertise and skill to the table and it's always a pleasure to work with you.

Many thanks to my agent Sam Morgan, who answers all of my questions patiently, keeps me pointed in the right direction, and who helped me craft the perfect name for this book.

All my love to Team Arsenic, because you're always ready to show your love over a five-hour brunch or a massive platter of steak. And to the Clarion West family as a whole, when I'm with all of you, I feel like a single thread in a rich tapestry of speculative writers. I value every one of you who teaches me how to be better at my craft.

To everyone down at the Pub, thank you for helping me name the *Well Actually* and for being caring friends during this tumultuous year. Codex Writers, you pull no punches and always let me know when I'm not doing the work. I look forward to spending more time with all of you in every city around the globe. Writing Excuses friends, you coaxed me to take breaks during revisions, but also brought me souvenirs from the beach as you went swimming and I continued editing. Next year, I'll be right there in the sand with you.

Warm appreciation to my sensitivity readers, who always see things that I've missed. As always, you should take credit for the good parts, but all of the mistakes are on me. And an appreciative high five to Jerry who always held things up, no matter how late I worked.

ABOUT THE AUTHOR

TJ Berry grew up between Repulse Bay, Hong Kong and the New Jersey shore. She has been a political blogger, bakery owner, and spent a disastrous two weeks working in a razor blade factory. TJ co-hosts the Warp Drives Podcast with her husband, in which they explore science fiction, fantasy, and horror. Her short fiction has appeared in *Pseudopod* and *PodCastle*.

Visit her at https://tjberrywrites.com and @TJaneBerry

HUMANITY'S LAST HOPE ... A MURDEROUS UNICORN

SPACE
Unicorn
BLUES

T.J.BERRY

UNDER THE PENDULUM SUN BY

JEANETTE NG

PAPERBACK & EBOOK
from all good stationers and book emporia

Two Victorian missionaries travel into darkest fairyland, to deliver
their uplifting message to the godless magical beings who dwell
there… at the risk of losing their own mortal souls.

*Winner of the Sydney J Bounds Award, the British Fantasy Award for
Best Newcomer*

Shortlisted for the John W Campbell Award

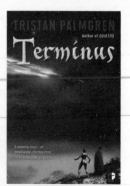
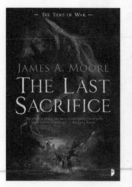
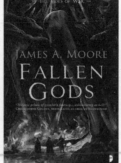
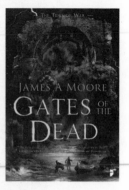

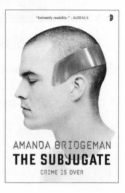

Science Fiction, Fantasy and WTF?!

@angryrobotbooks 📷 🐦 📘